A World
of
Expectations

A World
of
Expectations

By

Gayle Lynn Messick

This book is dedicated to the persons
I hold most dear:

My mother, Sarah Schofield

My sons, Edward and Stephen

My daughter-in-law, Christine

My granddaughter, Avery Anne

My best friend, Bert Dodman

Acknowledgements

Many persons supported me while writing my first story and I cannot publish without first thanking them.

Amanda taught be me to show not tell and encouraged me to write from the images in my mind.

Heather F. (Quill) kept me honest in all things British. I always admired the gentle way you offered suggestions. You stuck by me through every chapter and every posting. Heather is a writer who draws you in, wraps her beautiful prose around your heart, and makes you eagerly wish for more. I admire how she interprets a scene, the flow of the words and even the rhythm of the sentences. If my story had some charm of its own, thank Heather.

DebraAnne was my punctuation and grammar assistant on ths story. I could not complete a single sentence without her help but, alas, I have tinkered with the story so all mistakes are mine. I did try to follow your excellent examples.

KarenA read my story first and provided me with the encouragement and push I needed to finish.

Mary Ellen Shoemaker, my friend who pointed me in the perfect direction for the opening. I rewrote the first chapter many, many times, but after Mary Ellen worked so diligently to show me her opinion I was able to burst forth with it. Once done, I was finally satisfied.

Carol Blatnicky and Abbe Younghanz, two of my Qualla Village neighbors, read my story encouraging me to publish.

Bert Dodman helped me with the final review for mistakes. Still, I continued to tinker with the sentences. And so, as we say in the posting forums—all mistakes are mine.

To my friends and family that had to endure my excitement on a regular basis, thank you. I know I was a wee bit boring at times, but I do appreciate your patience.

Finally, thanks to all the many people who commented with their reactions to the postings and chapters. I learned a lot from what they said. I was pleased to have so many kind persons take time to respond.

A World
of
Expectations

Book I – The Alliance

By

Gayle Lynn Messick

Chapter One

Mr. Fitzwilliam Darcy is not a contented man.

He was three years short of thirty and life had become mundane. Everything had been done for him all his life—nannies granted his every demand, teaching masters answered his questions, footmen built his fires, maids cleaned his home, cooks prepared his meals, groomsmen watched over his horses, and a valet washed his body, tied his cravat, and even buttoned his breeches. As master, he also employees a butler to pour his drinks, a steward to manage his estate, a solicitor to handle every legal issue, and a secretary to write his letters and tell him where to go and when to be there. He existed for the singular purpose of procreating and passing down his great wealth to his male heir. Death by his fiftieth birthday, as when his father died, no longer seemed such a great punishment.

The season was over; the city was empty. The newspapers were bereft of stories on the social life of London. Many belles and beaus of elevated society, referred to as the *Ton*, had removed themselves to seaside resorts or country estates for the summer. He had chosen to remain in his London townhome instead of going to Pemberley, his Derbyshire estate.

Nighttime would be arriving soon. Darcy gazed out the window. The sky was bland, no vivid reds or oranges to mark the day's progression towards a blackened sky; yet to him the fading sunshine appeared like a graying veil covering the park outside.

His view overlooked Grosvenor Square, a prestigious location for a London home. The Darcy family had owned the house for several generations and with his father gone, the home was his. He, as every new master did, enhanced it by placing his collection of artwork on every available inch of wall space, but there was something vulgar about doing nothing else with one's time.

Lasciviousness, while discreet, was rampart. Men's clubs provided little activity other than food, drinks, gambling, and gossip. Nightlife meant attending parties with a crush of other sophisticated men and women. If there was room to spread your legs, sip your drink without being knocked about, or being able to hear the person standing in front of you, then the *Courier* announced the party was a failure. Today there were no parties, no soirees, nor any balls. He cared not. In fact, his disenchantment took hold before the season had ended.

"Humph." Darcy snorted. The women of the *Ton* were like identical twins, except instead of two ladies there were hundreds. It mattered not with whom he danced; it was the same woman in style, air, haughtiness, and speech. They dressed the same, they walked with their heads and chins held high, their backs straight, their fans opening and closing in a rhythm that never changed, and they gossiped. They strutted about in silken gowns of vivid hues; his favorites, light colors, were passé. Not one girl offered him a challenging conversation, preferring instead to fawn over him, tediously. He did enjoy a woman with a sly wit; yet, they seemed cruel and mean spirited in their chosen words and targets. This year, and for the first time, he experienced not an ounce of passion or even a tinge of lustful desire. He dreaded choosing a wife from amongst this insipid, characterless horde of useless partygoers.

Darcy stared at the passing carriage carrying its passenger home from perhaps a day spent shopping on Bond Street or from a gentleman's club on St. James. He was surprised the door displayed a crest. He thought every important person had departed town. This gentleman might prefer the actresses on Drury Lane or the brothels of St. Giles's at Covent Garden to the fashionable elite attending horse races at White Hawk Downs in Brighton.

Another carriage flew by at an unsafe speed. Darcy cringed. The passenger was one of the upstart tradesmen who had arrived in society. Always in a hurry, these interlopers bullied and battled their way into higher circles. They used money as the weapon. Their parties were the biggest, most expensive elaborate affairs. A difference existed between these men of wealth alone—the nouveau riche—and those gentlemen where breeding and lineage were more important. But these entrepreneurs were the men that lived. They did not subsist solely for the next party; they had a point, a purpose, something deeper than filling their schedules with various forms of entertainment.

He hungered for their fervor, coupled with his desire to achieve something not accomplished by his father or grandfather. He could not identify the precise triumph he sought, and this puzzled him exceedingly.

Darcy rushed to his desk determined to understand what gave the tradesmen that secret air of confidence. He searched through his papers, and pulled out a document that identified the enterprise capturing all their enthusiasm. Steam. This simplest, most abundant item turned out to be a magnificent power source. This was the future, and those men of not so high society had controlled it and made it their own property, their estates, their legacy.

The aristocrats and gentry ignored the world's fluidity. He did not. In fact, it was what caused him to lay awake at night. What was the value of being a gentleman landowner when the days ahead belonged to machinery? When steam-powered looms had begun to take over the textile industry, he felt frightened by the threat. In his tenants' homes the women converted wool from his sheep into woven cloth. They would lose their income if the textile mills improved, and from every indication, they would become more efficient. The cottage industry would be dead. What would his tenants do then? Would they abandon him for these new factories?

He had filled his days for six months learning everything about these inventions and the trends for the future. America, China, and Russia were the emerging trading partners of worth, but England needed a fast method of transportation to reach them. Steam, he believed, would be the power.

He had investigated investment opportunities only to discover the costs exceeded what he could afford. If he just knew any of the inventors, then perhaps he could obtain a better deal. Still, he could not reconcile letting the opportunity pass. Mortgaging his estate was one solution, but he was not willing to take that step. The recognition of what would be required—partnering with these young upstarts—caused him to shudder.

Gentlemen did not align themselves with tradesmen or their sons living off their father's fortune. Participating in trade was untenable. Friends, yes; business partners, no. The nation's wealth relied upon the profits realized from products produced by the ground—crops, gemstones, raw materials, and textiles. Aristocrats and non-titled gentlemen estate farmers, such as he, owned all the property and these were the men who ruled the country. The tradesmen were elbowing their way into control, powered by new riches made from sources other than the yield from miles and miles of acreage. They, not him, held the well-being of his descendants in their hands.

On this 16th day of August, Darcy closed himself off in his library and contemplated the correct road to take—partnering for shared wealth or borrowing against his home, but never once did he imagine the journey to his answer would begin at the point of a gun.

***

"Look here!" shouted the man bursting in the library; his rifle's muzzle pushing the door open.

Darcy jumped up and raised his hands above his head, dropping the paper in his hand. He hated to admit defeat to the words floating to the floor or surrender to the man pointing a gun at his chest. He strained to identify the person cloaked by the shimmering haze of twilight.

Geoffries, his butler, rushed into the room and attempted to grab the weapon. "Mr. Bingley has gone daft."

"Bingley? What is this? Are the one hundred thousand pounds your father left you not enough? Must you rob me of my wealth too?" Darcy dropped his arms down.

"No, no. I was excited about the rifle." A scarlet blush crept upwards from Bingley's neck as he lowered his rifle. He remained fixed on the spot, moving to his usual chair only after Darcy waved away the butler. He patted his firearm.

"Is this the gun you used last year to shoot more birds than I? The one you refused to let me hold?"

Bingley held out the rifle. "Yes, but much improved. My second cousin is the one responsible for the improvements. Ezekiel Baker's grandmother is his aunt."

"The Baker rifle?" Darcy's eyes fell upon the weapon; his brows rose upwards. "That is the Baker rifle?"

Bingley nodded, his grin spreading across his face.

Darcy accepted the rifle used exclusively by the 95th Regiment of the British Army and studied the gun's firing mechanism, which he found configured in an unusual manner. He gave it back, and then returned to his window. He locked his hands behind his back and gazed at nothing in particular.

"My father attempted to sell the modified version, but the negotiations ceased upon his death. Now the mission falls to me, and I... Darcy? Ahem."

He turned around and waited for him to continue.

"I do not know where to go or who best to contact. Much profit is to be had. I am hopeful that you..." Bingley dropped his head and glared at the pattern on the rug.

Following his friend's line of vision, Darcy saw the document lying on the floor. This was the precise second it happened. Amidst the final snippets of the day, he, wide-awake and sober, experienced an inspiration so at odds with his convictions that beckoned him down this uncommon and unfamiliar path. He had fought against it for so long but no more.

Darcy held up his palm, stopping his young friend from speaking, and then, without a single utterance, twisted around and concentrated on the view outside his window. This time, he gazed at no specific object. The windowpane reflected the light flickering in his eyes as his mind raced ahead. His heart raced. His palms felt as damp as the back of his tightly arranged cravat. The depth of his beathing decreased as images he had refused to imagine filled his mind. He was afraid to take a deep breath, move a finger, or speak a single syllable for fear the revelation would disappear into the blackening sky. A full five minutes elapsed before he marched to his desk, dropped in his chair, and scribbled notes on several pieces of paper.

Bingley fidgeted, watching in silence, his rapid breathing echoing with each dip of the quill.

"Thank you." Darcy lips unfurled which, within an instant, matched his friend's now beaming smile. "I have been pondering an idea for a long time; and with your visit today, I found my means—the modified Baker rifle." Darcy began a brief explanation of his idea for an alliance, one that defied social conventions—a true partnership between a gentleman and a tradesman. A share of the profits from the Baker rifle sale would provide the means to pursue his quest.

Bingley's jaw dropped. "I had only anticipated a letter of recommendation." He paused and scratched his head. "A partnership?"

"Yes." Darcy half-listened as his energized friend spoke. He often wished he could show excitement so openly, but his childhood training on always displaying a gentleman's mask of indifference had taken control. Instead, he listened to his friend's rambling, disorganized manner about inventions and machinery without showing a reaction of any sort, that is, until his friend divulged his uncle was James Watt. He flinched, and then confessed his ignorance of Bingley's relationship to the man many considered the inventor of the steam engine.

This new information ignited sparks in his mind. Bingley's connection allowed him to view this promising and emerging new industry not with the anxiety he had possessed before but with a successful mindset. He rubbed his temples; his head throbbing as possible opportunities bellowed for recognition.

The longer the two men spoke, the larger the venture grew, turning what started out as modest endeavor into a global enterprise. Bingley argued the partnership had to include other men to guarantee success.

They agreed on three friends: Lord Blake, Stephen Kent, and Gerald Rawlings.

Darcy settled back in his chair. The year was 1811, a time when old men, content with the way things were, would resist any changes. His alliance demanded partners willing to do what their fathers would not.

"Shall we test out the accuracy of the rifle on the birds flying high above my estate in Hertfordshire? Darcy?"

"I beg your pardon, Bingley. What did you say?"

"Shall we test the rifle in Hertfordshire? At Netherfield Park, the estate I leased recently."

"The country may be the perfect location to reveal our plans to our friends, but..." Darcy squeezed his brow together. "I wonder if they will agree to come. Many years have passed since we attended Cambridge, a few events transpired, and our close friendships waned. What could bring them to Netherfield?"

"I have an idea, and I am positive it will work."

Darcy raised his right brow.

"I will hold a competition at Netherfield Park. Blake will not pass up a chance to defeat you! Kent will want to prove a tradesman's son is the superior man."

"A competition? But what kind?"

Bingely grinned. "I will worry about that. You agonize over those dull and boring business details; I prefer to be social." He repositioned himself at Darcy's desk, picked up the quill, and began writing. He paused, a smirk developed. "Even if a lovely lady is nearby, I will not make you talk to her." He dipped the quill in the inkwell.

Darcy swirled the brandy in the bottom of his glass, mulling over the situation, but when the suggestion of a happy idea brightened his eyes, Bingley pounced—.

"Ah ha! I caught you thinking of meeting a pretty girl."

"My mind was more agreeable engaged on the possibilities this alliance will bring."

Bingley groaned. "The future may hold promise of a different union—one that smells good, is soft to the touch, and moves like an angel."

He had heard it all before. Darcy declined to comment with word or expression. He wore his mask of indifference.

Bingley returned to scratching the paper with the quill. Darcy pondered how it was possible any teaching master understood what his friend wrote when Bingley held up the blot-filled message and asked, "Would you look over my invitation? I do not want to make an error..

Chapter Two

Mr. John Cuffage studied an invitation a young man had slipped to him with a warning about Fitzwilliam Darcy's plans for a business alliance. He focused on the ramifications until the tinkling of his door's bell alerted him to someone entering his store, the New World Cigar and Wine Shop.

Cuffage hid the invitation under a journal and rushed up front to assist whichever gentleman had come to spend money. After the customer ordered his French wine and brandy, he returned to the back room to finish writing a report when he heard another bell, this time from the alley door leading into the back room. Unlike the other fashionable stores on Bond Stret, his backdoor opened as often as the front and by men from all classes—titled nobility down to the humble working men. Although their purpose was different, each man sought a private audience and none of the visits included the purchase of any of the products sold up front.

Cuffage stuffed his unfinished report inside a journal and placed it on the shelf next to three similar ones also stamped with a bird of prey. He presented his practiced, welcome smile on the gentleman walking towards him.

Fool, Cuffage thought as he considered this man who had used credit to purchase shares in his latest speculation. The investment appeared to have now failed, forcing full payment be made. He did not attempt to conceal his disgust towards yet another member of the gentry betting his estate money on a risky scheme, and then unable to produce the funds to cover his losses.

Cuffage reached up, retrieved one of the journals, this one entitled GAS LIGHT COMPANY, and opened it up to the first page. His eyes scanned the list of the ten gentlemen he had deceived. Combined, they owed him two hundred thousand pounds. He checked the time on his pocket timepiece, a George Clerke eighteen-carat rose-colored gold watch, and glanced at the inscription, *A foole and his money is soone parted.*

Twenty five years ago, he had rejected a future life as a clergyman the day he had read this quotation from *Defence of Government in the Church of England*. Many fools lived in the world and with so much money available to wrench out of their hands, he chose this occupation instead. The Wine and Cigar shop was a front for the real business taking place. Shaking his head to chase away his thoughts, he marked today's date and time in the journal.

"Bah!" He sneered while scrutinizing the ruined man who now stood slumped with his head slightly bowed, his hands fidgeting with his frayed beaver top hat. This addle-pate had once professed trade was worse than mud caked on the bottom of his boots while at the same time attempting to get rich in a business scheme run by him, a mere tradesman. Cuffage heard him sniffle or, at the least, simper. He shook his pointing finger. "No more time. Pay the twenty thousand pounds, or the magistrate will confiscate your estate. You have one week as stipulated."

"But my family! I have a wife and three children. Where would we live?"

"Sell her gowns and jewelry. Take possession of any dowry money. Do what you must do if you wish to remain living on the estate. I care not what happens to you." Droplets of spit escaped his mouth as he spoke the final words.

The man, his shoulders drooping, hurried out into the alley, sobbing and gasping for breath as he slammed the door behind him.

Cuffage returned the journal to its place and waited for his next customer. He cared not which door they entered.

Nigel, dressed in a faded brown jacket, stained work shirt, and rumbled trousers. He had come through the back door, not with his hat in his hand, but with a high step in his walk. He was busy figuring out his costs for providing the confidential service Cuffage sought. "I've been loyal," he mumbled as he added a few more shillings to the total. He handed over the sheet. "That's my price." He patted his pocket. "And I want my coin now so I can get started. Meryton is a small parish with hardly any place to stay."

Cuffage crossed his arms. "You ask too much. All you need to do is pick up documents in the hollow of an oak tree in the East Meadow of Netherfield Park."

"You also said to watch the men. That is a cost too."

"Send a report at least once a week, express any urgent news." Cuffage sighed, leaned down, and unlocked a drawer to retrieve coins from a metal box. He slapped them on the desk with a loud smack. "This should be enough for your needs."

"Is there anyone in particular I should focus my attention on?" Nigel winked as he scraped the coins into his hand. "Or someone I shouldn't worry 'bout? I wouldn't want to waste my time watching your spy."

"My contact will remain a secret. He is so well practiced at disguise you would not guess his identity. Just retrieve the documents from the oak tree, watch the men, and send me a weekly report."

"Yes sir, Mr. Cuffage." Nigel picked up his payment and exited out the same backroom door in which he came, his coins jingling in his pocket.

Cuffage wondered if Nigel would report anything worthwhile or if the extra coin he gave him was wasted. Any stolen documents would be helpful, but he doubted the five gentlemen would reveal any secrets for him to hear. The men would not get entangled in local society or be a party to any scandal. No one important resided in that small, backwoods parish.

He pulled a blank journal off the top shelf, used his signet ring to stamp the image of a falcon on it, and then wrote THE ALLIANCE in big bold letters. On the top of the first page, he entered the sum he had given Nigel. He prepared a long detailed message, addressed it, and sealed it with his ring.

"No one jeopardizes my operations. Certainly not a young, foolish man such as yourself, Mr. Fitzwilliam Darcy. I will bring you down just as I did to the Duke of Charnwood." Cuffage laughed. "I wonder how His Grace is enjoying his life now." He retrieved Bingley's invitation. "I will come after you, Darcy, of course, that is if you can persuade Lord Blake or Mr. Rawlings to sink below their stations and intermingle with the mud caked on the bottom of their boots. I think not, but I will be watching and preparing."

**

Nigel tied his horse to a tree in a wooded area of the East Meadow of Netherfield Park. He had arrived in Meryton the night before and found lodging at the Blake Bull Tavern. The accommodations were satisfactory, the furnishings adequate, and the meal in the dining room had been tasty. His first assignment was to drop a message in the hollow of the oak tree today.

The oak tree could not be missed. It was immense and stood alone. Nigel presumed it had been there at least one hundred years; the branches were the size of most tree trunks and stretched a good distance. He coud not see anyone in the East Meadow, and so even though it was day, he decided to take a chance. He ran to the tree with the message in his hand and once there he easily found the hollow opening. It was at eye level and large enough to hold packages if needed. But when he laid the note inside, the sound of hoofbeats startled him. He spied two horsemen fast approaching and much too close for him to run back to the wooded area. He scrambled up the tree, and hid among a section of multiple branches. He had just settled in when he spotted the edge of the message sticking out of the hollow. Before he could retrieve it, the two men stopped under the tree.

"Darcy, it is a wonderful spot for a picnic as there is enough shade to cool all the good people of London. Don't you agree?" the younger man exclaimed.

"Don't, Bingley? You have reverted to colloquial speech again. Say 'do you not agree?' Even in private!" Darcy continued his benevolent education with his reprimand. "The spoken word, along with the quality, age, and cut of the clothes, speak to the station of the man."

Nigel's eyes widened and a smile crossed his face when he realized who the two men were. He strained to hear what they were saying.

Bingley hung his head and sighed. "I know."

"I would not dare criticize anyone in such an overt manner, except you did plead for help in making a good impression.

Bingley groaned. "I do thank you, Darcy. Still I blundered again. In London I am much more careful."

Nigel felt a squirrel run across his arm and had to control his gasp when the two men dismounted and sat underneath the tree. The edge of the message was just above their heads. Their conversation turned away from Netherfield Park to an assessment of the Meryton society, which seemed to Nigel to please the younger man more.

"Have your neighbors called upon you?" Darcy asked.

"Yes, of course. They are not all savages. They were quick to welcome me. I do not believe I have met with more pleasanter people anywhere. Why, men from the four most prominent families came straight away. Sir William Lucas was the first gentleman to arrive. Oh. He announced that he attends St. James. Often."

"Humph." Darcy uttered. "Country gentlemen are the ones who would be impressed with an association with the Royal Court and would boorishly remark about their connection to it."

Bingley leaned his head back against the tree, his gaze focusing on branches above him. "I look forward to continuing my acquaintance with the Lucas family."

"How many?" Darcy asked.

"How many what?"

"Eligible daughters, of course!" Darcy slapped his friend's shoulder.

Bingley held up two fingers. "There are other families as well—the Longs, Bennets, and Gouldings. I am anxious to further my acquaintance with them as well."

"And?"

"Mr. Long has two nieces; Mr. Bennet has five daughters."

"Five? Are they all out?"

"Yes."

"Surely you jest. No one allows their five eligible daughters to be in society at the same time."

"They do, Darcy. And I have been assured that they are the most beautiful jewels in the country. But you will be more interested in Mr. Goulding."

"Why?"

"He has no daughters in a desperate search for a wealthy husband, only horses seeking an owner who will feed them the best oats. Mr. Goulding owns some of the finest horseflesh in the country. I understand the best families purchase their stock from him."

Darcy shrugged.

"Perhaps we can call upon Mr. Goulding after the others arrive. Blake has a keen interest in the fillies, but unlike you, he does not limit himself to pretty mares with four legs."

"I am not adverse to the ladies, but unlike you and Blake, I am more selective. I cannot imagine any woman worthy residing in this unknown, backwards little parish.

"Perhaps your opinion may be flawed in that regard. Now, I must give a warning. You may not enjoy the social events planned."

"Oh? We are to mingle with the locals?"

"Yes, there is an assembly dance tomorrow night, and a few days later Sir William Lucas is hosting a soiree. We are all invited."

"Must I?" Darcy sighed.

"I will not demand you attend, but then you chance the loss of future friendships and opportunities. They are charming people."

"Enough. Now when do our friends arrive?"

"After three."

"Are they are still unaware of the purpose for the invitation?"

Having grown bored with the men's conversation, Nigel's interest perked up. Finally, something of value of which might be included in his report to Cuffage.

Darcy stretched his arms above his head, his fingers touching the hollow. Nigel's eyes widened. The message was within reach. He leaned into the tree branch and held his breath.

"Well…" Bingley hemmed. "In my invitation I did not mention it. But in a separate letter to Kent, I wrote a little about the partnership aspect. He discussed it with Rawlings. I am unsure of Blake's knowledge."

"Blake must not know or he would not come."

Darcy reached to grab a handful of grass flapping in the sudden gust of cool air; although he pulled his hand back, placing it in his lap. "Finesse will be required to bring him into the partnership."

"When should we tell him about our plans?" Bingley asked, standing up.

"We should not wait too long. We need to know how he will respond. If he chooses to refuse, then we can use the friendly competition to show that we do not harbor any ill feelings. We do not want Blake to put up obstacles for us either."

They discussed what to say when the time arrived to reveal everything, agreeing to drop a hint during dinner that night. They talked in-depth about the Baker rifle and the many future possibilities for the steam engines. Darcy suggested they withhold bringing up the risky aspect of the venture at first.

Much to Nigel's dismay before Darcy could elaborate Bingley glanced towards the house and announced, "It is nearly noon. Shall we return to the house?"

Darcy agreed, jumped up, untied his horse and waited while Bingley, facing the hollow in the tree, brushed his hands together before smoothing down his riding clothes. Nigel gripped the tree branch and inhaled deeply when his gaze fell upon the edge of the message sticking out. It was in Bingley's direct line of sight.

Bingley turned. The two men mounted their horses. Nigel's taut shoulders relaxed, and as soon as the riders disappeared down the road, a burst of air escaped his mouth, causing the squirrel to leap to the branch below. After mumbling about what he heard and what Darcy had not said, he climbed down and hurried to the find his horse. He returned to his rented room at the Black Bull Tavern in Meryton where he prepared his report for Mr. Cuffage. He added all the new information he had heard. "He will be pleased I learned so much so quickly."

Chapter Three

"Your guests have arrived." Whitson, Bingley's butler, announced. Bingley and Darcy hurried to the front door to await the carriages. One's rank did matter—Blake's carriage led, Gerald Rawlings followed behind, and Kent was last in the small caravan progressing towards the house.

Blake's carriage did befit a lord with its gold-like metal trim, matching horses, and the appearance of the coachmen. They dressed in dark red-tailored coats, striped waistcoats, stark white cravats and shirts, and leather breeches. Hogskin gloves covered their hands and black hats topped their heads, although with his discerning eye, Darcy spotted the wear on their boots and the aging of the fabric. Still, no one failed to appreciate the station of the passenger inside—Robert Henry Schofield, Marquess of Blake, and eldest son of the Duke of Charnwood.

"Blake!" Bingley rushed to greet the man stepping down.

From his perch on the front steps, Darcy assessed him, and with the upcoming competition in mind, noted his friend's muscular body underneath the tight fitting clothes. The power in Blake's arms and legs had been due in the past to his habit of a sunrise gallop, and it was apparent that this practice had not changed. He knew Blake would be a formidable rival in Bingley's competition; the man to beat.

"Bingley," Blake called out. "How long has it been?"

"Too many years, my friend. I welcome you to my home." Bingley looked over his shoulder towards the massive brick building with three floors and the twenty-two windows.

"Netherfield Park is a fine prospect." Blake turned his attention on the house. "Darcy!" He shouted as his oldest friend ambled down the front steps.

"I hope your trip was comfortable."

"The weather was excellent and at four and twenty miles it did not strain my strength or temperament. I admit my thoughts have been focused on the competition and how you will feel when I am the victor."

The two men had finished their proper bows and civilities conducted for the audience of footmen, drivers, and doormen watching the scene, when the next carriage door opened.

Mr. Gerald Rawlings exited, his valet following behind. Logan had done his master's bidding without complaint or question. Rawlings liked to say they were two men—a gentleman and a gentleman's gentleman—and dared Darcy to guess who was who.

Bingley rushed to provide the proper civilities. The waiting friends joined Bingley and Rawlings as they had completed the usual courtesies.

Darcy studied the man he had not seen in four years. Rawlings, the opposite of Blake and Bingley in coloring, was the one who most resembled himself—olive complexion, midnight black hair, tall, and muscular. Their similarities diverged with the curl of their hair and color of their eyes. His were deep dark brown, which he had been told many times, blackened to match his hair whenever his temper flared. Rawlings viewed the world through much more vibrant ones, green, much like the distinctive tint materializing on tarnished copper and bronze.

"Here is Kent." Bingley separated himself from the group as soon as the final guest arrived.

Darcy admired Kent's mahogany wood coach with its azure, almost black, velvet fabric decorating the inside and the newness hinted at the enrichnment of the most modern enhancements. It was larger than his carriage. Kent may not be someone of the highest echelon as demonstrated by the lack of a family insignia, but no one would ever mistake it for a meager man's carriage. It was the newest, most expensive conveyance available.

To Darcy, the man disembarking had seemed taller than before, although he still had not equaled his own height. Although Kent's features were sharp—a nose too long, cheekbones too high, and a chin that jutted forward—creating a strong and powerful face. While Kent's walk mimicked his own, and, even though he imitated the same haughtiness and condescending attitude, this tradesman did not fool anyone as to his true station in life. Kent could do nothing to erase his heritage. On a regular basis, all the men whom he tried to impress jested that there was no accident in birth. Having himself joked in the same manner, now Darcy considered what a lifetime of enduring this callous remark did to a man's attitude.

The five men moved inside the house, each man in order of status. Lord Blake followed Bingley, the host, as protocol dictated. Darcy referred to him as Blake. When they were young, the marquess had forced him to bow and call him Lord Blake, that is, until one particular round of fisticuffs ended the ritual. Their friendship grew as did their rivalry and the title was dropped. Ever since Cambridge, Blake permitted all the men staying at Netherfield to call him thus, even though he had admitted to harboring a trace of resentment when the tradesmen's sons dropped using his title.

Next in line came Rawlings. He may not have a title, but his father, the Earl of Wolverly, did. The proper salutation for second born son was the Most Honorable Mr. Gerald Coronel Rawlings. This designation distinguished him as a man from a noble family, but not born as the titled heir. The Most Honorable, however, was not a moniker Rawlings felt befitting, nor did he believe all titled gentlemen deserved it—his eldest brother proved his point. But, because society used this measure to differentiate those of superior rank, Rawlings did not object too strongly.

In the great hierarchy of social status, Darcy fell in behind Rawlings. His father was a gentleman from an old and respected family with an immense northern estate that produced great wealth. The Darcy family's acceptance by the upper crust improved the moment his father married the daughter of an earl.

Kent and Bingley belong to the rising class—the wealthy children of merchants, bankers, and men of knowledge and the proper address for them was Mister, the same as Darcy. However, since they did not own estates, they were not a part of the landed gentry, or referred to as gentlemen, even though they attended the same schools, lived on the same streets in London, used the same tailors, and retained an equal number of servants. However, the mechanisms turning the world in the nineteenth century belong to this emerging group—scientists, inventors, industrialists, mercantilists, and tradesmen—while the old guard kept them at a distance in the hope that their own supremacy would remain.

Bingley gave a brief tour of the home, identifying the specific rooms assigned to his guests. Even though the men had expressed a desire to learn more about the competition, and while Darcy and Bingley wished to reveal the true purpose for their visit, they agreed to part and meet again for dinner, allowing the new arrivals a little rest. Several men went to their bedchambers, others to the library where brandy, wine, and refreshments were available.

Bingley, with Darcy at his side, instructed Whitson to ensure the footmen respond to any request the men may have. Whitson bowed and left to tend to business when he bumped into one of the new arrived guests dressed in riding clothes and heading out the door.

***

Dinner began at eight. Bingley led his friends into the dining room and as custom dictated, the other men followed by way of status—Blake, Rawlings, Darcy and, lastly, Kent. As they chose their seats, Darcy noted the absence of the objects women thought important—large bouquets of autumn flowers or even the popular fern or winter evergreen leaves. Which is why he and the other men, at first, were confused with the table setting; the butler had not included glasses for the wine, but instead they found a teapot and teacup completing each place setting.

Rawlings lifted the pot's top and smelled the smoky wood fragrance drifting upwards. "Bingley! You remembered our Tempest."

At Cambridge, they used teapots filled with brandy. They had all felt stranded at school much as Shakespeare's Prospero felt on his island in the play *The Tempest*, hence the nickname. They were avid drinkers, as were all similarly aged males, and used the teapots to conceal their drinking from their teaching masters. Whenever someone suggested tea, no one argued, regardless of the time. Other students had snickered at the woman's beverage, never learning the truth.

Darcy glanced around the table at his four friends.. When he attended the university with them, he had drunk, slept late, dressed in a hurry, and flirted with the local tavern maids. These memories caused him to feel a constriction in his chest, not a pain, but a dull sense of something lost or hidden away. He remembered the first time this dullness overcame him—the day the head master told him about his father's illness. He never resented his world of responsibility and duty, but a slight regret seized him when his carefree routine had ended. The morning after he finished his studies, his father had died, making him the Master of the Pemberley, the largest estate in his home county, Derbyshire.

"A toast." Bingley poured the fiery liquid into his cup. "To the renewal of old friends."

"To friends."

"To the competition," Blake said.

"To new pursuits," Darcy added. "And new opportunities for all of us."

"Hear, hear." The five men gulped their drink in one swallow.

Bingley motioned for Whitson to bring in glasses. "We are grown now, we shall drink as men."

Darcy sat back and at first listened as everyone talked over each other. The conversations focused on their Cambridge days until they had exhausted all their memories of women, teaching masters, and drinking.

Next, they addressed their rivalry, and an echo of excitement reverberated in their voices when they spoke about the invitation.

"You must tell us, Bingley. What is the competition and what will the victor receive?" Blake asked.

"My answer will come all in good time, but not tonight. I will tell you this; the competition will be up to you."

"Are we to vote on the game?" Rawlings asked.

"No." Bingley took a bite of roasted potatoes. He chewed it slowly and made a production of the swallow.

"You are making no sense. How can it be up to us?"

"It is, Kent, as you will discover. I suggest you weigh what uses your skills the best and your fellow competitor's talents the least. Strategy is needed to be successful."

"Then, I suggest boxing. I have practiced and never again will I be defeated in a match." Blake winked at Darcy. "When I win you will refer to me as Lord Blake again, bow to your knees in my presence, and not speak until I give you permission. I never forgot that loss." He rubbed his chin. "Do not underestimate my abilities."

"I would not dare." Darcy's right eye twitched as anxiety about the partnership pushed its way into his thoughts. He worried that he had overestimated Blake's willingness to discount rank and social standing. In fact, he seemed to have become more status concious than before. Although he had never paid attention to his attitude before today, it was possible nothing had changed.

"Darcy, do you know which game he has chosen?" Kent asked.

"No. I am as uninformed as you are. Our host has been deliberate in keeping this secret."

"Let me guess. A horserace?" Rawlings asked.

"Perhaps." Bingley replied.

"A game of skill?" Kent suggested.

"Perhaps."

"How can the choice of a game be fair since we possess different abilities?"

"It is perfectly fair, Blake. Each man will relish the opportunity to display his talents." Bingley sipped his drink.

Darcy returned to sizing up the men. Blake directed his conversation to either himself or Rawlings with a few questions about the competition going to Bingley. Kent avoided conversation, reclined in his chair, and kept his eyes trained on Blake and there was not a fraction of friendliness in his gaze. He turned his attention to Rawlings, whose eyes were darting from man to man. That friend used his sarcastic wit as a disguise for evaluating the others.

Bingley clicked his glass with his knife. Once quiet took possession of the room, he waved the remaining servants away. "Friends. I am honored you made the journey here and agreed to the competition, but first we must set aside a few days to enjoy our reunion. Besides, setting up the competition will take time. We have been invited to an assembly ball tomorrow night and a private party a few days later. The sporting season is upon us, and I look forward to a day or two rescuing a few birds from the warden's grasp in the sky. Let this first week be without rivalry."

"A dance? How are you going to get Darcy to attend? Tie him up and drag him by the boots?" Rawlings beamed at Darcy over the rim of his brandy glass.

"I dance."

"Not with strangers. Oh, have you met someone here?" Rawlings bent forward, his interest shown on his face. "Are there any pretty girls in this part of the country, Darcy?"

"I have not had the pleasure. He is best to answer your question." Darcy pointed his head to the host.

"Every man I met since my arrival spoke about the loveliness of the two eldest Bennet girls and the attractiveness of the two youngest." Bingley responded.

Darcy was not surprised the announcement had elevated the men's interest. All his friends would be delighted to be in the company of a beautiful woman.

Bingley leaned over his place, inhaled deeply before placing another forkful of roast beef in his mouth. He groaned with enjoyment while he chewed the meat into tiny slivers, swallowed, and then in a slow movement, wiped his mouth.

Rawlings bellowed, "Enough! Do not keep this to yourself."

"They did offer a caution that the middle child is plain and boorishly opinionated on propriety. Perhaps she might be a good choice for one of you." After the chuckles subsided, Bingley continued, "The two older girls own both grace and poise; the youngest are considered flirts."

Blake and Rawlings paid attention; Kent picked at the lint on the tablecloth, and from time to time lifted his eyes casting a dark, blackened glare towards Blake.

Unlike the flirting manner of the others, Darcy experienced an invisible hand squeezing his throat whenever he found himself in a room full of strangers and, in particular, a gathering of beautiful women. He never knew what to say since his particular wry humor did cause offense at times. As a result, he always remained silent, content with walking and watching, entertained by the foolishness of others.

Rawlings coughed several time bringing Darcy back from his thoughts.

The servants removed the dishes from the table, leaving the teapots and glasses in place. Bingley signaled the footmen to vacate the room.

"I have not heard your name matched with any lady, Darcy?" Blake asked. "What have you been involved in of late, although I suspect you spend your time working."

"True. I am pursing new endeavors. I feel this is a most exciting time and opportunities are ripe for expanding properties and holdings. Men must act with haste if they are to capitalize on the future's fortunes."

"But Darcy, you have no need to pursue further wealth. Are you not well situated now?" Blake leaned forward in his chair, pouring out his second brandy from the teapot.

"What is good now may not be adequate later. I cannot rest on my laurels… " Darcy held his hands up, wiggled his fingers and added, "or sit on these."

"Rest is unknown to you, for you are forever working," Kent said.

Darcy nodded. "True, but Chaucer said it best: *Nowhere so busy a man as he there n'as, And yet he seemed busier than he was.* Quite frankly, I am bored. My steward directs the day-to-day operations at Pemberley. My solicitor handles matters of legal interest, several men manage my shipping and mining interests, and a secretary conducts my London affairs."

"Come now, Darcy, you are busier than you are letting on. You are never without your papers and do not leave your study or library until demanded or required." Kent said.

"They call on me when the need is critical. While the responsibilities are great, I desire new challenges and even risky ventures. Perhaps it is true that I am busy, but I am bored and seek to pursue new interests."

"Might I be so bored? You are involved in the best investments." Blake said.

"In truth, you…" Darcy inhaled a deep breath, tightened his grip on the stem of the glass, and attempted to control the twitch in his right eye before continuing. "You were invited here to consider an offer to form a business partnership with Bingley and myself."

The announcement surprised neither Rawlings nor Kent; they displayed curious expressions.

Blake, however, jumped up, knocking over his glass, and presented Darcy with a befuddled expression. "You brought me here under false pretenses." He threw his napkin on the spilt liquid soiling the tablecloth, and marched to the door, his long legs pulling him out of the room. He continued down the hallway towards the staircase.

Chapter Four

Blake's foot had touched the first step when Darcy caught up and convinced him to join him in the library. Only Rawlings followed behind the two men. Once there, Blake separated himself and stood at the fireplace.

"I understand your concerns about connecting with Kent and Bingley." Darcy spoke to his friend's back, since Blake would not face him.

Blake whirled around. "You seemed to have surrounded yourself with tradesmen lately. First, Bingley, and now, Kent! He seemed to know a little too much of your daily habits."

"Let me assure you, I did not consider their involvement in a business venture without serious thought over the past six months."

"They are tradesmen, Darcy. How can I connect myself in such a way? How can you?"

"Do not be a fool and let this opportunity slip by." Rawlings scoffed, and then softened his voice saying, "The talk is plentiful around town."

Blake glowered at Rawlings. "You know not of what you speak." He faced Darcy and then relaxed his glare. "If our friends find out, we would be cast out, I tell you. Cast out! Blackballed at our clubs! There will be no... lady of any consequence willing to connect herself to me... us."

Darcy sensed that he must select his words with care. Finesse, he reminded himself, use finese. Any hope for creating the alliance would begin in this room at this moment. He placed his hand upon Blake's shoulder. "If a possibility existed to do business with only men of our stature, I would. I do not like this any more than you do, but progress without them is impossible. They are the ones busy inventing the machines and setting up alliances with foreign competitors. We must find ways to stay out in front. Otherwise, one day they will rule us. We cannot let that happen."

"Listen to him," Rawlings said. "Think man, what does the gentry do? Gamble, drink, engage in debaucheries and seductions, and spend their days socializing. Gentleman at leisure is as true a description as there ever was."

Darcy waited for Blake to speak.

Rawlings headed for the sideboard and the decanters filled with wine and brandy. A sputtering dying fire, which no longer contained sufficient warmth to heat the room, was the lone noise heard until the his cough gained the attention of Darcy and Blake.

Rawlings handed out filled brandy glasses. "The tradesmen have gone off to play a leisure game of billiards while we gentry have remained to discuss business. Perhaps their revolution has already been won."

Blake stared at Darcy. "I am surprised you feel comfortable to lower yourself to partnering with tradesmen. Have you no sense of duty or obligation to your name? Am I the only one in this room that respects our station in life?"

"Times change, and I no longer have a father to challenge my actions."

"Yes, you are your own man, Darcy." Blake nodded. "But, I am not."

"Your answer may come with a good night's sleep or after a few days enjoying the society here and demonstrating your prowess against the birds challenging your ability to shoot. You do not need to decide tonight. There will be no ill feelings if your wishes do not coincide with mine, and Bingley will hold the competition regardless. I look forward to the victory." Darcy revealed a smile on his typically blank mask.

Blake gulped the brandy down.

"When you hear the whole plan, and your role in it, you will find it easier to agree." Darcy said.

"Perhaps."

"Are you not concerned about my willingness to lower myself to their level?" Rawlings asked. "My father is an Earl."

"You do not seem as anxious. Why is that?" Darcy asked.

"I look forward towards the adventure. I have tired of the leisure life and acquiring any enormous profit is not to be ignored." Rawlings patted his pocket as he snuck a peek at Blake. "As a second son, I must make my own way in life. Recent experiences taught me what is genuinely important, and duty and obligation to one's name is not essential." He sipped his brandy, his eyes staring at an invisible image far away. "You are fortunate Darcy. Sometimes what a father may expect of his son is not for the best, nor what will make one happy. Sometimes they have their own agenda which can injure an entire family."

"We agree on that account." Blake said.

Darcy felt the dullness return and was envious of his friends whose fathers were still in their lives.

Rawlings cleared his throat. "Shall we join these new upstarts in the billiard room, and as gentlemen of the old world, teach them how leisure is done?"

***

After he finished his tasks, Rawlings' valet seated himself in one of his master's sitting room chairs. Logan had laid out the master's clothes, placed the *London Times* on the table, sorted out the important mail, filled the decanter to the top, and set a cigar next to his master's brandy glass. Satisfied with his work, he filled a glass for himself, picked up a book and waited for his master to return from dinner.

"Drinking my brandy, you craven, guts-griping malt-worm?" Rawlings cried out as he entered the room.

"That I am. What are you going to do about it, you gorbellied, hell-hated whey-face."

"Ah." Rawlings loosened his cravat, his laugh resounded throughout the room. "An exceptionally good insult, Mr. Logan. Shakespeare would be proud his words combined so. I concede to you tonight. I need to write it down."

Logan rose.

"Sit. Mr. Logan, I want to hear what you discovered." Rawlings eyed the decanter and waited for his man to pour him a drink. "We have been here long enough for you to have met your counterparts, although I do not think you can be compared to them."

"They are as expected." Logan peered at the door and imagined the puzzled or shocked expression on any of the other gentlemen or their valets if they walked in the room and witnessed the uncommon set up between them. He handed Rawlings his brandy before he took another sip of his own.

"Do not hold back on your opinion. How are they meeting your expectations?"

"Bingley will babble on and on, his man nodding in time with the words. He is your typical new valet—a head made up of eyes and ears but no brains or mouth. Bingley can talk enough for the two of them. He will have to endure many smiles and sighs if his master finds himself infatuated again."

Rawlings nodded. "Yes, yes, and no doubt he will. I suggest you engage the valet in meaningful conversation. He might even be interested in current events."

"He is young and inexperienced, and I doubt he is inclined to any discussion other than gossip. It is not my inclination to chat with the servants, Rawlings. Nevertheless, he may be a good source of information."

"Fine. What about Blake and Darcy's men? I suspect they have older, experienced manservants." Rawlings lit his cigar, settled back in his chair, and listened.

"We will get no information from those two. Both gentlemen will speak of nothing more important than the weather, the day's schedule, and the proper attire for the day. Lord Blake might, on a rare occasion, voice a few words on women, business, or family, all one-sided, but his man would never share the information."

"And Darcy?" Rawlings pushed his glass forward for a refill.

"As definite as the sun rising in the east, the words uttered by Darcy would be polite but not a single unnecessary syllable."

"I suppose Kent is different from the others?"

Logan set his glass down. He almost never had more than one drink with his master–almost. "Mr. Kent spends his time trying to emulate Darcy. Although, unlike most newly rich, he does not put on airs to his servants. Nevertheless, I am sure he has found a way to accentuate his higher station to his valet."

"And Kent's valet?"

"He is pleased to be employed."

Rawlings finished his cigar and gulped down his drink. "Logan, please draw me a bath."

Logan stood, reverting to his duties as a valet. "Yes sir, Mr. Rawlings."

As Logan prepared the bath, his thoughts dwelt on how he, a son of a valet from a long line of valets, had come to lead a life so different from any other valet of his acquaintance. He recalled his first meeting with Rawlings, then a strapping young lad of fifteen, one who had recently lost his mother to an unknown disease.

"Logan, tell me about your mother. Where is she from?" he had asked.

His valet had taken pity on him, then, for both had lost their mothers. That, and Rawlings reminded him of his younger brother. And that was how it had all started. They had been confidants after that. No matter how hard he had tried to be a well-trained valet, Mr. Rawlings seemed to prefer a loyal friend.

Logan performed his duties without conscious thought, instead he mused over various conversations they had had during the last twelve years. As Mr. Logan, they spoke of scandals, town gossip, women, gaming, current events, and business. He spent his free time reading books, Shakespeare most often, and all the London newspapers Rawlings had recommended. Thus, he was able to discuss issues in a meaningful way.

Rawlings had never sought a yes-sir, no-sir man, which suited Logan. Their unique relationship was much better now that his master wanted a drinking partner to help curb his habit of indulging to excess. Logan was not one to turn down a good brandy in the evening, and he did so admire his master's taste in fine wines.

"Logan, are you visiting with a sassy wench in your reflections or is there something I should be concerned about?"

At this moment, they were not drinking partners. Rawlings was the master busy contemplating his bath and Logan was the valet engaged in drawing it.

"No. I was recalling when I first came to work for you, Mr. Rawlings. Fond memories overcame me."

"Yes, I was an obnoxious little bastard."

"You were a young man with oats to sow, sir." His reply was a perfect answer from a well-trained valet.

Rawlings filled Logan in on the day's events. Blake, after a dramatic and pretentious show of disgust, had agreed to stay; but would delay any decision on the partnership until Darcy provided more information. Amd for now, he agreed to enjoy their reunion. He is curious about the competition.

Are there any requests for tomorrow, sir?"

"We will be attending a dance tomorrow night at the local assembly hall. Bingley guarantees beautiful women will attend and a few will be shameless flirts. Which waistcoat goes best with flirts, Logan? I do so love a feisty, brazen girl."

"The red one, sir. It always catches their eye."

"I dislike red; the green will do. It matches my eyes." Rawlings looked at his bedroom window, the one facing the East Meadow. "This will be the most amusing excursion and a profitable one, too."

Logan turned his head in the same direction. After a moment, his mouth curved with a slight twist upward, and he whispered, "Indeed."

Chapter Five

The assembly hall doorman held the door for the latest guests, the five men from Netherfield Park. He bowed, and then snapped his fingers, alerting others to help. While they removed their outerwear, he admired the fine fabric and modern cut of the items. In as quiet a voice as possible, he told the maids to place their belongings in the proprietor's office. The doorman tapped his pocket and felt the unexpected coins given to him by Nigel, who was hiding and waiting in the office to search the coats and hats.

Bingley faced his four friends. "Shall we?"

"Lead on." Darcy said. The men began the ascent up the two flights, and without a thought, followed in the order of their status, except as host, Bingley stepped in front.

Rawlings shouted over his shoulder to Darcy, "Duck! The beam is too low for the two of us." He continued up. "Why is it, do you suppose, all dances are held upstairs? Why can the ballrooms not be on the ground floor and save us this damned climb up?"

Blake scoffed. "Must you remark on every little annoyance of life? There will always be stairs leading to the dancing. That will never change."

"This is the nineteenth century. Cannot one of those foolish new inventors create an easier way to advance up the steps?"

"The music is pretty loud, and I must say I heard better, even in the south. Now this is something easily changed." Blake brushed the dust off his jacket. "I have been to cleaner places."

"This is a country dance, not one of the private balls held in town. Do not expect as much here." Darcy stopped, sniffing the air. Lavender. Someone is wearing lavender tonight.

"We are all familiar with your opinions about a dance, Darcy, regardless of its location." Bingley said.

Blake sighed. "Let us hope there are at least a few pretty lasses for our eyes. I am tired of looking at men's faces all day long. Alas, I have my doubts."

"May I remind you the Bennets will be here? The locals claim they are the most beautiful girls in Hertfordshire, perhaps even England."

"Well, Bingley, I assume you would know. Did any pretty girl not catch your eye?"

"Or yours, Blake. We both possess excellent vision, do you not agree?"

"That we do." He nodded.

"Darcy, do not look so grumpy. It is just a dance. You are not on trial here." Bingley said.

"Humph. Rawlings can tell you we are always on trial."

"Not true, but I will agree we are all veritable targets." At the top of the stairs, Rawlings placed his hands on his hips, leaned over and pulled in several deep breaths.

Darcy clapped his shoulder while they waited for the fifth man.

"I am fortunate. No one knows me here," Kent called out.

"No one knows you anywhere."

Kent sent Blake a sharp stare.

Bingley pointed to the door with his opened hand. "Shall we enter the proverbial den?"

Darcy felt his throat tightened as he walked through the door to with a room filled with strangers.

Those assembled hushed when the Netherfield party entered the Meryton hall. All were dressed in the finest clothes and appeared majestic in their manner. The five men gazed at nothing in particular while Meryton stared at them while they stood tall with their chins high, each man ignoring the whispers of wealth and family position. They had experienced such rudeness before as the focus of many society matrons in town. The *Ton* was more discreet – even if the words were the same.

The most important tittle-tattle circulating the room claimed the five wealthy gentlemen were not married. Every matron moved to her unmarried daughters, chastising them to stand straight, throw their shoulders back, and display a most pleasing smile. It is a truth universally acknowledged that an unmarried woman in need of a good fortune must exhibit herself to gain the attention of a wealthy man.

And so it was, when Mr. Bingley and his friends approached, Mrs. Bennet presented four of her daughters to the men: Jane and Elizabeth, the poised and graceful eldest girls, and Kitty and Lydia, her two youngest beautiful but giggly flirts.

***

Mrs. Bennet was in a heightened state of excitement. The morning light flooded through her window, but she had risen before sunrise to spend her time on reflecting on the minute details of the previous night's dance.

Five wealthy gentlemen! Mrs. Bennet sat at her desk designing ways to match the men with her like number of daughters. When her housekeeper tapped on the door, she gave the word, and Hill entered the room carrying several journals.

"Hill, what are we ever going to do?"

"Do, Mrs. Bennet? I have the housekeeping accounts. Shall we start with them, or would you prefer to begin with the menu?"

"What? Oh. Tomorrow's menu." After Mrs. Bennet had selected the meals—tea, coffee, toast, and rolls with butter for breakfast, and mutton and applesauce for dinner—she slammed her quill down on the desk. "It is my fault, having daughters. Why had not one been born male? Especially Lizzy. She is so like her father, she should have been his son. Not that she would save me, mind you."

"Miss Elizabeth loves you, ma'am." Mrs. Hill reached for the other journal she had placed on Mrs. Bennet's desk. "Shall we start on the household accounts now?"

"We must keep Mr. Bennet in good health. We must. I pray every night that he is not dead in the morning. Oh, my nerves, , my nerves."

Hill handed her the smelling salts. "There now, Mrs. Bennet."

After a moment, Mrs. Bennet recovered enough to say, "Now if Jane could secure one of these men! I think she has at least one gentleman interested. Shame he is the poorest —only five thousand a year, you know. Five thousand a year and an estate so close, and he is the poorest! It would set us up for life if my Jane became the Mistress of Netherfield Park."

"Yes, ma'am. Only five thousand a year." Hill rolled her eyes.

Barely taking a breath, Mrs. Bennet continued, "We must keep my dear, sweet Jane in good health, too. How my nerves act when either she or Mr. Bennet sneeze, cough, or show any sign of illness. You know, I was never nervous before I married. I was quite gay and happy. I had not a care in the world."

"You were the spirited one." Hill glanced at the cameo of the youngest daughter, Lydia, on Mrs. Bennet's desk. "Would you like to go over the household accounts now?"

"Oh, must we do that now? If Mr. Bennet died today, I would not have to worry about housekeeping accounts. Why, I would not be allowed to live in my own home. That hideous little man with the entail will take control over all our things: the furniture, my china, Mr. Bennet's books, and even you and all our servants! It is a disgrace that property passes down to the nearest male relative."

"Now Mrs. Bennet, you know that I shall not leave you. Shall we meet this afternoon to finish the household accounts?" So saying, Hill returned the housekeeping account books to Mrs. Bennet's desk.

"Household accounts? Why must I worry about household accounts now? I am worried about household accounts in the future. With no place to go and only the clothes in our closets, it would be horrid."

Hill remained silent.

"The world belongs to the men as you are well aware, I am sure. Women cannot work, not that I would want to do so, mind you.

"No, ma'am. Work isn't meant for you."

"Why must the laws be so cruel? Society's rules punish women! Men go anywhere they want, do any kind of work, live where they can afford, and even dally with the ladies without being scorned. It is not fair."

"No ma'am. Life does not seem fair to most people." Hill waited by the door.

"Thank goodness once married, a husband cannot cast off his bride with ease." Mrs. Bennet smirked to her reflection in the mirror. She had never been spoken truer words about herself. "But I hate that my friends will be scheming to set their girls up with the gentlemen. I hate that Jane may marry the poorest one of the five, and some other neighbor's girl may secure a better future."

Before Hill could respond, Mrs. Bennet jumped up "I must go down and convince Mr. Bennet to visit Mr. Bingley again. He must somehow become better acquainted. He must go if our Jane is to secure our future. Why, who could resist dear beautiful Jane as a wife? She is an angel! All the men say so."

"Yes, Miss Bennet is beautiful, as are you, Mrs. Bennet."

Mrs. Bennet looked herself over. At three and forty, she was still attractive enough to remarry, if necessary, unlike a few women she could name. She took great pains to retain her girlish figure—and this after given birth to five daughters!

Satisfied, she squared her shoulders and left to join the others for breakfast who were busy eating or occupied in toasting their bread.

"Mr. Bennet," she said, cooing as she placed a slice of bread on her toasting fork. "You should have seen the way our Jane was admired last night."

"Why? Was it so different than any other night?"

"Yes. Yes, sir, quite decidedly so. Jane danced with four of the Netherfield Park gentlemen, and with Mr. Bingley and Mr. Rawlings twice. I dare say she was the favorite amongst them." After thinking back on the assembly, she added, "but I would give not a moment's notice to that Mr. Darcy. He not only did not dance with any of our girls; he slighted poor Lizzy." She thrust her bread over the flames.

"Slighted my Lizzy?" Mr. Bennet eyed his favorite daughter.

"Yes, Papa, but I did not care for him either. But Lord Blake requested my hand for a dance, and he is a gentleman of the highest order."

"Highest order, Lizzy? Do not tell me you are letting your mother's silly ways affect you." He said, winking.

Elizabeth rolled her eyes.

Mrs. Bennet pursed her lips, and narrowed her gaze. Her husband hid behind his newspaper. A tight smile crossed Mrs. Bennet's lips. "My dear, when will you be paying a call on Mr. Bingley? Sir William, Mr. Long, and even Mr. Goulding visited more than once and you called upon him only the one time. And that was before his guests arrived."

He lowered the paper. "I am sorry to disappoint you, my dear, but I have no plans to bother Mr. Bingley again. It is my understanding he is here for sport, and I prefer he stick to the kind he can shoot. I will not go unless specifically invited... and by the man himself." He raised his newspaper and ruffled it several times.

"Why should you not attend to him?" She dropped her toast onto the plate. "Do you want to be an obstacle to Jane's happiness? And what about Lizzy? Even you must realize she is interested in Lord Blake. How can you not see to their future?"

He stopped reading, and made a performance of turning the newspaper page. "My mind is made up. You will not be able to work on me in such a way."

"If you do not go, Charlotte Lucas may capture the heart of one of the men. He may be a better choice for one of our girls." She switched her gaze to Lydia.

"I doubt they would admire such a silly girl."

"Phew. Men like silly girls today as much as men did three and twenty years ago, Mr. Bennet." Her eyes sparkled, her smile tightened. "Did you know Mr. Kent has at least five hundred a year more than Mr.

Bingley? His family comes from trade, but he does well for himself. I would not like Charlotte or Maria to keep any of our girls from getting him."

"But Charlotte is so plain and Maria is so young, is that not right, Mrs. Bennet?"

Her husband's comment reminded her that he was an experienced player in this game of theirs. She ignored his question, and he returned to reading his paper.

"And Mr. Rawlings is a good catch, too." She continued. "He was polite, and I could not make him out, but I understand he is the second son of the Earl of Wolverley. Second sons have to make their own way, and he made a fortune from a most convenient marriage. His wife died in childbirth and left him with all her money. Quite flush is what I heard. He's almost as rich as that Mr. Darcy. No one knows for certain about Lord Blake, but he must be wealthy, he is the eldest son of a Duke."

Mr. Bennet jumped up with the paper folded untidly under his arm. "Not all peers are rich, my dear."

"If he is friends with the others, then he must be rich. They wouldn't associate with him if he were poor. Rich men like to keep amongst themselves, you know." She paused, and then insisted in her most shrill voice, "Mr. Bennet, you simply must go and visit Mr. Bingley! You must not vex me so."

He glared at his wife. "I know what you are trying to do. I shall retire to my study." So saying he left the room without any further conversation and without finishing his breakfast.

Lydia laughed. "I care not for any of those men. None of them wore a red coat, so I shall not care what they do or who they choose."

Having laid in wait for this moment, Kitty cried out, "You care not because none of them danced with you. What are officers in red coats when a man of Mr. Rawlings' status prefers me to you?"

"But he kept glancing at me and smiling everytime you turned away. Still, he does not wear a red coat, so you may have him, sister."

They continued to argue while their mother lectured them to use their feminine wiles to ensnare a husband. Without a single word, the two eldest sisters retreated outside.

Jane led her sister to the garden. "They seemed happy with the assembly last night and have much to say to one another."

"And they will be talking for hours about fashion and flirting and everything except the proper comportment of a lady."

"Oh, Lizzy, do be serious."

"But, I am. Shall we cut a few flowers this morning? I need more lavender for my perfume."

When they reached the garden, the Jane shifted the conversation. "Mr. Bingley is what a young man ought to be. He is sensible, good-humored, and lively; and I never saw such happy manners! So much ease, with such perfect good-breeding!"

Elizabeth found the cutting shears and handed her sister the flower basket. "He is also handsome which a young man ought likewise to be, if he can. His character is thereby complete."

"I was very much flattered by his asking me to dance a second time. I did not expect such a compliment."

"Well, what about Mr. Rawlings? You danced two dances with him as well."

Jane sniffed and then placed a sprig of lavender her sister offered in the basket. "This one has a very potent scent for your perfume."

Lizzy held a branch up to her nose. "Very strong aroma this year. No one will mistake it for your rose oils." She knew Jane preferred Mr. Bingley simply by the way her sister blushed when she said his name. Now, shall we return to discussing Mr. Rawlings?"

"He was all politeness, it is true, but he did not entertain me quite as favorably as Mr. Bingley."

"Well, Mr. Bingley certainly is very agreeable, and I give you leave to like him. You have liked many a stupider person."

"Dear Lizzy!"

"You are a great deal too apt to like people in general. You never see a fault in anybody. The entire world is good and agreeable in your eyes. Why, I never heard you speak ill of any person in my life."

"I would wish not to be hasty in censuring any one; but I always speak what I think." Jane paused and then suggested, "But, you have not told me what your opinion of the gentleman who favored you."

"As much as I would like to be as happy as you, I cannot yet say that I am. I danced with Mr. Bingley once, but he kept his eyes trained on you. He broke my heart when the only conversation we shared was answering questions about Miss Jane Bennet!"

"Lizzy! Now tell me truthfully, what is your opinion about the other gentleman?" Jane shook her finger at her sister. "It has taken me years to realize the direct approach is what works on you. Do not be so reluctant to answer me."

"Well, Mr. Kent and Mr. Rawlings were excellent dancing partners; Lord Blake did show me much attention, although I know not why." She pulled a dead leaf from a flower. After a moment of reflection, she shook her garden shears at her sister.

Jane gasped and took a step backwards.

"However, who is Mr. Darcy to call me merely tolerable? He is tall and handsome, but he is the most arrogant man I have ever met. Lord Blake has more status than he does, and yet he was kind in his words and actions. I doubt if Mr. Darcy even spoke a single syllable to anyone outside his party the entire evening. Insufferable man!" Lizzy shook the shears again.

Jane relieved them from her sister in a simple graceful motion. "He did say Humph! But I do agree, Lizzy, that he was wrong to say what he said about you. It was not gentleman-like at all. Perhaps he was not in a mood for dancing. He might be shy around new people. Or something was troubling him or his mind was full of, well, hunting."

"Do not make excuses for his poor manners."

"Enough talk of Mr. Darcy. Tell me your thoughts about Lord Blake. Should I give you leave to like him?"

Elizabeth sighed. "I have never seen such a man."

They sat down on the bench. Jane waited while her sister remained engrossed in a private, but by her expression, a pleasant thought.

Elizabeth sighed. "Alas, he is the son of a Duke. I am not of his sphere. He will never go beyond small meaningless conversations and a few dances."

"You do not know that."

"We have nothing but our charms to recommend us, and that would not do for Lord Blake. I do find him to be charming and attentive, but," Elizabeth shrugged her shoulders, "what future is there with him?" She lowered her head. In a quiet voice said, "Did you know he questioned me regarding my blood lines during our dance?"

"I am sure he was trying to learn all about the lady who caught his eye. Our dowries are not that small." Jane patted Elizabeth's hand resting in her lap. "We may not have any connections, but we do have a dowry to complement our charms and a generous one, sister."

"True. My seven-thousand-pound dowry is significant for a country squire, or even a baron's son. Still, I am sorry to say the amount is a mere pittance compared to what daughters of nobility can offer."

"It is not too small for anyone especially when affection is also present."

"But in this case all he was interested in discovering the size of my dowry and my blood lines. And combined that with how low my connections are, Lord Blake will turn away from any serious intentions."

"Do not presuppose what the reason behind his questions is – you may be wrong, and it may cost you a great deal." Jane shook the shears at her sister.

Elizabeth made a pretense of shielded her face with her open hands. "But who sees the world as you do? Not I. You are too good, sister. I am willing to place a wager Lord Blake is trying his best to determine if I am worthy for his attentions.

"Lizzy! Betting is not proper activity for a lady."

"Yes, this is true, but gaming and gambling are sweeping the nation. You must accept that once he discovers I have little money and no titled relatives, I will never see him again. Nonetheless, I did find him to be a most congenial partner. He is well read and told me a little about his travels." Elizabeth gazed over her sister's shoulder at a distant point while she tapped her foot to a tune playing in her head. "He is an excellent dancer and his eyes are a radiant shade—"

"Girls!" Hill interrupted. "An express message has arrived London for your father.

"Did our Uncle Gardiner send it?"

"No miss. Mr. John Cuffage did. Your father seemed upset. I just wanted you to know."

They nodded, but both knew their father would never discuss bad news with them unless he called for them. They remained outside and focused their interest on the shots exploding over the skies at Netherfield Park and on two particular young men holding their guns.

Chapter Six

The five men at Netherfield agreed to a day of sport after their confined and crowded evening socializing at the Meryton assembly hall. The cloudy autumn horizon was otherwise dry—a good day for plucking the distinctive male Blackcock grouse from the skies. The bird's dark glossy blue, almost black, plumage contrasted with the grayness overhead. In flight, its wingtips stretched apart, much like fingers of wide-open hands, with a wide white stripe running across its back. The blackcock moved at faster speeds then most other breeds of grouse and proved difficult to hit with a common flintlock. Whenever it swooped or glided across the sky, the bird tilted its head downward exposing its bright red brows, thus making a perfect target for any shooter with a good eye and an accurate weapon—a Baker Rifle.

Bang.

"Damn Bingley. I never heard a firearm make such a noise." Rawlings said.

The servants who stood by to load the guns and collect the gentlemen's prey did not attempt to conceal their curiosity as they rose up on tiptoes to steal a glimpse at the strange looking flintlock with the exploding sound when fired.

"What caused your shot to sound so different?" Blake stepped closer.

"A family secret." Bingley said.

Blake fixed his eyes on the firearm. "You must tell us. Kind people always share."

"Yes, do." Kent huddled with the other men around Bingley and his gun. "You bagged the lead bird before my flintlock was loaded."

"I suppose he will be willing to tell if one of you kills the most birds in the next hour." Darcy patted the returning golden-haired retriever. The dog whined and frantically wagged his tail until Darcy pulled the dead bird from its mouth and handed it to Bingley. He rubbed the dog's ears. "Of course, you must snag more grouse than Bingley and he already has one in the hand. Otherwise, do not worry. You will be informed soon, because the rifle is important to my business proposition."

"He told you the secret, Darcy?" Blake asked. "Not going to tell?" He shoved his gun into Rawlings' chest. "Well then, you must shoot the bloody birds. Use my firearm; it is newer and better than yours. You are the best shot amongst the three of us." Rawlings, Kent, and Blake dashed away.

Darcy studied the retreating group. He hoped this was a harbinger of things to come—men with differing backgrounds coming together to succeed. He tapped Bingley on the arm. "How many do you think you will need to shoot to keep them at bay?"

"Eight or nine. The time is not enough for Rawlings to bag that many."

Darcy searched over the trees for any birds in flight. None were visible, but he did hear the strange sneezing sound unique to Blackcocks. The males were near. "You seem cock-sure you can out shoot him."

"The gun scares them. More fly by after I fire the shot. I should knock eight or nine out of the sky."

"Trumpeting your skill, Bingley, or your firearm? Well, go to it. I, unlike the others, realize how hopeless defeating you will be unless perchance you happened to bring another marvelous firearm with you?"

"You are on your own. Whom do you think… "

A loud bang sounded from Bingley's rifle. More shots rang out as the other men fired at the cluster of grouse soaring overhead.

"Well, another one for me! For shame, Darcy. Do not aim for the lead bird. I will beat you every time. As slow as you are, you should aim for one flying in the back."

"Do not give me ideas." Unable to squash his chuckle, Darcy pointed his finger and thumb at Bingley in a gun-like fashion before rushing away to join the other men. Once he caught up with his friends, he learned their shots missed their targets. "You are now down two birds." They winced at his pronouncement.

For the allotted time remaining, many shots were fired. They waited to score the killings when they all gathered to return to the house.

"Ahem." Bingley counted the birds held by the men and the servants. "Rawlings, you bagged five. Good job! And, Darcy, only three? I will be kind and not mention the other's total. The family secret is still safe; I shot eight."

"I used Rawlings' firearm. The aim was not right." Blake pointed his gun towards Kent. "I cannot imagine how I avoided shooting him."

"I do not fear you. You would miss even at this close range. Bingley, you are the winner today." Kent handed his lone grouse to the servant.

Rawlings grabbed Bingley's gun and aimed the muzzle at the sky. "You did hit your targets with precision last night, too. You danced with all the pretty girls. Which lovely dove do you believe was the most beautiful?"

"Oh! The eldest Miss Bennet, beyond any doubt; there cannot be two opinions on that point." Bingley answered. "Let us all go in for drinks and refreshments." He signaled the servants to proceed to the house.

Blake blocked Bingley's progress before the men walked any distance. "Not so fast. You tried to get Darcy to dance with Miss Elizabeth Bennet. Would you agree she is as handsome as your Miss Bennet?"

"It is not merely my opinion. Sir William and Mr. Goulding expressed their exuberance about Miss Jane Bennet's charms. Of course, all it takes is one peek at her to acknowledge they were the most astute gentlemen at the assembly." Bingley grabbed his firearm from Rawlings, "You danced with her," adding harshly, "twice."

"I was warning the lady to avoid gentlemen killing birds for the singular purpose of winning a bet."

"Speaking of warnings, Bingley," Darcy interrupted, "do you not believe Miss Bennet smiles too much? You must be cautious when a lady overly exhibits herself. I grant you she is a most handsome lady, but she smiles without rest."

"This would be a dreary world if people smiled only when you did, Darcy. I think Miss Bennet is an angel, and all angels smile."

"And devils do not?" Darcy winked at Rawlings.

"You mistake my meaning," Bingley said. "You go around giving offense wherever you go. I suspect you do not like the world or most people living on it. There is much to like."

"And you go around making friends with everyone. I see grave danger in that."

"Now Darcy, a happy medium exists. Look at him." Rawlings tilted his head at Blake. "Nevertheless, I would place him in the same wagon with Bingley after last night. Smiling all night long, he was!"

"I was being polite and being helpful to our host. Is it not our duty to help him win his place in Hertfordshire? "Is that not what friends do?" Blake held out his hand to Bingley, who held the gun behind his back and away from his eager friend.

"One should spend his time keeping his friends from making serious mistakes," Darcy said.

"Mistakes? To what mistakes do you refer?" Rawlings faced Darcy. Both men stood tall. No more than an inch difference separated their height, and except for Darcy's curly hair and eye color. Anyone would be forgiven for confusing them as twins.

Darcy stepped back and relaxed his rigid stance. "Why, toying with young women. You realize we were the birds last night, and every young lady was the bullet fired from their mercenary mama's rifle. They all hoped they would be successful."

"How did you get to be like this, Darcy? I never met more pleasanter people in all my life," Bingley said.

"Yes, so you said last night."

"When? Oh, I remember, when you refused to dance with Miss Elizabeth."

"It is a compliment which I never pay to any place if I can avoid it."

"Why, Darcy?" Rawlings asked. "You never explained your unfriendliness with the ladies."

"I do not dance unless I am particularly acquainted with my partner. There was no woman in the room for whom it would not have been a punishment for me to stand up with." Darcy shrugged. "I... I knew no one."

"Several uncommonly pretty girls attended. If you wanted an introduction, you should have spoken to me. I met many of them."

Darcy scoffed. "Bingley, you danced with them all, even the plain girls. I will admit that you also danced with the only handsome girl in the room twice and keep staring at her all evening. It appears Miss Bennet caught your fancy."

"I believe her sister, Miss Elizabeth, is another lovely girl," Blake said.

"Her? Humph. She has hardly a good feature in her face, more than one failure in her form, and her manners were not of the fashionable world."

"Darcy, where you envisioned a face without a single remarkable feature, I discovered the most beautiful expression in penetrating eyes, all lively and spirited." Blake paused, staring at an invisible object in the far distance. He closed his eyes, sighed, and then popped them opened. "Where you perceived an imperfect figure, I observed a light and pleasing form. Her manners may not be fashionable as you say, but they are full of easy playfulness when she speaks to anyone."

"Yes, Darcy we all agree. You are afraid of women," Rawlings said.

"Afraid? I am not afraid; I am not in the habit of toying with any lady."

"Having a dance at a ball is not toying, Darcy. You danced at Almack's many times." Rawlings tapped Darcy's shoulder several times.

Darcy brushed Rawlings' hand away. "Meryton is not London and this assembly hall dance cannot compare to the assembly rooms at the least exclusive social club in England, let alone at the most."

"True, but several ladies would be pursued by the finest men if they secured admittance to Almack's. You need not ignore all the women. No harm will come to you if you danced once." Rawlings said.

Darcy shook his head in disapproval. "In the country, a lady's imagination is rapid; jumping from admiration to love, from love to matrimony, in a flash. Gentleman must remain indifferent here. You displayed too much friendliness last night. All your smiling and laughing is toying, in my opinion."

"What is the point of a dance if not for smiling, dancing, and laughing? I suppose you would rather discuss books." Rawlings threw up his hands and spun away.

"All I saw was a collection of people in whom there was little beauty and no fashion. The room was full of mothers and their daughters, exhibiting themselves for our attention."

Rawlings twisted back around. "I was wrong. You are not a fool, Darcy. You, sir, are a pompous arse."

The other three men stood still with their mouths agape and brows raised. They waited to hear Darcy's reaction, but Rawlings spoke first.

"Do not appear so shocked. In the past, I was as arrogant as you. Admit the truth about yourself."

"How am I pompous?" Darcy's eyes turned black. "Do you believe it because I am neither captured by a pretty face nor do I allow a young lady to trap me?" He gasped at his own question, the heat rising on his cheeks.

Rawlings stood close enough to eye him. A full minute ticked by before he stepped back, relaxed his taut muscles, and answered, but this time with a gentler tone. "Some women do as you say. Gentlemen attended the dance as well. You did not speak to them either."

"What, those clod hoppers? I have not the smallest interest in any of them. All they want from me is money or an association they can use later. I do not lend my name freely."

"Sometimes you need something from those types of men." Kent said.

Darcy examined his four friends' faces, lined up together, shoulders almost touching, as they scrutinized his every twitch, a foreboding sense overtook him. He turned, his legs taking long strides towards the house; the others following behind. Darcy did not slow his step until he arrived at the door.

Bingley reached him first. "Everybody was most kind and attentive to me with no formality, nor stiffness; I soon felt acquainted with all in the room. They were accommodating people, and, Darcy, you must admit the number of pretty girls was unusual for a country dance."

"As I stated, I witnessed little beauty and no fashion."

"Surely you are not speaking about the Bennets?" Bingley asked.

Darcy paused, recognizing Bingley's anxiety by the pitch in his voice, mixed with half shock and half apprehension. "I grant you Miss Bennet is well-bred, but her mother is intolerable, and the younger sisters not worth speaking to."

"Including Miss Elizabeth? I dare say she is a beauty," Blake said.

"She a beauty? I should as soon call her mother a wit."

***

The men separated the moment they entered the house, forgoing the refreshments and the wine placed in the library for them. Darcy headed for his personal chambers where his valet was waiting with a hot bath. His thoughts replayed the angry words spoken at the morning hunt while he slipped into the heated and welcomed water. Without warning, Miss Jane Bennet's image appeared. Her elegance matched the best ladies in London, her fair complexion was without fault; her blue eyes sparkled much like icy crystal rather than a sunny summer sky whenever she gazed at or spoke to anyone, including himself. She was the most handsome woman in the room.

Bingley had claimed her before he even had the opportunity to present himself. He had planned to dance with her and had avoided everyone as he mentally practiced not only the words he would use to ask for the dance, but the depth of his smile to present to her. On this occasion, Bingley had told the truth. She was the image of an angel. And now she would be *his* angel. Proper etiquette demanded guests not compete with the host unless invited to do so, and when a woman was the prize, Bingley would not allow the competition.

"Humph." Darcy snorted as he recalled how Bingley had tried pushing the second sister on him. He remembered giving Miss Elizabeth a swift, flickering glance. She was not tall, her curls were almost unruly, her mouth was too large, and her complexion was not fair. She sat alone in a chair, tapping her foot to the beat of the music. She smiled to everyone, but when given the opportunity to treat him kindly, she chose to send a smirk his way, and then laughed at him with her friend.

Blake's defense nagged him. Light and pleasing? Bah. Darcy reminded himself to pay closer attention to her when they met next. "Blake must not be toying with the girl. I did not bring him here to cause ill-feelings with the locals."

"Sir?" The valet asked.

Darcy shook his head and then slunk further in the water as he tried to determine why Blake was so adamant about her beauty. He closed his eyes. Brown irises with steaks of gold gazed at him, her right brow raised and her lips curved upwards, not in a cruel manner, but a playful one, exactly as Blake suggested.

He realized he reacted to her image in other ways as well. He forced his thoughts to shift to tonight's drinks after dinner when he and Bingley would begin to reveal the terms for the partnership. Will they agree? Will Blake flee? Agree or flee? Darcy chuckled at the rhyme and then realized that this might be the most expensive venture of his life.

Chapter Seven

The purpose for being at Netherfield Park was not sport or leisure; it was business. Once the men finished their evening meal, they headed for the library. The servants built a crackling fire to remove the nighttime chill in the room, but not enough heat escaped to cause them to sweat or nod off after the six-course dinner, which grouse had overfilled one serving plate.

Darcy entered a few moments after Blake, Rawlings, and Kent had chosen their seats from chairs scattered around the room. Bingley followed close behind and placed his unusual rifle against the fireplace within clear view.

Rawlings rushed and picked up the gun, out-racing Blake by a single step. "This is an impressive firearm, Bingley." He inspected the trigger, muzzle, and firing mechanism and then held the gun in the shooting position, aimed at the ceiling, to check its site.

"Yes, without argument, it did the honors today. Why does it work so well?" Blake asked.

"Darcy, I cannot take anymore," Bingley said in a whining voice. "Blake is driving me daft. He followed me everywhere, hounding me. The rifle is all he talked about this afternoon."

Rawlings turned around and almost knocked Blake off his feet. "Here! Take the damn thing."

Blake grabbed the gun. "Bingley, tell us how it works?"

"For God's sake, answer him now. I cannot listen to any more questions about the blasted thing." Kent complained holding his hands over his ears.

"Is this how you won senior wrangler's honors at Cambridge? Did you question the professors to death? Did they run mad from the room?" Rawlings asked.

Bingley stayed busy stirring the fire as he waited.

Darcy was pleased Bingley had paid attention when he had explained how delaying an answer was a successful technique to gain interest.

The men stopped chatting. Bingley smoothed his jacket, uttered a loud "Ahem," and once all eyes were upon him, began with his story. "Blake is holding a modified Baker Rifle."

The men stared at the gun and then in unison said, "The Baker Rifle?"

"Yes, except more accurate."

"You demonstrated that today. You say modified; how so?" Blake asked.

"Look close. The Baker has been modified in the muzzle for better accuracy, and the firing mechanism is different." Bingley cringed when Blake aimed the rifle at his head to peer inside. "Stop." He grabbed the rifle away.

Blake's mouth dropped open.

Bingley pointed to the cap. "This is a percussion cap. It is almost certain to explode when struck causing the ball to be propelled out much quicker."

"That explains why my shots missed their targets," Blake said nonchalantly. "I aimed at the same birds as you and since your shot reached the bird first, you claimed the prize."

"Yes, he tried to use that exact reasoning." Bingley pointed to Darcy. Rawlings hooted and teased the two men calling their excuse pretentious.

"I can understand how these modifications helped you kill birds, but how does the rifle fit in Darcy's partnership?" Kent asked.

"Will we get to own one?"

"For the sake of God, Blake." Rawlings shouted. "What is it with you and that bloody gun? I am interested, but you are obsessed."

"Every year my father holds a shooting party for all his friends, and he is never kind about my lack of success. I purchase the finest firearms. Nonetheless, I cannot hit a cow standing still at three feet. Your rifle may make me competitive at the next shoot."

"Well, keep it then."

Blake's eyes widened. "Truly, Bingley?"

Bingley handed him the rifle, shouting, "But do not aim it at your head!" The men broke into laughter and once the noise quieted down, Bingley continued with his story. "My family is responsible for the improvements to the gun. My uncle has been unsuccessful in the negotiations that my father had begun with the British army so I have taken over the effort. If I am successful then so shall you be."

"Oh, so our partnership would benefit from the sale of the gun?" Rawlings asked.

Darcy stood. "In fact, gentlemen, I believe the firearms transaction will generate needed capital from the profits with which to pursue other ventures."

"Since you are the person bringing this group together, Darcy, tell us what you envision as our roles?" Blake asked.

"I spent the last year studying the advances in machinery which will revolutionize our lives and transform society. Machines will bring plentiful profits, yet the start-up costs are so staggering, no one gentleman could afford it. I believe a business alliance is, therefore, necessary."

Rawlings pointed to himself, Blake and Kent. "But, why us?"

"When Bingley brought me the rifle, I knew who else I wanted to join with me. You all provide a critical component to the overall group. Bingley is offering up his family talent, allowing us to participate in the profits."

"Why?" Rawlings and Blake asked in unison.

"Bingley lacks connections." Darcy directed his gaze at Blake. "Your uncle is associated with the man who oversees the military—"

"I assume you speak of my Uncle Harrowby?" Blake interrupted. He glanced at the other men. "Lord Liverpool is a great friend of his."

"Precisely. Present our ideas to him at your one of Lord Harrowby's dinners, especially if Lord Liverpool is there. Discuss the issue over brandy and cigars. You are well connected to powerful and influential politicians, Lord Liverpool the most critical for our needs. This is helpful to Bingley's family." Darcy hoped Blake accepted the simplified description of the role for him. He had to convince him that a tradesman could not do this only someone of a higher station.

"Darcy, is this connection all you want? I am to acquire a great profit by drinking a brandy or two. I doubt this is all you want."

"There is much more to my plan but enough of this for tonight. The billiards table is waiting our evening game. Tomorrow, I will explain everything." Darcy sensed a pullback was necessary. He would mull over his approach tonight. At least Blake was interested.

***

Darcy stared out the library window the following morning. The Netherfield men, meeting an hour earlier than intended, were convening for a full day of serious talks. The plan to remain indoors was a good one; the clouds releasing a horrendous soaking to anyone brave enough to venture out of doors. He squared his shoulders, turned around, and faced the empty room.

He could still pursue the effort albeit at a slower pace without Kent's agreement; however, Blake was essential for obtaining the profits from the sale of the Baker rifle and bankrolling the venture. Otherwise, two choices remained—the other men would need to invest heavily, or he must mortgage his family estate to cover the funding.

Darcy paused to assess the readiness of the library. The staff had prepared the library while the men had slept. They arranged the most comfortable chairs around the fireplace in such a way to allow for open conversation and a table, complete with coffee, tea, fruits, and sweet treats, hugged the far wall. On the other side of the room a sideboard had been stocked with various types of liquors, which were to be kept ready at all times—the coffee and tea hot at one table and the liquor carafes full at the other.

He turned back towards the window, this time his focus was on what would happen. He anticipated which chairs his friends would chose, their reactions, and the answers they would give. He reminded himself of the importance of coming to an accord before requesting the legal agreements be drawn up.

The men's reflections became visible in the glass of the window as they filed in the room. Blake did sit in the largest chair, nearest the fire, and an anxious and fidgeting Bingley stood by the fireplace. Rawlings and Kent elected to sit nearer the window. Satisfied the time had arrived he turned around and gave the signal to start the conversation.

Bingley coughed several times to gain everyone's attention. "I feel like a teacher standing in front of a room full of bad boys biding their time until they can go outside to play."

"We are listening. I suspect what we want most is to learn more about the partnership." Rawlings answered.

Darcy sensed a seriousness take hold of the room.

"Where do the profits from the Baker rifle go?" Blake asked.

"In machinery and the products they create, which we will ship overseas in a global path, trading as we go." Bingley looked at his friends' faces, shook his head. "Yes, like school—confusion reigns. Very well, I shall explain first about the machines."

"Machines?"

"Steam-powered engines are the type of machines we will use to manufacture goods at significantly lower cost. Many believe my uncle, James Watt, is the inventor of the steam engine. He does build steam engines, but much more efficient ones by using a condenser he designed than those simpler models invented by others."

"Who uses Watt's engines?" Rawlings asked.

"His machines are found in more than five hundred factories and mines throughout England," Bingley inclined his head towards his friend and added, "including Darcy's mines. While my uncle was not the inventor of the steam engine, he is credited with inventing the parts necessary for the locomotive."

Rawlings and Blake scoffed and then argued with Bingley over its lack of safety, unreliability and, in particular, the slowness. A long discussion followed on the future of the railroad in England.

"Perhaps the faster speed will not happen at first, but one day I am positive, and long before our children are full grown, we will rely upon the railroad for moving goods and passengers at an accelerated pace, which we do not enjoy today."

"Do you believe people are willing to sit in a strange conveyance which requires a fire to make it move? Blake exaggerated a shudder.

Bingley turned his head towards the window. "Today is a rainy day. I want you to think of the comfort of a locomotive carriage speeding along a track. Locomotives will not travel on muddy, bumpy roads as we do nowadays."

"Any other uses for this steam-powered engine?" Rawlings asked. "The locomotion seem risky to me."

"Today, many inventors are trying to modify ships to speed across the oceans. Do not scoff. Steamboats exist today that travel down the river. So you see, steam-powered ships are not as farfetched as you may think. Great profit will be the outcome for anyone investing now. The faster the product reaches the buyer, the quicker the payment and the higher the profit. Now you know where my money comes from – machinery. To attend a Bingley gathering, you had best be able to distinguish pistons from cylinders and flyball governors from rotary engines. My pedigree is rich with inventors." Bingley released a long breath and plopped into his chair.

"Who are these people? Do we know of them?" Rawlings asked.

"A few, such as Watt, but only our friends and family within our circle know the rest."

"A circle exists among inventors?"

"Yes, Blake. Circles exist among us much as they do with the aristocracy and gentry. Many newspapers saturate the pages with stories on the elite in London society, and most people know who is included in your circles. Little is written about the other persons of merit so only a few are aware of a similar ranking of engineers, architects, and even inventors. The Royal Society invites the most successful inventors and men with the highest level of knowledge in the sciences to join. My uncle's portrait hangs in the gallery and most of my family belongs to that sphere. There are also other groups with their own distinctions."

"Other groups?" Blake leaned forward.

"Certainly." Bingley glanced at the other tradesman's son. "Kent hails from a successful assortment of shipbuilders and mercantilists. He resides at the top."

Rawlings and Blake turned towards Kent, who shrugged his shoulders in a casual manner.

"One day machines will do the most tedious work and do away with using unskilled laborer."

Rawlings jeered, "Surely, Bingley, machinery will not replace servants? How will these things launder the clothes, cook the meals, clean the house, or pull our carriages? You are not saying your steam engines will accomplish all that?"

To temper Bingley's enthusiasm, Darcy jumped up, forcing the attention on him. He believed the time had come to take control over the conversation. "Perhaps not. Nevertheless, major changes are coming from these new inventions." He spoke at length about the types of machines involved in textiles, including the power looms used at his own facility and other current uses.

A debate ensued on the merits of jeopardizing money on steam-powered engines. Blake ignored the conversation, settled back into his chair, aiming and firing an invisible Baker rifle until he heard his name attached to a discussion of insurance.

"Is underwriting what I am to do in this alliance? And with what money? Mine? Or do you plan to announce 'purchase your insurance for all your machinery here' and everyone will give us money?" Blake rolled his eyes.

"Of course not." Darcy paused while he formulated a reply. He readied himself for his friends' reactions, which would follow as soon as the words left his mouth. "We can disguise the types of insurance we are selling—"

"Ha!" Bingley interrupted. "I am surprised. You hate disguise of any sort."

Darcy detected the conspiratorial smile shared among his friends. He controlled his sigh and then promised himself to try a different word than disguise, perhaps conceal or cloak, even mask might work. One evening years ago after many mugs of ale, he had pronounced his disdain for disguise, in fact, he abhorred it. With the conceit of a young man, he declared he would never participate in any such deception. And so, his friends, also drunk, but sober enough to remember, chose Bingley to be the one to call him out.

"Disguise? You?" Bingley asked causing a round of laughter from the other three men.

Darcy paid no heed to their chiding and forged ahead. "It may be a long time coming, but we will be setting up the foundation and would get a jump on all our competitors if we include insuring machines as well as the common fire and shipping insurances. This is business and, yes, concealment is an important factor at the start of a new venture. At least until it is too late for anyone to do better than we can. Now, I would not lie to anyone who asked but," he paused and then tried to speak with conviction, "I would respond in an appropriate manner to safeguard our investments."

Blake crossed his arms. "And the money, Darcy, where exactly does that come from for this venture and especially the insurance? I am not in the position to underwrite all these types of insurance."

The men stilled in their chairs, not a twitch of a finger or blink of an eye occurred. After a second of absolute deadness, Rawlings began to fidget before finally interrupting the empty air. "Yes, do explain. We are all..." he glanced around, "all of us are interested in how to finance everything."

Darcy squared his shoulders and stood erect. "I have thought this through. About your question Blake, I made many friends among investors when I invested in shipping insurance. I know many of them wish to expand their activities, but we need to make the largest part of the investment if we wish to realize the majority of the profit. A successful ocean crossing equates to all profit, which would be available for the other endeavors. Every arrangement begins with the profit from the sale of the Baker rifle."

"None of our money will be used?"

"We may need to fund a portion of the costs for developing the new products."

"How much?" Rawlings asked.

"With the sale of the rifle, perhaps one thousand pounds."

"And without the sale?" Blake asked.

"We would have to make up for the lost profit, which I total to be over one hundred thousand pounds."

Blake jumped up. "Twenty thousand each, Darcy?"

"Yes. So you see, Blake, you are important to the venture."

"You could say I was the most important one."

"In the beginning, yes."

Heavy breathing reverberated throughout the room. Rawlings tapped the arms of his chair, Kent kept glancing at Bingley, and Blake paced the floor.

"Could you explain everything now?" Rawlings asked.

Darcy began a long speech about his plans for the alliance.

After a minute, Blake stopped listening to the conversation, closed his eyes, tapped his foot to a tune heard only by him, wet his lips with his tongue, sniffed the air, and took slow deep breaths until Kent shouted——.

"I will not be involved in treason!"

Chapter Eight

"Treason?"

Rawlings and Blake gawked at each other; Bingley grimaced. Even the servants flinched at the word, but Whitson shooed the footmen out the room and with as little noise as possible returned to restocking the sideboard with hot tea, brandy, and some of Rawlings' favorite sweet pastries.

The rain smashed against the window increasing in intensity as the seconds passed. The normal crackling sounds filling the room were absent since the fire had diminished. Whitson was quick to rebuild the fire.

Darcy spotted the tense muscles jutting out on Rawlings' neck and glanced around at the other friends who also appeared stressed. He answered in what he hoped was a calm, confident voice; this was not the time to hesitate for very long. "No. I doubt the government would consider this proposition to be treason. Yes, we will be doing business with a prohibited country, but we are not at war with them nor are we selling the Baker rifle to anyone other than our own military. Finally, actual trading would not start until England lifts their trade embargo. We must set up the deal now, and not wait for the politicians."

Rawlings jumped up and took long strides over to the sideboard. "Do any of you gents want brandy? Damn, I may pour myself two! I do not care what bloody time of day it is." The men mumbled their agreement. Bingley rushed to help fill the glasses.

Kent hands clasped the arms of his chair squeezing until his knuckles turned white. His voice sounded shrill to Darcy's ears. "Why this deal? There must be some other way. I am not in a position to risk my future on a chance your assumptions might be correct. I am not a member of the protected class. I can be charged with a crime since I do not have any noble peers in my family."

"When everything is settled, the fur trading business owned by Mr. John Jacob Astor will be the one left standing in North America. He will prevail over our cousins in British America. We must negotiate a deal with Astor now."

Rawlings swallowed a large gulp of his drink. "There are conflicts still between our countries. They talk of war again. Will dealing with this American cause us problems? "

Darcy nodded. "Yes, some risks do exist. For now, we must keep our efforts in secret. Contracts will be written in such a way to conceal our connection with Astor to protect us if the problems escalated into war."

Rawlings, Blake, and Kent, coughed in unison. Bingley stopped pouring the brandy into the glasses long enough to utter the oft-repeated teasing phrase Darcy knew was coming. "I am shocked that you still profess that disguise of every sort is your abhorrence."

Darcy maintained a blank expression, although he sensed the tiniest evidence of a smile forming at the corners of his mouth. He realized now that using a word other than disguise would not stop the taunts.

Rawlings took another large gulp. "Darcy, how are we to accomplish this?"

"It will be necessary to operate through one of Astor's London connections,"

"And which one of us is to meet this person and make the necessary arrangements?" Rawlings glanced around the room and noted the other men had turned their heads away.

When Rawlings, with both brows, raised pointed his finger at his own chest, Darcy raised his hands upwards a little and, with a small shrug, mouthed the word, yes. Rawlings scoffed loudly.

Darcy felt it was an insincere gesture and assumed Rawlings was interested, perhaps excited, at the prospect of going to America. He decided to speak with him apart from the others, if possible that night.

The three men, stunned by the information, walked around the room and stretched their legs. They huddled around the refreshments murmuring among themselves. Bingley sat in his chair glaring at his hands, while Darcy settled back in his chair sipping his brandy. He tried to give off an air of confidence while he worried if he had used enough finesse with Blake. At this moment, he also wondered if even Rawlings would agree.

Rawlings returned to his seat. "Who is this man in London, Astor's connection? What is his background, and can he be trusted? And finally, why would he do this?"

"He is a tradesman established in the import and export business in town. He has a reputation as an honorable and trustworthy man. He will take risks to better himself and his family. I am assured he is the best of men."

"Does this man have a name and why is he not here?" Rawlings asked.

"I did not invite him because I wanted us to decide if we should pursue this risky venture first.

"Well, what is his name? Perhaps I might know of him." Kent asked.

"Mr. John Cuffage."

"Cuffage? In import and export?" Rawlings furrowed his brow and rubbed his forehead. "Kent, do you know him? You family is in that business, surely you have met him."

"Not I. Perhaps my uncle has had dealings with him. I am not acquainted with anyone by that name."

"Mr. Rogers suggested him," Darcy answered.

"Ah." The men relaxed.

Darcy knew this information would relieve their anxiety since his secretary had been the most sought after of all the men of the profession. So much so, when Mr. Rogers accepted working for him, London gossips whispered that he attempted to secure a lifetime position since the two men were the same age.

"How does he know this man?" Rawlings asked.

"Mr. Cuffage approached my secretary, offering to provide special services, cigars, and wine. Well, during their meeting, Mr. Rogers learned he had befriended Astor when he lived in London. Today Cuffage is Astor's contact point for all trading between our countries. Once Mr. Rogers heard of my recent interest in Astor, he remembered the conversation and made the suggestion."

"That is all to the good, but will he maintain the secrecy we need?" Rawlings asked.

"Mr. Cuffage is very discreet in his business dealings. I can assure you that each one of you has come into contact with him." When they all objected, Darcy swallowed the last remnants of his brandy and held up his glass. "Have you not been to the New World Cigar and Wine shop on Bond Street? Mr. Cuffage is the lone source for French liquors and has been so ever since we began fighting with Napoleon." His friends affirmed that they had been to the shop, as had all gentlemen in town, Darcy announced with what he knew was a smug tone, "He is the owner."

"Oh, I still do not think I know him," Kent replied.

Rawlings scanned through a few articles dealing with the fur business, while Darcy expounded on the risks involved. "Nevertheless, is the fur trade a profitable business? What do you see happening with all these furs?" He pointed to the paper in his hand. "This article is not so positive."

Darcy squared his shoulders, and lifted his chin. The time had arrived to announce, in the simplest terms, his global strategy. "I own interests in two different shipping lines and as such I plan to ship our finished textiles to America in trade for the furs, and then ship Astor's furs to Russia, the Continent, and even China one day. There, I assure you, we shall find a great demand for them. We will obtain items of trade from each of these areas and move on to the next trading place. The pattern will repeat until we have circumvented the entire world without having the expense or the risk of returning to the home base. And with our investments and ownership in the future railroads and steamships, we will realize unimaginable profits."

Darcy held up a handful of orders. "North America is the only major supplier left for these furs. We must start there and I have no doubt John Jacob Astor will prevail over our British cousins. The sale of Bingley's modified Baker rifles to our military will provide the needed capital to begin our quest around the world. Another critical reason for establishing an arrangement with Astor is his efforts to open a fort on the west coast of the continent. Economically, we would need to use that port as a part of the route to reach China."

"Is this not too grand of an idea?" Blake asked.

"All great alliances start with a grand idea. Otherwise, there would be no need for a partnership of any kind. Individuals could proceed and be successful."

"How will your ships make their way to the Americas?" Rawlings asked. "I understand British cargo ships are in danger if they appear anywhere near their shores, let alone dock there."

"Some of the states do not agree with the embargo and have the secret blessing of the United States government to allow them docking privileges. It is my understanding that the USS Constitution has even escorted ships to and from New England ports. England's politicians are aware of this situation." Darcy glanced at Blake. "Here is another example of how you can help the partnership. We need the prohibition lifted."

"I presume you are again referring to my uncle Lord Harrowby?" Blake glanced at Kent and Rawlings. "He is a force in Parliament and could help with the politics if needed."

Darcy nodded.

"It may be better to keep this among ourselves until we become established," Blake said. "I for one do not wish my father to know about it. He does not think too kindly on business."

"Nor the people involved in trade I suspect," Kent added.

Whitson entered the room carrying a silver plate with a single letter placed on it. He thrust the plate forward to his master. "An urgent message has arrived."

Bingley grabbed the letter, broke open the seal, and as he read it, frowned. He did not provide any information, instead remained quiet the rest of the day, diverting his eyes whenever anyone glanced his way. Darcy grew concerned, but said nothing.

Darcy spent the remainder of the day discussing the endeavor until each man was satisfied they understood the entire plan. Rawlings seemed eager to partner. Kent maintained an unreadable face. Blake remained engrossed in his own thoughts.

The men integrated their evening meal with the lighthearted talk they had shared upon their arrival, but had been missing that morning, although the conversation did not stray far from their earlier discussion.

"Bingley, did I mention I saw a steam locomotive three years ago?" Blake asked. "The name of the blasted thing was *Catch-Me-Who-Can.* What a childish name! I never forgot it. If my memory is correct, there was not much enthusiasm for it. I did not ride on it."

"Was that the gigantic monstrosity that went around a circle at Torrington Square off Gower Street?" Rawlings scoffed.

"Yes, it went in a circle." Blake drew an imaginary circle in the air and rolled his head in unison. "And on the... what did they call those things that kept breaking? Oh, yes, rails."

"That was an early model. There are better ones now."

"I rode on it and found it fascinating. I am not afraid of it." Kent glanced at Blake and then turned to Darcy. "Did you not take a turn on it, too? Did you not pay your shilling to take a ride the same day?"

"Yes, it is true, I did ride it as did my young sister, Georgiana. I could see the possibilities even then. One day, I wager, even you, Blake, will willingly ride one of his locomotives!"

"I think I shall stick with my horses or my carriage." Blake turned his head towards Rawlings and waggled his brows.

Rawlings raised and lowered his in return. "Yes, a little oats and some sugar, and we are good to go fifty miles in a single day."

Bingley scoffed. "Fifty miles in a day? Locomotives will one day go that far in a single hour, and without the need for a long stop for a change of horses. Even the early model you mentioned traveled at fifteen miles per hour."

"Well *it* did not travel fifty miles an hour that day. Why my horse can gallop faster." Blake said.

"Yes, but he would be dead in no time if he had to run at that speed nonstop for any period." Kent replied.

"Unless, of course, the horse is named Conqueror." Darcy toasted Blake with his wine glass.

Blake grimaced at the mention of Darcy's horse from their childhood. "One day Darcy, I will own a steed capable of challenging and defeating you in a race."

Chapter Nine

Bingley's stable, an average size for a country estate, provided sufficient stalls for his guests' horses and conveyances—barely. The men had arrived in carriages, pulled by a team of four, and they brought along their favorite riding horse. After a few days, the stable hands discovered the habits of the men: Lord Blake favored riding more than the others did, preferring an early morning ride and then a second one before sunset; Mr. Kent chose mid-afternoon. Mr. Rawlings did not venture out of the house often, while Mr. Bingley rode when estate business required it and only when accompanied by his steward and Mr. Darcy.

And so, when Darcy walked through the stable door before the sun had risen, the stable hands were surprised.

Blake caught sight of him out of the corner of his eyes and delayed his leaving. "Did you come for a sunrise ride?"

"I did." Darcy signaled to the boy who dashed off to fetch his horse. He looked around. "I believe we are the ones who ride in the early morning."

"You mean we are the men who wake up in the early morning."

"True. They come for breakfast when the afternoon is near."

Blake, sitting atop his horse, pulled himself up to his full-seated height. He lifted the reins. "Shall we race? Or would you prefer to trot like an old dowager?"

"It is still dark. Are you not respectful of your horse? You do not know the area well enough to avoid some hidden rut." Darcy mounted his stallion, sighing as he settled into the saddle. Blake was the most competitive friend of his acquaintance.

"As you say, old woman. We shall trot, but at first light, we shall race." Blake winked.

They nudged their horses forward and progressed down a well-worn path. Darcy assumed the route would end at an area suitable for a gallop. He was correct as his friend did lead him to the wide-open fields of the East Meadow.

They had arrived there the moment the sun rose. Blake glanced at Darcy, shook his reins, pushed his heels in the horse, and shouted, "Now!"

Darcy, well prepared for a sudden race, urged his horse forward. They came to a stop ten minutes later at the far side of the meadow and with Blake more than a horse's length behind. Darcy spun around on his saddle. "I enjoyed the race. I hope the dust from my stallion did not distract you."

"One day, I will find a horse worthy enough to beat yours. What is his name again?" Blake asked.

"Bouchain."

"Do you always name your horses after military battles?"

"No. For my mares I choose Shakespearean names, such as Rosalind or Juliet."

"Well, I name mine after favorite places." Blake patted his horse.

Darcy eyed Blake's horse and then lifted his eyes up at his friend, with a questioning gaze.

"Chesterfield." Blake admitted.

Remembering the rumors flying around London two years ago, Darcy shook his head. He rarely listened to malicious talk, but the gossip centered on Blake dallying with Lady Beatrice while visiting friends in Chesterfield. It was his manner to discount rumors, yet this time he had believed some of this could be true. He wondered if this was a partial reason for the name.

"Shall we rest over there?" Darcy pointed to left side of the field where the grand oak tree stood.

"No!" Blake caught his breath and then added, "No, the… horses need to drink." He pointed to the water flowing on the other side of the trees lining the western part of the meadow.

"You were somewhat quiet yesterday." Darcy said as they dismounted and led their horses to the bubbling creek.

"The business was all very interesting, but…" Blake searched the trees lining the end of the meadow. He leaned forward, furrowed his brow as he focused in on a specific point, and then relaxed.

Darcy waited; hoping his silence would encourage his friend to continue. He reminded himself to use finesse. He would not pressure him.

Blake whirled around to face Darcy. "Surely you are not saying tradesmen are on an equal level with gentry?"

"The gentry are structured around class distinctions of, well, farmers. Of course, most of our income comes from all the land and natural resources we own."

"Come, come, Darcy. That is much different from selling items to the commoners. We do not sell; we collect the rents from our tenants who do the selling."

"Even so then, is it not business keeping us rich through them? What purpose is raising sheep, mining, or growing crops if not for putting the by-products up for sale? And to the masses! Is that not trade of sorts? Or is it accepted because the gentry do it?"

"I understand what you say, but do not forget who I am. With privilege comes social responsibility as well. Your uncle is an Earl. What does he think of your partnering with Bingley? Does he even know?"

Darcy glanced at his boots.

"See! You are as reluctant to reveal the truth to your own family as I would be to tell mine. And yet, you seem excited to subordinate yourself to trade."

"Do not concern yourself about me, Blake. I asked Bingley to manage the new inventions, and, I am asking Kent to handle the import and export business and all modes of selling the goods. Both their families possess expertise in these areas. You see, we need them."

"But as partners? Can we not simply hire them?"

"Hire them to do what? Hand us money? If we wish to benefit from the substantial profits from the sale of their rifle we must partner. Otherwise we would only receive a fee, too small to fund the other ventures."

Blake leaned down and cupped a palm full of water. "And my role?"

"Your responsibility will not require anything more than bringing in the connections and managing some of the financial aspects. No doubt your mathematical prowess will be used mostly to count the profits."

"Who will draw up the legal papers? Every lawyer and solicitor owe their livelihood to the self-same people we do not want to know. Darcy, you cannot keep this a secret in town."

"Mr. Phillips an attorney in Meryton handled the Netherfield lease agreements for Bingley. He appears very capable of drawing up the documents for the partnership."

"You cannot guarantee his confidence."

"In his eyes, we are very rich and powerful men. If so much as a single word leaked about our activities, he assumes we would destroy him. Of course, the obscene amount of money we will pay him is another incentive for maintaining silence. We are his most notable clients, and, do not forget, he cannot afford to jeopardize the loss of Netherfield Park revenue after we leave either. I doubt anyone here will think ill of you."

"Not this place, Darcy. I care not what the families in Meryton discover. I care about the important people in London."

"Your partnering will remain a secret. I promise you, Blake. No one in London will find out. With all these questions, does this mean you are considering joining with us?"

"I will give you my decision later."

"I do have one more request."

Blake crossed his arms.

"If you decide to join us, please not another word about tradesmen, rank, class, or any mention of how they are beneath us. Keep those thoughts to yourself. Division among the partners would destroy it from within.

Without responding, Blake lined his horse up for mounting. "Shall we head back?"

As they leapt upon their horses to return to Netherfield, Darcy, detecting a faint scent, lifted his chin, sniffed the air, and thought lavender—I smell lavender. Darcy twisted around and, seeing no one, began to worry Miss Elizabeth Bennet had crept into his thoughts again. She had worn that exact fragrance at the assembly hall dance and he had not been able to forget the light aroma. He turned away from the wooded area, assuming he had imagined the scent. What he had not anticipated was the sight of his friend poised to race again.

Before Blake could move, Darcy yelled, "Now."

Neither man nor horse slowed or stopped until they reached the stables.

"Will you be joining me tomorrow? You must give me another chance to best you in a race." Blake handed his reins over to the stable hand.

"You had two chances this morning." Darcy dismounted. "Well, I am truly sorry. I have Pemberley business that I must address. Perhaps in the afternoon or the next day?"

"I am always available for riding, even twice a day suits me well. I do not mind going alone in the morning." Blake stepped with a brisker stride towards the house mumbling, "If I must join this alliance in order to spend more time with Miss Elizabeth Bennet, the risks might be worth it."

Darcy felt a sudden sense of uneasiness as he made sense of his friend's mutterings. He had not imagined smelling the lavender fragrance in the air. Miss Elizabeth Bennet had been nearby.

***

Rawlings loathed early morning rides. He preferred drinking a pot of coffee while reading letters and the latest newspapers from town. This morning he did not require coffee as the newspaper was old and there was but a single letter, expressed from his father. He grumbled as he handed the message to Logan. "I have no choice. I must return to town."

"Perhaps a short visit will suffice."

"As short as possible. Plan to leave the morning after Sir William's party. I will not forgo a chance to flirt with Miss Lydia." He smiled. "No carriage. Now, let me tell you about this alliance."

Logan handed the opened letter back while Rawlings explained the whole of Darcy's business scheme to his valet as he took his morning bath. He omitted nothing while Logan remained silent throughout the soliloquy.

"Have you come to any conclusions?" Rawlings asked.

"I am sure you will be tasked to handle the fur trade. Kent is not up to it."

"Darcy hinted as much. I pretended to be annoyed, but in truth I am excited for the opportunity to sail to the new world and spend a little time getting to know the business and this man, John Jacob Astor."

"How long would that take? Ocean voyages can be very lengthy." Logan said.

"Kent indicated at least nine weeks is needed for the crossing. I will stay another month or two before returning home. All totaled no more than five or six months should be necessary. If we leave in December, we could be back by spring, which will be excellent timing. I have no desire to be in England during the London season."

Rawlings had grown tired of the annual parade of debutants fostered on the unmarried men through parties, dances, dinners, and theater outings. It started in February when Parliament opened and ended before summer commenced. No one wanted to be in London in the heat, preferring instead to shift to their country estates or stay at one of the fashionable seaside locations, such as Bath or Bristol.

"I am curious about this new land of opportunity. But is that not a long time to be away?"

Rawlings shrugged. "Perhaps if we can get passage on the *Lively*, the transatlantic journey would take less than forty days. Kent's family built the ship. A cousin, I believe. His name is Watt as well; an Edward Watt. I do not know if he is a relative of Bingley's uncle. I assume they forge marriage alliances in their circle, much like us in ours.

"For our comfort's sake, let us hope the *Lively* is headed our way."

"We must go," Rawlings said, the strength of his voice increasing with each word. "Bingley suggested I investigate Robert Fulton. He has built a commercial steam vessel using a Watt engine. Once in New York, we need to take a ride on Fulton's North River Steamboat to Albany. Bingley is anxious to learn all he can. Make a note of that."

Logan scribbled in a journal. "Bingley and Kent seem to be well connected."

"Kent and Bingley are attached to some of the most progressive families. Although I suspect Kent is the better-connected man of the two. His family is involved in shipping, textiles, import, export, gems, and what else, I know not. He is from an exceedingly ambitious family."

"Yes, it seems so." Logan stood to stir the fire.

"I will never be able to repay Darcy for including me in this venture. I suppose he thought he was returning a favor from that night."

Logan turned around, his brows raised. "Yes. Where would Mr. Darcy be if not for you?"

"Forty thousand pounds richer, I imagine."

"But, he would not have survived the ordeal. He is not as strong as you."

"He is stronger than I and has the markings of a true gentleman." Rawlings said.

Finished with the fire, Logan returned to his chair. "Fur trade? Is that the true reason you want to journey to America?"

"No, you are quite right again. I would like to look for further opportunities." Rawlings tapped his fingers in a marching rhythm. "I wonder at the lack of concern most Englishmen have of America's competitiveness. They will push us unlike any other country has. I do possess uneasiness about the supposed British superiority."

"How so?" Logan asked.

"We were unable to be victorious in battle which was not an accurate indication of our strength. Although, I fear, it may be tested again soon."

"Let us hope it does not happen while we are there seeking to do business with them."

Rawlings stood to stretch out his back. "They are but our uncouth, uneducated offspring, but still we must be wary of them."

"Perhaps. Do the opportunities include women or simply business?" Logan asked.

"Both, of course. I seek investments everywhere. Nonetheless, in the Americas, I am sure to be sought, even if they pretend not to care that I am a son of an Earl. Now the women, conversely, will be enthralled by my noble bloodlines."

"I understand Americans are not as rigid about dalliances with the ladies," Logan said. "You will not have to marry if you go beyond a stolen kiss."

Rawlings shook his head. "I do not know how one functions without a class structure. I assume their social standing is based on money."

"I suspect so. They have no monarchy to rule them now. Well, shall I look for appropriate reading material for such a journey? Do you have any preferences or recommendations?"

"No, gather what you can. I must attend my father's birthday dinner. I will not leave before Sir William's party and miss a chance to flirt with a delightful young lady. Oh, once we arrive in London, you must purchase every book about the new world, the fur trade, steamboats and machinery. We have much to learn."

"Very good, sir. How long will we stay in town?"

"Not a second longer than necessary for a dutiful son's appearance. We should be able to return the next morning. Oh, one more thing. Bingley received an urgent message yesterday. Find out what the upshot may have on the alliance."

"I already know the contents, sir. It is not of dire import nor does it impact you; at least, I do not think so." Logan revealed what he had learned.

Rawlings chuckled. "I agree, not a problem for me, but most unfortunate for Darcy. Well, I am off to breakfast, Logan."

***

Darcy, having seen to the care of his horse, hurried from the stable to locate Rawlings. He wished to ask him to handle the business in America. As he reached the entrance hall, Kent emerged holding a large satchel and was on route to the door.

"Heading to Meryton?"

"Nothing so entertaining. Mail arrived from my uncle in London. I must approve all the contracts and go through the many unpaid invoices from the... privileged class. You understand the tediousness of business and the difficulties in receiving payment."

"And yet the stacks of work never diminish."

Kent's eyes searched for listeners in the vestibule. He whispered, "Blake's father is the worst offender. I hate that any lord with a seat in the Parliament is exempt from obligations to us *tradesmen*."

Darcy took a step backwards. "I was not fully aware of the situation."

"It is common knowledge." Kent said.

"Humph." Darcy's eyes fell upon the satchel. "Your bag is bulging."

Kent patted his satchel. "True. The damn attorneys can force a simple agreement to turn into a volume of undecipherable paragraphs."

"I offer my help."

"Perhaps another time."

"Where are you going if not to town? Darcy asked.

"My normal custom is to sit in my garden and let the air and sunshine keep me awake as I suffer through the reading. Somehow being outside makes all the 'whereas' sentences seem not so… boring. I will be sitting in a quiet spot on the estate trying to recreate the mood of my home."

"The East Meadow is home to a remarkable oak tree."

Kent caught his breath. "No, no. Too much shade. I have discovered a wonderful location near a creek in the northern area, with a large fallen tree branch nearby that I can use as a chair."

"Well, I will not impede your progress. I am expected in the dining room."

They tipped their heads to each other and left in separate directions.

Kent headed for the stable, bumping into Rawlings' valet coming out of the building. Kent asked the stablehand if Logan had been riding. The lad indicated with a shake of head no, but stated that he had requested his mare without indicating where his destination might be. Kent did not respond other than to thank the boy for the information and patted his sachel while he waited for his horse.

Within fifteen minutes, he mounted his stallion and departed into the morning sun, checking over his shoulder the entire way.

✳✳✳

That night once the sun had set and the road in front of him was impossible to see, Nigel raced at a breakneck speed. His bulging satchel included a lengthy message and some documents he had retrieved from the oak tree. It outlined the full extent of the partnership. He hoped Mr. Cuffage would be most pleased with the two startling pieces of information—the men sought a business arrangement with Astor and, more importantly, they intended to use Mr. Phillips as their attorney.

Nigel arrived at the Cigar and Wine shop as Cuffage unlocked the front door, opening up for the days' business, who was quick to hustle him to the back room where he spit out the news about Astor.

"Hm. Mr. Phillips? They chose him to be their attorney?" Cuffage shrugged. "I must get my hands on the agreement he draws up before any of them sign. Will he be willing to sell the document?"

"But, sir, Mr. Phillips is Mr. Thomas Bennet's brother-in-law!"

"Damn." Cuffage slammed his fist on the desk. "I cannot risk using Phillips as an intermediary now." He paced the room for several minutes. "When the time comes, I must travel to Meryton and handle my own affairs.

Chapter Ten

Blake rose an hour early for his sunrise outing as sleep had not been his companion. Restless the entire night, he heard every bush-cricket until they quieted at three in the morning. What kept him awake was not the screeching of the insect's summer love call, but his own shricking words filling his ears. He dressed in haste and without disturbing the household, rushed to the stable. He relied upon a long, jolting gallop to clear his head.

After the sun rose and the warmth hit his face, he slowed his horse down to a trot. He reflected on Rawlings' position on the partnership. His friend appeared willing to join with Darcy and collaborate with Kent and Bingley.

Blake led his horse further into the wooded path as he weighed the temptation for future wealth. He sighed. Darcy needed his decision soon.

His mind was thus occupied when Miss Elizabeth Bennet, walking along the exact path, diverted his attention. His memory the day before had not failed him; he looked around and discovered he had arrived at the precise location in the woods where he had caught sight of her walking between the trees.

Blake jumped down and greeted her. "Miss Bennet!"

"Lord Blake," She replied with no sign of ill-will, curtsying and lifting her eyes to meet his bright smile.

"I do not mean to interrupt your walk. Pray continue," he said in all politeness, although he hoped that she would invite him along.

"It is not unwelcome, my lord."

She turned to resume ahead, but glanced back and smiled at him. With such encouragement before him, he tied his horse to a tree branch and ran to catch up with her.

As soon as he reached her, Lord Blake offered his arm. "What brings you out here so early in the day?"

She took his arm. "The day seems most promising when the sun begins its ascent."

He breathed easier and attempted to keep his eyes on the path before them as they continued walking, but caught himself stealing repeated glances at her hand resting atop his arm. Tempted to caress the small delicate hand within such easy reach, he chose to place his other hand behind his back and squeezed it many times.

Blake stared at the sky. "I, too, love the sunrise. Weather permitting I ride every morning. It helps to clear my head of all unnecessary tedious details of late."

Elizabeth raised her right eyebrow. "There are tedious details at Netherfield Park?" She chuckled when he squirmed.

Blake gazed down at her, debating whether to tell her the truth. He must do something his friends, and in particular, Darcy, would not appreciate. He felt trapped by the uncontrolled disorder in his life. His eyes locked with hers. He admired her unique manner of raising her brows as she gazed up at him with her head tilted downward. She was teasing him for a clever answer.

"A secret perhaps?" She asked.

"I will admit, tedious details abound when the room is empty of the sweeter sex." His smile softened at the sight of her uncommonly arresting eyes.

"Ha! You would not say so if you found your way to Longbourn and its many tiresome female residents." She shuddered in an exaggerated manner, diverted her eyes, and released a short sigh.

"You tiresome? I shall say not. You are quite easily excited and amused, I think. Your eyes give away the truth." His own smile deepened as he watched her lower her head, but not enough for him to miss her mischievous countenance. Emboldened, he breathed in a deep breath, gasping at the light fragrance filling his nose. "Do you often walk this way, or do other paths exist which you can recommend to a kindred spirit?" He glanced around the forest until his eyes returned to hers.

"I know a few. I am curious though, are you interested in the paths used for foot or saddle?"

"Saddle, of course. I ride and do not typically walk. Do you not ride, Miss Bennet?"

"Not if I can help it. I do know how, but I would rather walk. I feel apart from nature when I sit high upon a horse." She waved her hand towards the trees. "I prefer to stop and admire all the forest's entertainments and its many decorations."

Blake took a step closer. "You confirmed my theory. Not even the quiet forest is tedious to you. And I daresay, you decorate the forest with an interesting blend of elegance and loveliness." His interest increased when he surveyed the entirety of her.

She turned away from him, but continued to sneak peeks at him.

After some moments of silence, he stopped, reached down, picked a tiny pale yellow wildflower, and held it out to her. His palms began to sweat as she, glancing at him with half hidden eyes, twirled it under her nose. He again offered his arm as they continued along the path. Again, he held his hand behind his back and repeatedly made a tight fist. She took his arm.

He cleared his throat, drawing her eyes to him, "I see what you mean. I could not have given this to you from the height of a horse. My guess is you prefer wildflowers to those tended in a garden."

"I like both, my lord, for each has its place. Do you not agree?"

"True. Nothing is as sweet as the perfume or loveliness of a garden flower. Yet no greater surprise occurs than to find the unexpected blossom along the unkempt forest floor."

"Which is your favorite?

"Ah, the unexpected surprise is the greater joy. The garden flower is displayed for all to enjoy," Blake said, then eyed the tiny bell-shaped flower whirling in her hand and added, "while the wildflower is reserved for those fortunate and wise enough to venture into its path." He snuck a quick peek to catch her reaction even though she had attempted to shift her face from his view. "I admit to one advantage of a garden flower." She gazed up at him with a questioning stare; he responded by making a show of sniffing the air. "Lavender makes the sweetest perfume."

Even though she released a slight chuckle, he spied the crimson color deepening on her cheeks and neck before she turned her face from his view and did not look back until her composure had returned.

They continued their walk, but he steered clear of any more awkward chitchat. They discussed books, travel, and the many attractions of London. After an hour, they parted to fill their stomachs as full as they had filled their heads.

***

Blake arrived for breakfast, noticing everyone at the table. Their talk centered on neither business nor the competition, but on the next social event. Sir William had invited the entire household to a party at Lucas Lodge and his friends were chiding each other about the Bennet sisters, who would be attending.

Filling his plate from the buffet, Blake's thoughts drifted back to his encounter with Miss Elizabeth. *I was such an addle-pate. What drivel did*

I say to her? I must guard my actions more strictly and not be so forward. Flowers. What overcame me? What power took possession of my tongue? He slid into his chair as the others spoke of the meeting later that day. He jumped into the conversation. "Darcy, I am anxious to attend Sir William's—

Rawlings interrupted Blake, and before Darcy responded. "Yes, indeed. Who would want to miss a chance to visit with certain ladies of this county? Blake, you cannot possess all the pleasure. I shall seek some enjoyment as well."

Blake did not bother to reward Rawlings with any comment, preferring to smile at his own thoughts of his walk this morning.

Bingley dropped his fork. "I warn you Rawlings, my sights are set on one particular fine lady. You are welcome to find pleasure elsewhere."

"I look forward to the opportunity." Rawlings finished a bite of his pastry, an apple-filled tart with a dash of cinnamon and sugar on top. "These are delightful; I must give my cook this recipe." He dabbed his mouth and wiped his hands. "I will be leaving after Sir William's little gathering. I cannot delay the trip to London beyond then. Rest assured though, I will return on the following day if for no other reason than to indulge myself in more of these wonderful sweet treats."

Darcy tapped his glass with his spoon to gain Rawlings' attention. "Oh, do not forget your mission on your return to town. Time is of dire import."

Rawlings tipped his head in agreement before picking up his second pastry. He wondered why his friend thought he would forget something they agreed to just yesterday. Perhaps the announcement was made to alert Blake of his willingness to participate. Anyway, he was curious about Cuffage, and once he arrived in London, he had planned to hire an investigator. Two brothers skilled in prying and spying came to mind: Nathaniel and Nigel. Either man would do. He had used Nathaniel once before when his suspicions of his wife's transgressions occurred and had been satisfied with his work. London's best families hired either him or his brother, Nigel, when seeking a confidential investigation. He would share his plan with Darcy.

The men finished their eggs and pork chops and drank the remains of their coffee before separating into two groups and heading out in different directions—Rawlings, Blake, and Darcy moved to the library while Bingley and Kent retreated to the billiards room to play a game of Twenty Points.

Two individuals or partners played in the traditional billiards game, which did not suit Bingley. He designed this game so any number of men could play together. The rules were simple. The shooter received a point for a ball falling into the pocket and lost a point when he missed. The man who sunk the last one in each rack obtained three extra points. The cue ball slipping into a pocket cost the player a hefty five points. Play continued until someone reached twenty points forcing the elimination of the one with the lowest score. The game repeated and did not end until one man remained to collect his winnings from the losers. Wagering was as much a part of the rules as was the method of elimination.

Even though the billiard room connected directly to the library, the closed door between the two allowed for privacy. Kent and Bingley spoke freely while continuing an ongoing private competition. They were tied. The two men had spent a quarter of an hour playing before Kent called his friend on his lack of focus.

"Bingley. Bingley! It is your shot."

"I beg your pardon. I was not attending." He lined up his shot and was quick to thrust his cue stick. "I was remembering how Blake and Rawlings reacted when Darcy told them about the fur trade. I never knew anyone who could open their eyes so wide."

"Yes, quite a fright for them." Kent studied the angles for his friend's shot.

"And you! Treason? Come, come. Did you believe Darcy would dirty his hands in such a manner? Are you pleased with the arrangements?"

"All is well, except I dare say I am not happy with Blake. He is like so many others of his kind." He glared at the cue ball on the table. "I do not trust him nor do I think he will join us." Kent uttered a small groan. "We need him. Your family needs him, but he is condescending to me and you, and his attitude is not encouraging for partnering with him."

Bingley paused to allow his friend to take his shot and then studied the choices Kent left for him. "I am sure he means well. They are taught arrogance from their childhood. Do you feel Darcy is more accepting then?"

"Yes, but he is not titled himself, although his uncle is an Earl. He is a little more accommodating. Of course, I hold something he wants. I doubt I own anything Blake wants."

"You enjoy many assets he does not possess. Many times, you have pronounced that the world is changing. Blake may change. It is hard to overcome a lifetime of prejudice."

"Bah! He will never change. If it were not for Darcy, then Blake, as with all peers, would never agree to connect themselves to me," Kent glared at his friend, "or with you for that matter. You heard him talking to Darcy." Kent imitated Blake's tone and attitude. "Surely you are not saying tradesmen are on an equal level with gentry." Kent knocked the ball in the pocket with great intensity.

"Do not be quick to judge. I think he is deserving of our friendship. How do you find Rawlings?"

"Now, he is one gentleman with whom I can do business. Rawlings does not seem affected by status, although he does have his moments too. Curiously though, I witnessed how he speaks to his man, Logan, and am surprised by their relationship."

"Kent, promise me this talk of rank and superiority will not go beyond us. The alliance cannot withstand this type of class hatred. We are all important to the success."

He tipped his head and when pressed by Bingley provided a verbal agreement.

Bingley, relaxed, took his shot, and then grinning from ear to ear announced, "Game, Kent. I am now one ahead again. Of course, you can seethe over my superiority with a cue stick if you like."

"Till tomorrow, my friend. Till tomorrow." Kent left with the excuse it was time for his afternoon ride. Bingley's thoughts swirled in his head.

Thus, when Darcy entered the billiard room, he found his friend alone and leaning on a cue stick, staring out into the distance. "Twenty Points, Bingley?"

"At your service. I am surprised you prefer to play it over the usual game of billiards."

"I know I cannot beat you at the traditional game." Darcy admitted.

"I do not think you can defeat me at this one either!"

Darcy fidgeted with his stick as he waited for Bingley to rack up the balls. "I believe everything went as expected with our business discussions."

"It went smoothly considering the persons attending, and the fact that I was the one that introduced them to the plan." Bingley offered Darcy the first shot.

"Everyone is quite impressed by your family background." Darcy missed the shot. "Perhaps I should not be so confident in my ability to hit the balls.

"Perhaps not as certain as I am of my skill." Bingley leaned down, aimed, and flicked his cue stick. He made his shot and two balls fell into the same pocket. "So, how are your two charges doing?"

"Rawlings is not a problem. He is willing to handle the fur trade. Blake is a little shaky, but we discussed that possibility before.

"Yes, you were correct about Blake. I am hopeful he will become more accepting of Kent and me if we all partner in the alliance."

"Giving Blake the rifle did help."

Bingley tipped his head. "I had the most difficult time convincing Kent not to take offense at the tradesmen stabs Blake made."

"Is there a problem? I have not focused on it as much, but Kent is as critical to the alliance as Blake."

"Kent wants to connect himself to a higher society; he will learn to hide his contempt for peers. I spoke with him. He has agreed not to speak of his prejudices."

"Let us hope so. I, too, cautioned Blake. Well, tomorrow we attend Sir William Lucas' party, is that not correct?" Darcy pushed his cue stick forward. "Blast!"

Bingley released a long sigh, relaxed both his shoulders and stance. "Yes, and tomorrow I will leave behind these heavy discussions. I do not understand how you enjoy such serious talk."

"Then it is better I am the one worrying about the many details, and not you." Darcy flashed his own customary smile in response to Bingley's usual grin. Those who did not know him well could mistake Darcy's smile as a smirk; Bingley's grin was all that was pleasant.

"Yes, the details are all yours. Another point for me," Bingley said as his ball fell into the pocket. "My total is now nine points."

Darcy concentrated on the shot left for him. After a moment of careful study, he hit the cue ball, chuckling when three balls rolled into their pockets. "Three more points for me taking my total to ten, I do like this game of yours."

"Good shot. I repeat myself when I say that I am glad to be of service."

Bingley leaned down to examine the positions of the balls to find his best shot. He grinned. His shot placed two balls in the pocket and left impossible shooting angles for Darcy. The two men continued to study the table, take their turns, and keep account of their points. Play continued until Bingley demonstrated to a now frowning friend how the real master at billiards played the game. "Twenty points. Game!"

Darcy put away their cue sticks and poured drinks. "To the victor." He bowed in deference to Bingley's win. Afterwards, he looked up, and with unrestrained interest in his eyes, asked, "I hope all is well with your family."

"Yes, all is well." Bingley answered in an uncommon cool voice.

"And your relatives up north? All goes well with them?"

"They are quite fine. Thank you for inquiring."

"I suspect the Netherfield tenants have many concerns at this time of year."

"I suspect you are correct..." Bingley smiled, his eyes twinkling, and then, with his recently learned vacant expression, he added "but I did not hear of any."

Darcy shifted his weight back and forth and coughed several times. "I believe all is well in London too. I have not read anything of interest in the papers all the while we have been here."

"Darcy, stop being coy!" Bingley's grin stretched to a smile as his friend's face reddened. "If you want to know about the message, ask. I would not hold anything back from you."

"All right. Did it reveal anything which might affect the alliance?"

"Indirectly."

"Oh, is it anything I need to know?" Darcy's neck muscles tensed.

"I suppose I should warn you."

"A problem?"

"Not for me, but it is a problem for you."

Darcy leaned forward, grabbing the side of the table with his eyes boring into his friend. "For God's sake, speak up man. What was in the message?"

Bingley locked his eyes on Darcy. "Caroline will be joining us, as will my other sister and her husband."

Darcy dropped his head, shaking it side to side in slow motion. "Ah. Yes, a problem for me." He glanced at the door leading to the library. "It might be a problem for several of the others as well."

"Yes. As I said, it is not a problem for me."

"When will they arrive?"

"Sometime next month. Around the twelfth of November."

"We have more than a fortnight. Why was it so urgent?"Darcy asked.

"It was not urgent on my part. It was urgent on Caroline's. My sister heard about our little foray into this area."

"All of us?"

"No. Just me and... you." Bingley finished his drink. "I am off to handle some urgent estate business." He snorted. "A most useful excuse as you said. I do wish you pleasant thoughts."

"Pleasant thoughts, indeed not!" Darcy muttered as his friend left the room.

Chapter Eleven

The Netherfield Park library had become the room of choice for the men. It served as the meeting place for business discussions as well as the favorite place to share wine and brandy. It was not conducive to reading since only one of the ten bookcases housed any books. Upon entering, Rawlings joked how it must have taken the work of lifetime of a small child to fill this room. In this room, the men found the London newspapers as Darcy and Kent insisted.

Rawlings made himself comfortable while waiting for his friends to finish dressing for Sir William's party. Two newspapers rested on the table next to him— the *London Times* with its serious content and the tittle-tattle *Courier*. Rawlings, tired of the serious talks of late, chose to dwindle away his wait time by reading amusing stories. He picked up the gossipy paper where he found an article, which piqued his imagination.

"Good evening, Rawlings."

"I beg your pardon, Blake. I did not hear you enter." Rawlings tossed the newspaper on the table.

"Have you decided if you will partner?"

"Yes, based on what I know now. Will you?"

Blake sat down. "You did not hesitate. Do you not have reservations? I would have thought you at least would have had at least one concern."

"What would that be?"

"I have met your father. He is not likely to approve of this alliance."

"Phew! Are you saying you will not join because of your family? Does your father hold your hand when you cross the road?" Rawlings said, sneering. He turned his body away from Blake.

"Do not be a horse's arse. What is bothering you? Me?".

"Since your role is critical to forming an alliance, the rest of us are dependent upon your decision. I, as do the others, must wait while you tease us with the direction you will take.."

Blake shrugged. "I have not yet decided. I am not pleased with the lack of respect shown to me."

"I am not aware of any disrespect."

"Bah! I am not treated any better than Kent or Bingley. Darcy places us on the same level."

"It is a new era." Rawlings kept a close watch on Blake's hands. They had a slight shake to them whenever he let go of the arms of the chair. He forced himself to remain nonchalant when he wanted to slap Blake and make him accept the deal. .

"For some reason Darcy does not respect my station in life." Blake said, his voice trailing off at the end.

"I am not aware of any disrespect on his part. How difficult is it to decide?"

"I have not made up my mind. Why are pushing me?"

"I look forward to the adventure, and that is why I desire to learn of your decision. I must make plans soon."

"You do not fear a voyage to America?"

"No. I am excited for the opportunity that, however, might not come to be. It is up to you." Rawlings grabbed the *Courier* and held it up high while he read the back page, ending any further discussion. Blake twiddled his thumbs.

"You seemed to enjoy the assembly the other night." Blake said breaking the quiet in the room.

Rawlings placed the paper in his lap. "Yes I did. As Bingley said, some uncommonly pretty girls attended. I am pleased I went, if for no other reason than meeting one young lady I would like to get to know better."

"You would not connect yourself here, would you? Such an alliance would be quite a humiliation for your family."

"Ah. Humiliation. If you feel any of the young ladies are below your notice, you should be more like Darcy. He believes these country people are beneath him, and he made his attitude known."

"You consider Darcy's behavior as appropriate?"

"As he said, he does not toy with the ladies and has maintained his distance, therefore not a single family believes Darcy would lower himself to their level. They are correct to think so because he made a deliberate point to ignore everyone—men . They will not seek a connection with him, in fact, I wager he is not at all liked." Rawlings pointed to Blake. "You, in contrast, set yourself up to be pursued."

"Pursued? By whom? They understand my status and recognize I will not allow it." Blake leaned back in his chair.

"You know very well which mother and daughter to which I refer."

"But a dance, Rawlings, it was nothing more than a dance. You said so to Darcy, if my memory is accurate."

"Yes, I did; but the conversation had meaning only between him and me." Rawlings stood and then headed to the sidebar to refill his glass.

"Do you suggest I separate myself from everyone except our party here?"

"No, Blake. I am suggesting you show less attention to Miss Elizabeth Bennet. She may well be expecting more from you than what you are willing to give."

"You think she is not worthy?"

"I believe she is worthy, but my opinion is not important. She is an admirable gentlewoman; as is her eldest sister, Jane. Your idea of quality people would not frown if they met them. They conduct themselves most properly."

"Again I ask, would you consider allying yourself in marriage to any of these women here?" Blake leaned forward.

"I would have no qualms if I chose to do so. My marriage was an alliance without love and since Margaret passed I view life with a new outlook. I am free to pursue my own happiness, and I plan to seek a lady who might interest me." Rawlings settled back into his chair, downing a large gulp of brandy.

"I was sorry to learn of the death of your wife."

Rawlings shrugged. "Not to worry. I will marry again."

"Are you challenging Bingley for his fair maiden? You did dance with her twice."

"I am not that sort of friend."

"You indicated a preference for someone. So, if not Miss Bennet, perhaps Miss Elizabeth?"

"As I said, I am not that sort of friend. I prefer a different type of lady."

Blake tapped his fingers on the arm of the chair. "I mean, the Long girls were nonsensical. Two minutes in a conversation and I would be asleep." He sat back, closed his eyes in an attempt to recall who attended the assembly. "I suppose the Lucas daughters are tolerable, but Miss Lucas is rather plain with few other charms."

"You mean money and connections?"

"Money. Her father does attend St. James."

Both men shared a laugh about the place where social climbers go to be seen. Rawlings moved to the sideboard for another brandy and Blake motioned for one as well.

"Miss Lucas might be acceptable to Kent or Bingley."

"Bingley has already chosen to pursue one lady."

"Yes, Miss Bennet is his choice." Blake accepted the glass, but set it down after one sip.

Rawlings plopped into the chair. "She is the choice of most men."

"I think Kent would do well to consider Miss Lucas. He needs a steady, practical partner. He can be a little hotheaded, and they are both well matched in rank."

"He is not hotheaded, merely ambitious, and Charlotte Lucas would not suit him. He has someone else in mind."

"Oh, who?" Blake leaned towards his friend.

"I shall not say, for I might be wrong."

"Fine," Blake said with a brusqueness. "That leaves the younger Bennets?"

"Did we dispose of Miss Elizabeth?" Rawlings winked.

"No. I assume she is still in the mix. She is delightful, if you like an amusing, lively sort of girl."

"Lively? I believe the youngest Bennets, Miss Lydia and Miss Catherine, are the liveliest."

"Yes. Quite true. However, Miss Elizabeth is spirited, but within the standards of propriety," Blake said.

"And quite pretty. Regardless of what Darcy says, she is a beauty."

Blake sighed. "That she is." His lips spread across his face.

The three other men appeared at the appointed time. The five men left together, climbed into the carriage, and set off for Lucas Lodge.

***

The ride was bumpy over the well-traveled road even though they were seated in Kent's Town Coach. The red and orange sky of twilight could be seen though the glass in the vehicle. The upper part of the windows slid down inside the carriage side, allowing fresh air to stream in unobstructed. The dark navy blue velvet cushions, trimmed with leather and brass buttons, felt expensive to the touch. Behind the forward facing seat were two brass trimmed wooden cabinets. One housed several glasses and many decanters, each filled to the top with brandy, wine, port, and sherry. The other was home to the sheepskin leg and lap blankets. The floorboard had slits where the passenger could feel the heat from warmed bricks unlike the cumbersome design of their own carriages—

bricks placed on the carriage floor taking up most of the foot room. Small glass enclosed candle lanterns graced each corner with small openings to the outside for the smoke. The men tried to assess the carriage without the outward appearance of a gawker. Blake mentioned his admiration on the efficient design of the space while covertly calculating the cost of the richness of the materials.

"Rawlings, what were you and Blake whispering about? I thought I heard the names of a few of the lovely ladies of Meryton." Kent asked.

"Dancing." Blake answered, his tone even. "We were speaking of dancing. Darcy's favorite amusement."

"In fact I was about to discuss the Waltz, the shocking dance sweeping the ballrooms in the continent," Rawlings replied. "The current chatter about it and who is engaged in doing it is jumping off the tongues of the *Ton*. Imagine our fine friend here," Rawlings directed his gaze at Darcy before continuing, "swirling around the room with a pretty damsel in his arms."

"Scandalous!" Blake replied.

"I danced it." Kent smirked. "It is all the rage in my circles."

"Of that I have no doubt. It is not done in refined society." Blake paused, squished his nose. "Well, unless you consider the Carlton House set polite. I heard a rumor Prinny himself danced it some time ago. He must not been sober for even he has yet to repeat the performance."

"Do not be such a clapper-clawed puritan. Even I would like to learn it. I have found something the Prince of Wales and I agree with! Imagine that. Prinny and me!" Rawlings turned to the quietest man in the carriage. "How do you feel about it?"

Everyone turned towards Darcy whose expression remained blank. "Kent, Bingley, and I learned it a year ago. I own no strong objection to the dance. Of course, I believe it is not appropriate unless you know your partner well and have some type of arrangement."

"Not true," Kent said. "Darcy was dancing with a woman with whom he did not have any sort of understanding."

"She instructed us on the steps is all. I needed to hold her in such a fashion to learn the dance." Darcy peeked at his friends' open mouths. "Good God. She is almost fifty years old! And one of my father's cousins. She was visiting Pemberley from Vienna. She is the instructor! She demanded we learn the confounded dance."

Rawlings turned to Kent. "Tell us! Is it as tantalizing as they say?"

"You will think of nothing except what it would be like to dance with someone young and pretty." Kent replied.

"Can you imagine dancing the Waltz tonight? What a scandal!" Blake said.

"Is there no one who makes you want to hold her in such a way?" Rawlings asked.

Blake shook his head. "You misunderstand me. Holding a lady of the *Ton* is one thing. But to hold one of these country girls would cause her mother to run to town that second to purchase her daughter's bridal gown."

"Any mother in particular?" Rawlings watched Blake shrug. "Ah, so if given the chance you would not dance the Waltz with any of the Meryton ladies?"

"Certainly not. No." Blake brushed something unseen from his jacket until he jolted his head up and with narrowed eyes, glared at Rawlings. "Would you?"

"I might like to take a twirl with one little lass. She would know how to respond to such a dance; she would not be shocked. With her, the dance would be quite enjoyable."

"You must dye your coat red first, Rawlings," Kent said. "Miss Lydia and Miss Catherine Bennet would react as you say."

"Yes, they are the most obvious ones. Miss Lydia prefers the officers of the Militia." When Darcy glanced at him with a questioning look, Rawlings nodded, and ignored his other friends' reaction to his confession. "Perhaps, the only ones willing to respond to her flirting games are the men wearing the redcoats. We would not. None of us. Well, at least not in public."

Kent whispered to Blake, "The redcoats do not seem to mind what kind of uncontrolled passion Miss Lydia displays. She will either convince one of them to offer or perhaps be compromised to gain a husband."

"Bingley, you have not identified who you would dance with yet. Do we need to ask?"

"Of course not, Kent. Now unlike Blake, I look forward to the day the Waltz is commonplace. Only pleasure will be felt when a gentleman can lead the lady around the floor in his arms at every ball."

"Darcy, you are quiet. Do you not have an opinion?" Rawlings asked.

"I prefer to listen. It is most enlightening. I learned much."

"And what have you learned?"

"The Waltz causes some men to become as silly as incorrigible young girls."

Blake turned to Rawlings. "And are you such a man?"

Rawlings nodded, his head moving vigorously. "Yes, yes. I am and most eagerly if permitted to hold a certain voluptuous female when the music plays."

"Oh my. So, you would dance with Miss Lydia?" Blake asked.

"I would rather dance with Miss Lydia than with anyone resembling my late wife."

"But she is so, so… " Blake paused.

"Coarse? Flirty? Immature? Silly? I think she is beautiful, fun, and passionate." Rawlings breathed in deep, and then released a long sigh.

"Surely you would not consider connecting yourself to her? She does not show proper decorum at all."

"Why should I not connect myself, Blake?"

"She is not of your station."

"What station do you refer to?" Rawlings sat upright.

"Well, Rawlings, you belong to a much higher level of society than you find here. You have a responsibility to your family."

"And?"

"It is not acceptable." Blake replied.

"Perhaps you can tell me why, you white-livered dewberry!" Rawlings laughed heartedly before his countenance shifted into a serious mien. "I am a widower. Why can I not marry for love, passion, and partake hungrily of her fruitful vine the next time? Is there anything wrong with finding a strong, healthy young woman with whom to enjoy a little crinkum crankum?"

Blake paused to formulate a polite response. "What you speak of can be purchased any night or day."

Rawlings glared at Blake. "You cannot procure a gentleman's daughter in such a way. Of course, one could wait for her to make a marriage for convenience and afterwards be free to dally around. Although she should produce the heir first, but some women do not wait."

"You are too cynical."

"I can offer proof many women fit the description." Rawlings waved his hand in a careless manner.

"I am sure you can find an acceptable wife among the *Ton*," Darcy said.

"Darcy," Kent said, "what is amiss with the Bennets? I do not understand why you feel Rawlings should not pursue Miss Lydia if that is his desire.".

Blake blurted the words out in a quick and loud voice, "Because her mother has a brother in trade, who lives in Cheapside."

Darcy cringed. He assumed Blake was not aware Kent's London home was located in that part of town. Most tradesmen lived close to their warehouses and the Kent family was no exception. "How do you know this?"

"I asked Miss Elizabeth at the assembly."

"You asked about her relatives at the dance?"

Blake shrugged at Darcy's shocked expression. "During the dance to be precise. How else was I to discover her bloodlines?"

Rawlings said. "I found out as much when I danced with Miss Catherine." He nudged Blake. "Otherwise you would be pursuing Miss Elizabeth in your normal manner."

"And what exactly is my normal pursuit?"

"Typically, you bring her flowers and other little gifts." When Blake remained silent, Rawlings continued. "Well, if I choose to pursue Miss Lydia, I will do so without regard to the *Ton*, my family, or my friends. But I must wait a few years! For now, Miss Lydia is too young."

"That she is." Darcy nodded.

Rawlings tapped him. "You have not said with whom you would dance the Waltz. I assume no one in this parish is tolerable enough to tempt you?"

Darcy glowered. "When are you scheduled to return from London, Rawlings?"

"Avoiding my question on purpose, Darcy?" Rawlings laughed. "I shall answer yours. I will return in three days time, on Friday late."

"Well then, at the party I shall invite Mr. Phillips to visit Netherfield Saturday to draw up the legal papers." Darcy glanced sideways at Blake. I will expect everyone's decision about the partnership then. Ah. We have arrived at Lucas Lodge."

Chapter Twelve

The Netherfield party arrived fashionably late to Sir William's party; everyone else was already in attendance. The addition of Colonel Forster and several redcoats to the usual amalgam of Meryton society created a mix of festive red among the blue, black, and green coats and pastel colors of the ladies gowns. While Darcy was relieved that this evening included more men than ladies, Rawlings, smoothing his jacket, had hoped blue would have been the most becoming color of the night.

Sir William bowed politely; the gentlemen returned the gesture in kind. "Ah, gentlemen, good evening. I am honored by your presence. Meryton welcomes you as we have at least four and twenty families mingling in the grand parlor."

Rawlings quietly hummed a tune which he continued doing for the rest of the evening.

Sing a song of sixpence, A pocket full of rye.
Four and twenty blackbirds, Baked in a pie.

Sir William directed the men's attention to a small group of officers standing to the left. "Let me introduce you to our newest resident, Colonel Forster. You may be interested in his stories, as he has returned from the continent."

After making the introductions, Rawlings, Kent, and Darcy engaged in an enlightening conversation with the colonel while Bingley sought out Miss Jane Bennet, Blake looked for Miss Elizabeth.

Darcy transferred his attention away from the colonel's retelling of a battle onto Miss Elizabeth Bennet's eyes, which brightened, no, burst with streaks of golden light emanating from her brown irises when she directed them on a swiftly approaching Blake. Darcy had planned to assess her tonight and determine if Blake had spoken the truth of her beauty. He inspected her form, the unruly curl of her hair, the strong features of her face, and the elegance of her movement. Her hands and arms never seemed lost, moving through the air as graceful as the great ballerinas he had witnessed dancing at the King's Theatre in London. His gaze darted from Miss Elizabeth to her older sister and back again. He concluded Miss Jane Bennet was the more handsome of the two as defined by society. However, Miss Elizabeth possessed something enchanting. The flickering slivers of gold in her eyes, the wispy curls bouncing on her neck, the sun caressed skin shimmering in the candlelight, and her poise in speaking to others all bode well for her, but her absolute delight in the world around her is what enticed him. He could not identify the specific feature or gesture, although it distinguished her from all other women he had met. He decided Blake had not defended her sufficiently.

Rawlings poked his arm.

Realizing he was not attending to the Colonel's discussion, Darcy removed himself away from the group to a solitary spot at the fireplace. Rawlings slid beside him, pointing his glance towards Blake and Elizabeth and then sang so low only Darcy could hear him:

When the pie was opened the bird began to sing,
Oh wasn't that a dainty dish to set before the king?

Darcy scoffed. "Is there not a silly girl somewhere here tonight who can tempt you?"

"Yes there is. But I shall find another branch to watch my own delicious little blackbird sing and flit around. Perhaps I shall bestow upon her one of your lustful, cold black stares." Rawlings ambled over to the refreshment table, humming as he went.

Darcy positioned himself so he could hear Elizabeth and view her expressions and reactions. Blake spoke first which she responded with a raised right brow. Blake had described her as playful. She was indeed a teasing girl, but the happy expression proved she was not mean. He leaned his arm against the mantle. He wondered what inane, trivial matter they would discuss. He maintained his gaze on her features as her facial expressions changed with her reactions. She was playful, no, charming.

"Miss Elizabeth, I am the fortunate one today." Blake said

"How so, my lord?"

"Why, you have not only attended this gathering today, but you have also honored me with your smile. Are those wildflowers?"

Nodding, she touched the delicate blossoms in her hair. "Lord Blake, have you long been friends with Mr. Bingley and the others?"

"Yes, we all attended Cambridge together and shared the same lodgings. The five of us shared a bond between us, you see, as we were all without mothers."

"I do not quite see. How did that bind you?" Elizabeth asked.

"Mothers are the necessary ingredient to civilize the beasts! We all laughed about our being wild without restraint, you understand. One day while sipping our, ahem, tea, we decided we needed to civilize each other. We agreed that each of us would dress up as a mother for another man. Mother would then lecture her adopted son about his uncivilized ways – gambling, drinking, cursing, and, umm, other things that wild gentlemen do. Of course, Mother would have to partake of much drink to wear the dress."

Elizabeth opened her eyes wide. "A dress?"

"Perhaps not literally," Blake confessed lowering his head to conceal his grin.

"But there are five of you here. Or was one of you left without even a substitute mother?"

"You are correct. We each have one mother, except Bingley who has four. He joined us at Cambridge after we chose the mothers. We all reserve the right to lecture him! He is the youngest among us."

"So mothers lecture, is that what you think, Lord Blake?"

"Well, lecture may not be the correct term. Shall we say educate instead?"

Elizabeth smiled. She tipped her head. "And in what subject did your substitute mother educate you?"

Blake shook his head. "No, Miss Elizabeth. You know very well that a mother's conversation with her children is confidential. I am sure your mother has taught you, and you would not wish to reveal any of it."

"True. Nevertheless, did your mother try to match make you a wife? Did she tell you to smile and blink your eyes and hide away your wit and intelligence?" Elizabeth dropped her head, and then raised it up in a unhurried manner, displaying a very broad smile and rapidly blinking her eyes.

He chuckled. "No, but if you could have heard Mother Fitzwilliam humorously lecture me, excuse me, educate me about women, you would be laughing now."

"Fitzwilliam? And which gentleman is Mother Fitzwilliam?"

Blake inclined his head towards the man leaning against the fireplace mantle. "Why, Mr. Darcy of course. I need the very best to educate me."

Darcy fought his smile when he caught sight of Miss Elizabeth's expression. He diverted his focus on to other guests.

Blake returned his gaze upon Elizabeth. "Sorry, we all agreed to use our given names when posing as the fairer sex."

"You mean the wiser sex!"

"Wiser, Miss Elizabeth?"

"Yes, you have said that your role as mother is to educate. Does that not make the female gender wiser?"

"You are right; I stand corrected. As I said, we use our given names when we pose or direct a question to Mother. I guess it is a code of sorts."

"So, Mr. Darcy was lecturing you about women?" Elizabeth asked, her eyes focusing on the man in question. "With humor?"

"Yes, precisely, and you would have found the witiness in it as well, I am sure."

"And to whom were you the mother?"

"I, Mother Robert, dressed up for the Honorable Gerald Rawlings, second son of the Earl of Wolverly." He almost curtsied as he spoke. While wearing a dress was not required, all the men did curtsey at least once when they portrayed a mother. The depth of the curtsey corresponded with the amount of drink consumed beforehand.

"Mr. Rawlings?" She searched the room for Blake's friend.

"Miss Elizabeth, I must assure you that I have behaved properly by cautioning Mr. Rawlings about the evils of women," Blake said drawing her eyes back on him.

"And what evils are those, Mother Robert?"

For the briefest of moments the air was still before Blake answered, "Why the evils of beautiful eyes in a beautiful face with a smile that lights up a person's heart. A woman so unique she would cause the man to lose sight of all his goals in life; a woman so special, he could do nothing but follow her command."

"And would this mother have an evil woman in mind?"

"Yes, Miss Bennet, Mother Robert does." Blake lowered his chin towards his chest. "And Mother Robert has decided she is best suited to someone other than Mr. Rawlings, or Mr. Bingley, or Mr. Kent or even Mr. Darcy."

Darcy, surprised by Elizabeth's blush at something Blake said but too low for him to hear, believed that even from a slight distance away he could detect the sound of her heart pounding. Placing his hand upon his own chest, he conceded it was not hers alone beating at such a speed. Darcy glared at Blake's back. What is he doing? He hurried to join them and positioned himself close enough to Elizabeth to take in her lavender scent.

Charlotte Lucas also approached the group. "I am going to open the instrument, Eliza, and you know what follows."

With a brief glance at Mr. Darcy, Elizabeth answered, "You are a very strange creature by way of a friend! Always wanting me to play and sing before anybody and everybody! If my vanity had taken a musical turn, you would have been invaluable; but as it is, I would rather not sit down before those who must be in the habit of hearing the very best performers."

Darcy opened his mouth to speak when Blake offered his arm. "Please, Miss Elizabeth? I would dearly love to hear you play."

"For you, I shall make an exception." Elizabeth slipped her hand around his arm.

Darcy met her eyes. He could feel the heat emanating from his eyes and knew he must be giving her one of his black stares Rawlings spoke about, but he could not control his reaction. She enticed him with her tease. He fought an outward showing of his smile when he realized she was unable to discern his interest. She must have understood the intensity of his gaze. He could not stop. His eyes bored into hers even as she turned her back to approach the instrument.

"What is amiss about me, tonight? Elizabeth mumbled. "Well, Mr. Darcy can simmer in his own thoughts. As she moved to the piano, "What did Lord Blake say? Humorous advice. Bah!"

Blake, planning to turn the pages for her, led her towards the pianoforte and then sat down next to her.

"I play from memory, Lord Blake," Elizabeth whispered.

He retreated to Darcy's side.

"Her performance is acceptable, though by no means on the level of many London ladies." Darcy spoke quietly to his friend.

"Is there nothing these people can do to please you?" Blake asked, whispering.

"You seem to be pleased. Too much, in my opinion. Take care and remember our discussion when we were hunting the other day. Do not give her false hopes."

Darcy stood alone, his eyes never leaving Elizabeth. She moved to allow her sister, Mary, a turn. His lips turned up at the edges when Blake arrived at the piano a little too late and in the end, had to turn pages for the younger girl. Darcy moved across the room where Kent had just handed Rawlings a glass of wine. He stopped and joined them but instead of engaging in the converstion, he glanced around the room until he located Miss Elizabeth. He half-heartedly listened to what his friends were saying.

"What time do you leave?" Kent asked.

Rawlings winced at the tartness as he swallowed his first sip. "In the morning, before breakfast. I delayed my journey until the last second."

"Is there much festivity planned?"

Rawlings exhaled. "My father is celebrating his birthday, and we all must attend. He will be five and fifty. I believe there is to be a family dinner one night and a ball the next, not for my father but for my self-indulgent brother, Thomas. They have negotiated a bride for him; or, shall we say, rather sold him to the highest bidder."

"You seem concerned; I did not think you were close to your brother."

"No, it is not my brother that concerns me. I fear they will place me on the auction block as well," Rawlings admitted with a self-conscious laugh.

Having finished turning the pages for Mary, Blake joined them, interrupting the easygoing conversation between them. "So, you are off in the morning, Rawlings? Do you know when Bingley plans to hold the competition? I have grown tired waiting for it."

Rawlings diverted their attention to Bingley and Jane standing alone and deep in conversation. "I expected it to be right way, but—"

"Bingley said he would announce the competition on Satuday after we meet with Mr. Phillips. He decided to wait for your return, Rawlings."

"But Kent that was before he found his lady of the moment. I suspect it might be longer now that he is so pleasantly diverted." Rawlings inclined his head towards Elizabeth. "You do not own a similar diversion, do you, Blake?"

Darcy stood upright. He held his breath. He did not turn towards Blake; he kept his eyes on Elizabeth. He waited, but Blake did not answer.

"Blake, I noticed you were having an intense conversation earlier," Kent said breaking the silence.

"You notice too much. Perhaps if you filled your time with your own activity you would not focus so often on mine."

"I beg your pardon. I did not mean any offense. I was concerned when Miss Elizabeth appeared flustered.".

When Blake opened his mouth to respond, Rawlings coughed. "Tell me, Blake, will you be visiting Goulding's stables tomorrow?"

"I was not aware that a visit was on the agenda. I am at Bingley's mercy there. "

"Pardon me. You were busy flirting at the time."

Darcy stiffened.

Rawlings brushed an imaginary speck of lint from his coat. "Bingley made arrangements with Mr. Goulding earlier tonight when Darcy was speaking to Mr. Phillips about drawing up the legal documents for our alliance."

Darcy coughed."I understand the prized stallion is sought after by many people."

"It will be interesting then, to hear of your visit when I return," Rawlings said.

"And you, Kent. Will you be going to see the magnificent stallion everyone has been discussing tonight?" Darcy asked.

"No. I have received another satchel of mail that must be dealt with quickly."

"Excuse me." Blake tipped his head and walked passed Darcy as he left to stand alone at the window.

Darcy searched for Elizabeth. She was busy laughing with Colonel Forster and his wife. He relaxed when she did not make a move towards Blake.

"Kent, you seem lost in thought," Rawlings said.

"Perhaps, but then I am not alone. I noticed earlier you seemed fascinated by something. Or someone."

"We are such a pair. One is a thinking man and another is an enjoying man. What holds your mind?"

Kent tilted his head towards Bingley. "To be honest, I was thinking of how often Bingley finds a new lady. It is his usual habit."

"Yes, he does seem smitten again." Rawlings eyes found Bingley, who, of course, was deep in conversation with Miss Bennet.

"It looks like Blake is friendlier tonight."

"I was prepared for Bingley to find a new love, but not Blake. I suspect his friendliness is due to the second Bennet girl; Miss Elizabeth."

"You noticed that too?" Rawlings asked.

"It seems the two of us are most discerning tonight. Nevertheless, it is obvious enough for anyone to detect. Except, perhaps Bingley who I doubt even knows we are in the same room with him." He glanced over to Blake. "This time it appears the lady prefers Blake over Darcy. He is not standing in line for the women ignored by him, as is his customary practice." Kent laughed and slapped Darcy's shoulder.

"As we all do. Except Bingley. He always seems to do very well. No Darcy castoffs for him." Rawlings laughed.

"What about you?" Kent nudged him with his elbow. "What has caught your eye? Or should I say whom and is she dressed in a blue or dotted brown gown?" He pointed his gaze at Kitty and Lydia who were giggling and circling two officers dressed as he had described.

Darcy chuckled. "Shall I hum a tune for you? *Now isn't that a dainty dish to set before a king.*"

"I surrender. It is true, I was watching the youngest Bennet girls. I cannot quite make out how they are so different from the two eldest. They are so animated – unlike any gentleman's daughters I have ever known."

"By animated do you mean laughing, flirting, and spilling their wine?" Kent sipped his drink.

"Yes, they do seem to be having more fun than the others."

"Especially the youngest, Miss Lydia."

"Yes, the taller, prettier one." Rawlings examined the young girl's form, fixing his gaze on the spot where skin and fabric intersected.

Darcy followed his line of sight. "She does wear the most revealing of dresses."

"She has much to reveal. In fact, she is the most well-endowed of all the Bennets." Kent said.

Rawlings shook his head. "Not if you consider her mother."

Kent laughed a little too loudly, causing the Lydia to turn and gaze at them. Rawlings openly smiled at her. She did not return his smile, preferring to flirt with the handsome red-coated officer by her side.

Rawlings exhaled and shrugged his shoulders.

"Mrs. Bennet puzzles me. She wants her daughters to marry well, and yet she does nothing to temper their actions," Kent said.

"Nor push them towards men of means," Rawlings mumbled.

"Humph." Darcy spotted Mrs. Bennet encouraging Elizabeth to speak to Blake. "Humph."

When Miss Mary began to play a tune well suited for dancing, Kent grinned at Rawlings. "Shame it is not a waltz. You would not have to wait to enjoy that well endowed figure!"

It was Kitty, and not Lydia, that looked towards Rawlings and smiled. He secured her hand for the dance. They lined up next to Lydia and her officer, who stood next to Bingley and Jane. Finally, two other guests joined the group and they began to dance.

Pleased that several of the young men had chosen to dance, Sir William approached Darcy for the very purpose of encouraging him to follow suit. Elizabeth passed by and, seeing the opportunity, recommended her to him. When she turned down Darcy's offer, Sir William hastily removed himself elsewhere.

Darcy released the breath he had held while waiting for her answer and although disappointed he was intrigued by her rejection having never been turned down before. He kept his eyes on her and studied her walk as she made her way to the other side of the room. Most unusual. He heard Blake mutter a curse. For the first time, Darcy appreciated the unwritten rule that once a lady turned down an offer she could not dance again that night with any man. Blake would not have a turn with her this evening.

"I can guess the subject of your reverie." Kent said as he drew next to Darcy.

"I should imagine not."

"You are wishing we were back in Bingley's library working on tedious business matters!"

"Your conjecture is entirely wrong, I assure you. My mind was more agreeably engaged. I have been meditating on the very great pleasure which a pair of fine eyes in the face of a pretty woman can bestow."

"Dare I ask whose eyes might they be?" Kent asked.

"Miss Elizabeth Bennet."

"Miss Elizabeth Bennet!" Kent repeated, his tone unmistakenly insincere. "Her eyes are fine, indeed, especially as she casts them on another." He inclined his head towards Blake.

"Humph." Darcy's forehead creased when his noticed Blake moving towards Elizabeth.

Chapter Thirteen

The empty breakfast table greeted Darcy as he sat down with his coffee and a small stack of mail. Blake, as usual, was out riding before sunrise; Bingley and Kent were sleeping late, their habit following a party; and Rawlings was preparing to leave for London.

Darcy had barely cracked the seal on the first letter when Whitson informed him Rawlings wished a word with him. He gulped the rest of his coffee and then rushed to meet his friend. The library door was open enough to hear the sound of humming. Oh, he is in a jolly good mood Darcy surmised as he entered and found Rawlings dressed in a riding outfit, sitting in his favorite chair by the window, nodding his head and tapping his fingers in time with the beat of some tune only his friend could hear.

"Four and twenty blackbirds?"

Rawlings jumped up. "Yes, indeed. And she is a dainty dish to set before a king," Rawlings paused and then pointed to himself. "And the king is in his counting house, counting out his money. A wonderful rhyme."

"You wished to speak to me?"

Rawlings nodded.

They settled into chairs across from each other. Darcy lifted his eyebrows, but he waited for his friend to compose his words.

"I want to thank you for inviting me into the alliance; although, I must admit I do not understand why. I bring nothing of any consequence."

Darcy locked eyes with Rawlings. "I owe you much."

Rawlings held up his open palm and swung his head wide when he shook it.

"Why not join me for breakfast? We can speak openly since no else is present." Darcy asked.

"Not this morning. I had a tray sent up early. Although, I am tempted to pack up a few of cook's sweet pastries before I leave."

Rawlings patted his stomach. "No! I ate too many treats already. If I keep this up no one will ever confuse us again!"

"Why did you wish to see me?"

"I am leaving in a few minutes. Is there anything you need for me to do in town?"

"Nothing more is needed than to make inquires about Mr. Cuffage. I was not pleased Kent did not know of the man. Find out what you can before we attempt to pursue global trading. We can concentrate on the railroads and steam powered riverboats for transporting our goods in our own country first if he does not check out."

"Oh, I will." Rawlings tapped his pocket. "I have the last known address of Nathaniel and Nigel."

"Are you planning on booking passage while in London? We do not have signed agreements yet."

"Yes, if all is well with Cuffage. I can always cancel later if needed."

Darcy moved to the window.

"Meryton has surprised me." Rawlings said.

"How so?"

"The men believe we are here as a shooting party."

Darcy caught sight of Blake riding up the driveway in a slow trot. "And the women presume it is to find ourselves brides, I suspect."

Rawlings shrugged. "Is marriage not what all women think about?"

"And fashion. Even Georgiana would not forgo dresses and shopping." Darcy thought of his younger sister rushing through the many expensive London shops on Bond Street.

"Spending money is women's business. Men are the necessary evils who provide the funds." Rawlings joined Darcy by the window. "I suppose that is why a woman pursues gentleman the way she does, and if the man desires her, then he will seek a way to offer her a fortune." He narrowed his eyes. "Not all methods used by women are honorable."

"Nor all men when a women is desired," Darcy added.

For a short time, the two men wordlessly eyed Blake.

"Are you worried about him?" Rawlings pointed his his head to the figure retreating to the stable.

"Blake? No. I am more worried about you." Darcy clasped Rawlings' shoulder. "The voyage is dangerous enough without having to worry about the shipping embargo and the Americans."

"True, but the Royal Navy worries me more. I hope to be riding on a fast moving American-owned ship. Kent provided me information about the *Lively*." Rawlings gave his friend a half frown. "The Navy boards American cargo ships and captures the men."

"You should not worry. They would not dare conscript the son of an Earl."

"But, Logan may be pressed into service." Rawlings said. "He has served me admirably."

"And me also." Darcy again clasped his friends shoulder, this time he gave it a slight squeeze. "Logan would not be taken on your say so alone."

"Perhaps." Rawlings relaxed. "Regardless, I do admit that I crave the adventure all the same. Well, I must be off."

"I beg your pardon for detaining you from family duties at this time."

"I detest them." Rawlings' body became rigid when a sideward glance revealed a frowning friend. "Darcy, do not suffer any guilt. Unwilling people cannot be detained unless guns and shackles and the like are used."

"Many kinds of guns and shackles exist," Darcy said, his words barely discernable.

"I can attest to that!" Rawlings nudged his friend. "Do you have any letters for me to take to town?"

Darcy reached in his coat pocket.

"My pleasure." Rawlings smiled as he accepted the thick letter. He pretended to weigh it with his hand as an imaginary scale. "I assume its weight is due to those four syllable words you are so fond of using."

Darcy maintained his noncommittal mask.

Rawlings bowed, placed it in his pocket beside the other important documents, fingered them, and hurried outside where Logan was waiting with horses saddled and ready to leave.

***

An unhappy Blake, returning from his morning ride, followed Darcy into the dining room where Bingley and Kent held their first forkfuls of sliced ham and eggs.

Kent winced as he swallowed his coddled eggs. "Not an agreeable ride this morning?" He put his fork down and summoned the footman over to remove his plate.

"It was adequate. The scenery was dull—not a single object of interest." Blake sat in his usual chair after serving himself from the buffet. His plate held a small amount of food, of which he pushed around the edges. He sipped his coffee, ignoring the conversation until Bingley addressed him.

"Blake, perhaps this afternoon will cheer you when we go to Goulding's horse farm to inspect the stallion."

"Yes, I understand he expects us at two. I look forward to it." Blake peered over the top of his coffee cup. He had spent years inspecting and purchasing thoroughbred horses, and had grown skilled at recognizing the unmistakable signs of what is not a suitable animal: one that laid it ears back; shied away when approached; had a runny nose; stood on limp or crooked legs, or had pupils that would not dilate in light. If a horse passed this short test, he then examined the size of its chest. If one side were larger, the horse would favor one lead over the other, which was never a desirable attribute. Most sellers allowed for one ride—not a fair measurement —and after years of experience, Blake discovered it was not even necessary. He required no more than three minutes to assess the worth of any horse.

"Bingley, it is with regret, I must decline," Kent said. "I need to attend to some pressing business that cannot wait until tomorrow. Alas, my responses must be sent today."

"I believe the proper phrase is 'I have urgent business that must not be delayed' as I have been schooled." Bingley winked at Darcy. "Is that not the correct wording?"

Kent tipped his head towards Darcy. "Consider me educated."

"I will not delay you." Bingley grinned. "Please do not hesitate to ask my staff to assist you in any way. Darcy has them all well trained."

"The correspondence would not take long if there were not so much." Kent snuck a peek at Darcy. "I do not labor over finding the right or longest word or phrase."

"True, I do spend time choosing my words. Other men use the first thought that comes to mind; I try to find the most accurate one for the purpose at hand. Usage of the correct word conveys an unmistakable acumen. I can even guess which words each of you would use to portray your feelings about being around a beautiful lady?"

"I can think of a few!" Bingley exclaimed.

"Now, Bingley, you say glad." Darcy turned to Kent. "Yours is happy, Rawlings always uses delighted, and Blake, pleased is how you describe everything."

"And you, Darcy, what is your choice?" Kent walked to the door. "My guess is you would be petrified!"

"I believe in high spirits sounds better, do you not agree? Which one best conveys the situation?" Darcy asked.

Bingley grinned. "They all sound like glad to me! I do not care since it is I who will be around the beautiful lady."

"I, too, have some work keeping me busy this morning," Darcy said. He unsuccessfully hid a smirk behind his coffee cup. "However, I will be able to join you on your visit to Gouldings for I shall not need to search for big words today."

"Blake, do you wish to go?" Bingley asked.

"I have no work to do. I finished my correspondence yesterday. I do not drag my feet as these fellows do!"

Everyone laughed, but Blake did not flinch.

"You finished fast only when it involved mathematics." Darcy stood to leave.

"True, it does come effortlessly to me. I multiplied three digit numbers at age five."

"Yes and Mr. Rudolph reproached you for the methods used many times."

"Not a single master, particularly not Mr. Rudolph, convinced me my method was wrong. I always came up with the exact answer!" Blake shrugged his shoulders. "What does it matter how you accomplish the task as long as, in the end, you are successful?"

"A gentleman follows the proper way of all things," Darcy said.

Soon thereafter, Kent and Darcy left to attend to business; Bingley and Blake remained. They spoke about the challenges in completing difficult literature assignments from the boring masters and laughed at many of the funny and embarrassing recitations of poetry recited in front of the old men.

As young men, Blake and Bingley liked each other, both possessing similar charming natures, and in particular, they displayed it around the opposite sex. Each preferred to spend time in the company of the ladies, and neither man felt compelled to apologize for it. Both attended many balls in town, and they danced every dance. They flirted with and wooed women the entire night. Most importantly, they both enjoyed smiling, and that had not changed with the passage of time.

Their conversation took a different direction, which focused on their friends at Netherfield Park.

"I do not understand Darcy sometimes. I mean, he shies away from practically all ladies." Bingley settled back into the chair and waited for an answer.

"Yes, he can be aloof around them." Blake glanced at the door. "When he is well acquainted with a lady he will flirt a little."

"I have never seen him act in such a fashion."

"His idea of flirting is no more than the way we would say hello."

"Ah." Bingley nodded. "Kent is also reserved."

"His sole purpose is to imitate Darcy. Now, Rawlings became more reserved after he wed."

"I was surprised when he married Margaret Stevens. Why, he had just finished university!" Bingley said.

"Within a month, I believe. We may never know the reason why. Rawlings does not suffer a single word to be spoken about it."

"True. One time I remember his friend, Lord Dembrey, asked him, and he simply walked away." Bingley said. "But he seems happier now."

"Yes, as a widower he does smile and tease more."

***

Bingley's carriage pulled into the Goulding estate. Absent from the driveway were the reddish leaves from the area's common oak trees. Instead, a shining yellow adorned the sawtooth oak trees, which stood in a line along the road to the house and gave off the appearance of glowing rounded, pyramid-shaped torches. The brightened golden color had not yet begun to fade to the brown hue that occurred right before the leaves fell off the trees. It was still early autumn.

Bingley, Blake, and Darcy eyed the many handsome looking horses grazing in the fields, each man searching for the stallion. Some horses raced about, and a few of them stopped to view the carriage as it passed. The horses were of every color, size and shape. The men agreed the owner took meticulous care of the animals, for no other reason than their healthy appearance.

Bingley pointed to the horses on the hillside. "Does it not feel like an orphanage? They are trying to display themselves for adoption."

Blake gazed out the window. "I do believe they are!"

"That one, with his majestic posture, is not easily owned by any man." Darcy identified the stallion they came to inspect, standing alone in the field, far away from the hillside.

"Welcome, good sirs," Mr. Goulding said as the three men exited the carriage. They exchanged the usual polite pleasantries before he directed them to the stables.

For an older man, Mr. Goulding had the physique of a young one. He worked the horses daily. After breaking the wild ones, he, and the now tamed horse, tore across the countryside. It was his true pleasure. He chuckled as the astonished visitors eyed the size of his stable.

"Oh my, this is far more than I expected." Blake gaped at the building size.

"Excellent, Mr. Goulding." Darcy viewed the stable housing over fifty beautiful thoroughbreds, not including the ones in the field. "From where do they come?"

"Places such as Arabia, Germany, Russia and even a few made their way here from the Americas. They have developed some interesting breeds; the Morgan in particular. Must be because of those wide open spaces they brag about so much."

Darcy turned to Goulding. "I believe I caught sight of the stallion you made mention of last night. He was alone in the open field. A beautiful white horse that stands sixteen hands tall?"

"Yes, I suppose you did get a glimpse of him. However, good sir, he measures a full seventeen hands. A tall one he is even for one of his type. He is as close as you can get to a purebred Andalusian, one of the world's ancient breeds. In earlier times, these sturdy horses were mixed with Arab and Barbary strains. Today's breed has a bit of Oriental blood but not this one.

"If my recollection is correct, Romans made use of them in several ways," Darcy said.

"Yes sir. The horses had the strength and agility needed for various military activities. The Romans not only rode them into battle, they made them pull their chariots as well. Few horses are able to accomplish both successfully."

Since two of the gentlemen showed no interest in the history, Goulding waved to a stable hand brushing down a chestnut mare. "I will send a boy to get the stallion."

"I am surprised you do not need to send a man. In fact, several men." Bingley chuckled.

"He is strong, you are correct, but if you treat him right he is gentle, too. Shall we take a tour of my stable and examine the many other fine breeds available?" Mr. Goulding pointed to the building.

The men agreed promptly and spent the next half hour viewing, patting and otherwise inspecting the horses. The men were fascinated with the Justin Morgan horse from America until they discovered the white stallion in the next stall.

"Is that horse an Andalusian as well?" Blake asked. The horse owned the same strong build and haughty air about him as the one they saw in the field.

"You have an exceptional eye, my lord, but no. He is a Lipizzaner. However, they bred Andalusian with these horses, and that is why they appear so much alike. He comes from lowlands of the Carpathian Mountains in Lipizza, Archduke Maximillion's royal stud farm."

Blake eyed the quality thoroughbreds in the stalls. "I am surprised Londoners are not aware of your business. I would have heard of it, Mr. Goulding, if so."

"Oh, some do. They choose to keep it a secret, wishing for no competition for my finest steeds. I provide my horses to the best of families, and, might I add, I hope to furnish a few more in the near future?" He bestowed them with a pleasant smile.

As they progressed to the horse corral to wait for the stallion, Bingley spied a young man speaking to a lady. "Blake, I believe Miss Elizabeth Bennet is here." Squinting, he looked around the area for any other visitors.

Blake gasped. "Oh, my. Yes, it is her."

Mr. Goulding nodded. "Yes, Mr. Bingley, you are correct. Miss Bennet often comes to visit Mrs. Goulding. In spite of the age difference, they are firm friends. Neither suffers fools kindly. It does appear she is engaged in some argument with my son, Robert. This has been their way—always arguing—even as youngsters. They end up laughing, of course. The two are, beyond doubt, most fond of one another."

Blake's eyes widened at hearing this, keeping them aimed on Elizabeth and the younger Goulding son as they spoke so warmly with each other. He caught himself clenching his fists and not concealing his frowns. Embarrassed, he hastily turned away to look for the stallion.

The servants brought the four-legged object of the trip to the men and drew their attention. Nevertheless, when Robert Goulding and Elizabeth walked out of view, any interest Blake had in horses evaporated. He left the others and went in search of the couple. Bingley followed close on his heels.

After taking a turn around the garden, Robert Goulding led the young lady to a bench. "Pray tell me Miss Elizabeth, how is Miss Bennet?"

"She is doing well. She was sorry to miss the visit, but it could not be helped."

"I wished she was able to come today. My, um, mother would have enjoyed it very much." He lowered his head and added, "And I would have, too."

Blake and Bingley joined them, cutting off any further conversation between the two long time friends.

"Forgive me for interrupting, but I could not miss giving my regards to you, Miss Bennet." Blake bowed politely.

"Lord Blake, how exceedingly kind." Elizabeth curtseyed. "And you as well, Mr. Bingley. Have you met Mr. Goulding?" Elizabeth proceeded with the proper introductions, and for several minutes, the group spoke of the many fine horses on the farm and in the stable.

A footman approached and addressed Robert Goulding, interrupting his amusing story about runaway ponies. "Please excuse me; I am called away. Miss Elizabeth if you would be so kind to send Miss Bennet my good wishes, I would be most grateful. Goulding bowed to the group and left.

Mr. Bingley's eyes followed him into the house, his concern growing over a perceived relationship between Miss Bennet and Mr. Goulding. "I overheard you earlier saying your sister, Miss Bennet, was unable to come. I hope she is not ill."

"She is well. Thank you for asking."

"Does she visit here often, I mean, to behold the new arrivals? Is she fond of horses?"

"No, she rarely visits, but yes, she does have a fondness for them. Then again, I am found here more often, yet I care naught for the creatures."

"Mrs. Goulding must be pleased you come to visit," Blake said his voice without enthusiasm.

"Yes, she and her family. Her son taught me how to shoot arrows, fish, and even climb trees."

Blake smiled. "Do you come here to play like that still?"

"No, I come to abuse and tease young men who dearly want to ask pointed questions but cannot."

"All the young men or just a few?" Blake glanced over to Bingley and then back to her.

"Certain men, for they all desire what I know. You see, I am a member of the wiser sex."

Blake could not conceal his smile. She nodded in return.

Bingley shifted his weight from one foot to the other. "And what is that information you hold so dear?"

"Why, Mr. Robert Goulding will soon be engaged. Her father has an estate eight miles west."

A collective sigh was released from both men; Bingley was relieved Mr. Goulding did not have any understanding with Miss Jane while Blake was grateful that their childhood friendship had not left him with an interest in Elizabeth.

Elizabeth turned to look toward the stable. "I am surprised you are not inspecting the beasts?"

"I did want to pay my respects as soon as I became aware of your presence. I knew not if you would be coming to view the horses." Blake led the way toward the corral. "We have come to inspect a new stallion. It took me but a second to decide to purchase the magnificent beast— even if Mr. Goulding prices the horse high."

Elizabeth looked at Blake with raised brows.

Blake whispered, "I am willing to pay handsomely for things of exceptional value."

When the corral came into view, the marquess pointed to the spectacular horse. Bingley turned away from Blake and Elizabeth and watched Darcy continue his inspection.

"Mr. Darcy seems interested too. Are you not concerned he may purchase him first?" Elizabeth asked.

"No. he takes too long to make a decision." Blake chuckled, and then with a serious expression leaned into her. "I, conversely, move with great speed." Looking back towards Darcy, he scoffed. "I will outbid him if need be. Perhaps though, we should join him just in case he fools me this once." Blake attempted to lead her to the corral.

Elizabeth stopped abruptly. "Oh, I rarely go near the large stallions. I prefer the gentler, smaller horses. I stay at the house or here in the garden." She inclined her head towards several small bushes. "As you see, my lord, there are many winter roses beginning to grow."

"I am not surprised. This is a place where things of beauty are on display." Blake gazed at the horses, then upon the flowers and finally when his eyes fell on Elizabeth's face, his smile deepened until her eyes sparkled in return.

Bingley maintained his attention on Darcy inspecting the, horse; but when a special messenger arrived and the senior Goulding hurried to the house, he turned to his friends and bowed. "Miss Elizabeth, Lord Blake. Please excuse me." .

The eldest Goulding son replaced his father and stood by while Mr. Darcy patted the horse, checked his teeth and eyes, and tested the strength in its legs.

Darcy's countenance changed from a relaxed, controlled state to a tense rigid stance when Bingley left Blake and Elizabeth unchaperoned. He experienced a familiar dullness filling his chest at the sight of the easy camaraderie of the couple smiling and laughing with each other.

"Mr. Darcy, with such a scowl, are you imagining losing the race to this magnificent horse?" Goulding asked.

Without turning, Darcy said, "You mistake my mind. There is no race I cannot win. All I need are two things."

"Two things, sir? May I ask what they are?"

"One, I must be willing to sacrifice what I hold dear."

"And the second?" Goulding leaned in, hoping to gain perspective.

"Knowing the exact moment to make my move."

"And has that time arrived; is this the moment to make your move?"

Darcy shook his head. "You ask the wrong question. You should be asking me if I am willing to sacrifice."

"Oh, and are you willing to sacrifice today?"

While he contemplated his answer, he stared hard at Elizabeth who was now speaking in an animated fashion Blake. Without changing the direction of his gaze, he gently rubbed the horse's coat. "I have not made up my mind, but if I do, I will be like the wind at your back: invisible, yet determined. No man can ever stop the wind, and no man shall ever stop me from succeeding in a race I choose to win."

Goulding's father returned from the house just as Darcy finished speaking. "I am sorry to inform you, sir. The stallion has been sold."

Chapter Fourteen

The tap of his boots echoed throughout the foyer as Darcy walked down the stairs. The hustle and bustle of the day had not yet begun. This was his favorite time—the sun had scarcely appeared at the tip of the horizon and the nighttime mist had begun lifting much like a sleepy child removes the comforter—unhurriedly and with a speck of resentment. He sniffed the smell of sage and rosemary wafting though the house, which grew stronger with each step he took towards the dining room. At Netherfield Park, there was always some form of pork for breakfast: bacon, ham, or this browned mishmash with the most unusual spices added to it. He had come to fancy the jumbled mess, mixing it with the tasteless scrambled eggs. Rawlings may favor sweet, but he preferred spice.

He filled his plate, happy the cook offered the peppery hodgepodge this morning. He placed the first forkful in his mouth the instant he sat down, savoring the taste as he swallowed it in a slow and deliberate manner followed by equally slowly eaten forkfuls. He returned to the buffet, not for seconds even though his plate was now empty, but to pour a cup of coffee and stand in his usual spot at the window. He gazed out at the animals beginning their day, although none of the birds, the dogs, or even the horses registered on his thoughts. Mr. Phillips would arrive later this morning to draw up the papers and, hence, this day his life would take on a new direction. He called his emotions an anthill of anticipation and a mountain of anxiety.

Rawlings entered the dining room exhibiting more enthusiasm than he had shown before he had journeyed to London. Darcy turned around, a smile across his face. They were alone as had become the norm until either Blake returned from his ride or the other two men emerged from a late sleep, scraping their feet as they made their way to the coffee urn.

"Good morning."

"Welcome back, Rawlings. When did you arrive?"

"After all the little boys had been tucked into bed."

"How was your visit?"

"My brother's fiancé is exactly what he deserves. He has not shown any interest in her now that my father made the arrangements."

"And Mr. Cuffage?"

"I spoke to Nathanial. He had performed a few investigations for him. He said Cuffage is a good sort and offered up his recommendation for his character. I was unable to question his brother. Nigel was out of town. Nathanial assured me that his brother was of the same opinion."

Darcy released a deep breath, stood, and moved to the buffet to refill his coffee. "I am satisfied, then. We can proceed. Do you wish a sweet pastry?"

"Thank you, but I am hungry for a full dish of food this morning." He moved to the buffet and placed two apple-filled pastries next to his eggs. He did not add any of the spicy pork to his plate, instead choosing several large ham slices. "I am pleased to be back here."

"Why is that?" Blake asked as he, Kent and Bingley strolled in the room.

"I am now happily ensconced in a house no one knows, in a town no one has heard of, and in a county few travel to."

Everyone was keen to hear the latest gossip. Rawlings told them the current talk from the antics of the Prince Regent to Lord Byron's newest escapade. Cheerfulness, shocked expressions, and even a bit of solemnity filled the room. Gentlemen from the highest circles were as much interested in the comings and goings of the society in which they live as the Meryton community was in theirs.

"Was the trip to Goulding's successful?" Rawlings glanced towards Darcy.

"Not for us. The stallion was sold while we were inspecting him."

Blake dropped in his chair almost spilling the eggs from his plate. "Mr. Goulding was dishonorable. We arrived at his invitation and he sold the horse before we finished our inspection."

"Were you planning on purchasing it?"

"Indeed I was." Blake glared at Darcy. "I would have enjoyed defeating you in a race for the first time." He looked back at Rawlings. "The stallion was the most excellent specimen. I am seriously disappointed." Blake slammed his fork on the table. "I am more than displeased. I am quite angry, in fact. I wanted that damn horse."

"What type of horse was it?" Rawlings asked.

In unison, Darcy and Blake answered, "An Andalusian."

Rawlings blinked. He, as a member of the Four Horse Club, knew its worth. "Blake, I would have purchased him sight unseen if I had known Goulding owned one."

"I asked him to identify the new owner, but he declined. I offered twice as much, but Goulding refused, except he kept babbling that all hope of owning the horse was not lost." Blake shrugged. "Needless to say, I am still annoyed." He mumbled he would even pay triple the price if he must. In a final word on the subject, he announced without any hint of joviality, "I would pay or do anything to beat Darcy at a horse race."

"Gentlemen." Darcy clicked his knife on his glass until everyone gave him their full attention. "Mr. Phillips will be here at ten to draw up the alliance agreement. Have you decided to unite with Bingley and me?"

Kent and Rawlings responded with a hearty yes. Blake, however, drank a full goblet of water, stared at his plate, and remained silent until Darcy clicked his glass again.

"Blake? It is up to you. What is your decision?"

Blake did nod his agreement, although slowly and without comment. With sweat trickling down his temple, he kept his eyes focus on his plate and ignored the salty droplet falling on his plate. His subdued approval deflated everyone else's enthusiasm.

"It is almost ten now," Bingley said and then stood. "It is best we move to the library." The others swallowed their coffee and fell in behind Bingley. The voices of the men, except for Blake, were slightly raised, their stride purposeful, and their words tinged with a forced laughter. Darcy sensed something, but he could not identify it. However, he did acknowledge it was due to Blake who diverted his eyes when any of the other men glanced at him.

Upon entering the library, they noticed how different the room appeared. Before, the servants had arranged the chairs in a circle around the fireplace, but now they had placed them at a very large table. Rawlings was pleased to spy a tray full of the sweet pastries next to the fruits on the sideboard. The men spoke of many things, none of which was business related, until there was a knock on the door and Whitson announced, "Mr. Phillips."

The local attorney stepped into the room, bowing as deeply as possible without dropping the disordered documents in his hands. Maintaining control, he pulled himself erect with his shoulders back and head held high.

Bingley rose to greet him. "Welcome, Mr. Phillips. Would you care to take a seat here? You could spread your papers out and be more comfortable that way."

Stacking them on the table, Mr. Phillips waited as Bingley stood beside Mr. Darcy. "Good day, Mr. Bingley, Mr. Darcy."

Bowing, Darcy introduced the other three gentlemen. "Thank you for coming, Mr. Phillips."

"It is an honor to be of service." He bowed to each of the men and the depth of his bow showed them the greatest of respect.

The men took their seats and waited for Darcy to begin, and once he did, he began the discussion in his most serious tone. "Secrecy is the key. I will explain our plans to you in sufficient detail to draw up the legal documents. We, none of us, want any news of this alliance to find its way to London, or even around Meryton."

The men nodded in unison.

Rawlings enjoyed the scene in front of him. It resembled a pack of lions and a newly born, wobbly lamb. The king lion was in charge and the lamb was happy not to be sliced for dinner. He caught himself chuckling aloud. Darcy, he noted, sat in the largest wingback chair with his friends lined up in a semi-circle of sorts. There was a table between them, and a simpler chair for Mr. Phillips on the other side. More like a lion's cave than a den thought Rawlings. Poor man! I do not believe I could think clearly with such a wealthy, united, and powerful front staring directly at me. Well now, let us discover what makes this man!

After organizing his papers into specific stacks, Mr. Phillips sat rigidly in his chair and spoke with confidence. "You can be assured of my silence, good sirs. I will take all precautions to ensure none of my acquaintances will be aware of this. Not one of my acquaintances, sirs, will be privileged to this information."

"Thank you for your assurances. Now, we need a document drawn up that explicitly states the finite detail of this alliance." Darcy paused until Mr. Phillips had his writing instruments ready.

Finally, with his quill and inkwell in place and many sheets of blank paper in front of him, Mr. Phillips gave the sign to continue.

Looking around the room, Darcy's neck and shoulder muscles relaxed when he spotted Blake's slight nod. "We have come to an accord as to what to include.

The meeting continued for several hours with a more composed solicitor furiously taking notes as the men described their role and what they wanted included in the written contract. He shrugged or nodded at each of their demands, his expression remaining calm until he heard the words prohibition and embargo. His eyes burst wide open; he halted all writing. Placing his pen down, he crossed his arms tightly against his chest and inclined backwards in his chair.

Rawlings, enjoying the entertaining moment, kept his focus on Darcy who had leaned forward, presented a confident smile and spoke in a reassuring calm tone. "Do not worry, Mr. Phillips. We are looking toward the future. In all sincerety, we doubt any trading would occur before the embargo is lifted. By that time, we would not be going against England. We seek a jump on establishing our association with American traders. All we desire is to beat the competition!"

Darcy may have settled into the back cushion with his hands clasped together and resting in his lap, however, this tranquil picture did not negate how his darkened eyes bore into Mr. Phillips. "That is why this information requires the most secrecy. We would not want any misunderstanding by our government to jeopardize the mission."

"I see. I do understand now." Picking up his pen, a startled Mr. Phillips nodded. "Secrecy is the key in circumstances such as these."

"Will you be able to attend to these matters?" Rawlings asked.

"Yes, I do not see any immediate obstacles on my part that cannot be overcome."

"When will the documents be ready?" Darcy asked as Mr. Phillips put away his writing pens and collect his papers together.

"To ensure the secrecy you desire, I must be circumspect in my actions and research some areas, although, as I have said, I do not perceive of any major obstacles." He rummaged through his papers. "I imagine this will take at least a fortnight."

Bowing his head, Darcy said, "We are available at Netherfield Park if any need should arise."

As Mr. Phillips stood to leave, all the men rose in unison. Mr. Phillips bowed and then jerked upright. "Oh! I seek one more particular bit of information. How does the alliance plan to divide the profits?"

Darcy answered, "Equ—"

"It has not been decided," Blake interrupted in a loud and unyielding voice. "You may leave that part of the agreement blank until later." He held his chin high, his shoulders back, and showed no expression on his face, much like Darcy's normal mask of indifference.

The identical reaction appeared on the other four men's faces— shock—as they turned to gawk at Blake. No one blinked; no one breathed, causing them to appear as statues. Mr. Phillips busied himself with searching through his papers. He did not look up.

Darcy's glare tuned into a scowl aimed at Blake and then he rose, seizing control of the situation,. "Ahem. Mr. Phillips, Lord Blake is correct. We have not yet come to agreement on that aspect, but I assure you all is well."

Bingley jumped up, directing the attorney's attention to the sideboard table's array of pleasurable treats. "Mr. Phillips, will you stay for some refreshment? Perhaps, a glass of wine?"

Phillips shared a drink and a toast to the future, which was quickly completed and without the zeal displayed earlier. He indicated he was anxious to start and hurried to gather his documents together. He left the room with Bingley on his heels, praising him for his good work and patience. Everyone else remained quiet until the footman closed the door to the hallway shut.

"A pox o' your throat, you bawling, blasphemous, incharitable dog! Rawlings yelled, marching towards Blake. "I suspected something by the cowardly manner in which you agreed."

Blake kept his chin high, his shoulders squared. He held up his hand to stop him from coming closer. "I do not fear insults, Rawlings. Darcy, you remarked many times how critical I am to your alliance. You cannot go forward without me. So, I have calculated my worth and arrived at a figure."

"Let us hear it."

"I want one third of the profits." Blake waved his hand at the other men and added, "The rest of you can split among yourselves in any manner you agree."

"One third?" Darcy winced.

"Otherwise, I will not participate."

"No!" Kent slammed his fist on the table. Not one ha'penny more than I receive." He turned his glare on Darcy. "I am as critical to the success as Blake. You cannot do this without me. I am his equal in this partnership. You led me to believe rank has no extra privileges here."

"Why must you base every problem on rank and status?" Blake asked.

Kent leaned towards Blake. "Because I must always walk last and you always go first. Perhaps, socially the nobility is treated as such, but when it comes to business," he shook his pointer finger, "you are not superior to me."

"Phew. This is not about my nobility. If you want one third because you are critical to the partnership, then negotiate for it as I am."

Kent twisted around to face Darcy. "I will withdraw if Blake receives a larger share of the profits. Do you understand?"

Bingley's hands trembled; his head dropped downward, but when his shoulders began to shake, Darcy jumped up, placing his hands on his hips and boring his darkest state at Blake who had also risen from his chair.

Rawlings positioned himself next to Darcy.

Blake took a step towards Darcy, then stopped and crossed his arms. "That is my price for my connections to Lord Liverpool. He is the sole person able to approve the purchase."

Kent whispered in Bingley's ear and when Bingley responded in the same manner, Kent's gasp was audible enough for everyone to catch.

Darcy bellowed. "No. Either everyone shares equally or there is no alliance."

"Equally? Bah. Even we are not equals. Take my offer or send me on my way." Blake approached Darcy, their black stares joined. "If I must sell my services like a... commoner does, then I place a high premium on them." Blake backed off and stepped around the table. "You cannot purchase a marquess on the cheap."

Bingley opened his mouth and had almost announced his agreement but stopped at the sight of Rawlings' wink, which was done in a manner that Blake could not see.

Darcy stepped close to Rawlings, speaking to him in a low whisper. Rawlings shook his head in exaggerated manner, but this time he performed it for Blake's eyes. When Darcy was about to speak, Rawlings grabbed his arm and squeezed it.

When no one spoke, Blake shrugged. "Very well. I shall tell my man to pack up and we will be gone within the hour." He turned and headed to the door. His walked away assured and while not swift, he did not crawl. He stopped abruptly just as he reached the doorframe when Rawlings called his name. "Blake!"

Without turning, he waited. He pulled himself up to his full height.

With a calm voice, Rawlings said, "Lord Liverpool owes my father a deep financial debt. You are not the only one with access to him."

Blake's shoulders twitched slightly, but enough for Rawlings to catch sight of it.

"So you see, I have an even better connection than do you. So go on and leave. We will not stop you from going. However, we will enjoy the riches that will come our way without regard to your current situation in life."

Blake stared down the hallway, remaining silent for a full minute. No one else spoke. He knew without turning around that their eyes were aimed at his back. Thoughts clicked through his mind as a trickle of sweat rolled down his neck and under his cravat. "Wait!" He called out and then turned to face his friends. He slackened his muscles.

Everyone looked forward, hints of smiles appearing on their mouths.

"Rawlings, I do not believe your father would assist you once he learns the truth. He would not approve of your partnering with tradesmen. Even Darcy admitted to me he would not tell his uncle of the alliance. So, I do not fear your bluff."

Rawlings gazed at Blake, a smile hinted on his mouth. "But you are unaware that my father owes *me* a great favor from four years ago. I am the unknown beast in the room, Blake. You do not know what I can do." He slid into his chair and in a nonchalant manner, brushed unseen dust from the table.

The men understood this pretense and they recognized the ploy when others did it to them. This time, no one knew if Rawlings was being truthful—he did not share Darcy's belief that all disguise is abhorrence.

The room stilled. Blake plopped into a chair and tapped his fingers on the table. A speck of light flickered in Blake's eyes as he calculated the possibilities until the corners of his mouth curved upwards.

"I doubt you will approach your father, but I will make a deal with everyone. It concerns Bingley's competition." Blake replied.

"How so? Rawlings asked.

"If I am the victor I get thirty percent, but I demand two conditions."

"We are blindfolded?" Rawlings said with more of a jeer than a tease. "With our hands and feet tied?"

"No. I demand that the competition does not include shooting or a race where Darcy can use his own horse." Blake glared at Rawlings. "One game for the thirty percent—the four of you against me. That puts the odds in your favor, not mine. Ask Bingley for the name of the game and then decide." When all eyes switched to Bingley, Blake continued, "No more evasive answers. What is the game we are to compete in?"

Bingley sighed. "I do not know what the game is exactly."

"Explain yourself. We are all anxious to hear."

"It is not one game, Blake, it is five."

"Five?"

"Yes. Five. I do not know what they are because each one of us is entitled to name a game of his choice. It is like the Greek Olympics. The man who earned the most points after all five games wins."

Kent sneered at Blake. "It appears you would have to beat us at our own particular game. Not a single game, but four games of our choosing to your one. Now it is your decision. Do you still wish to offer the deal?"

Blake squirmed as he calculated the possibilities. His eyes darted up and down and his fingers danced as he added and subtracted unseen numbers. "Not necessarily true, Kent. The competition will not be about who wins the games, but who places second and third the most times. Total points can be acquired in a multitude of schemes."

"Bingley, were you planning on awarding something to the winner?" Kent asked, although he knew the answer. He whirled his head back to catch Blake's expression.

"Goulding's Andalusian. I bought it." Bingley announced.

Darcy gasped.

Blake's eyes widened. "Oh my! The horse!"

Rawlings rapped on the table. "Ah! The Spanish horse. Excellent. But now we have a new deal Blake. You do not get to compete for the horse if you do not agree to join us at equal shares if you lose."

"But, as victor you will agree that I would get one third the profit and the magnificent stallion?"

"Thirty percent, you said." Rawlings said.

"Yes. Thirty percent. Then I consent to your terms as long as my other two conditions remain—no one chooses a shooting competition or any game using Darcy's horse."

Darcy, Kent, and Bingley glanced at each other; Rawlings pointed his head to the billiard room door encouraging a separate meeting.

"No. I need your decision now!" Blake crossed his arms. "Or I walk out the door."

Darcy, Kent, and Bingley turned their eyes toward Rawlings, each man holding his breath. Rawlings knew the truth; he must decide.

When Blake took a step backwards and whirled around to leave, Rawlings called out—

"We will take the damn deal!"

"Not quite." Kent's fist slammed on the table. "I propose whoever wins the horse acquires the thirty percent and becomes the leader of the alliance. If that is not acceptable, then I will not join."

Bingley, Darcy and Rawlings' brows rose in unison, but they nodded their agreement.

After a momentary pause, Rawlings said, "We agree. Blake, do you?"

"Yes, I do. And may the most superior man win."

Chapter Fifteen

The men, upset and angry at Blake and his demands, approached the games with a seriousness than had it been the friendly competition as intended. The design of Bingley's plan was simple—the awarding of points for each game based on results: one point to the man in last place with increasing number of points up to five for the first place finisher. Whichever man receiving the most points for the five games won the horse and the larger share of the alliance earnings.

The prize of the additional ten percent profit represented hundreds of thousands of pounds, not to mention the lower percentage to be split among the other four men. This created an uneasy atmosphere around the proceedings. The men feared the winner of any game might be decided on a dispute. Therefore, they charged Bingley with finding independent judges, one to approve the rules and others to monitor every game.

And so it was, as early in the morning as socially permitted, Bingley mounted his gentle black and white spotted mare, India Treasures, and headed towards Meryton to obtain judges for the most challenging competition of his life. He had settled on asking several men and hoped they would be amenable. He decided to first approach Sir William Lucas. Once the question left his mouth, he received an immediate agreement as well as one from Mr. Phillips, who was visiting at the time. Next, he rode to Mr. Gouldings followed by a visit to Mr. Long's estate. The acceptances were swift from both men. Now he headed towards the estate he had saved for last, hoping to couple this call with visiting the eldest daughter. He glanced down the driveway to the two-story brick home of Longbourn. He wished to catch a glimpse of a beautiful blonde-haired lady.

The clopping of a horse's hoofs alerted Mr. Bennet to the approaching visitor. He laid down the now tattered letter, which had conveyed the horrific news days ago. The damage from investing in Mr. Cuffage's scheme would not change no matter how many times he reread the message or glared at his brother-in-law's signature, Edw. Gardiner. Mr. Bennet shouted to himself about how he should have listened to his warning about Cuffage. He folded the letter in half, and then he pulled it back open. He retrieved the first message he had received on this problem, this one from Cuffage demanding payment. He had just begun to read it anew when he heard a knock on the door. He placed the letters in the left drawer and locked it with a key he kept on his person at all times.

"Mr. Bingley," Hill announced.

Mr. Bennet rose to greet the young man. After dispensing with the required civilities, he offered, and Mr. Bingley accepted, a glass of port.

Bingley chose to sit in the chair next to the window with a clear view of the garden. He thought the house was quiet, too quiet. Nothing caught his interest outside. He glanced around the study. Along the wall was a most comfortable looking sofa. Books of all types overfilled the shelves, some of them lying horizontally on top of vertically placed ones. Bingley imagined the eldest Bennet daughters sitting in the two chairs facing their father's desk. He wondered if they were ever as nervous as he was at this moment.

Mr. Bennet beheld the young man examining the room. "How may I be of service?" With his practiced devilish smile he added, "I have many fine things to offer a young man such as you. All you need is to ask." His eyes fell upon the cameo of his eldest daughter sitting on his desk.

"Thank you. I do ask you for a favor," Bingley said.

With his hands clasped together. Mr. Bennet tapped his lips as he waited for the young man to speak. This morning he had enjoyed the quietude of the house while his wife and daughters had gone visiting. He smiled at Bingley, who appeared to be struggling to find the words.

Bingley licked his lips. "Ahem. My friends have agreed to participate in a competition I am hosting for them, and I came to ask if you would like to be involved."

Mr. Bennet raised both brows. "A competition?"

Bingley fidgeted in the chair. "Yes, sir."

"Well, I understand you have a magnificent new firearm, so how can I refuse? I would have to run quite a distance to avoid the range of the bullets."

Bingley cried out, "Oh no, sir. I would never risk your health. I want you to act as judge."

"And what would I be judging?" Mr. Bennet leaned forward entertained by the range of emotions crossing Bingley's face.

Bingley cast his eyes downward, noticing his boots were too dusty to be in a gentleman's study. He pushed them far under the chair. "It is complicated."

"As are all things where young people are concerned. I think I will be able to keep up!" Mr. Bennet covered his smirk with his closed hand as Bingley's feet tangled up in the chair legs.

"The competition is made up of five games; a different one each day."

"Games?" Mr. Bennet jerked his head upright. He leaned back in his chair and gazed at the ceiling. He raised his open palm to stop Bingley from continuing. "You want me to judge five games? Shall I move into Netherfield Park? That way, Mr. Bingley, I could be available all day and night."

Mr. Bingley's eyes grew wider, but before he could speak, Mr. Bennet said, "My family would never permit it, sir. Please go on."

Bingley exhaled a deep breath. "Yes, well, my friends must select a game of their choosing, plan their game, acquire the equipment needed, if any, and get the rules approved by a judge. You, if you agree."

"So I do not know what I will be judging?" Unable to conceal an amused and slightly befuddled expression, Mr. Bennet settled back in his seat in anticipation of a response.

"In the beginning, I need someone to review the rules for the games. I want to ensure no one manipulates the game to their own advantage. It is imperative that no one manipulates the game."

"But you are all friends, is that not true?"

"Yes." Bingley fidgeted in the chair. He took a deep breath, released a slow exhale through puffed out cheeks. He did not want Mr. Bennet to think ill of his friends; nonetheless, he recognized the financial importance that none of his friends obtains an unfair advantage. "But we are all competitive. Any problem would be coincidental. You could help us avoid any such situation."

Mr. Bennet stood and walked to the far wall where his own flintlock hung. "Does the judge get a rifle to keep the peace if things get a little out of hand?"

Bingley sighed. "Ah, a modified Baker might be available."

Mr. Bennet patted his firearm, turned back towards Bingley, and smiled. "Now young man, how will I get the rules?" Mr. Bennet returned to his seat, resuming his earlier position—clasping his hands together, lightly tapping his chin.

"Each man will bring them to you."

"I am surprised you are not the one who brings all the rules, Mr. Bingley."

"Their game remains a secret until the morning it is played. For my game, I will bring the rules to you on another day." Bingley snuck another peek out the window.

"Yes, I see. Another day. I quite understand." Mr. Bennet rushed to cover his snicker with his hand.

"I asked Sir William Lucas to judge as well. He agreed to assist during the actual game."

"Oh. He is needed to help keep the peace between friends?"

Bingley tapped his fingers on the chair. "Um. Between… " he paused, "between competitors, yes. It is most important to have independent judges." He felt his cravat become wet when the older man stared at him with his twinkling icy blue eyes. "You will be invited to the games and perhaps be called upon to be a game judge as well. The competition should be terrific fun. I also acquired agreement from Mr. Goulding, Mr. Long, and Mr. Phillips to be judges too."

"Ah, one peacekeeper for each young man. But who will keep the peace between the peacekeepers? Old men are a competitive lot themselves." Mr. Bennet did not hide his smirk this time.

Bingley grinned for the first time, feeling the examination was over. The other requests for judges had gone smoothly, but Mr. Bennet had teased him without mercy.

"Mr. Bingley is there anything more I should know about the games. You did say how important peacekeeping was for them. I, mean, it is a friendly competition? Nothing critical is weighing on the outcome, is there?"

Bingley studied his hands as if he had recently purchased them, and he needed to figure out how they worked. He lifted his eyes up. "No, sir. I have planned for a friendly competition with a great stallion for the prize." Damn, he thought at the falsehood he had just said. He supposed this is why Darcy abhors disguise of any sort and he did not like this deception. The alliance was a secret, so should the profit be. "There will also be scotch whiskey given to the losers. A case of it."

"The prize is a horse? Of course. Men can be very," he paused, "manipulative, pardon me, competitive, over anything walking on legs. I look forward to it, then. May I refill your glass?"

"Yes, please." Content now that he had secured his independent judges to watch over the proceedings, Bingley settled back into the chair and let his mind wander on sweeter thoughts. With each sip of his wine, Bingley checked out the window, which the older gentleman noticed.

The young man questioned Mr. Bennet on local farming issues for some time. He continued to give his attention to the garden, and then stared at the study door, and back to Mr. Bennet who continued to refill their glasses. Mr. Bennet did not conceal his amusement as they sipped away the afternoon.

When Bingley's questions became more general and even repetitive, Mr. Bennet took pity on him. "I hope you are able to remain for refreshments, Mr. Bingley. I am sure Mrs. Bennet will return with all our daughters from her visits in short while."

"Yes, thank you. I would like that very much." Bingley no longer felt the need to look out the window and sunk his back further into the chair.

A less anxious Bingley then identified the game he had chosen for the competition. Mr. Bennet was quite surprised. Moreover, when he explained the reason why he chose it, the older man stared at the young man with a new level of respect. In fact, he asked if there would be a chance for others, including himself, to try their hand at the game. Bingley agreed but only after the competition was complete.

"Then I suggest you provide the opportunity at your harvest Feast."

Bingley face lit up. "A harvest feast?"

"Most estate owners provide a celebration for their tenants at the end of the harvest. It is a little late for Netherfield Park, but it would help establish you as a neighbor."

"Indeed. Excellent suggestion, Mr. Bennet. I will consider it."

"Perhaps a competition for the locals could be done. If you do hold one, I suggest you offer one of your magnificent rifles. It is the talk of the parish."

Bingley sighed. How many of his rifle must he give away? An estate owner has many responsibilities, some Darcy had not explained.

Soon thereafter, the Bennet ladies returned, and the study no longer held Bingley's interest.

"Go on, young man, you have earned it." Mr. Bennet waved his hand towards the door.

Bingley tripped as he stood.

Mr. Bennet leapt up to catch the man. "Well, perhaps you should spend the rest of your time here, Mr. Bingley. Shall I ring for some coffee or tea?"

"No sir. I will be fine. I need a bit of fresh air."

The two men advanced to the door. Mr. Bennet spied his housekeeper in the hallway. "Hill, please ask Jane to show Mr. Bingley the garden. He has been most interested in it all morning." As Hill left to carry out the request, Mr. Bennet chuckled at the blushing young man taking quick strides down the hallway.

Bingley, waiting by the front door, could not stop beaming which increased when Jane was quick to appear.

She led him around the side of the house to the garden that he had stared at from her father's study. He had memorized every inch of the yard.

"Mr. Bingley, I am surprised to see you here today. To what do we owe this honor?"

"I came to ask your father a favor."

"Oh." Jane blushed. He neck muscles bulged. She lowered her eyes, breathing in shallow gulps while she waited for him to continue.

"I asked him to be a competition judge," Mr. Bingley blurted out. Hiccup.

Jane lifted her eyes. She suggested they sit on the bench; Mr. Bingley agreed.

Bingley prattled on about balls, and judges and shooting and ruts. He thought she was content to sit and listen to him talk although he could not discern if she understood anything he said. Once they exhausted the subject, he returned to Netherfield Park.

Bingley rushed to the billiard room. He had hoped to practice before Kent appeared for their daily game. He called for a pot of tea and a bit of refreshments. He needed to overcome the effects of the afternoon glasses of port. He had racked the balls and prepared to take his practice shot when Kent stepped in the room. Their ongoing competition found them tied. Bingley studied the shooting angles for the ball he wanted to sink.

"I was remembering Rawlings and Darcy reaction when Blake made his demands for the thirty percent. I feared for his safety. I expected a few fists to be thrown."

"I would have readily joined in." Kent said.

"I did not anticipate it. Did you?" Bingley said.

Kent banged his cue stick on the floor. "No! And I do not trust Blake nor do I think he will join us if he loses the competition."

"Do not think so unkindly, Kent. What bothers you more? If he gains the extra profit or becomes the leader?"

"It is not the giving up some of the profit that bothers me as I have no need for fortune, but our having to need him is what makes me angry. Your family needs this sale. He is a condescending prig to us, and his attitude is not welcomed."

"I suspect he may have a need for the money more than he wants to admit." Bingley studied the choices, took his shot, and missed and lost a point. "I have heard rumors."

"If they are true, I would not be sorry. I despise him for the manner in which he blackmailed us. If it were not for Rawlings, I would have... " Kent paused. "Nothing. I would have done not one damn thing. It is illegal to strike a noble." He hit the cue ball so hard it bounced off the table.

"Did you believe Rawlings? He will not say if he could have obtained the contract from Lord Liverpool."

Kent shook his head. "Blake was smart in demanding our decision before he could tell us the truth. He accepted the agreement, so I assume he was bluffing."

Bingley took his shot. "True. Only Darcy abhors disguise of any sort."

"Rawlings is more Machiavellian. I think I shall nickname him The Prince." Kent laughed at his own joke. "What is done is done. In fact, I might be the victor and the recipient of the thirty percent. And I would enjoy him being subservient to me." Kent's cue stick connected and sent the ball in the pocket. "I would be pleased to take the lead."

Bingley studied the angle of for a particular shot, took it, and winked as the final three balls he needed fell into the pockets. "Game, Kent. I am now one ahead again. Of course, seethe over my superiority with a cue stick if you like, or better yet, you can pay me an additional thirty percent of our wager."

"I hope you do not expect to defeat me for the stallion. I will surprise our gentlemen friends."

Before he could respond, Darcy and Rawlings joined them, each man selecting a cue stick.

"Twenty Points?" Darcy fidgeted with his stick as he waited for Bingley to rack up the balls. "I expect that you have secured Mr. Bennet as a judge."

Bingley nodded. He offered Darcy the first shot. "Sir William, Mr. Long, Mr. Goulding, and Mr. Phillips have agreed as well. It has been a long day. Did you know they each hinted for a Baker rifle? Even Mr. Phillips!"

Darcy stopped abruptly. "I am not surprised. We all want one!" His shoulders rose and dropped with a heavy sigh. He took his shot and missed. "Blake is a problem, and if he loses, I fear his attitude may create problems in the future.".

Bingley drew the attention with a tap on the floor with his cue stick. "If Blake wins, I am optimistic he will become more accepting of Kent and me. He would be able to maintain is elevated status. Oh, and I appreciate your efforts, Rawlings. If we could have avoided this, I would have felt more at ease."

Rawlings took his shot, placing the cue ball in the pocket. "You are not planning to choose this game, are you? Blake has improved of late."

Bingley shook his head. "I have a much better one in mind."

Rawlings leaned on his cue stick. "I know we promised to keep the games a secret; however, a great deal of money is at stake. I propose we strategize our methods to keep Blake from winning."

"And provide you with the means to win? I think not." Kent answered. "I have as much of an opportunity to win as does Blake."

Darcy furrowed his brow. "Will this competition create a problem among even us?"

Bingley shook his head. "Not with me. I can be excessively delighted with twenty percent."

"Seventeen and half." Darcy corrected him.

"Will Blake remain if he loses? I do not trust him." Kent said.

"That is why I think it would be best not to work together to defeat him. He may bolt if he feels his loss was due to our conniving. If it is an honest competition, I suspect he will uphold his agreement. I will query Blake, although he is not someone I favor at the moment." Darcy pushed his cue stick forward. "Blast!"

"Nor I. I do not wish to socialize with him either," Rawlings said. "He should be made to take his meals in his bedchambers. Perhaps the stable hands could lose his horse. Or perhaps," he glanced at Darcy, "someone else could flirt with Miss Elizabeth."

"Stop unless you have a great desire to offer up large sums of seed money. I suggest we not treat him as the enemy," Darcy said. "He was negotiating for a better deal. It is my error in emphasizing the importance of his role. I apologize for not being more prudent."

"Bah! He would have asked for it regardless. As he said, he is a marquess!" Kent's shot hit the cue ball so hard it jumped off the table.

Rawlings picked it up, handed it to Bingley. "I suggest Kent lose ten points for making me bend down and pick up the ball from the floor." He faced the other men, "Look, I am willing to conceal my distrust. I can disguise my feelings; can you, Darcy?"

"I am just as angry; but I do not hate Blake if for no other reason than the twenty thousand pounds it will cost each of us if we do not secure the order for the Baker rifles." Darcy patted his pocket. Inside was the letter he had written for this solicitor to begin procedures for obtaining loans against Pemberley. He dared not leave it anywhere else. Now, if Blake walked away from the alliance, then he would send it. He would not ask the other men to fund the endeavor. His own need to pursue this venture had become greater than was his anxiety over keeping his fortune. His concern at this moment was to keep the others on friendly terms with Blake and he felt an honest competition was imperative.

"I will try." Rawlings glared at Kent and Bingley. "And you two?"

Kent nodded, but he did not show any enthusiasm.

Bingley took his shot. Another point for me," he said when his ball fell into the pocket. "My total is now nine points. And yes, I too will pretend as if there is no ill will."

"We are all agreed then. We shall enjoy the games as if the horse was the single reward."

"Agreed." Rawlings, Kent, and Bingley said in unison and then Rawlings added, "We agree to disguise our true feelings." They laughed aloud.

"I shall like riding my Andalusian in front of Blake. What is its name, Bingley?" Kent asked.

"Heracles. His name is Heracles. Oh, and a case of Oban whiskey for the losers awaits."

"A very fine name for my horse!" Rawlings said.

"You will be drinking the scotch whiskey while I am atop the Andalusian, regardless of its name." Kent laughed. "Whiskey is a fitting prize for the losers. You can drink yourself into a stupor while I parade in front of you."

The men continued to tease and argue about who would be the proud owner of the stallion while they continued to play.

Kent leaned down to find his best shot. He grinned. His shot placed two balls in the pocket and left terrible angles for Darcy who followed him in the playing order. The men continued to study the table, take their turns, profess their superiority, and keep account of their points. Play continued until Kent shouted, "Twenty points. Game!"

Darcy sensed anxiousness about the wedge between his friends but pushed his fears aside. It was not that long ago when his friends lined up against him at the bird hunting and now everyone has forgotten that argument. So shall this one be too, he told himself.

***

Preparations for the competition began in earnest the following morning with a whirlwind of activity from writing rules to putting together the necessary equipment for their games. With significant money from the profits weighing on the outcome, the men sought to find a game that would ensure Blake ended on the bottom.

Kent remained in his bedchambers with a breakfast tray and sent furiously written messages by express post. By noon, he summoned the butler.

Whitson had agreed to provide him a footman who was familiar with carpentry, but with concern about Kent's requests, he rushed to speak to Mr. Bingley.

"Unless it is illegal I do not wish to hear about it. I approve of his changes," Bingley replied in a nonchalant manner.

"Mr. Bingley, sir? You do not wish to know the extent of the effort?"

"No. It will be fine. It is most important not to deny any one of my guests their requests. Give him, and the others, what is requested and without comment. "

"As you wish." Whitson bowed, shook his head, left the room and mumbled, "I hope he remembers this conversation after these games are done."

Darcy sought out Bingley's steward. They had become well acquainted when he was guiding an inexperienced Bingley at running an estate. The steward had complained that the tenants unfairly gave Mr. Bingley all the credit. Darcy told the steward to let the impression stand. Therefore, when he appeared that morning with a request, the steward agreed without hesitation to offer his assistance in any manner possible. They spent his first day riding towards the eastern part of Netherfield Park, in fact, towards the East Meadow. They did not return until very late. Darcy spent the evening writing his message which was, like Kent's, sent by express post.

Bingley spent his time in the library making drawings of something on several sheets of paper. If the drawing made him unhappy, he discarded it in the fire, ensuring every trace of the paper turned to ash.

Blake remained at leisure and even lingered in the dining room enjoying the bountiful food left behind while his friends spent the day in earnest planning their games. He sipped his coffee and imagined himself riding the stallion, Heracles, while all his friends were sipping the Oban scotch whiskey. Blake was not concerned about his game, having known immediately what he would choose. He needed just one day to prepare his rules for Mr. Bennet. No other effort was required.

Rawlings had much to discuss with his valet, who would have plenty to do.

"Mr. Logan, I need your help." Mr. Rawlings motioned for Logan to sit in the chair by the desk.

"I suspect this is about the Olympics?"

"Of course. It is imperative Blake not win. I care not whether any of the other men win, but he must be stopped."

Logan nodded for him to continue and as his master recounted the event, his eyes grew wider.

"I did not suspect Blake was capable of such duplicity." Rawlings sighed.

"He must have been planning this all along. Pretending the connection to tradesmen was beneath him just to make them cater to him. Phew! I would wager his demand is about money and not status. He was sly," Logan said."

"If I was not involved I would have found it amusing and would have admired Blake's boldness. Anyway, I will need you to acquire a few things." Rawlings began to scribble a list of items.

"Are four sufficient?" Logan sat patiently, waiting for the list.

"You know me too well. Yes, I suspect so depending on what we find in the surrounding country. Did I bring my blue and yellow striped waistcoat and other clothes?"

"I pack for any situation."

Rawlings relaxed a bit. He handed Logan the completed list. "Bingley is quite the sportsman, I say."

"I suspect he has not had any responsibilities or obligations in his life. Sports are just one way to fill time." Reclining in his chair, Logan sipped his tea.

"Some of the other ways are a lot more fun." Reaching for the cigar, Rawlings ignored the teacup in front of him. "Bingley is an amicable man. He gets bored too easily, and I suspect that is the reason for his devising activities for us all. Twenty Points, shooting birds, and now this competition."

"Amicable is not the most useful trait when it comes to running an estate." Logan looked up from his cup.

"Are you aware of something amiss here in this," Rawlings waved his hand about the room and added, "coliseum?"

"His servants are undisciplined, to say the least." Logan leaned towards his master. "They gossip worse than the old dowagers in town."

"Anything important that might impact my stay here?"

"Perhaps. The rumors are about the Bennets and a letter received from London."

"Oh." Rawlings sat erect and clasped the arms of the chair. He furrowed his brows and listened without interruption as Logan filled him in on all the latest tittle-tattle, revelations that focused on how Mr. Bennet's brother-in-law, Mr. Gardiner, had risked the Bennet girl's dowries on a risky scheme of some sort. The rumors did not have anything more specific other than the income from the estate remained safe.

"I do not know if any of the gossip is accurate, but it is of little importance to me." Rawlings gulped his wine. "I never bothered to learn the amount of Miss Lydia's dowry. Her lack of wealth makes no difference to me."

"None?"

"None! Perhaps, I will be the favorite one now that the pert Miss Lydia's seven-thousand-pound dowry has been lost as well as the reason for those red-coated leeches to hang on her every flirtation."

They discussed the effect on the alliance and the impact on the men. Finally, returning his focus on the competition, Rawlings provided Logan with the funds he would need to purchase the items needed for his game.

He blew a smoke ring in the air. "Let the games begin."

Chapter Sixteen

The back rooms of the largest tavern in the town's center had served as the men's club. It was not overly large, yet all the essentials were there: bar, small dining area, and the card playing room. Since no other establishment existed as a men's club Meryton or in any of the surrounding area, the proprietor had added a billiard room and private gathering section, thereby rendering his men's club and tavern complete. It had all the elements needed to remind the patrons they were men first, before they were husbands, farmers, shopkeepers, or soldiers. Visitors to the clubrooms included more than just the four and twenty estate owners and distinguished gentlemen of Hertfordshire. The militia officers, the well-to-do tradesmen, and those gentlemen servicing the intellectual and spiritual needs of the community also found solace within the tavern's private area.

In keeping with manly traditions, men liked to wager and the favorite place to do so, without the disapproving reactions of the womenfolk, was at this dwelling; identified by a sign hanging above the door, which included a painting of a magnificent bull and the large sized saying BLACK BULL.

Mr. Roger Staunton, the proprietor, was ever ready with his betting book. All the men recognized it instantly—a large black journal with a fierce looking bull stenciled in gold on the cover. Inside were the names of all the local men; all their losses circled and winnings checkmarked. Since a drink or two accompanied every bet, Roger Staunton annotated his journal regardless of the purpose of the wager.

Men visited the tavern on a regular basis. They stood around the bar area, drank, and talked loudly. Some men played cards or billiards. Others were content to sit and argue over the most mundane things, even placing bets on the truth about the latest gossip.

When news about Mr. Bingley's competition reached the neighborhood, husky voices, musky scents, and the sound of heavy boots on the dusty floor flooded the Black Bull. All the talk focused on the five men, five games and one grand prize—the Andalusian stallion. London, renowned for its wagers of vast fortunes, could not compete with the frenzied behavior taking hold in this little parish called Meryton.

One man in particular, Nigel, who was staying at the Black Bull Tavern, showed more interest in the gentlemen than in the games, spending his time bothering patrons for any shred of information on their activities. Staunton had assumed the purpose of his questions aimed at finding that advantage all gamblers wanted before they placed their money down. However, this man paid for the information with coin.

The night before the first game, Staunton invited Sir William Lucas and Mr. Bennet to the tavern. As judges, they were his best sources about the event, other than the actual competitors who were very unlikely to visit the Black Bull.

The patrons, their eager faces searching for any betting advantage, swarmed the two men as they attempted to find a spot to sit. They peppered both men with questions; each hoping for any tidbit for placing the winning bet.

"You must tell us about this competition. We understand you are the judges."

"Which man looks the most fit? Who is the smartest?"

"I want to place a bet on the marquess. I am sure he had the best master instructors in England, being the son of a duke."

"What are the games, Mr. Bennet?"

"Will we be allowed to witness the competitions?"

"You know we will continue hounding you until you talk. I promise you we will."

Raising his hand to stem the questions, Mr. Bennet sat in the nearest chair. "Please give us some room. Let us get comfortable if you wish to learn about the competition." He smirked at the impatient men crowding around them. "Someone buy me a drink, and I will tell all."

"Pour me two, and I will make sure he does not stray from the truth," Sir William said as he sat in the chair next to Mr. Bennet.

Roger Staunton nodded his head to the servant to fill their glasses quickly; he, too, awaited the information with considerable interest.

Mr. Bennet began his story after he took his first swig of ale. "They will play five games. The men drew straws to decide the order. Lord Blake's game will open the competitions." Mr. Bennet waited for the murmur to die down.

"Tell us about Lord Blake's game, Mr. Bennet. We have heard snippets."

All the men found chairs for themselves for they knew they had a story coming. Mr. Bennet never bored them when he was in a talkative mood, and today he certainly was.

"I remember my meeting with Lord Blake when he brought the rules for his game. I am the approving judge, you understand, and all the men had to do so." Sighing, Mr. Bennet thought back on the day he hosted these men in his study, followed in the late afternoon by an irate wife who had been kept in the dark. "He was well prepared. He carried with him many charts, numbers, and rules upon rules." Chuckling he took another nip of the ale. "This young man does not understand the value of economy with the written word."

"Well, what game did he chose?"

"Chess. Lord Blake chose chess," Sir William blurted out.

"Why chess?"

Smiling, Mr. Bennet leaned forward. "He is the master at Parsloe's, the London Chess Club. In fact, he won every game he has played in the last three years."

The background hum of whispered conversation rose as the other patrons discussed this new piece of information. "Well what are the rules?" someone yelled.

"The game, drawn out on several diagrams, is to be played on two chess tables in the library." Mr. Bennet chuckled as he recalled the flawlessly hand drawn illustrations. "Lord Blake maintained that we must separate the tables to the far sides of the room. He wanted the players to be able to concentrate on their match without disruption by the other game. He insisted the tables had to be thirty inches high and the chairs had to be just so. With such attention to frivolous detail, I suggested Lord Blake enter the diplomatic profession, but he did not respond."

"Mr. Bennet, who plays? I think someone has to sit out the first match."

"Yes, now about the playing order. Lord Blake made this one chart, all colored, to show the rounds and the players for each round. Quite elaborate! I never saw such work in all my years," Mr. Bennet revealed a slight smile as he stared at his empty glass. He nodded his appreciation for the refill. "I decided the playing order. Lord Blake and Mr. Kent will play at one table; Mr. Darcy and Mr. Rawlings at the other."

"What about Mr. Bingley?"

"He will sit out the first round. Do not worry they all play each competitor once. Each man will sit out a turn."

"Stop! Let us at least have time to bet. I want Lord Blake."

"We all want Lord Blake you bloody fool. Did you not hear Mr. Bennet tell us that no one has beaten him in three years? Let us bet on who comes in second. I want that man, Mr. Rawlings. He is an earl's son. That should be worth something."

The conversation between the patrons and Roger Staunton escalated. After a time, Staunton annotated the Black Bull's book with all the wagers. Rawlings and Bingley received the most bets. Kent garnered many supporters, as well. Mr. Darcy, on the other hand, had a fraction.

***

Not a single man at Netherfield was late for breakfast the morning of the first game. They had prepared for a long day of competition. When Blake handed out the rules to his friends, his choice did not surprise any of them; they were more interested in how he organized the tournament. Once the judges arrived, they removed themselves to the library. The servants brought in coffee, wine, cigars, and plates of food. The men agreed they would dress comfortably—no cravats and no jackets.

The timepiece on the mantle ticked away as the men took their seats. Sir William stood by one table and Mr. Goulding by another. Mr. Phillips and Mr. Long sat in chairs situated near the game tables. Bingley, who was sitting out this round, decided to observe the match between Darcy and Rawlings. He was glad for the opportunity to study these two men rather than the others. He had no hope of defeating a master such as Blake, and through the years, he had had plenty of practice playing chess with Kent.

Mr. Bennet found a comfortable chair near the fire. He sipped his coffee, read the latest London newspapers, and took pleasure in the sound of men's voices. The first round began. Immersed in reading an article about Parliament's actions on land enclosures, he jerked his head up when Mr. Rawlings shouted—

"Blast! You win, Darcy."

"True." Darcy said offering his hand to his friend. "It is called the Queen's Gambit. I was pleased to get a chance to play someone that had not experienced it before. The Gambit works very well! You did admirably for never having played against it."

"Someone wrote that the pawns are the life of the game. I do believe he was wrong."

"Philador said it. He is the best chess master. I would not dispute him."

"You could have been kind and attacked less aggressively."

"Can I expect that sort of kindness during your game?"

Rawlings shook his head in amusement. "Not after today!"

Bingley congratulated Darcy and consoled Rawlings before they joined the judges at the other match. Blake and Kent's game continued. Blake possessed all his back rank pieces and a few pawns as well. Kent was down to six pieces: his king, queen, one bishop, one knight, and two pawns. Kent shook his head. Every move seemed a disaster. How can I be losing? I won many a game in many a tavern in my day. Kent moved his queen down the board only to watch Blake move his rook in line with the king.

"Check"

"Damn." Kent continued to play defensively until there was no defense left. He laid his king down and stood to shake Blake's hand.

"Excellent game, Blake. I bow to your skill."

"Thank you, Kent. You did better than I expected. Where did you learn? I was amazed at your plays. Quite unorthodox."

"While you were sweating over your math studies, I was playing in the taverns!" Kent laughed. "Perhaps I should have concentrated on math!"

"Fortunately for you there are three more rounds. Which round do you sit out?

"You do not know? We follow your rules."

Blake's face colored. "Mr. Bennet established the order of play."

"Oh. I sit out the last round. I need to win the next three games if I am to come in second."

As the two reset the chessboard for the next game, Bingley and Rawlings approached them.

Sir William announced, "Time for round two."

Rawlings took his seat to play against Blake, and Bingley and Kent left for the table across the room. Sitting out, Darcy poured himself a coffee and joined Mr. Bennet near the fireplace far away from the chess games.

Surprised when Darcy sat down with him, Mr. Bennet cleared his throat. "You are a most confident fellow."

Darcy looked at him with wide eyes. "I beg your pardon?"

"You are not studying your competitors to gain that all important advantage."

Without so much as a smile, Darcy responded. "I have played them many times in the past. I suspect the day will be long. I prefer to relax."

As the games progressed elsewhere in the room, Mr. Bennet's conversation changed from the chess game to a subject that every landed gentry understood. "I understand your estate is quite large. Did you as the landowner enclose all your fields or do you provide common land for your tenants?" Mr. Bennet pointed out the article in the newspaper as he offered the young man another coffee.

Darcy nodded. "Enclosure in Derbyshire happened many decades ago, nevertheless it was conducted by agreement among the landholders and the land users. While there are arable common fields, the enclosed land is used as pastureland for sheep."

"So you are a sheep farmer, Mr. Darcy, on enclosed fields?" Mr. Bennet lifted one eyebrow.

"Yes, to a great degree." Darcy tapped the arm of the chair, the beat escalating. Most sheep do graze in enclosed fields. I found that to be more efficient."

"And more profitable I should say." Mr. Bennet said, his right brow raised. .

"At Pemberley we did enclose some land for selective breeding experiments. I hope to produce bigger and more profitable livestock. That would not be possible in common fields." He gripped the arms of the chair.

"No farming, then, on enclosed land?"

"Of late, we experimented with four-crop rotation on a portion of the enclosed farmland. However, most arable fields are still common land." He did not elaborate on how much of Pemberley was enclosed.

"Both of your experiments are very progressive. I am not sure that is wise. There are times when it best not to pursue wild schemes." Mr. Bennet scoffed.

"Crop rotation is not new. Livestock breeding has been tried through the ages. Perhaps it is just the scientific methods that concern you." Relaxing his grip on the chair arms, Darcy settled further back into the seat.

"Scientific methods. Hah! I caution you Mr. Darcy to be wary. Nevertheless, I will admit enclosure is not new. The land in Hertfordshire has not yet faced that situation. I do not look forward to the day it happens. The tenants will not be consoled." Mr. Bennet shook his head. Sipping his coffee, he watched the expression change on the young man's face.

"Derbyshire landholders have opened a cotton mill in Matlock Bath to help the displaced tenants." Darcy leaned forward. "Are you familiar with Arkwright?"

Mr. Bennet threw his hands up. "You speak about another progressive scheme. Arkwright's new machines may be productive;

however, the mills using these machines employ children younger than ten years!" Sneering, he waved the paper in his hand. "I have no desire to see a mill opened here and bring us the Luddite problem. There is also an article covering their latest attacks on the stocking frames and power looms. I believe it is in your neck of the woods."

"Major landholders have a say in how the mills are run."

Just as Mr. Bennet was about to speak, their attention was diverted to the table occupied by Blake and Rawlings.

"Damn. That was quick." Standing, Rawlings shook Blake's hand. "What was that? Fifteen minutes? Even Kent took twice as long!"

"You made a mere single mistake."

"Yes, the mistake was playing this game! I could have had myself a few good drinks if I had just forfeited from the start." Rawlings eyed the sideboard, filled with good wine and brandy.

Blake reset the chess pieces for the next game. "I do not recall you preferring games of strategy."

"True, so true." Rawlings looked at Blake with a sparkle in his eyes. "I like the simpler games, such as shooting birds."

"Well, I am skilled in a different way. You are good at hunting." Placing his hand over his heart, Blake pleaded with him. "I am relieved that is not the game you would have chosen."

Rawlings selected a sweet pastry from the table and poured himself a coffee. "No, it was not. You did spare yourself that embarrassment when you conditioned your demands."

Blake, declining any food or drink, inclined his head towards the other match. "Well, shall we join the others? It seems everyone else is engrossed in that game."

Kent and Bingley continued play for over an hour. Blake had positioned himself to scrutinize Bingley's play since they played each other in the next round. Searching for the slightest telltale signs, he paid close attention to his eye movements, his body posture, breathing pattern, and reactions to any unexpected move Kent made. He groaned when Bingley made a move, and other times he smiled. Blake did not attempt to conceal his surprise at how well Bingley played.

Kent held his own against Bingley, and everyone found it hard to determine the better player. After many moves, the two competitors agreed it would not end satisfactorily for either of them. Blake nodded his agreement. He, too, could not discern any means for either man to win. Mr. Long called the game a draw.

Sir William announced the round two chess match scores. Blake was in the lead with four points, two points for each win. Darcy had two points for the match he played. Bingley and Kent held one point each, and Rawlings had none. The number of points won in the chess games determined the finishing order of tournament, and subsequently, the ranking for the stallion.

All the men took a break at the end of the second round. After excusing himself, Mr. Phillips left to attend to some urgent business. He assured them he would return before the final game. Although he did not explain, his 'business' was with his wife. Many ladies of the area, including all of the Bennet women, gathered at his home, awaiting some news.

The servants brought in trays filled with cold meats, fruits, and cheeses. They lingered in the room trying valiantly to discover how the game was going. A young boy was waiting outside the kitchen for any information he could obtain. He was ready to bolt to the Black Bull. He dearly wanted the penny the proprietor was paying for match results.

The third round began one hour after the break had started. The older men changed positions: Mr. Bennet and Mr. Goulding were the judges for the matches. Blake and Bingley sat at one chess table and Darcy played Kent at the other. Rawlings, whose turn it was to sit out, approached the refreshment table where Sir William was standing.

"Do not look so forlorn, Mr. Rawlings. You still have two chances left."

"Thank you, Sir William. I did not expect to do well. I have not played chess in years. I took part for the one point I will earn for last place. Bingley warned us we must play or not recive any points. So here I am, allowing my friends to humiliate me, which I would never allow them to do otherwise." Rawlings followed his pronouncement with a laugh and a slap on the Sir William's back, putting the older man at ease.

"You may do better if you win just one game. Mr. Bingley and Mr. Kent are tied. I believe you have not played either man yet."

"True. That is something to consider. I hope the fine people of Meryton did not bet their future on me today."

"Oh. You know about the betting."

"Who could not? Is it not the latest craze?"

Nodding, Sir William wondered what was happening at the Black Bull Tavern.

***

"Here you go, boy. You earned your penny." Roger Staunton threw the boy a coin, turned to his patrons, and shouted, "I have the results for round three."

"Who played?"

"Lord Blake played Mr. Bingley and—"

"Did Blake win again?"

"Yes, he defeated our Mr. Bingley." Mr. Staunton waited until the crowd quieted to announce the other match. "Mr. Darcy played Mr. Kent and—"

"Did Mr. Kent win?"

"No, Mr. Darcy won."

There was a collective, "Oh."

"What is the score for the chess tournament now?"

"Lord Blake is in the lead with his three victories." He waited for the crowd to quiet. "Mr. Darcy is next with his two victories, Mr. Kent and Mr. Bingley are tied for third place for their game that ended in a draw, and Mr. Rawlings is in last place. He did not win any games yet."

"I need to change my bet. I want Mr. Darcy now. Although I cannot stand that man he seems to have better skills than my favorite, Mr. Rawlings."

"It is getting late. Do you think they will finish today?"

"They had better. I cannot stay here all night." The other patrons laughed, just the same none left to return home.

***

There was a small break after round three. Rawlings, Bingley, and Kent all chose wine. They huddled together whispering about Darcy's chances, and the importance a win for him would be for the alliance.

Blake and Darcy preferred to avoid drinking. They were the most serious players. They sat across from one another, and without a word, studied each other until Sir William announced round four. Darcy took his seat opposite Bingley. He chose the table nearest the windows, knowing his friend lost concentration when there was a view to admire. It is a shame Mr. Bennet did not bring his two eldest daughters with him, he thought as he glanced at Bingley, and then turned to Blake who was sitting out this round.

Rawlings and Kent took their seats along the far wall. Someone lit the candles as dusk was just beginning. The matches started. The judges studied the players carefully, searching for any infraction while the competitors concentrated on their own moves. It was not long before both games finished.

Round four ended with Darcy and Kent winning their games over Bingley and Rawlings. Darcy, having played three games, tied for the lead with Blake. Kent, whose turn it was to sit out the final round, ended the tournament with three points. Bingley had one point and Rawlings, as he expected, had none.

The final round of the tournament was about to start. Rawlings and Bingley were playing to avoid last place, which Rawlings had to win to move up. A draw would give Bingley the fourth place rank. Also, the game for which everyone had been impatient to begin had arrived: Blake against Darcy.

Rawlings and Bingley played for one hour before Rawlings laid down his king. "Good game, Bingley. With the draw, you are the proud owner of two points. I wish you great success."

"I was fortunate to have played you in the final round. The results would have been much different had we met earlier."

"I doubt it is so. I rarely play chess. Still, I congratulate you, my friend. You did very well. Truth be told, I am surprised you did not beat Kent."

Mr. Bennet offered his congratulations for a game well play and then directed their attention to the other match. "Shall we hurry over to watch the chess master and the challenger?" They agreed with alacrity, and all three found their way across the room. They did not stop for drinks or food.

Servants milled about, taking their time replenishing the refreshments and refilling the carafes. Roger Staunton's boy was back and waiting for more information. One servant dusted away some invisible lint from the sofa nearest to the chess table in an effort to gain any advantage since he had wagered his own money on the outcome. No one bothered with or cared about the servants. They kept their eyes on one chessboard and two very determined men. The men suggested to forgo any break for dinner, preferring to sustain their focus on the remaining match.

A relaxed Blake observed Darcy, whose countenance had changed into a serious mien, replacing all the ease and relaxation from the prior games.

Darcy did not look around. He did not speak. He barely breathed. He did not eat any food brought in for the men. He did not partake of any alcohol. He had spent several evenings studying the chess books written by Francois-Andre Danican Philidor. Blake admired the man, often calling him the greatest player that ever lived. And, if his friend spoke so highly of him, then he needed to know as much about how Philidor played the game as Blake did.

Blake made a move, Darcy countered, and then attempted an aggressive attack which was crushed immediately. Blake remained calm for the first two hours. The third hour proved to be difficult and it was not until the fourth hour when it finished.

My, this is getting interesting, a most amused Mr. Bennet thought. Blake shook Darcy's hand, and then waved all the judges over.

Chapter Seventeen

All day long, patrons filled the Black Bull Tavern. Word spread throughout the neighborhood that two judges planned to stop by to describe the final round. By this time, every man, from servant to landowner, was cognizant of Mr. Bingley's competition.

In the beginning, the bettors were interested in all aspects of the competitions, now they desired to know the name of the man who came in second place. Collecting their winnings was important, but as is the usual nature of men, they also coveted their ability to crow about their cleverness, at least until the next game.

Mr. Bennet and Sir William entered the tavern; Mr. Staunton slammed the journal shut. A servant led the two judges to the same chairs they had occupied the previous day. Two tankards of ale appeared before the men took their seats while the patrons crowded around them. Some sat, others stood close.

Mr. Bennet tapped impatiently on his mug; waiting until all murmuring died down before he revealed the results. "Those betting on Mr. Rawlings to win, you must pay up. He did not thrash Mr. Bingley as you boasted, instead the game ended in a draw. Mr. Rawlings is in last place for the stallion with one point." Mr. Bennet waited for the jeers to subside. "Mr. Bingley has two points and Kent sat out having played his four games and ended the chess match with three points."

"Do not drag this out, Bennet! Tell us the victor in the other match—Lord Blake or Mr. Darcy."

"Now, that was the game of the day, taking over four hours to complete. Mr. Darcy was a man focused; there could be no different opinion on that."

"Who won? Tell us man, who won?"

"Neither. It ended in a tie. An excellent game I might add; and it was, perhaps, the best match I have witnessed in many years. Lord Blake may be a master, but Mr. Darcy gave him fits throughout the game."

The patrons' chatter grew louder. Surrounded by men confused about their wagers, Roger Staunton closed the betting journal and shouted over the din, "I figure Lord Blake and Mr. Darcy both ended with the same number of points. Was that allowed to stand? Did no one come in first for the stallion?"

"True, those two did tie the chess tournament with seven points after the five rounds. Mr. Kent did well to finish with three points, Mr. Bingley managed to gain two, and Mr. Rawlings was last with one."

"I am sorry Mr. Bingley did not do better. I was hoping he would win the stallion. This will make it harder for him."

"What is the rule for ties?"

"The overall competition did not provide such a situation. I, as rule judge, suggested Lord Blake and Mr. Darcy play until one either won or bowed out."

"Well, did they play?"

"They are stubborn men. Lord Blake might be more charming and talkative, but he is every bit as proud as Mr. Darcy."

"So they played?"

"Yes and no. The games will be held tomorrow."

When the next day arrived, a smiling Mr. Staunton observed the increased quantity of men in his tavern. The men drank, ate, and continued to bet while they waited out the results. The wager changed. This time who won garnered the most bets. More men bet on the Lord Blake than on the man disliked by almost everyone, Darcy. Both these men treated the locals with a similar arrogant superiority; however, Lord Blake smiled at them from time to time. He had even danced with several young ladies at the recent Assembly ball, while Mr. Darcy ignored anyone not in his own party that night. Nor had the townspeople overlooked his dismissal of their Miss Elizabeth Bennet at the dance. Mrs. Bennet had made certain for the entire town heard about the slight. Men used any morsel before placing a bet, and this particular crumb of gossip did not cause any kind feelings towards Mr. Darcy.

The news about this extra game was scant since the persons permitted in the library for the game were limited to the competitors and the five judges. Everyone waited; their eyes glued to the tavern door. As soon as someone won, Mr. Bennet promised he would hurry to reveal the winner.

The final match ended and when enough time had passed to take their leave politely, Mr. Bennet and Sir William hurried to the Black Bull, each looking forward to the free ale. The two men smiled and waved their hands at the patrons when a cheer erupted at their entrance. Once settled in the two chairs reserved for them and overflowing tankards handed to them, Mr. Bennet began his story.

"After ending in a tie the day before, today's match started down the same path. The first and second attempts again ended in ties." He waited for the murmur to die down before continuing. "It was exciting to watch. Mr. Rawlings and Mr. Kent were drinking and cheering on their favorite."

"Which one favored Lord Blake?"

"Mr. Rawlings and Mr. Kent rooted for Mr. Darcy. I suspect they had something riding on the outcome other than the horse. From the sounds they made, the stakes must have been significant," Mr. Bennet said, smiling. "Mr. Bingley remained neutral, claiming, as host, he would be too uncomfortable choosing sides, although I did see him smile with every winning move Mr. Darcy made."

"So, Mr. Bennet, what happened? How did it end?"

"A winner emerged in the third match."

"Ah! Just tell us who!"

The room grew silent. No one dared take a sip or a bite to eat, in case anyone missed Mr. Bennet's announcement. All eyes focused on the eccentric, teasing master of Longbourn.

Sir William yelled out, "Lord Blake!"

A cheer went out for those who had bet on Lord Blake.

Mr. Bennet sipped his drink unhurriedly before continuing with his story. "Lord Blake was having sport with his friend. He won in the shortest game of the day. In my opinion, he could have won any of them. He is a master of chess, and the best player I have ever witnessed."

Enjoying his ale, Mr. Bennet recalled an odd comment Mr. Rawlings told one of the players—I suspect, one day soon, you will be in a different sort of match; one of greater significance. In the same manner as chess, you must plan your moves. Be aware the other competitor will have his own plans and allies. And be careful, my friend, not to lose one day because you underestimated your rival. He is tenacious, and he will be willing to sacrifice to win.

Mr. Bennet found the dynamics among the men to be the most diverting. Most diverting indeed.

Mr. Staunton posed a question, bringing Mr. Bennet's attention back to the tavern. "When is the next game? I thought Mr. Kent's game was to start today?" He waited for the response as he wrote the number scores for the stallion on the wall: Olympic Points: Chess: Blake 5, Darcy 4, Kent 3, Bingley 2, and Rawlings 1.

"They agreed to play tomorrow."

"Do you know what game is to be played?" A successful patron asked. He was anxious to extend his winnings.

"I do, but I promised to keep the games a secret. You see, the other gentlemen do not know, and the game along with the rules will be named at breakfast on the morning it is to be played. It does create tension between them, I imagine."

"I suspect their valets are working overtime to gain that information," one patron chuckled as he noted the servant refilled Mr. Bennet's tankard for the fourth time.

"Yes, I suppose you are correct."

***

"Mr. Logan, do not tell me you failed. You…you… soulless knotty-pated scullion!" Rawlings relaxed in his chair near the fireplace as he waited for Logan's reply. The solitary noise in the room was the sound of his valet fiddling with the fire.

"I have tried everything! What do you suggest?" Logan answered after a short pause.

Rawlings removed his cravat and wiped his brow while Logan poured the tea. He had been successful in including the calming beverage in Rawlings schedule. However, unbeknownst to him, his master slipped a little rum in the teapot from a flask he kept hidden in the room.

"Have you tried giving the valet a woman for the night?"

"I did. I swear the man is more afraid to be released from service than desirous of having the fine pleasures of a silky soft woman to cuddle up to all night long."

"I suspect you have received many gifts?"

Placing his cup down, Logan began his evening chores, "Not one of them thought of a sweet miss though. I might have revealed all if they had presented me with a beautiful, silky body of a woman."

"Just the body? You want a dead woman. I do not wish you to sell me out for such a thing. I will buy you a damn live chit if need be!"

"Do not be such a spongey puisny-tilted eunuch."

Tipping his invisible hat to his valet, Rawlings chose to let him win the best insult for this night.

"Very good, sir. I will not sell you out for anything less." Bowing to Rawlings, Logan left the room chuckling and headed to the stable. He spied Darcy entering just as Blake shouted something to a stable hand. Logan found a spot in which to watch unnoticed.

Blake was about to mount his horse for an afternoon gallop when Darcy called out his name.

"Darcy! I am surprised to see you. Are you planning to ride? Do you wish to best me in something today?" He laughed as he patted his filly, Chesterfield.

"Not today."

"If you do not plan to ride, what brings you to the stables? Come to inspect my Heracles?" Blake glanced toward the beautiful white stallion in the far stall. "You must catch me now. I have begun the games with the most points."

"That will not be so in a few days."

"Well, what is it? I can see by your expression you wish to have a word with me."

"You toyed with me," Darcy said without a hint of displeasure in his tone.

"True, but you were so determined. I did not wish to lower any regard you held for yourself."

"Ha. You are enjoying your small win. Nonetheless, each day it will be more difficult for you to gain points. In fact, I doubt you will score more than one point when my day comes."

"What is your game? You knew full well that I would choose chess."

"I will not tell you now. Remember, do not come naked." Darcy displayed his trademark smile as they both recalled the earlier conversation about the competition. Someone had remarked about playing the games naked as they had in the original Olympics. Bingley had joked and said they could.

"Have I ever played this game before?"

"If I tell, that could be giving you an unfair advantage."

"Can I not bribe you?"

"Perhaps. One-third profits might be sufficient." Darcy released an uncharacteristic laugh when he noted how Blake's back stiffened. He continued, "Money cannot compensate for the pleasure of witnessing your expression when I announce the game. It is not money that is an inducement for me for forming this alliance, but you realize you are causing ill-feelings with the other men."

"I must do what is best for me without regard to others. I mean no offense to them."

Darcy's countenance changed, his brow hardened into a scowl. "I have the strength of mind to endure your toying." His eyes narrowed. "Not everyone does. I beseech you to not trifle with others."

"I am not playing games with the other men."

"I do not speak of them. I speak about a local girl."

You do not understand at all." Blake said brusquely, squeezing his hands into fists and standing in a rigid upright position.

"Understand what? That you are enjoying all the country has to offer?" Darcy asked.

Blake started. "Of what are you referring? Naturally, I am enjoying all that is available here."

"Will you leave it all behind when we return to London? And leave her—"

"Do not think about me like that," Blake interrupted, agitated..

"Why not? I know your past with women like Miss Elizabeth."

"You are not aware of my actions in life. As I said, you do not understand at all."

"Exactly what do I not understand?"

"My attentions to her."

"What are your intentions, Blake?" Darcy asked, anger rising in his voice.

"I cannot say. Or rather, I will not say." Blake did not drop his stare.

"Or are you are embarrassed to say the words aloud?"

Blake leaned in close enough for Darcy to feel his breath. "I am my own man. My relationships are no concern of yours and neither are Miss Bennet's." His eyes turned black. "Stay out of this."

Darcy mirrored Blake.. "I will not let you dally with her." With a quick movement, he stepped back and added, "Or any other lady here, for that matter. We did not come here to enjoy the attentions of a pretty face. We are here for business." Darcy stormed towards the door as Blake yelled—

"Darcy, stop!"

Halting mid stride, Darcy slowly turned to face Blake.

Blake shook his head, and in a softer tone said, "I will not be distracted from the alliance or my commitments to you. I promise you."

"Or the one-third profits." Darcy mumbled as he walked to the house.

***

The next morning found the all the men, except one, waiting at the breakfast table and curious, eager, and excited for learning about Kent's game. No one had been able to find out or even imagine what he had chosen. Kent was not the best in billiards, fencing, archery, or target shooting.

"Where is Blake?" Darcy asked moving to the dining room window with his coffee in hand.

"I believe he is returning from the stable," Bingley said.

Darcy focused his attention on the path leading to the house. "Did the man go riding again this morning?

Bingley shook his head. "No, he wanted to check on his horse. He said something about soothing his mare's jealousy when he wins Heracles."

Darcy's sighed and relaxed shoulders. Rawlings noted it but kept the focus on the game. "Win Heracles? He counts his chickens I should say!"

"I was the best at Cambridge, Rawlings," Blake said, walking into the room. "Perhaps I do count my chickens. You, sir, are still trying to locate your eggs. How many points do you have now? Oh yes, one."

Rawlings and Kent shared a questioning glance when Blake chose to sit at the opposite end, far away from Darcy.

"Do not be so cock-sure, Blake. Today's game may not suit you at all," Kent said.

"Well, what is it, Kent? What is to be the game?" Blake asked.

"We must wait for the judges. The ballroom is sct up, and we will meet there in a half hour."

"So, we play your game indoors?" Blake asked.

"Games, more like" Kent said, a delightful gleam twinkling in his eyes.

When the judges arrived at the allotted time, all the men removed themselves to the ballroom. Surprise was evident on all their faces, for before them was the best looking tavern they would ever enter.

Kent had spared no expense. His footman-turned-carpenter had placed beams along the walls with wooden planks fastened between them. Five chairs, typical to those found in a tavern, had been lined up in a row in front of a bar set up against the back wall. A servant, dressed in a scruffy outfit, was obviously the *proprietor*. He stood at the bar with bottles of brandy, wine, rum, and even Oban whisky with the appropriate drinking glasses lined up on the shelving behind him. They stared at him when he held up a black journal similar to the betting books found in men's clubs in town. He opened the journal and held up a quill.

Signs typical for this type establishment hung on the walls. However, the floorspace reserved for dancing held the most interest for the men. Four different games were on display.

"Welcome to the Netherfield Park's Five Alls!" Kent announced, pointing to the plaque hanging behind them above the door. Five figures appeared on the sign with a slogan under each one.

"First figure is a king in all his finery, with the pronouncement, I *govern all*," Kent said, as the men moved closer to inspect the figures and the mottos painted upon it.

"He must be Darcy. He is here to lead us, is that not so?" Rawlings asked. The others nodded in agreement.

Mr. Bennet stood next to Mr. Goulding and studied the interplay between the young men. "Hmmm, this could prove quite enlightening. I wonder where Mr. Darcy is leading these men."

"Second one is undoubtedly a pontiff or bishop. You can tell by his vestments and insignia, and the inscription, I *pray for all.*"

"That would be you, Rawlings. You are always quick to tell us where we go wrong," Darcy said. When Rawlings sent him an exaggerated glowered, he added, "And then you forgive us our sins, pour us a drink, and make us laugh at ourselves."

"Third one is a lawyer in a gown declaring, I *plead for all.*" Kent laughed, and then gazed at Bingley.

"I suspect that would be you, Bingley," Rawlings said. "We can do wrong in your mind."

"I cannot help it if I am fond of all of my friends," Bingley said, shrugging.

"Fourth one is a soldier in his dress uniform, stating I *fight for all.*" As he read the motto, Kent aimed an invisible Baker rifle at the men.

Everyone yelled out, "Kent!" Rawlings followed up by saying, "Of course it is more like fighting us!" The men laughed. Kent did not appear amused.

"Finally, a poor countryman with his farming implements crying, I *pay for all*. That leaves you, Blake," Kent said. "However, I do not think that is quite true. I would say we tradesmen pay for you, but soon the money will flow in a different direction when I win the stallion."

The friends argued in half whispers and mumbles, which amused two judges. Mr. Bennet whispered, "I daresay each one could be any one of the figures."

"I agree, and any us as well," Mr. Goulding replied.

Kent drew their attention back on the day's purpose—his competition. He pointed to the games set up in the dancing space. Rawlings was the quickest to follow him to the first table.

"Why, it is shove ha'penny. I have not played that in years." The other games set up—skittles, quoits, and cribbage—could be found in any of the pubs and taverns he had visited many times over the past four years.

"I should have guessed!" Bingley exclaimed. "Kent, you did spend many an evening at the taverns. I thought all this time you were up to something else!"

Kent waved the others over and handed out the rules to his friends.

Sir William coughed loud enough to gain everyone's attention and then announced, "Game two shall now begin."

Chapter Eighteen

The second game was held behind closed and guarded doors. Two footmen stationed at the entrance had explicit orders that no one enter the room except the judges, the competitors, and the lone servant posing as the bar keep. Those instructions, however, did not keep these two doormen from straining to hear talk of winners and losers. Amongst the shouts and cheers, they heard chuckles and guffaws. On one occasion, the room grew silent, followed by an enormous burst of sound.

Waiting for news, the makeshift sentries listened with their ears upon the door and viewed the action by peering through the keyhole. After a particularly excessive hilarity passed, the guards shook their heads, gave up hope, and returned to the proper doormen's stance.

"The quality folks is a queer lot."

"That they are."

"Which gent did you wager on to be second?"

"Mr. Bingley." The footman raised his brows in question to the other guard.

"I put a thruppence on Mr. Rawlings."

The morning had been filled with competing on the tavern games, to be followed by drinks at the bar, and refreshments shared by all the attendees. The men took on a competitive spirit: cheering when they did well and moaning alibis when they did not. When the doors opened, the men spilled into the hallway with voices raised in merriment. The doormen barely breathed as they kept their ears trained on the men's conversation.

"I must tell you, my friends, this was a most enjoyable morning. I am especially partial now to our counting the points for the stallion. Yes, indeed. A most splendid day." Laughing, the game two victor slapped the back of his friend when he led all the men out.

"Yes, you did well today. Remember though, there are still three more games left. The real game is who wins the most seconds and thirds."

"I will be sorry to see the tavern decorations removed. I rather like having a gentleman's club so close." Darcy pointed with his head back towards the ballroom. He had witnessed how the tension disappeared among his friends when they entered the ballroom tavern.

Turning around, the men beheld the comfortable room. The afternoon sunbeams pointed down upon the games in the middle of the floor. Without ceremony, one servant put away the brandy, port, and ale while the other servants retrieved the trays of uneaten food.

"Now this is worth the trouble of climbing several flights of stairs!" Rawlings exclaimed.

Bingley decided to leave the ballroom decorated for a while, and the men concurred with alacrity when Darcy suggested the servants move the billiard table into the room.

The Five All's Tavern would become their own unique men's club, where they invited the judges to stop by from time to time. Here they would continue to challenge one another in a friendly game of Twenty Points. The drinks flowed and the friends behaved in the manner of men without the civilizing women present. They spoke and sang in masculine tones, the arguments ended in mocking duels, and the language filled with words never spoken in polite company. They had returned to their Cambridge days when life was carefree and responsibilities were few. In this most private of all clubs, all was well between the men. No one mentioned a single word about the high stakes riding on the competition.

After this second day of competition, and when the older gentlemen departed for their homes, the young men separated. Several chose quiet surroundings while three others opted for the outdoors. Two men left for Longbourn and the other rode his horse to the open fields of the East Meadow.

***

Riding Chesterfield calmed Blake after his performance at Kent's game that morning. He refused to spend this clear and bright day shackled to a book in the library with Darcy and Kent. He preferred to ride in a fast gallop when he needed to ponder concerns encroaching on his thoughts.

However, nothing—not even the competition—could erase the vision he saw in his head as he raced towards the open meadow. He tried not to search for Miss Elizabeth, as had become his newest habit on his morning rides. He found himself drawn to the hidden path he had previously discovered, *her* path.

He sought time to think about the situation with her, and he wanted to consider Darcy's interest in the whole affair. However, when the loveliness of a gown fluttered along a side path, all thoughts abandoned him as he dismounted from his horse and rushed to her.

"Miss Bennet." A pleased Blake bowed and without a hint of remorse for his small falsehood said, "I had hoped to find you today."

"Looking for solace, Lord Blake?" Elizabeth picked a yellowish-orange leaf from the tree and did not peek at him. Instead, she kept her eyes on a snow-white furry squirrel with the brightest red eyes, until the animal scurried away.

"If consolation is needed for me to remain in your company, then yes, I accept," Blake whispered as he leaned closer to her than was proper.

Elizabeth turned, smiled at Lord Blake, and then stepped back a little. She played with the leaf in her hand, twirling it under her nose while they continued walking along the path. "First one eliminated this morning, I understand."

"Your father talks too much." Keeping his eyes on the trail ahead, Blake offered his arm.

"He did say you are the best chess master he ever witnessed. Did he talk too much then, as well?" Elizabeth gazed at him with the most arresting eyes he had beheld.

"He should be a little more selective when he speaks about my abilities to others. I would not wish to lose any good impressions I had garnered."

"Much can be learned about a person when they lose, as well. You, I understand, make a charming loser."

"No one loses charmingly. They merely pretend to do so while all the time seething inside. We are taught how to smile at our losses at a dreadfully young age, as you are well aware."

"My father spoke about Mr. Kent's skills with commendable appreciation. Had you never played any tavern games before, Lord Blake?"

"It is true I have some experience, but Mr. Kent grew up on them. He should be superior to us who found time to only dabble at them."

"Tell me about the games, if you can do so without becoming cross with yourself."

"Galloping through the open meadow released all my irritation to the wind. So how shall I begin?"

"I have never even dabbled, my lord." Elizabeth found a large tree stump, which she used as a bench. "Perhaps you could describe each game and how it is played."

"As always, for you, I shall endeavor to do my best." Blake sat down beside her. "Kent set up four tavern games in Mr. Bingley's ballroom. I must say it was quite a sight. He spared no expense in decorating it to look like an authentic tavern. The old King's Head near my home could learn a few lessons from him." Blake stared straight ahead, remembering how surprised he was when he saw the room.

"Where is your home?"

"Leicestershire. Have you ever traveled there?" Blake asked.

"No, other than London, I have not ventured beyond Hertfordshire. We digress. Please continue with the competition as I am quite captivated by it."

Blake narrowed his eyes. "You and Hertfordshire are absorbed. I understand many have hiked to Meryton to place bets on the games."

"Are you stalling, my lord? I know you lost in the first elimination. I will admit you have not been diminished in my eyes." Elizabeth studied the leaf in her hand.

Leaning closer, Blake inhaled her familiar lavender fragrance mixed with her own personal scent that had become forever impressed upon his consciousness. "Thank you. I would never wish that." Sitting upright, he cleared his throat. "You are correct. I am stalling. I do not like telling how I could not succeed on the initial game. Oh well, we began with shove ha'penny. Have you ever played it?"

"No. Please tell me more. Is it difficult?"

"I think luck is needed. Mr. Kent insists skill is required." Blake rolled his eyes. "It is a game with a board and a few ha'pennies."

"How do you play?"

"Exactly like the name. You shove a half penny across the board. Well, slide or push it to be precise. May I take your arm?"

Elizabeth held out her arm and rose, gasping when he grabbed turned her arm, pulled her down. He turned it over and pretended it was a game board. She remained seated in absolute stillness while he used his finger tip to draw imaginary lines from her elbow crick to her wrist.

He described the board, and how a penny should slide and stop near the top. He ignored the growing huskiness of his voice. He snuck a peek up at her. She was sitting very still and did not appear listening as his fingers continued to move with a light touch across her arm, causing her goose bumps to rise underneath his fingertips. He heard her shallow breaths. When his knee rubbed against her thigh, as he turned to demonstrate the game, it excited him in ways he had never before encountered. He lifted his eyes and started at the blush cascading down her neck. He felt his own face on fire and assumed his cheeks had deepened into a bright crimson color of his own.

Elizabeth cleared her throat. "I understand now, please go on." She retrieved her arm and he turned to sit more appropriately.

For a few moments, they avoided eye contact, until their breathing had returned to normal and their faces were no longer flush.

"You will get to try this game for yourself. In fact, Mr. Bingley will include them at the harvest feast. I will watch to see how you do."

"Harvest Feast? I had not heard about any such event. And is not the harvest long finished? Why, this is November?"

"Oh. Bingley told us at dinner last night he was planning to hold a celebration for his tenants. Even though he did not let the estate until the time had passed to hold such an event, he is most desirous to show his tenants how attentive he is for all those things. Perhaps Celebration Feast would have been a better name."

"Perhaps. It is commendable regardless when it is held."

"I agree. I suppose you will be learning the particulars later. As I said, he desired all the tavern games made available for the attendees of the Feast. Your family is to be invited."

"I await it with pleasure. Now tell me more about the games. I am like everyone else, obsessed. My father did not tell us anything more, except how you and Mr. Bingley fared."

"Mr. Kent had a competition with four games—shove ha'penny, skittles, quoits, and cribbage. I will show them to you at the Harvest Feast.

"Go on. How did the scoring work?"

"A simple scheme, in fact. We played the first game and if you ended in last place then you were excluded from moving on to the next one." Blake's muscles in his neck twitched and his hands balled into fists. "I was eliminated after the first game, when my penny flew right off the..." He threw his hands up in expiration as he mumbled, "...blasted... board. This is costing me a great deal."

After taking several deep breaths, he shook his head. "Please excuse my ungentlemanly outburst. I forgot myself, but all the same, I am confounded by my inability to push a penny on a board."

"Shall I release you to go galloping about in the meadow, Lord Blake? Elizabeth asked, snickering. "Do you need to release all this new irritation to the wind?"

Smiling, Blake shook his head.

"Well, you are forgiven. Please go on. Did the others win points for each tavern game?"

"No, nothing so complicated as that. Although, I did receive one point towards winning the stallion, because I was the first one eliminated from the rest of Mr. Kent's games. Whoever was eliminated in the next game received two points, and so forth."

"What was the next game, and who lost?"

"Skittles and Mr. Darcy lost. I am glad he did not do well, for it would have made it difficult for me to best him for the victor's prize. He was none too happy either!"

"Why do gentlemen make things so complicated?"

"We must keep our senses sharp in order to deal with ladies. They are the wiser sex as you know." Blake presented her with the most charming smile he could muster.

"Lord Blake! You use my own words against me." Elizabeth smiled at his tease. She made the motion of throwing the leaf at him, instead she released it to the ground.

"Not true! I use them against me. Well, I shall continue to describe the games. Apparently, Mr. Darcy is no more skilled than I am. He failed at Skittles. Mr. Rawlings has had more practice as he patronized taverns and public houses for several years after we completed school. I learned today that Mr. Bingley and Mr. Kent spent their youth playing these games. You, I guess, can surmise how the points went?"

"Not everything. I imagine Mr. Rawlings placed third when eliminated from quoits and the final game came down to Mr. Kent and Mr. Bingley in cribbage. Remember, my father told us Mr. Bingley's result. I assume Mr. Kent won."

"Yes, he did. I am surprised your father did not tell you all the standings."

Elizabeth dropped her head to hide her blush she could feel rising on her cheeks. "Jane and I asked only about you and Mr. Bingley."

"Oh! Now, Mr. Bingley played exceedingly well; still, Mr. Kent was the victor. The standings for the stallion have Mr. Kent in the lead with eight points and Mr. Rawlings last with four. The rest of us are tied with six points."

"I would have liked to watch the games."

"Miss Elizabeth, I will be interested to witness how well you play these games at the Harvest Feast."

"I have attempted a little cribbage before."

"Then it shall be quite entertaining to observe you playing the other pub games. I assure you, there is nothing untoward in playing them." Blake looked at Elizabeth's arm and felt his face grow hot again.

"Mr. Bingley is most kind to hold this Harvest Feast."

Blake nodded. "He is the most amiable gentleman of my acquaintance. He seems to thrive around people and everyone likes him. He never says any unkind word about anyone, except he does rather tease Mr. Darcy at times."

"Does Mr. Darcy not take any offense?"

"No, Mr. Darcy is especially fond of Mr. Bingley. They became best of friends when their fathers died. Rather sad."

"Yes, dreadfully sad, indeed."

"Mr. Darcy was expecting his father's death, for he had grown ill over many months, perhaps even years. Such was not the case for Mr. Bingley whose father, stricken with pneumonia, passed within a few days. Mr. Darcy was a grand friend to him during that time, and since that day, Bingley has relied on him on matters of major significance."

"And that is why they are particular friends?"

"Yes, and Bingley stood by Mr. Darcy when it was his turn to bury a father. They do have a unique relationship. He allows Mr. Bingley to tease him and never takes offense at the jests. I believe, his unreserved friendliness fills some void for Mr. Darcy."

"Mr. Bingley appears to have survived his loss with his humor and sunny disposition intact. I am afraid Mr. Darcy lost his."

"When he is in comfortable surroundings, Mr. Darcy can be surprisingly amusing. He possess a clever wit. Do not be too hard on him."

"I am surprised. You seem to admire Mr. Darcy."

"I do not comprehend how he accomplishes everything; run an estate and a home in London. He has many investment responsibilities, and is his young sister's guardian."

"He is proud just the same; too proud to mix with the likes of us!"

"He has a right to be proud, do you not think?"

"But, he... let us return, for I am sure they are expecting you." Elizabeth rose from the makeshift bench and began down the path without waiting for Blake.

"I know what Mr. Rawlings is planning," Blake shouted.

Elizabeth stopped and turned to him with a curious expression. She walked back towards him. "I thought it was a secret. How did you find out?" Her eyes widened.

"I know his passion. In truth, I am speculating, of course." Blake moved closer to her. He could sense her breath upon his person. He lowered his head to gain a better view of her face.

"Which game do you guess?" She asked softly, catching her breath when their gazes locked.

Blake leaned closer, his breathing slowed. He took a whiff of the lavender scent that now overpowered all other senses. His palms started sweating and he felt blazing hot underneath all his layers of clothes.

"He will have us race through Meryton in chariots!" Blake pulled back, shaking his hands and then rubbing them dry against his jacket.

"No! Like the Romans?" Elizabeth said, without attempting to hide her surprise.

Blake nodded. "Just like the Romans."

"Is there a reason why he chose this game?"

"He is a member of the Four Horse Club, and races all the time. Rawlings will use his favorite pastime as his game, as I did with the chess game."

"What is the Four Horse Club?"

"Terror on wheels! Certain gentlemen have formed a club who drive barouches five and twenty miles to Salt Lake where they eat, drink and, well, do other things. They are not supposed to travel faster than a trot nor overtake another, but I understand once they pass the half way point and have feasted on their noon meal and had much to drink, the rule is discarded."

"Might he be defeated?" Elizabeth took Blake's arm. They turned to make their way back to his horse.

"I think not. We will be lucky not to be knocked over."

"If you do not win this game, are you concerned you will not win the stallion?"

"The competition is not about who wins every game, but who can achieve the most seconds and thirds. That is the true game."

"Well, Lord Blake. I wish you luck."

Blake released her hand from his arm as he examined the path. "And perhaps if I find an object to carry with me for luck, I may do well." He stooped to find either the leaf she discarded earlier or a wildflower like the one he picked for her before.

Smiling, Elizabeth dropped her kerchief over his shoulder. "Perhaps this will suffice."

Lord Blake picked up the handkerchief carrying the lavender scent. Adorning one corner was the very same wildflower he was searching for, and along the other was a single garden rose.

***

Rawlings requested to seek Mr. Bennet's assistance for his game and Bingley suggested he accompany him to Longbourn. The main road in Meryton must remain open and clear of travelers to avoid serious problems for his race, and as the rules judge, Mr. Bennet would be the one to ask. Rawlings purposely neglected to request it when he had his rules approved. At that time he planned on using it as another reason for going to Longbourn. Bingley, as well, would venture to Miss Jane Bennet's home for the slimmest excuse. Within moments, Bingley sat atop his gentle mare. He was not entirely sure he wanted to win the stallion, and he was concerned about Blake not remaining with the alliance if he lost. No one had signed any agreement, yet.

Miss Bennet was home when the two men called. Bingley was quick with his visit to her father. Leaving Rawlings to conclude the arrangements, he immediately searched for the eldest daughter.

Jane was gracious in showing him the garden. Mary, their chaperon, again commented to him on the evils of sport; nonetheless, nothing she said could dissuade him from being in Miss Bennet's company. It did not take long before Mary found a bench suitable for reading and observing her sister and visitor take a turn around the garden.

When Mr. Bingley leaned in and whispered his guess for Rawlings' game, Jane's brow wrinkled. "Are you concerned about the game? You may be injured." She promised to keep it a secret even from her favorite sister.

"I will take care. If I do well, I will be competitive with the others."

"I am anxious no one be hurt. Is your game as dangerous as this? Jane was no different from any other resident in the parish. She enjoyed knowing more than anyone else, excepting her father, who knew all the games, of course. She bestowed upon him many smiles before Bingley revealed his game.

"My game is not dangerous at all. I suppose tomorrow's race will be the most perilous game, but I do not think we will take unsafe chances. Although I must say, Mr. Darcy has been quite wily about his game, so I am not positive his would not be perilous. Miss Bennet, let me assure you, my friends will not take any undue risks."

"I am glad to hear it is a friendly game with nothing more on the line than a horse."

Bingley glanced at the ground and then whispered, "And perhaps a little more."

They walked in silence for several minutes. When Jane looked at Bingley, she noticed there was sweat upon his brow when he glimpsed at her neckline.

He raised his head and gazed into her eyes. "Do you remember in the days of old, young maidens provided their favorites with a scarf for luck?" He dropped his gaze onto an object around her neck, which covered her neckline.

"Oh, yes I do recall those stories. Blushing, she removed her scarf and handed it to him. "I wish you luck, and I hope this will help, Mr. Bingley."

"I have won with this on my person, even if I lose the race." Busy gazing at a tiny spot where the scarf had laid, Bingley did not discern Rawlings' approaching. "Miss Bennet, do not count me out for I may yet surprise Mr. Rawlings at his own game."

"I look forward to it." Rawlings bowed as he joined the two. "All the arrangements are finished."

As the men departed Longbourn, Rawlings kept his eye on the slip of light blue fabric peeking out of his Bingley's coat. Rawlings guessed what it was and laughed heartedly when his friend pushed the scarf further into its hiding place.

Bingley chuckled. "Do not look disheartened at missing Miss Lydia today. I heard the youngest Bennets walked to town, their goal was to purchase some pretty ribbons. Are you seeking your own good luck charm? "

"Oh? A ribbon would make a lucky token."

"You will need more than a flimsy good luck object, my friend. I warn you."

Rawlings scoffed. "I have wasted enough time listening to your idle threats." He stared down the path. "However, if I must lose the stallion, I hope it is to anyone other than Blake."

Bingley's nod did not convince Rawlings. He recalled Bingley's reaction to Blake's demand. What had he whispered to Kent? He figured it was not good news. At the time, Kent did not seem pleased. In fact, he seemed a bit shocked.

"All will be well, my friend." Rawlings nudged his horse forward, but before they reached the turn for Netherfield Park, he confessed his desire to go into town. He feared the shops would have closed, and the ladies returned home using a different path. Determined they pushed on. He refused to miss an opportunity to speak to a pert Lydia away from her family and, in particular, Colonel Forster's officers.

After a half hour, they had not found the youngest Bennets, so they agreed to return to Netherfield; one man happily patting his pocket, and the other a little frustrated.

The bright afternoon sun lit the words on the pages of the books Kent and Darcy were reading. They sought a little quiet time in the library after the boisterous, noisy tavern games. Tomorrow was Rawlings' competition and they expected another long day.

Kent trudged through a Shakespeare's tragedy. How does Darcy read this? If I must think about each line as I read, I will go mad. He turned another unread page.

Kent's thoughts wandered when he looked up at the bookshelves. Now, I prefer *Wealth of Nations* or anything by Tom Paine. Of course, I cannot read such books here. I would be imprisoned for sedition. Kent snorted. I can well imagine these men's peevish reactions, especially how Blake would recoil. Well, Paine does not specifically call for the overthrow of the aristocracy. Not specifically!

He peeked at what Darcy was reading. John Donne. Poetry! I cannot stand what he reads other than his books depicting Admiral Nelson's sea battles. His thoughts gravitated onto Blake and Bingley as he continued to *read* his book. Their behavior around the two eldest Bennet girls worried him, as well as their tête-à-tête, often spoken in hushed voices. They whisper too much. God, they still discuss their flirtations like young schoolboys experiencing first love.

All afternoon as the mantle clock announced time's passing with a chime each half hour. Kent waited for the right time to address Darcy. The sunlight began to lessen and the words on the book lost their sharpness. He sensed the time had come. He shut his book, leaned forward, and directed a concern, in his calmest voice he summon up, to the other man sitting across from him who seemed lost in his book.

"Darcy, are you not apprehensive that two friends are spending too much time with a couple of young ladies? Will this diversion interfere with our business plans?"

Setting his book in his lap, Darcy bestowed his full attentiveness upon Kent's concern. "I do not see how their latest flirtations will cause any disadvantage to our alliance. There is no other society in which to focus their interest. Both men are prone to fancy the ladies; they have fancied them since our school years."

Kent did not drop his eyes or settle back in his chair. He was trying to make out the sincerity of Darcy's response, although his friend seemed to be feigning confidence.

"When they notice a particular lady, Kent, they often dance with her more than once, fetch her drinks, sweet talk in such ridiculous ways, and otherwise flirt and flatter the woman."

"Do they not raise false expectations for the young ladies?" "I should hope not. I do not think they go beyond what society views as harmless flirtation."

"So, you believe they are not serious over their latest interests?" Kent asked, leaning forward.

"Bingley is behaving as, well, Bingley. He falls in love every other month, as he cannot be without the companionship of a beautiful woman. I have no doubt he will fall in love with another as soon as we return to London."

"And Blake? Are you at all concerned with him?"

"Blake? He is not under the same obligations or circumstances as Bingley." Darcy paused to sip his wine and compose his words. "While he also engages in many flirtations, he does respect his situation in life. Most young ladies understand his attentions are just a flirtation. They do not object and in actuality, seek the notice since any singular treatment by a marquess will help her move up in her own circle. In contrast, Bingley must marry to help him advance to a higher status. Being new to London society, his open behavior towards the ladies is his way to find out who might serve that purpose.

Kent studied Darcy who was, by his furrowed brow, wrestling with his thoughts.

"Blake will connect himself in marriage to increase his fortune and holdings; he must marry an heiress, someone worthy of a future duke. No one here is suitable for Blake's needs. This is the way of our world, Kent."

He caught the hint of regret in Darcy's voice and his desire to end the conversation, but Kent took a chance and continued. "You believe marrying up for social reasons is acceptable? I mean, Bingley must marry into some titled or near titled family in order to move up in society. He has quite the wealth on his own. Would that be possible with his relatives being from trade?"

"Yes, he could find himself married to an earl's daughter or granddaughter. Of course, the family would need fresh funds. Those not requiring financial support will never allow such a union. It is just not done."

"Not even if he was a long standing family friend? Would Bingley become more acceptable, especially if he is enormously successful with this alliance?"

"Even then that is most unlikely." Darcy leaned his head back and closed his eyes cutting off any further discussion.

Kent frowned. He was deeply disappointed to hear this.

The two sat, lost in reflection, as they sipped their wine for a time. Kent reflected on the London season before he returned to his book. It mattered not that the afternoon sunlight was fading away. He turned another unread page.

Chapter Nineteen

Rawlings appeared at breakfast humming and smiling, with the rules of his game in one hand and accompanying maps in the other. Not finding Blake in his usual seat, he glanced about the room but to no avail. However, he did detect Darcy fidgeting with his food, uncommon behavior for his friend. He was pushing the eggs mixed with the spicy pork bits around the plate, without a single morsel ever finding its way into his mouth.

He studied Darcy while he handed out the rules and opened a large map on the dining room table. He noticed how Darcy kept an attentive eye on the door and appeared uneasy by something in particular. Aware of a troublesome situation brewing, Rawlings became acutely sensitive to it when an exhilarated Blake returned from his afternoon ride yesterday. Darcy had maintained a puzzled expression all evening and ever so often Rawlings had caught him sniffing the air around Blake. Rawlings asked Logan if there had been a fire in the kitchen or if something had spilled on Blake's clothes. Logan indicated his ignorance; however, he did reveal Darcy and Blake's heated exchange about Miss Bennet.

Rawlings turned toward the door when he heard Blake's voice in the hallway. Darcy greeted the late arriving man with a cold, dark stare, while Blake proceeded straight to the breakfast buffet table.

"I assume we are to participate in a Chariot race today." Blake said indifference in his tone.

Rawlings kept his eyes trained on Blake as he took his usual seat. My God, Darcy is sniffing the man, again! Curiosity overcame him. Handing Blake the rules, he, too, tried secretly to distinguish any particular smell about Blake. He detected the musky scent of a man except for a delicate hint of a flower. He returned—albeit a little bewildered—to discussing the game. He stopped speaking. Ah! Lavender! Miss Elizabeth wears a lavender perfume. Where does Blake go on his morning ride? He scoffed. No wonder Darcy is disturbed.

"Did you bribe someone, Blake?" Kent asked.

"No, did I not win senior wrangler's honors at Cambridge? I used my logical, mathematical mind." Blake tapped his head. When everyone else looked confused, he looked at Rawlings. "What else would *you* have chosen? You are a member of the Four-Horse Club! So what are the rules? And where do we race? And remember our deal." Blake pointed his head at Darcy.

Rawlings pointed to the map everyone else had looked at seconds before. "I was ready to credit some mysterious mathematical calculation or skill." Nibbling on his favorite sweet pasty, he viewed the men studying the map in between eating bites of food. The cook had filled the pastries this morning with a delightful lemon filling. He shamelessly licked the sweetened but tart gel-like substance from his lips before devouring the remaining bite.

"The race way will be marked by flags." Rawlings held up the map when he explained his game.

Putting his fork down, Bingley lowered his eyes and stared at his plate. "None will be necessary; the townspeople will line the path. Mr. Goulding and Mr. Long are handling the crowd."

"We are to be their entertainment today, I suppose." Kent sighed.

"Yes, you could describe it as such. Oh, tomorrow, they will be present for Darcy's game, and then again for his." Rawlings pointed to Bingley. "Mr. Bennet teased and badgered him before he would grant permission for anyone interested to observe the race."

"Why allow the public now?" An annoyed Blake fidgeted in his seat. "Should we not be asked if we would consent to be become spectacles for them?"

Rawlings set his map down. "Come now, Blake. I recall you saying that Bingley is the newest member of this community and, as his friends, we should help him with his neighbors. He needed to agree, and, I am proud to reveal, he did with great alacrity."

"Why not agree, Blake?" Bingley gulped his coffee. "Mr. Bennet argued that the remaining games are to be conducted outdoors. It will permit large crowds to gather, unlike the indoor chess and pub competitions. There was not a fair way to limit who could view them."

"Bingley, were you informed of Darcy's game?" Blake asked.

"No, I only know where it will be played. I am as much in the dark as you," Bingley said. "For today's game, I knew about the map. Of course, I did assume it was a horse race of sorts; I had no idea we would be using carriages. Besides, secrecy is optional."

"Who chooses the horses? Not Darcy I hope. That would break our deal."

Rawlings pointed at his chest. "I chose them, and none of Darcy's horses will be used. And besides which set of horses you get will be due to luck."

The men studied their maps, scrutinizing each mark in an attempt to recognize any familiar landmarks and the path of the race. Rawlings had drawn a sophisticated, easy to follow map with distinguishable well-known trees and accurate depictions of houses and other establishments on the street in Meryton where the race will end.

Darcy placed his folded up map in his jacket pocket. "Were the *chariots* brought down from London, Rawlings?"

"No, I did not wish to divulge our location to anyone in town."

"I suspect they will hear about all this presently," Blake said. "On the other hand, the competition will be finished long before word reaches our friends and family!"

"Where did you find the carriages for the race?" Darcy asked. "What type will be used, and will they all be the same?"

"We will be using two-horse curricles. Logan was exceedingly creative and discrete. I am aware I may have to purchase the chariots if you fellows cannot race without crashing." Laughing Rawlings looked at Bingley. "Each one is slightly different; the same goes for the horses, although we did try to make sure they were equal."

"Who decides who gets what?"

Before Rawlings responded, Whitson walked in with the straws in his hand.

"Ah, the drawing of straws! We should invent our own special straw to be used for choosing important matters!" Kent laughed. "Of course Bingley would then have to be responsible for setting up games all over the country."

"Well, this competition will be exciting and surprising." Bingley winked at Kent, and then spoke quietly to Blake. "I understand a few lovely ladies plan to cheer us on." He patted his coat pocket.

***

The sunny blue and cloudless sky favored Meryton while its residents lined up at first light, eager to secure a spot to view the competition. The route would take them through the main street in Meryton where many spectators stood waiting; although men, women, and children converged along the entire course. No one grasped that the shops had closed. They concentrated on staking out the best spot to root for the men. Everyone sensed the excitement building for the race. Even the ladies had their preferences, and placed wagers for ribbons, gloves, and in one case, a much-admired bonnet.

The Black Bull Tavern had emptied out well before the start. Unlike the women, the men wagered heavily, and again, they bet on who would come in second. The locals believed those with a superior lifestyle were not capable to win this race since driving a carriage took experience. Hence, Kent and Bingley were the favorites, and even a few bet on them to win.

The time for the race arrived. The stable hands brought the horse curricles to the starting line. The five competitors stepped forward to inspect their chariots. Kent spied one man waving what he perceived as a scarf, and the other, a handkerchief.

Rawlings called out to his friends, now standing by their makeshift chariots ready to race. He wished them God speed and good luck in arriving at the finish line in one piece. They had drawn straws twice, once for the curricle, and again for the horses they would use. Rawlings was not concerned. He knew it was neither the horses' speed nor the vehicle's shape that would guarantee him victory. His experience would triumph against the other lesser skilled gentlemen.

"Watch out for the arrows, shots, and darts that might find its way into our path," Rawlings teased his friends.

The local men practiced daily to win the modified Baker rifle at Bingley's Harvest Feast. Their competition included archery, darts, and target shooting, and the Black Bull patrons wagered on that contest as well. Word had spread once Mr. Goulding made the announcement. Thanks to the enterprising servants at Netherfield Park, every citizen of Meryton had heard of the modified Baker Rifle. In their minds, it was a most worthy prize; almost as sought after as the monetary prize that would accompany it.

Finally, Sir William held the starting pistol high in the air, signaling the men to climb aboard their carriages.

Mr. Rawlings bowed to the crowd as they applauded his apparel. He had worn the racing club's customary drab long coat that reached his ankles. It had three tiers of pockets with mother-of-pearl buttons as large as five-shilling pieces. He opened his coat to show off his blue waistcoat with yellow stripes and breeches, plush with strings and rosettes clear to the knee. He tipped a hat that was more than three inches to the crown, and bowed again. The crowd cheered when he took up his position. He snapped the reins; the horses became alert. They had rosettes at their heads, the harness silver-mounted. With the exception that the carriage was not a yellow barouche, he felt properly attired for a Four Horse Club race. Rawlings spotted Logan giving him a nod.

Sir William waited until the men indicated their readiness. He held the pistol above his head. The horses were anxious. The crowd grew quiet. The five gentlemen began to sweat.

A single bang sounded to start the race.

The crowds cheered while the men snapped their reins, and the horses bolted forward.

The first carriage in the lead was Kent's, much to Rawlings' surprise. Kent advanced to his left while Bingley charged ahead on his right.

"Damn. Get moving you lazy mules," Rawlings muttered, snapping the reins several times before the horses engaged.

Blake and Darcy trailed behind, too close to determine which man led. Both concentrated hard, their own horses failing to match the others' horses pulling away.

Darcy yelled "Charge" to no avail.

Blake laughed when the horse slowed.

Darcy smacked them hard with the reins. "Move!" He found the magic word, and his horses pushed him in front of Blake. Darcy glanced back at Blake with his customary smirk of a smile.

Blake cursed his horses when he found it difficult keep up in his rackety carriage. He focused his efforts on the race until several lovely young maidens standing along the path called out his name.

Darcy winced when his friend smiled at Miss Elizabeth, who had directed her captivating eyes towards Blake. She tapped several small rose buds in her hair. He, like Blake, could not divert their eyes away while they proceeded down the path.

A second later, Blake cracked his reins. While he and Darcy were struggling not to be last, Rawlings, Kent and Bingley were battling it out for first place. The contest was two miles long. When Blake clicked the reins a little harder, and his horses responded, Darcy was thankful they reacted not as explosively as Blake had wished.

The three frontrunners charged ahead, exchanging positions several times; each one enjoying overtaking the others before another man jumped in front. The finish line was within sight for the leaders. It was a furious battle. Kent was a whole carriage in front; Bingley and Rawlings were pushing hard upon his lead.

Rawlings was placing third in his own game. Damn! He thought. Who would have thought these two tradesman boys could beat a member of the Four Horse Club? We are the best racers in England! He whipped his horses one more time, sparing no energy.

The crowds along Meryton murmured louder as they spied the three men turn down the main street.

"Two hundred yards to go," Mr. Goulding yelled. The crowd cheered on their favorite man.

The men in the lead shook their reins as hard as possible and remained on the curricle seat as best they could.

***

"I never imagined such a race would have happened on our little roads. It was most exciting," Sir William said to his long-standing friends—Mr. Bennet, Mr. Goulding, and Mr. Long. While the competitors changed into proper dress, the judges waited for them in the library. Everyone, except Mr. Phillips; he would arrive last, having the most distance to travel from his judging spot.

Mr. Bennet surveyed the room, which appeared orderly; yet, he surmised the men relaxed here. He identified the signs of it all around. The chairs and sofa were located for conversing, not for show. The table in the corner seemed out of place. I suppose they have refreshments placed there. He noticed the sideboard on the room's other side filled with many different liquors.

Sir William approached Mr Bennet after he made his way to the sideboard. "Quite the choice, would you say?"

"All good brands, as well. I wonder who drinks the whiskey." Mr. Bennet fingered the bottle from Oban. "I never acquired a taste for Scotch whiskey."

"I have it on good authority that Mr. Bingley does. I believe some members of his family are from Scotland."

"At least I see some good port as well. Shall we?" Mr. Bennet asked. Sir William nodded. Mr. Goulding and Mr. Long were quick to join the two.

While they sipped their drinks mingled with excited conversation, the young competitors entered. Although dressed in fresh clothes, they did appear somewhat tired after the race.

Rawlings entered, smiled, and bowed to everyone when applause filled his ears.

"Congratulations on your win, Mr. Rawlings." Sir William patted his back.

Surely you are relieved sir." Mr. Bennet said, inviting the young men to join them in some port.

Mr. Rawlings pointed to the brandy.

"Yes, I am most fortunate." He turned to speak to Kent. "Where did you and Bingley learn to drive so? You must join the Four Horse club. You simply must! You are both excellent drivers. I will sponsor you. We will be unbeatable! Of course, no one knows we race. We never admit it."

A bemused Mr. Bennet watched Rawlings' sincere reaction to the close race before turning his attention on Kent. "Sorry young man, Mr. Bingley's spill that took you out must have been a disappointment. And after you were in the lead at the end, it was a shame to have such a tumble and come in fourth."

Kent nodded. "I might have won had Bingley's carriage not slid into me after hitting that that damn rut in the road. Fortunately, the horses were not hurt. I hate to see any animal suffer."

"Nor you or Mr. Bingley." Mr. Goulding nodded.

"I could tell you and Mr. Bingley surprised Mr. Rawlings with your skills."

Kent glanced at Rawlings. "True, he was unaware we had raced each other for years. Neither of us are novices at that activity."

"How so?" Mr. Bennet asked.

"Our uncles were in business together, and we have known each other all our lives and attended the same schools. Bingley would visit my family during the summer. My family builds carriages, if that helps you to understand." Kent refrained from mentioning all the items his family manufactured.

"No. I was not aware. But, how did this help you learn to race?" Mr. Bennet asked.

"Why, someone had to test them!" Kent laughed. "We gladly raced one another. We broke many carriages, as a result. That is why we were able to jump away unharmed. I am most proficient at extricating myself from a tumbling carriage."

"At the end, I believed either you or Mr. Bingley were going to beat Mr. Rawlings at his own game. Now that would have been an interesting twist to this competition," Mr. Goulding said.

"Perhaps, but it would not be as interesting to me!" Rawlings chuckled.

"Mr. Darcy, you did well to come in second," Sir William turned to the man standing apart from the rest.

"My strategy is still intact to win the stallion," Darcy said, coolly.

"What would you do if you won the Andalusian?"

"Why, I might choose to gallop in the early sunrise and calculate my winnings." Darcy tipped his head at Blake. "I would be greatly profited by such a victory."

"Darcy, tomorrow is the day we play your game." Blake retuned the nod. "After today's third place, I am now tied in fourth place for the stallion with nine points, and I need a better finish tomorrow at least."

Sir William, overhearing the remark, decided it was a good moment to record the scores. With a clap, he gained everyone's attention. "Now that all the competitors are here, I shall annotate the journal with today's results and announce the rankings for the stallion." He waited for everyone to quiet down.

"Mr. Darcy and Mr. Kent are in the lead with ten points." Sir William raised his glass, and all the men cheered. "Lord Blake and Mr. Rawlings are tied with nine points, and Mr. Bingley is in last place with six. Do not fret Mr. Bingley; anyone might win the prize depending upon the next two games!"

Bingley shrugged. "I agree."

"I must do well tomorrow, if I am to stay competitive." Blake begged, "Darcy, will you not give me a hint?"

"I gave you one." Darcy remained expressionless except for the gleam in his eyes.

"When? What did you say?" Blake furrowed his brow.

"I advised you not to come naked."

"Being naked is not a hint. You know I covet the stallion more than any other prize." Blake laughed as Darcy rolled his eyes. It had become a game between the two. Blake would make the pronouncement, and Darcy would roll his eyes. Blake would laugh, and Darcy would sigh without comment. This time, however, Darcy did not let the statement go unchallenged.

"Heracles will be mine." Darcy pointed to himself. "I am determined."

The men continued to focus their conversations on the race just completed, speculation on the games left to play, and the possibilities for winning the stallion. Afterwards some men chose to sit in the chairs, others stood by the sideboard, and then, a few opted to peruse the bookshelves.

Yes, this going quite well, quite well indeed, Bingley thought as he watched the room full with men happy in conversation until he heard some loud voices by the library shelves. Everyone rushed to join Mr. Darcy and Mr. Goulding.

"Believe me, sir. I tried inbreeding many times. You will not succeed by mixing the two," Mr. Goulding said in an insisting tone with his voice sounding louder than he had intended.

"You know horses. I know sheep." Darcy eyes bore into Mr. Goulding, who unlike many, did not step back. In fact, he narrowed his eyes into tiny slits and glared back at the young man.

No one else listening understood the argument. They at first believed the two men were talking about breeding horses with sheep. The discussion was too technical for them. Time had not long passed before the talk turned to how modern methods were changing the country and the others responded to the discussion.

"Progress is not always the solution," Mr. Goulding spoke in a forceful timbre. "Young men always want to change everything. Why cannot they just be satisfied? I have been successful in running my horse farm. There is nothing wrong with the methods I use. Young men!"

"These are different times. More people exist now, and the old ways will not be able to sustain this increased population," Kent replied matching Mr. Goulding's forcefulness.

"Perhaps, then, we should not train so many doctors!" Mr. Bennet said, his tone sarcastic. "I see no need for many changes."

"Are not the new inventions exciting?" Kent arugued. "Will they not change everything? Mr. Goulding, we cannot remain stagnant. No great nation can survive without progress."

"Progress?" Mr. Bennet said. "Bah! I might have some say about progress. Is it progress to force families from their homes into the squalor of the cities? Now that is a step forward!"

Standing erect, with his hands balled into fists behind his back, Kent glared at Mr. Bennet. "You need to prepare for the day when machinery will replace your labor. The creation of new tools and farming methods will continue and be more efficient than what we do today."

Mr. Long cleared his throat. "I doubt that. Laborers will always be needed. In addition, we do not use little ones mercilessly to tend our crops. You cannot say so at the mills." Having traveled last month to a mill town, he discussed the appalling conditions he witnessed.

"Not all mills are the same." Darcy moved to stand next to Kent.

"If the mill owners increased wages, families would live better. Progress will ruin this noble nation." Finishing his drink in a single gulp, Mr. Bennet stood beside Mr. Goulding and Mr. Long.

"This country will not be the greatest for long if we do not move forward. Other countries will not stand still as you propose we do." Kent glared at Mr. Bennet.

"Stand still?" Mr. Bennet cried out. "I am not proclaiming we do that. I am suggesting we not move at a breakneck speed. Schemes abound everywhere."

Rawlings moved to stand next to Mr. Bennet. "Not all speculations are advantageous; that much is true. You must carefully choose which people you rely upon when involved in some of the new industries."

Mr. Bennet shook his head. "Even people we trust can prove unworthy. Money. It is greed. Furthermore, we all are a greedy lot." He glared at the older men, and they all appeared to agree. He turned to the young men. "One day you will learn how money-oriented you have become."

Everyone stood still at Mr. Bennet's pronouncement. Sir William and Bingley both stared at the men with widen eyes and mouths open. Neither man spoke, coughed, or relaxed their eyes. They did, however, take a slight step backwards. Blake listened in the background.

Mr. Rawlings placed his hand on Mr. Bennet's shoulder giving it a small squeeze. After a few moments, he glanced at the others. The men had separated into the two age groups: the young ones on his left and older ones on his right and each group held rigid stances, casting cold stares at each other. Rawlings imagined a line drawn between the two generations, each side aiming modified Baker rifles at the others.

After a long wait, he spoke. "Mr. Bennet is correct. Greed has moved the world ahead in every instance. Yet, I do not believe it is the sole reason men to try to improve themselves. Sometimes the goal is to help loved ones." He glimpsed at Mr. Bennet before turning to look at Darcy, and with a softer tone said, "Other times boredom is the incentive."

When he felt the tension in the room relax, he continued. "Both reasons can be good. The actions you do not take are the ones you regret in life, and those are the thoughts that return time and time again to haunt you. Men must try new things. It is what we do."

Mr. Phillips had been quiet throughout this discussion. He peered down at the wine swirling in his glass. When his hands shook, he returned to the seating area where he pulled out a worn and tattered message. His eyes darted from the letter to the young men several times before he leaned back with closed eyes.

When all the other judges departed, Darcy noted Mr. Phillips fidgeting in his chair before returning a document to his coat pocket. After a moment, he again pulled it out to revisit its contents.

"Gentlemen," Darcy said, calling the others to attention. He inclined his head towards the seated area. "I believe Mr. Phillips lingered here for a reason. Let us allow him a moment to speak."

Upon hearing his name, Mr. Phillips rose from the chair. He returned the letter to his coat pocket and joined the men by the beverage table.

"Mr. Phillips, is there a problem? Do you need something for the alliance?" Darcy spoke in a calm voice, which belied his anxiousness. His experience in dealing with distraught tenants had prepared him in the art of emotional concealment.

"Beg your pardon. Some paperwork is causing a slight delay. I am waiting for information from London." Mr. Phillips did not raise his eyes.

"What can we do?"

"I have an issue that I cannot resolve, and I am not sure if I should even bring it to your attention." Mr. Phillips raised his head, sighed, and then shifted his weight back and forth.

"Speak up, man. It is better to disclose problems than cover them up." Agitation caused Rawlings' voice to rise.

Mr. Phillips glanced at the men. All five were now in a semi-circle, staring at him with alarmed expressions. "I... I received a warning. It is about Mr. John Cuffage."

"Cuffage? What is it you have heard?" Darcy asked.

"He is not as trustworthy as you were led to believe."

Darcy frowned and transferred his attention onto Rawlings. "Did you not investigate the man?"

"Yes, everything seemed in order."

Turning back to Mr. Phillips, Darcy asked, using his most commanding tone, "From whence is this allegation coming?

"I cannot say. The warning came from a conversation about a wholly different contract. I am bound to remain silent. However, I fear if this man is not trustworthy, you all may be hurt."

"Perhaps there is a vengeful reason for this man to make this allegation?" Kent asked.

"No, sir. My source does not resemble that sort of fellow; he is honorable in all he does. He came across this information, and for reasons I cannot say, wished to inform me of the situation. Yesterday he sent me an express from London confirming his suspicions."

"What is it you want, Mr. Phillips?" Darcy asked.

"I sent word to my contacts to investigate the man, Mr. Darcy. You would be wise to also contact your secretary in London and request he take a closer scrutiny, as well."

"Is there anything else that can be done?"

"Nothing else is needed, except I have withheld preparing the papers for Mr. Cuffage. I wanted to speak to you first. I assume the delay is acceptable and will continue until we put this warning to rest."

"Yes, yes. Very good, Mr. Phillips," Rawlings said,

While Mr. Phillips spoke to the other gentlemen about a few miscellaneous items in their own legal documents, Darcy prepared an urgent request to his secretary, Mr. Rogers.

As he wrote the message, defeat echoed in his head. Without Cuffage, they could not reach Astor and, without him, the global trading strategy would not succeed. Damn. His estate would be at risk if Blake walked away. The men had competed without any animosity as agreed, yet Kent's concern remained, would Blake reject the alliance if he did not win? Perhaps this country attorney is not as experienced at understanding the workings of a much higher society. Perhaps the information was a deliberate ruse to disrupt us.

Darcy sealed the letter, addressed it, and requested Whitson send it by express post. "Mr. Phillips, we should be hearing from Mr. Rogers quickly."

"Thank you, sir. I am relieved."

Bingley felt the need to lessen the tension in the room by offering Mr. Phillips another glass of wine. He agreed, sharing his wine with the gentlemen before leaving for his home.

Alone again, the partners put aside their concern over Mr. Phillips' news, and congratulated Rawlings on his win. He opened a special French wine, sent to him by express post for his win, and asked his friends to join him.

"Did you see the way not one of them thought well of progress?" Kent asked, incredulous.

"We may be the same ourselves when we reach their ages." Bingley laughed. "I cannot even imagine how stubborn we will be when that time comes."

"I, for one, cannot understand how they cannot see the future. Changes are coming, and even the old men will be affected." Kent sipped his wine. "This is excellent wine, Rawlings, where did you find it? From the forbidden country, I assume?" He held his glass for a refill.

"Mr. Cuffage sent it in advance of my race. He assumed I would win."

"How did he know about the competition?" Darcy asked.

"He did not say."

"Rawlings, what was that gibberish you spouted about regrets and all?" Blake said abruptly

"Gibberish? It was not," Rawlings bristled at the insult before softening his tone. "I have my own reasons for my remarks. These men are from a different era, and they would not be as free with their choices as we are. Think on how life must be for them, Blake."

"So, do you think our families may hold the same opinions? Has anyone worried about how this alliance will set with them?" Blake's gaze circled the group; his friends looked down. "You know we will face harsher criticism when our fathers and uncles present their arguments."

"Not all families will look down on progress," Kent said.

"We shall help one another if need be," Darcy said. "I will stand by my friends."

"We are in this together," Blake added.

"Here, here." said Rawlings as he lifted his glass. "To the alliance."

The others followed suit.

"To the alliance!"

***

"To Mr. Bingley and his Olympics."

The Blake Bull Tavern patrons lifted their mugs for the final cheer. Nighttime had arrived and the place was quieting down after hours of drinking, wagering, and bragging. The race had been so close until the end, men who had bet on Lord Blake moaned in their ale. Now the Lord's victory for the horse was not as secure as many once believed. First, fifth, and third place finishes left him in next to last place along with Mr. Rawlings.

Nigel had spent the day in the crowd watching the race as the townspeople had, except his attention was drawn to the two men in the rear—Darcy and Blake. They appeared to be attracted to the same Bennet daughter. Nigel did not misunderstand the rivalry brewing and decided to include this information in his weekly report along with the document he picked up in the oak tree hollow at dusk. He had to be careful going to the East Meadow ever since the area had been set up for someone's game and servants were often around.

Tonight he lifted his glass with the others. He guzzled the ale, set the mug down and headed for his room. "Cuffage will appreciate hearing that they have been told not to trust him, and Mr. Darcy has begun an investigation."

Chapter Twenty

The men fidgeted in their chairs while they waited for the announcement for Darcy's game. The stakes were high. While they sensed that Blake would not win, the rankings were too close to count him out. He was a mere one point behind Rawlings, Darcy, and Kent. Bingley's chances seemed gone.

The men came to attention in perfect military precision when Darcy entered the dining room. He had been very secretive in preparing for his game; sending an express message to a location none of the men discovered. He continued to steal away to talk to stable hands and the gardener and steward daily and was the first one to glance at the letters received each morning. Moreover, he smiled every day for a week and that was what worried them the most.

Blake had guessed fencing, since Darcy was downright unbeatable. However, he did acknowledge to the others he wanted that sport since he had an excellent chance of placing second. In addition he reasoned, thrusting foils, rapiers, or perhaps sabers fit the naked jests.

"Tup Running." Darcy announced.

"What the hell is Tup Running?" Kent searched through the document Darcy handed out. It did not take long. No maps were provided, and no charts similar to the one Blake had used for the chess tournament. Kent scrutinized every word on the single page of instructions.

Leaning back in his chair, Rawlings coughed until he gained everyone's attention. "In my neck of the wood, 'tup' is the equivalent to the 'beast with two backs'. Are we to get a little crinkum-crankum, Darcy?"

"It cannot be. Remember we were not to be naked!" Blake chuckled and then glared at Darcy. "Explain yourself. We need to know what this is."

"Pray tell us, how do rams fit in?" Rawlings asked, his eyes darting from one friend to the others.

"Rams? What about rams?" Bingley's eyes grew wide.

Rawlings did not hide his snicker. "Yes. I witnessed four such creatures arriving the other day. The boy said they were yours, Darcy. Come clean and tell us all.

"Tup running is a Derbyshire activity played at wakes and fairs."

"People bring rams to funerals in Derbyshire? Quite the thing for sheep country, I must say," Rawlings remarked.

"Do not be absurd, the wakes are merely church festival and fairs. Tup Running is amusing and agreeably entertaining," Darcy answered.

Rawlings rolled his eyes. "You take me too seriously at times."

"What do we do with these smelly animals?" Bingley asked, confusion on his face. "Riding would be too easy, and shearing would be too risky for both us and the beasts."

Darcy pointed to the paper. "Read the rules, I did not use any four or five syllable words for you to decipher. I turned a large area in the East Meadow into a pen. The rams will be inside the circle. You must catch the ram by its tail, and hold tight until a judge taps you on the shoulder. The first one to be tapped wins five points, and next one four points, and so on."

"This seems too easy, Darcy." Kent glanced through the rules again, looking for something more.

"Oh, I neglected to mention that the rams will be thoroughly soaped and greased around the end parts. You will discover the difficulty in holding on, I assure you."

Rawlings nodded to Bingley who said quickly, "Again, you attempt disguise, Darcy."

Darcy frowned; his expression and long sigh revealed his regret for long ago making the statement to his teasing friends.

"Now I understand your caution about being naked, Darcy," Blake said as the others chuckled, and then hooted at the image racing in their minds. He glowered at them. "I am pleased you are amused. I never so much as patted a ram on the rear. Once before have I touched its head, and I was a silly child at the time. I will not grab the tail of any animal."

"Blake, the townspeople will remark on your absence," Darcy said.

"I have no care to what they say."

"You agreed to all the games regardless of the choice," Rawlings said. "Or are you now willing to forgo the thirty percent?"

"But to grab a ram in such a way. Darcy, I cannot believe you perform such a hideous deed!" Blake asked.

"I chose neither guns nor my horses. You did not forbid any other animal. I have been exceptionally victorious doing this; otherwise, I would not have chosen this sport."

"Since you do own all the sheep in Derbyshire, your proficiency is unsurprising." Rawlings concentrated on the food on his plate, keeping his head down to conceal his expression.

Darcy scoffed. "I do not own all the sheep. Where do you get such ideas?"

"It is all the talk: Mr. Darcy owns half of Derbyshire, all the mines, and all the sheep," Rawlings said in an exaggerated imitation of the locals.

"Well, the speculation is not true. Oh yes, one last rule."

"Are we to kiss their furry bums too?" Blake asked.

Darcy chuckled. "If you so desire, Blake. Now, inside the pen will be four rams and when one is caught, that ram will be removed. This is to ensure the ram you catch will still be greased and difficult to hold onto."

"Could you have not chosen a different game? Fencing is an excellent sport, Blake suggested, then added, "Tup Running is rather disgusting."

"Perhaps the game we play at our fairs in Leicester might have suited you better," Kent said.

Blake eyed Kent. "You are from Leicester? That is my county."

Kent sent a cold stare in return, and then replied, "Yes, I have known that since our Cambridge days."

Blake diverted his eyes away from Kent onto his empty plate. "What is the game they play there?"

"It is called Whip the Cock," Kent said.

"Whip the what?" Rawlings asked. "Tup Running, Whip the Cock! I am surprised someone does not get thrown in the stockade at these northern fairs."

"What is, umm, Whip the Cock, Kent?" a grinning Bingley asked. His eyes drifted downward into his lap.

"They place a rope around—"

"Whoa. This is not a game I would be willing to play." Rawlings covered his lap with his napkin as if it had the strength of a knight's shield. "Not around anything of mine, I can assure you of that."

Kent laughed. "A rooster, Rawlings, they place a rope around a rooster and tie him to a post. The judges hand all the gentlemen whips. The first one to whip the poor feathered fowl and make him squawk wins it as the prize."

"What else is there? You and Darcy are so much alike." Rawlings shook his head.

"Thank you, for the compliment. They blindfold the contestants, spin them around, and then release them with whips in their hands. They wind up thrashing each other before anyone finds the rooster. The whipping is amusing to watch."

"A brilliant idea. Maybe we should all be blindfolded and spun in circles for Darcy's game too." Rawlings searched the rules for the word blindfolded.

"I wager Darcy would have included it if he had known about it. Speaking of wagers, are the locals aware of this game, Darcy?" Kent asked.

"They are being told about it as we speak."

"Will all those people come?" Kent knew the answer; nonetheless, he wished to take pleasure in Blake's reaction.

"I forgot this is to be public." Blake crossed his arms as he leaned back in his seat. "Are we to perform this humiliating activity in front of women and children? I may avoid this game."

"There is no reason you cannot drop out. Mmmm. If you do, then you will have garnered a nine-point total for four competitions. Remember, you only earn them, Blake, when you participate; and I will challenge giving points for not playing. Now let us see. My total for three games is ten, and if I win, I will be ahead with fifteen. All I would need for the last game is one and the stallion will not be..."—Darcy turned to glare at Blake—"Yours. Not to mention the unimaginable additional profits you would lose."

When Blake flinched, and then calculated the possibilities, Darcy knew that he had won his argument.

Bingley coughed. "Ahem. Before I forget, I did invite the judges to share refreshments following the game."

Rawlings looked up. "And, I hope the judges' family members will attend."

Bingley nodded, his grin indicated his pleasure.

Everyone turned to look at Blake just as the man pulled a lady's handkerchief from his pocket. Blake closed his eyes, and then gently caressed the linen cloth between his thumb and fingers. He raised it to his nose, and then popped open his eyes, smiled to Darcy. "I agree to play the blasted game."

***

The crowds at the Black Bull were lively and more animated than usual even since the competition began. The men complained to Roger Staunton about not having any tavern games at his establishment. Staunton promised to approach Mr. Bingley and Mr. Kent with an offer to purchase the ones used for competition, satisfying the men. Talk ended when the patrons spied one of the judges making his way through the door.

"Do you know the game for today?" A patron yelled.

"I do." Mr. Goulding announced the game and explained the rules.

The crowd talked and snickered until the novelty ran its course. Many men expressed surprise that a gentleman of Mr. Darcy's caliber would select such a game. Side bets on the naming of his game had included fencing, croquet, archery, pitching horseshoes, and one even for jousting. Not a single person considered Tup Running although with the knowledge Mr. Darcy owned an estate in sheep country, many suggested activities with those animals: shearing, roping, herding, and even tossing the beasts. But the most unusual bets were for bailing hay, plowing, ram jumping, wool naming, trimming a ram's hooves or horn, and Mr. Staunton's favorite—head butting with a ram.

"Where is this Tup Running being played? Are we allowed to watch?" A patron standing next to Staunton asked. He had placed his wager for second place on Mr. Kent, who was gaining popularity daily. However, Blake still led in the betting on the winner for the horse.

"Mr. Bingley invites anyone interested to come to the East Meadow at Netherfield Park at two." When Mr. Goulding completed his announcement, the crowd cheered. Not wishing to miss the event, the men made haste to gulp the last drop of their drinks, wrap up conversations, or finish the card or billiard game in order to scurry away to discharge their tasks for the day. They did not want to forgo witnessing such distinquished men lowering themselves to do such a frivolous activity.

Meryton was like any other small village. And so it was, within one-half hour, there was not a single person unaware of the particulars for the game. A large turnout did find their way to the East Meadow.

The generously greased rams pranced in the makeshift pen with their hind parts sparkling in the sun. They snorted and then butted heads with the tipped over wagons and makeshift fence circling the pens. The rams did not like the crowd that surrounded them. Darcy had paid several rather large and beefy stable hands to stand inside the circle holding pitchforks to control any charging ram. He did not wish any friend to be hurt. This event, he had told them, was to be pleasurable.

The five gentlemen, dressed as appropriate for the activity, entered the improvised wagon-type fence, causing the now hushed spectators to crowd around the circle. Also entering alongside the competitors were Mr. Goulding and Mr. Long who had agreed to tap the men once they caught a ram. Darcy had told his friends they must hold on until the tap. Mr. Bennet and Mr. Phillips walked along the pen, ensuring the makeshift pen held up. Standing safely behind the largest wagon, but in plain sight of the contestants, Sir William shouted to the young men to ready themselves.

Each one found a strategic spot from which to begin. Blake, frustrated with the crowd, relaxed when he spied Miss Elizabeth leaning against a wagon. She smiled when their eyes made contact.

Rawlings resolved to hold back, letting Darcy show how to be successful, before he attempted to flop his body around a ram's rear end. He had no doubt his friend would win this game; he was the one with any experience.

Shrugging, Bingley and Kent glanced at each other, then at the rather annoyed rams, and finally at the excited and talkative crowd.

Sir William dropped the flag.

Darcy was first to move, running straight for the largest ram. Within three minutes, he grasped the ram; however, he was not able to hold on, thereby slipping to the ground. Bingley and Kent both reached other rams, but were unable to grab a hold as the creatures ran away too quickly. The frustrated expressions displayed by the men signified to the onlookers that this competition was not going to be easy.

The crowd cheered while the gentlemen chased the rams. The pitchforks proved unnecessary; the animals stayed busy running away from the men.

Blake spied Elizabeth twirling a rose in her fingers, he smiled openly, and made a dash for one of the rams. He missed, but caught her nod. She had directed her sparkling eyes at him, with encouragement to try again. On his next attempt, he grabbed the ram, although the beast bucked and broke the hold when the crowd shouted for him.

Tap.

Mr. Goulding tapped Darcy, holding the tail tight, pronouncing him the winner and the proud owner of five points for this game. Darcy appeared unaware of the crowd's silence after the announcement.

Rawlings made his first effort at catching a ram. His hand clutched the tail just as he tripped and fell face down, causing him to let go. He was fortunate the angry ram did not trample him; preferring to dash to the other side of the pen away from the men. Nevertheless, from his spot on the ground, he determined Blake was having more success than either he or Bingley. Rising abruptly, Rawlings ran to catch the ram Bingley was chasing. He grabbed the beast, but before Mr. Long made his way to him, he spied Mr. Goulding approaching Blake, who was resolutely holding onto the largest ram.

Tap.

"Mr. Rawlings you have come in second." Mr. Long announced.

Rawlings heard Blake mumbling a few curse words. The ram he had caught pulled away a second before Mr. Goulding could tap him.

Blake zeroed in on a ram moving away from Bingley. He had reached the beast when he heard Mr. Long

"Mr. Kent, you have come in third."

The ram Blake was chasing had run away from him. With renewed determination and the crowd cheering him on, he sped forward, attacking the final ram.

"Lord Blake, you have come in fourth."

Meryton's finest families moaned. He was such a polite young man smiling to them on occasion that even the less sophisticated residents liked him as much as Mr. Bingley, almost.

When the crowd offered him applause, Lord Blake bowed before turning towards Darcy. "The stallion will be mine. I am not in last place. I shall win the Andalusian in the end."

Darcy, feeling a sense of satisfaction, offered Blake one of his rarely shown wide smiles.

Rawlings yelled, "We did it, Darcy. We did it!"

Darcy watched Blake's expression change from smugness to shock when he calculated the points.

After forty minutes, four of the men caught their rams, causing the game to be finished. Nevertheless, Bingley kept trying to catch Blake's ram. There were no more points to win, as he had earned his one point for coming in fifth. The crowd awarded him with riotous shouts of encouragement, and when he caught the beast, Mr. Goulding was quick to tap him on the shoulder. Bingley, like Blake had, bowed low to the applauding onlookers. He, however, went a step further by clapping for his friends and for the judges as well.

Sir William stood in the middle of the pen, once they removed the last ram, and announced the scores for the stallion.

"Mr. Darcy leads with fifteen points; Mr. Kent and Mr. Rawlings are tied with thirteen; Lord Blake has won eleven, and Mr. Bingley has eight points." The spectators murmured amongst themselves for several minutes longer calculating who to bet on for the next and final game.

When the crowd dispersed, the five men left to change into clothing presentable for the families staying for refreshments. The invited families meandered to the house where the staff directed the guests to the still tavern decorated ballroom. Shocked upon entering, a few women fanned their faces, and several men began to whistle. Once accustomed to the sight, some attendees wandered over to the skittles area, while others tested their skills at quoits.

The Bennet ladies, however, tried their hands at shove ha'penny. The youngest two Bennets had just finished a game.

"La, did you see Mr. Rawlings fall flat on his face? What a sight." Lydia snorted.

Kitty nodded. "At least he did not come in last."

"If they had allowed the redcoats to try, they would have just shot the rams first. Now, that is how to play the game."

Mr. Rawlings joined them just as she finished. He laughed at Lydia's comment,while thinking he should have done just that. Darcy did not expressly deny it. What fun it would have been if he had shot one of the bloody beasts! Hmmm, Lydia has such a keen mind. "Good afternoon, ladies."

The girls curtsied first before they began to giggle.

"Mr. Rawlings. I thought you were going to catch your ram and come in first."

"That was my hope, Miss Catherine. Alas, it was not to be."

"Would it not be funny if we were all soaped up and some redcoats raced and tried to hold on to us,Kitty? La, what a sight that would be."

Mr. Rawlings cringed. Can she think about nothing but redcoats?

"I was happy you won your chariot race yesterday." Kitty said. You looked so fierce when you crossed the finish line."

"Thank you, Miss Catherine. It was quite a race. I was surprised that Mr. Kent and Mr. Bingley were so skilled. I had expected competition from Mr. Darcy."

"I do believe Mr. Darcy was happy to be second in that race," Kitty said. "He smiled."

"Today's game was such fun. And to watch that Mr. Darcy chase a ram. I am surprised he would even attempt such a thing! He got all dirty like the rest of you." Lydia eyed Rawlings from his head to his feet.

"Darcy is experienced in this game. He told us he plays it every year in Derbyshire. It is a regular activity there."

"That would explain why he won. Kitty, did you notice that he did not bow to the crowd? He just walked off and ignored us all." Lydia glared straight at Rawlings with her right brow raised high and her head tilted to the left.

Rawlings mirrored her stare. "Perhaps he, like myself, was more interested in seeing who would come in next. Now, do you young ladies want more punch? It appears your glasses are empty."

They agreed through giggles and snorts. He left to acquire the drinks a moment before Lizzy and Jane joined their sisters.

"Jane, your gentleman did not do so well. He seemed silly running after that ram," Lydia teased her blushing sister. She whispered to Kitty, that their eldest sister was such an easy target.

"I suspect he was not at his best today." Jane said. "He had much on his mind. He must see to the invited guests."

"Lord Blake smiled at you, Lizzy. Is he sweet on you? Do you wish he would grab you like that ram?"

"Lydia! Do not be so coarse."

Mr. Rawlings returned with the drinks and with Mr. Bingley by his side. Overhearing Lydia's remark, he could not get the image of Lydia all greased up and running in circles from his mind. *Oh, how I like this girl. She is more akin to a bawdy barmaid than a gentleman's daughter. I would hear no pretense spoken by this little lady. She has much passion about her. She would not lie still with eyes closed tight, and, most definitely, not be almost fully dressed. Greased rear parts indeed!*

The group discussed the competition and the games played so far. Elizabeth spotted Lord Blake sitting alone, but when she stepped forward to approach him, Mr. Rawlings stopped her.

"Miss Elizabeth, it may be best to give Lord Blake a few minutes. I daresay he would not be the best company at the moment."

"I do not understand?"

"Lord Blake can only be in contention for the stallion by besting Bingley at his own game. Remember, we each chose a game that matched our strengths. Lord Blake has now determined that a win for him is a problem."

"Thank you, Mr. Rawlings. I will leave him be for now and wait for him to approach me."

"Thank you. That would be most kind."

The two returned their attention to the group conversation. Without realizing that he could not win the competition now, Lydia, in her normal teasing fashion, chided Mr. Bingley about his play today. The most points he could win after his game would be thirteen. There would most likely be at least one other with sixteen. Nevertheless, Mr. Bingley assured them that he was not a man prone to unhappiness nor was he that keen about competition. He was happy just to observe his friends so agreeably engaged.

As the afternoon wore on, Mr. Bennet proved the best judge to keep the final competition hush-hush. Everyone did his or her best to guess the game for next day. He enjoyed how his friends and families used all their arts to try to discover it. If either Sir William or Mr. Goulding had known the game, the secret would not have held so fast.

Mr. Bennet smiled when he considered Bingley's choice and thought how this game will cause more excitement than the others put together. He always wanted to witness such a game, and now he thrilled at the chance to play it.

Rawlings and Darcy snuck away to a quiet spot in Bingley's seldom used study. With brandies in hand, they chose seats near the blazing fire. The autumn evening chill had arrived.

"We did it. Blake cannot win now." Rawlings exclaimed.

"There is still a small possibility."

"Slight. Did you hear him suggest that we paid Mr. Goulding not to tap him in a timely fashion?"

Darcy shrugged. "He was upset. He did not believe it. He found me later and apologized."

"He did not apologize to me. Have we lost the alliance? I do fear him not living up to his agreement."

"I am not concerned." Darcy said. "Blake did not state that in any specifics, but he did leave the impression he would."

Well, again, I cannot tell you how honored I was to be included in this alliance. I still do not think I bring any value."

"I would not attempt such an endeavor without you. I trust you implicitly. I also need your sense of things. Sometimes I do not pay attention to the overall state of affairs since I tend to concentrate mainly on the small details. You possess remarkable insight."

"There is little else I bring to this group. I could not rely upon my father to help us with the Baker rifle sale. I am sorry Blake did not fall for my tactic."

"But he did. We are at least competing to keep him from the extra profit. He called your bluff, although he was not sure. It was a risk."

Rawlings darted his eyes towards the door. "I am concerned that I will not be as worthy a contributor as the others."

"Who else would venture to the Americas? Not I. Blake suffers from seasickness except in the smallest boats, and Bingley and Kent are more valuable here."

"Just the same, I thank you. This is exciting."

"When in London, did you secure passage for your trip?"

"Yes, on Kent's family ship, the *Lively*. The crossing will take thirty days or so unlike the normal two months trip. I need to thank Kent for his letter of recommendation. The captain indicated they would sail the moment Logan and I board. We will not wait for a full cargo, as is the usual way.

"When will you leave?

"Early December."

"Are your arrangements to meet with Astor underway?"

"Cuffage will be in charge over those matters I do not need to do anything. Although I am concerned with what Mr. Phillips said about the man, I do think he will serve us well. I heard nothing adverse from my investigator, Nathaniel, or his brother Nigel. I asked them to notify me if any worrisome information became known. "

"I am relieved to hear so. I wish you an easy voyage. The Atlantic can be a bit rough at times."

"As long as the ship arrives, I know I will."

"I will worry." Darcy spoke again after a few minutes of silence "I owe you much, Rawlings. I should have—"

"Nonsense. I needed what Margaret possessed, Darcy, not you."

Darcy dropped his head and glared at his hands. He remained lost in his thoughts for a few minutes without interruption until he sighed deeply. He stood. "Well, I am off to join the others. I plan to win the stallion. And you?"

"I, too, desire to own the horse; he is a beauty, and every single Four-Horse club member would envy me," Rawlings said. "If I come in second, you will need to finish in third place to win. So, I caution you, my excellent friend; I trust I will win the competition."

"I do not wish for you to think any other way." Darcy said as he and Rawlings left for the library.

Chapter Twenty-one

The noise level at Netherfield Park plummeted once all the guests had departed, although the men's baritone voices in the library kept it from becoming soundless. Tonight, spoken words were all that were feasible. Their arms and legs ached after spending the morning chasing the tails of irritated and uninviting rams. And when followed by a chase of a different nature in a house occupied by attractive and captivating women, their backs burned from pushing shoulders back, standing at full height, and sucking in stomachs. The men welcomed the opportunity to cast off the refined appearance for a brief moment of casual relaxation.

Blake remained sullen and sat in the far corner, lowering his eyes as everyone whispered that he was contemplating his loss. Elizabeth had lifted his spirits; nonetheless, her gentle conversation had not been enough to quell his dissatisfaction with his performance. He had counted on winning, no; he bragged about his prowess and had banked on his future earnings.

The other men had refrained from pointing out the current situation in the competition to Blake. First, Bingley would have to lose his own—and the final—game and second, Darcy must place last for Blake to have the slimmest chance. Blake finally lifted his head, shrugged his shoulders, and joined the others in conversation. He laughed, although subdued, at Rawlings' witty descriptions of the rams from his particular spot on the ground.

The men, slumped in their chairs with their limp arms fallen at their sides and their legs outstretched, enjoyed the camaraderie until Whitson entered the library and addressed Bingley, who, without delay, bolted to the door. "Please excuse me. It appears my family arrived a week early."

Bingley stood on the steps when the unexpected carriage came to a stop and rushed to greet his sisters and brother-in-law in his customary heartfelt manner. He had worried Caroline would be difficult after the journey; but she showed an exuberance he had never witnessed.

"Charles, I was so anxious to come. Why did you ask that I not arrive earlier to be your hostess?"

"Caroline, I recall you said you would not set one foot in Hertfordshire while those silly games were being played." Bingley ignored her sneer. "Louisa, Jonathan, I hope your trip was comfortable."

"You could have invited me to participate," his brother in law grumbled. "I enjoy playing games myself. We read the articles describing the contest in the papers. Although I admit, I would never grab any animal's tail, let alone a ram."

"How did you hear about Darcy's game? We played this morning."

"There were many persons who witnessed the event. They talked about the event at the inn where we stopped to change the horses. What was Darcy thinking?"

"I was thinking about winning points, Hurst. Nevertheless, it was delightful to watch my friends and four spirited rams run away from each other in a small, confined space." Darcy appraised Bingley's stout brother-in-law. "I suspect you will want to take part in the Harvest Feast games; a modified Baker Rifle is the prize. I am aware of your attempts to attain one."

Hurst's head shot up. "Charles, must I win some silly competition to get my own rifle? Well, what contest do you plan? Does it require strenuous activity?"

"No. The contests are archery, darts, and target shooting. If you wish to compete, you will need to practice. Meryton's men are preparing for them."

"Darts? Archery?" I think not." Hurst snorted. "I shall be keen on observing the riff-raff, though. It should be amusing to discover if they can hit the target and not each other.

"You may be surprised at the local mens' skills." Bingley bowed his head.

"Mr. Darcy." Caroline presented him with her often-practiced smile. "I am sorry to have not witnessed your game."

Darcy tipped his head, but kept his eyes directed at the Hursts while Caroline stared at his cravat for a moment longer than he thought proper.

"The newspapers described the informal manner in which you dressed for their games. Scandalous. I am displeased to have missed it." Caroline glared at his neck and then allowed her gaze to slide down his body in a slow meandering manner.

"I am sorry for any loss of entertainment, Miss Bingley." Darcy turned sideways to suggest they go inside. He anticipated this one particular new guest would create obstacles to his daily routine. He fell behind the group as Bingley led his relatives into the house, introduced his butler and several other members of the staff. The new arrivals ascended the stairs to the family quarters for a short rest after their journey.

Darcy spoke to Bingley about certain arrangements necessary to accommodate the two women, and then suggested the difficulties keeping Hurst unaware of the business venture. The decorated ballroom would remain intact and serve as a place to meet without the ladies present much like Brook's club in London provided a masculine-only haven.

Bingley ordered Whitson to ensure the tavern was guarded and the doors kept closed to his sisters. He and Darcy hurried to the library where the other three friends were waiting, deep in conversation.

Rawlings poked Blake with his elbow. "Have you met Miss Bingley?"

"I have not." Blake turned to Kent. "You have known Bingley the longest."

"She was a young girl the last time I saw her. She was like Bingley, except she did not possess his hideous grin. Even then, she cultivated a refined appearance, including the London tight lip smile. Unlike Bingley, she enjoyed reading. However, she does share his ability to tell the most entertaining stories. She was her father's favorite."

"And, does she possess a large—

Before Blake could finish his question, Bingley entered the room followed by Darcy. "My family has retired to their rooms to refresh themselves after the journey, but they will join us for dinner. I hope you find my sister to your liking. She is witty, pretty, and owns a fortune of twenty thousand pounds. Of course, I am always trying to marry her off. She is anxious to meet my friends."

Out of the corner of his eye, Rawlings glimpsed Kent chuckling and Blake calculating while Darcy cringed.

***

With Caroline and the Hursts added, dinner was polite above what had been. The men avoided any mention of the alliance in Hurst's presence. He would never sully his hands by becoming intimately involved in trade. His opinion that marriage to one so richly connected to a tradesman is the acceptable exception was evidenced by his wife, Louisa—the eldest daughter of one such family. He maintained the appearance of a gentleman if no other means by the clothes he wore, the social manners he used, and his possessing a townhome located in London's better section.

Caroline chose the seat next to Darcy rather than taking the customary position at the opposite end. Louisa sat beside her while her husband, Hurst, chose the seat at the other end where he entertained Kent and Rawlings with stories from London.

While the servants served the dinner, Caroline appraised the quality of the service, the taste of the food, and the table decorations. The unhidden scorn in her voice exposed her true opinion—the servants had not performed to her liking. Changes were coming for the staff.

The main topic during the first course centered on the games and continued until the servants served dessert.

Caroline glanced at her brother. "Charles, many people declared what an exciting amusement the contests have become to everyone in town. Why, my friends talk of nothing else and of no gentleman more so than yourself."

"I am seriously displeased our activities are discussed in London and written up in the newspapers. How did this come about?"

"Well." Caroline grabbed her wine glass, and then took a long drawn out sip.

Bingley tapped his fingers. All conversation at the table ceased.

"Several days ago, I attended Almack's with a friend. I suppose it was my remark to her brother that started the frenzy. He asked about you and wondered where you and Mr. Darcy were hiding. I told him the truth."

"Which was?"

"You and Mr. Darcy squirreled yourselves away in some backwater place playing silly games to win a horse. He asked about others in attendance, and I did reveal that Lord Blake, Mr. Rawlings, and Mr. Kent were here as well." Caroline lips formed a dramatic pout at her brother's frown. "Charles, you did tell me everything in your letter. You did not mention it was a secret."

"Go on."

"It did not take long for Mr. Johnson from the Four Horse Club to join us. He knows you very well, Mr. Rawlings.

Rawlings scoffed. "You told him? Sorry, Bingley. The man is such a rattle. I am positive the entire London society was informed before the sun rose the next morning."

Caroline pointed her head at Louisa's husband. "And he is also responsible for the rumors. He mentioned it at his club and even provided specific details. He had many visitors interested in learning more. Louisa, is that correct?"

Louisa paled. She did not answer; she peeked at her husband.

"Caroline speaks the truth," Hurst said, without an unapologetical tone. "I can no longer visit my club without being accosted for information. The London papers and all the clubs are paying a handsome sum to express messengers to bring the news of the games and the results. The betting on the stallion has become more frenzied with each contest, and I suspect the final competition will be the most heavily wagered."

"Caroline, what else?" Bingley asked.

"I know that night at Almack's I was surrounded by attendees wanting more information. I believe the *Ton* became infatuated with the event. I could not turn away the many ladies calling upon me at the townhouse for a tidbit or two to help them place their wagers. They were frantic."

Bingley shrugged. "There is nothing to be done about it. I suppose you were not at fault, Caroline. But in the letter, I did ask you to not share the information." He glanced around the table. "I am surprised at the interest. My intention was not to create such a reaction. I only attempted to be hospitable to my friends."

"And hospitable you are, Bingley." Rawlings lifted his glass. All the others followed suit as he toasted the host.

Darcy settled back in his chair, pleased. The favorable effect of the games concealed the real reason for their trip. The business interests of the men were well protected and remained unknown to the London crowd.

"My dear brother, when will the final game be made known?" Caroline used her napkin to dab her mouth, content he would not upbraid her any further. Free to flirt with Mr. Darcy, she blinked her eyes at him as she sipped her wine.

"Tomorrow I will announce the game. At breakfast, sunrise, in fact."

***

The competitors filled the dining room just as the curve of the rising sun appeared on the horizon. The full moon remained in view, not yet losing its prominence to sunlight. Bingley's daybreak start succeeded in avoiding interference by his family—and in particular his meddlesome sister—as he expected it would. Caroline never left her bedchambers before ten.

With great anticipation, Bingley studied the faces of his friends. "Gentlemen, welcome to the honorable *Company of Netherfield Park Golfers.*"

"We are to play golf, Bingley?" Blake asked, his enthusiasm lacking.

"I admit I heard much about the game but have never seen an actual competition," Rawlings said.

"Nor I. I did hear it is played at the Royal Blackheath club."

Darcy nodded in agreement. "Yes, Kent. Even I tried playing the game at the club, although I was a young lad at the time."

"Is there anything you cannot do, Darcy?" Blake asked.

"Beat you at chess!"

Bingley tapped his glass with his spoon. "Today we will not play the game, but spend our time practicing." His friend's curious expressions turned to surprised reactions.

Rawlings scoffed. "We do not need practice, Bingley. To hit a ball cannot possibly be that hard."

"You will be surprised at the difficulty and thank me before you attempt the game."

"Surely you jest," Kent said. "Why, I play cricket. You must hit a ball with a stick in that sport too."

"You shall discover the truth of what I say."

Bingley handed out the rules for tomorrow's game and the map making up the golf course. He explained whoever finished with the least number of strokes would win and thereby gain five points toward the competition for the stallion. The men, anxious to begin, asked many questions and then departed for the practice field.

They had scarcely begun when a dusty trail heralded the arrival of a fast moving gig, containing a much-tussled Miss Bingley, grabbing her hat and carriage. The servant pushed the horses forward by snapping the reins with her every scream to hurry.

"I did so long to witness the practice," Caroline said when Bingley assisted her from the gig. She smoothed her dress, patted her hair, and waited for her brother to speak.

The four other men stood with their mouths agape.

"I apologize for missing breakfast this morning." Caroline directed her attention on Darcy and away from her brother's scowling face. "I played before, and rather well, too. I shall be pleased to provide assistance to anyone."

Bingley eyes widen; stunned into silence. His mouth twisted downwards to make a frown. He found his voice, but mumbled to

Caroline, "You hit the ball one time and ran away crying when it did not go more than ten yards."

Rawlings, startled by the reaction, studied Caroline who possessed the habit of lifting her chin, throwing her shoulders back, and walking with that unmistakable London air whenever her brother scolded her. "An excellent jaunt, Miss Bingley. Perhaps I should recommend you to the Four Horse Club. Not many ladies are willing to become altogether disheveled for the mere thrill of a fast ride." When she narrowed her cold stare, Rawlings added, "Do you normally go riding with such reckless abandon? I would be honored to race you."

Bingley, regaining his composure, pointed to the trunks brought by his servants. The four men all gathered around, leaning forward to get a better look. Caroline wheedled her way next to Darcy in a pretense to peek at the contents.

Many bizarre looking items lay inside. Bingley explained their different usage while a servant started handing out the objects.

"Why, golf must be easy with sticks having such big ends." Blake said.

Caroline plowed her way to the trunk, picked up several clubs, offering them to Darcy. "These are yours. They are designed for taller men."

"I am tall, too, Miss Bingley." Rawlings snickered at her when she turned around. "Are there others like those for me? Or is Mr. Darcy the only fortunate one today?"

"Caroline!" Bingley sputtered. "Without regard to a player's height, the clubs are the same length. If you wish to be helpful, perhaps you would hand out the golf balls. Each man gets ten."

Caroline huffed, but did as he asked.

Bingley turned back to the men. "Try not to lose any balls during practice. A few local young lads will chase them down for you; but be careful with your shots as no more are available."

"I am positive someone else is eager to make a dash for someone's." Rawlings held out a golf ball. "Miss Bingley, pray tell me, of what are they made?"

Caroline hesitated. Bingley answered. "Leather stuffed with feathers. If tomorrow is sunny and the ground is dry, a ball will fly 180 yards or 150 if it is a wet day. Of course, first you must hit the ball."

"Miss Bingley, I find I need a little assistance with understanding this game. Do we use two balls for each hole? I see five holes on the map." Rawlings pointed to the map Bingley had drawn showing the course of play. "And I cannot imagine how many strokes are needed?

Have you perfected the hit to get the ball to fall in the hole with one try, Miss Bingley?"

Bingley eyed Rawlings with an admonishment type glare. "I am the best to answer, Mr. Rawlings. I am the one who designed this course. Please direct your questions to me."

Rawlings bowed. "I beg your pardon, Miss Bingley; I assumed all golf courses were the same."

As her face colored, she glowered at him. He sent her a quick unrepentant smile. She glared at him even harder than before. Rawlings chuckled, shrugged, and practiced swinging his club.

Bingley showed the proper way to hold the club and how to stand with their feet placed back from the ball. He soon motioned for them to move to the spot designated at the end of the open meadow. Once they mastered making contact with the ball, the men discovered it did fly long distances. Bingley had a separate area set aside for putting which they would use in the afternoon.

Caroline kept her eyes upon the men. She walked behind them, and, more than once, Rawlings caught her eyeing the men's backsides. When she drew near to him, he wiggled his hips, and then, with abruptness, twisted around to face her asking, "Am I standing correctly?

She lowered her eyes, and nodded in the affirmative as she left to instruct a servant to have a picnic lunch prepared. Mr. Rawlings leaned on his club watching her every move. Caroline called the footman back and whispered another task before sending him on his way again. She squared her shoulders, lifted her chin high, and returned his sneer with one likewise insufferable.

He did not cower from her; he laughed aloud.

The Hursts arrived after the servant left, but before the picnic began. Bingley, noticing his brother-in-law's interest, offered Hurst the opportunity to practice, and handed over his own equipment.

The two sisters found a useful occupation by handing the men different clubs when so requested. Caroline signaled to Louisa to help Mr. Rawlings, and was thus able to avoid any more contact with him.

"Will all Meryton's residents be attending your Harvest Feast?" Rawlings asked Bingley, glancing sideways at Caroline.

"What?" Caroline shrieked

"Damn!" Kent's club missed the ball.

Darcy had not taken his shot, but it was not a moment later before he also muttered under his breath, "Blast," as his attempt veered to the left with her second screech.

"When?" Caroline asked.

"The date is set for the twenty-fifth of November." Bingley answered his sister without as much as a blink.

"That is ten days away!"

Rawlings leaned on his club, following Caroline with his eyes as she moved closer to her brother. Her delicate hands furled and unfurled as she spoke. Rawlings feared for Bingley's safety, although he appeared indifferent to her pleas, grinning with every word hurled his way.

"What, pray tell, is a Harvest Feast?" She asked in a tone no one mistook for sweetness.

"We will hold a fair with a big feast for the Netherfield Park tenants and many citizens of Meryton. Following the feast, I arranged for a fireworks display. Managing such an affair would not prove too difficult for you, Caroline. You possess magnificent talents running these affairs."

"Me?"

Louisa touched her arm, and glanced over to Mr. Darcy, who was leaning on his club with his eyes focused on her.

"Why yes, Charles. I thank you for the compliment. I am sure we can host a wonderful harvest fair and feast. I do so love to entertain," Caroline said, the words sounding sugary sweet even to her own ears.

When the servants arrived with the meal, Caroline and Louisa excused themselves to attend to the preparations. The men relaxed once the ladies had left. The men uttered many oaths rarely heard spoken by the servants, but then again the sound of their chuckles in response was equally unprecedented.

"Damn."

"Damn ball. Bloody club."

"Blast."

"You are more than evil, Bingley," Rawlings said.

Bingley approached Rawlings, leaned in. He kept his voice low. "I may be evil, but I am not mean or cruel."

Rawlings bowed his head. "I shall endeavor to follow your lead."

Bingley slapped his back and moved to assist Kent.

"Why did the bloody ball veer to the left? It was just a straight shot. Why is this so blasted hard?" Kent sneered as he grabbed another ball.

A servant halted Bingley's progress to announce the picnic was ready. Although the men would have preferred light refreshments, they resigned themselves to a feast. Nonetheless, they were delighted with the food and the many bottles of wine.

The men took pleasure in the comfort provided when they slid down on the cool, silken blankets. The shade from several large oak trees beside a small pond and with the slight breeze flowing through the air cooled them after the hot sun had left its impact. Roast beef and fresh baked bread filled the air, and the opened wine bottles enticed their lips.

Rawlings chose to sit next to Miss Bingley as he directed a question to her brother. "Do you play this game often, Bingley?"

"I am a member of the Royal Blackheath. I participate in tournaments whenever I can, and I practice regularly while in London."

Rawlings nudged Caroline. "Are ladies allowed to join and play there as well?"

Bingley coughed several times until he gained Rawlings' attention. "No, the club limits membership to men. I understand ladies are learning the game, and do participate in games among themselves, but they are not admitted in the club. "

Miss Bingley handed a special basket to Rawlings and said in a syrupy sweet voice, "I had this meal made in particular for you, Mr. Rawlings."

Rawlings lifted the lid and then let out a loud laugh as he beheld a rather large piece of brawn. He leaned down to Caroline. "Touché, Miss Bingley. I bow to your ingenuity in retribution." He assumed she overheard him at dinner the previous evening when he announced how much he detested pork flesh and especially if soused into this pickled form. He took a gigantic bite. He leaned down and whispered, "I, too, claim inventiveness as one of my best assets. Although for me, the perfectly placed question is retribution enough." He chuckled at her gasp and her deepening blush.

"I cannot go long without playing golf," Bingley said. "You may regret learning the game. Your failure to succeed will make you daft. I assure you."

"So, that is where you disappear to so often?" Darcy asked.

"Yes, I confess. To where did you think I was escaping?"

"I did not know, but I assumed it was not a bookshop! You must believe, my friend, that I would have joined you had you divulged your secret passion."

"I was unsure whether you would think this was an acceptable pastime... You do prefer to read in your spare time," Bingley said

Rawlings dabbed his mouth with a napkin. "Ahem. Bingley, you did not mention all the festivities after the Harvest Feast. I am fascinated and wish to learn more."

"Oh, Caroline, as Mr. Rawlings has so kindly mentioned, we are to host a ball the day after the feast. We will need to invite all the best families."

"In eleven days? Here, in this place?"

Rawlings enjoyed the entertainment provided by the siblings as he nibbled on the brawn, washing it down with large swallows of wine.

"Yes, here," Bingley said in what he hoped was a stern voice.

Caroline leaned in close to her brother and whispered, "Charles, are you sincere about hosting a dance at Netherfield? I advise you, before you proceed, to consult the wishes of the present party." Caroline inclined her head towards Darcy and added, "I am much mistaken if there is not at least one among us to whom a ball would be rather a punishment than a pleasure."

"If you mean Darcy, he may go to bed before it begins, if he chooses, but as for the ball, it is quite a settled thing." Bingley glowered at Rawlings. "Caroline, I believe Mr. Rawlings has a request."

"I do?" Rawlings asked through clenched teeth. He caught on to Bingley's meaning and turned to Caroline. "If I might be so bold, I seek the pleasure of a dance at your ball. I would be honored if you accept."

"Thank you, Mr. Rawlings." Caroline answered, although her frown preceded her acceptance.

Bingley informed her that the housekeeper had begun the planning and was looking forward to it. And once given the word, she should send round the invitations as soon as practical.

"Oh, my dear sister, I want to give a special invitation to a certain family."

"Charles, is a young woman involved? Yes. I see it is true. I assume she is pretty," Caroline said.

"Ahem. I have decided to call on the Bennets with a personal invitation and I would like to introduce you, Caroline." Bingley turned to Louisa. "And you, as well."

"Bennets? I have not heard of that family. Do they venture to London?"

"No, Caroline. I do not believe they go to town at all. Their estate is called Longbourn, three miles from here."

She did not smile, her shoulders drooped, and she did not hold her head so high. Her face held no emotions as she turned to listen to her brother.

"Longbourn?" Lord Blake asked, suddenly interested in the conversation. "Are you to visit? I will join you, Bingley."

"Yes, count me in as well," Rawlings said as he sipped his wine. "It would give me much pleasure to meet with Mr. Bennet's young daughters. They are such remarkable ladies."

"Young ladies? Dare I ask how many there are?" Caroline asked.

"Five," Bingley said.

"Are they all out?"

"Yes, and all are quite pretty," Kent said.

"The eldest is the most handsome, is that not correct, Bingley?"

"It is not just my opinion, Rawlings. We previously established Miss Jane Bennet is the loveliest of the ladies." Bingley insisted.

Caroline noted the name and her brother's reaction. However, her brows rose when Mr. Kent stared at Darcy and said, "I daresay, she is not the one with the fine eyes! Do you not agree?"

Darcy response was limited to a deep sigh.

***

After the picnic, the men left to practice their putting on the other side of the meadow. Caroline and Louisa chose to stay by the pond, under the shadey trees. Unusual for November, the day had become somewhat warm, and the air was now still. The servants left the wine and fruit after clearing away the rest. Now with the men absent, Caroline sprawled upon the blanket with a glass in one hand and her head propped up by the other. Louisa filled their glasses.

"Louisa, look at what Charles has done now!"

"It cannot be helped. I understand our brother has already made the announcement about the Harvest Feast he is holding for his tenants and all the residents of this little parish."

"When did Jonathon hear about it?"

"Charles informed him during the gentlemen's brandy last night."

"No! So, how many families do you think he intends to invite?" Will he include all the riff raff too?"

Louisa shrugged. "I imagine the housekeeper will be the best one to answer that question."

"Did he learn anything else?"

As Louisa told her sister all she knew about the upcoming competitions and feast, Caroline's hands shook. "I may need smelling salts. Charles has so vexed me this time I do not know if I can survive."

"Be brave. I suspect we will be very busy. Nevertheless, you must be cautious, my dear sister. I noted Mr. Darcy's eyes when Charles spoke about your responsibilities."

"How could I not react? You should have warned me."

"I did not remember until we were surrounded by the others."

"Do you mean, Lord Blake?"

Louisa nodded. "Yes, he seemed rather attentive."

"He has twenty thousand reasons to be interested!"

They laughed. Their discussion moved on to the latest tittle-tattle about Blake's father. Both woman had previously spread a little bit of the gossip about the duke with their friends.

"Oh, Lord Blake is such a handsome man, almost as fine-looking as your particular interest!" Louisa said.

"And if the marquess was able to keep me in jewels and gowns without depleting my dowry, I may have been persuaded to change my attentions. Alas, the rumors are too widespread to be false."

"I suspect it is even worse."

"Oh. Louisa, what are we to do with Charles' latest infatuation?"

"Wait until he grows bored, I suppose. He always does."

"This is the first time I saw him blush when teased about a lady. He always laughed or disregarded my taunts."

Louisa refilled their glasses. "He was not the only one. Did you not see Mr. Darcy's reaction to Mr. Kent when he mentioned the fine eyes? I am positive Mr. Darcy was the target."

"What are we to make about that? And which lady owns them, I wonder?"

"I must say, there is a charming collection of fine eyes in Netherfield Park."

Caroline gulped her wine and held her glass out for more. "Very attractive looking men, too. Every single one of them."

"Yes, indeed there are. Of all the men, Lord Blake is as eye-catching as Mr. Darcy, although his coloring is fair. Mr. Kent has a way about him, although he thinks highly of his background in trade. He may be as wealthy as Mr. Darcy, but he would only be desirable if he owned an estate. I wish he was in a higher circle, alas, marriage to him would not elevate my status. Therefore, Mr. Darcy is the best of the men."

"Mr. Rawlings is the closest in appearance to Mr. Darcy; I just cannot stand the man."

"Be careful, Caroline. He seems to possess great sway with your Mr. Darcy."

"Perhaps. Nonetheless, I think our brother does have excellent taste in friends. Now which one has the best... "

All the servants fetching the balls could hear laughter as Caroline and Louisa tallied up the gentlemen's outstanding attributes.

Chapter Twenty-two

The golfers appeared at the Black Bull Tavern at eight in the morning to pay their shilling to the proprietor. Mr. Staunton had invited his regular patrons to witness the traditional payment made to the hosting establishment for the meal after the game. The men from Netherfield had bestowed this honor on him.

Shouts of encouragement rang throughout the building for each man, although Mr. Bingley received the loudest roar when he placed his coin on the bar. Instead of leaving straight away to the golf course, as tradition demanded, the men shared ale, toasted one another, and spoke to the attendees. The air sizzled with electricity with the fifth and final game deciding the winner of the stallion.

The men remained for a short period until the time came to begin the match. The servants had earlier brought the clubs and balls to the first tee. Spectators surrounded the entire first hole, having made their way to the course in the first morning light. Arguments arose over the most advantageous spot to stand.

The Bennets daughters had arrived at the course. The eldest two came to cheer on two of the men, whilst the younger girls came to flirt with the militia scattered amongst the crowd made up of shopkeepers, tenants, and gentry.

Bingley's footmen had pushed the mob back, waving pitchforks to discourage them from stepping on the playing field.

"Hey, we are not greased up rams, fella," one member of the crowd yelled out. The others laughed and snorted, and some even placed one index finger on each side of their head and grunted. The footman just pointed the pitchfork at them shouting, "Back off, you simpletons."

The spectators quieted; not for fear over the pitchforks, but because Bingley waved his hands with open palms downward at the crowd. He turned and shrugged his shoulders at his friends and indicated the time had arrived to determine the playing order.

Whitson held the straws as each man drew. Rawlings would tee off first, followed by Kent, Darcy, Bingley, and lastly, Blake. The throng cheered; they knew this signaled the beginning of the game.

Rawlings placed his ball on the designated spot identified as the tee. The other four men stepped back, giving him room for his swing. With his friends scrutinizing his every movement, he felt unsettled. He inhaled deeply and shook off the sensations of acute humiliation the way he would shake off unpleasant drops of rain. He studied the fairway, lined up, and swung his club in the long reaching motion he had been taught.

"That was interesting, Rawlings." Darcy pointed to the ball, which had not left the tee. The crowd snickered. Bingley held his hands up again to admonish them.

"Wait until you must perform in front of these strangers, Darcy." Rawlings glared at him before turning his hard, cold eyes to Bingley. "You said I would not sense the crowd. You are wrong. They are looming large in my line of sight. I fear I will hear their laughter in my sleep."

By the fourth shot, Rawlings's club connected, causing the stubborn ball to fly at least one hundred eighty yards, much to everyone's surprise.

"We are fortunate you did not hit so well on the first try, old man," Kent said as he approached the tee.

The spectators hushed as Kent swung his club.

Whosh.

Cheers sprinkled throughout the crowd as their eyes followed the flight of the ball, which fell short of Rawlings' shot.

"Good shot." Darcy wasted no time teeing up. He shook his head as his stroke landed close to, but behind, Kent's ball.

"Excellent." Bingley approached the tee, his walk casual. After preparing for his turn, he bowed, rewarding the cheering crowd. He lined his club up and swung. His shot sailed the farthest, although not as far as he had wished.

Lord Blake stepped up to the tee, amidst the townspeople's scattered cheers. He stood, hands on his hips, and peered down the fairway with a furrowed brow and glower sufficient to quiet the crowd until he twisted around and faced the other competitors. He flashed a smile his friends would later describe as wicked. He grabbed the club from the servant and swung away.

"Ohhhhh," the crowd cried out in unison.

Blake chuckled when his ball traveled over two hundred yards, well beyond Bingley's attempt. He spun around to take in his friends' stunned expressions. He winked. "Do not look so shocked. I am an avid player. I played golf since I was ten and, of late, visit St. Andrews every year."

Bingley shook his head. "I suppose my advantage in this game has been thrown to the wind."

"That, my friend, depends upon your skills as a player." Blake patted Bingley on the back. "May the best golfer win? My victory may still be in jeopardy."

Bingley sighed. He knew the other men were counting on him to win in order to keep Blake from collecting his thirty percent profit and leadership of the alliance. He had not anticipated any friend to be an experienced golfer.

"Shall we all advance?" Rawlings said. "I believe it is your shot, Darcy. Your ball is the furthest away from the hole.

As they walked ahead, the judges followed, chuckling at the unexpected turn of events.

Each man's next attempt arrived near the area surrounding the hole. Bingley reminded his friends to use the correct club.

"Putting separates the novice from the champions." Bingley crossed his arms.

Bingley and Blake sized each other up. Neither man had any problem as they sank their long putts in one shot. Today, two excellent players would entertain the crowd.

Even though the shots landed closer to the hole than Blake and Bingley's had, Rawlings and Kent had to putt three times before sinking their shots.

Mr. Darcy cursed, albeit beyond the spectator's hearing range, until his fourth try slipped into the opening. "Blast!" he yelled and then turned to glare at Bingley whose eyebrows had shot up. "You had better win. This is your game. It is your turn to win the five points." Still scowling, Darcy walked to his assigned servant-caddie and handed him the putter.

Rawlings approached his discouraged friend. "I may never overcome those three missed shots off the tee."

"And I may never learn to putt." Darcy shrugged. "If Bingley does not win, we are in trouble. I will do my best not to come in last. Blake kept his secret yesterday.?"

"I was surprised, since he missed as many shots as we did at practice. Well now, if you wish to be philosophical, Bingley must be feeling a wee bit of the shock I felt when he nearly beat me at my race."

"Ah. I shall hope the same result applies here. As long as Bingley wins this game, I am in the running for the horse. If Blake defeats him,

I fear my putting will sink my hopes unless I can bribe you into losing." Darcy was half-laughing at his own jest.

"Fear not, sirs." Mr. Bennet joined them. "By my calculations, a three -way tie for the stallion is possible. Of course, for such a situation, I am sorry to say..." He pointed his head at Darcy. "You sir, would finish in last place." He left to rejoin the other judges, but turned back and yelled, "Remember all hope is not lost. Many possibilities exist."

The crowd's murmuring indicated they too were calculating every way their chosen man would win. Nevertheless, once the players had begun to walk towards the next hole, the spectators took off in a run. Some went to the tee area, others to the putting hole. The rest just filled in the fairway.

As soon as the competitors reached the second tee, Sir William announced, "The number of strokes after the first hole are as follows: Lord Blake and Mr. Bingley each have three; Mr. Kent has five; Mr. Darcy has seven, and Mr. Rawlings finished with eight."

This hole proved more difficult for the novices. While Blake and Bingley took the same number of shots, no more strokes than the minimum expected for a long hole, the other men discovered why practice is critical to success.

Mr. Darcy's first shot fell into a deep rut beside the fairway. Rawlings' attempt to reach the putting green failed when his ball sliced right into the trees. Kent's ball dropped well short of its intended destination. While the men struggled, Blake and Bingley leaned on their clubs; smiling at their own memories. They had faced the same dilemmas many times before: ruts, trees, and lost balls.

Kent was able to finish the hole with six strokes. He handed his putter to his servant-caddie. "Blake, I am surprised to see you so adept at the game."

"No more than I," Bingley chuckled. "I never thought to discover if any of my friends had played before. I assumed they did not. Where do you play, Lord Blake?"

"At my father's estate."

"Excuse me. Do you play golf at your home?" an astonished Kent asked.

"Yes. I do truly enjoy the game as does my father and two uncles. We had one section set aside for the game after playing St. Andrews course years ago; although our area is limited to eight holes."

"Is the course difficult?" Bingley asked.

"Dreadfully so," Blake answered. "You are most welcome to come and visit. You play with brilliance. In some ways, golf is similar to billiards. You excel at that game too, which explains your ability to putt successfully. Finding the hole or the pocket requires knowledge of angles." Hearing Kent cough, Blake turned around. "Oh, excuse me, Kent. You are invited, as well. I did not mean to leave you out. The course is excellent to learn on, although it may take many rounds to do well."

They watched Darcy and Rawlings finish the second hole. Mr. Rawlings was pleased to tie with Mr. Darcy. His eight strokes closed the gap for fourth place since Darcy ended with nine.

Sir William shouted the scores: "Lord Blake and Mr. Bingley are tied with seven strokes after two holes; Mr. Kent is next with thirteen; Mr. Darcy and Mr. Rawlings have a total of sixteen."

Frustrated, Darcy whispered to Bingley, "Hebrews 10:30. Vengeance is mine says the Lord. Vengeance is mine. Pemberley awaits you, my former friend. I shall serve mutton every night."

Bingley exaggerated a shudder.

While their audience hastened to the next hole, the five competitors discussed their play so far. The townspeople argued amongst themselves, and bets between the men were flying furiously. This time, no one wagered on who would come in second; they bet on first place. Even the judges joined in, although no money was involved in the wager, only bragging rights of superiority. Sir William and Mr. Long both chose Mr. Bingley. Mr. Bennet and Mr. Goulding preferred Lord Blake. Mr. Phillips surprised them all and favored them both. He believed it would remain a tie. As they walked to the next hole, the judges discussed a resolution for any tie that might result.

The third hole resulted in the most excitement. Blake and Bingley did not end with the same number of strokes. Blake's first putt missed and Bingley found himself in the lead. Kent remained in third place, Rawlings moved into fourth, leaving Darcy to face his worse fears. Three strokes separated the three after Darcy sliced the ball into the trees with his shot off the tee. Since it was not found within the five minute timeframe allowed under the rules, he was penalized a stroke in addition to the penalty for having to use another ball. Darcy glared at the townspeople mulling around the area, diverting their gazes and turning away from him.

With two more holes remaining, the crowd grew restless. Those who had not bet on Blake or Bingley became rowdy. They shouted encouraging words as the men trudged to the fourth hole. Concerned, Bingley tried his best to quiet them, and in desperation, he asked his footmen to stay alert. The crowed size had swelled with each hole, causing pushing and shoving everywhere. Angry voices crying out for the men losing rose above the laughter of those who were more apt to win.

Bingley wondered if anyone remained in Meryton or if at least one man stayed to drink and wait comfortably at the Black Bull.

Mr. Roger Staunton stood alone at his tavern. With the bar set up, the tables ready to go, and extra chairs placed everywhere, he waited by the entrance. He noticed the quietness. Everywhere closed signs appeared—every door but his. Families living outside of Meryton sent at least one representative. There were no rooms available in the inns. The gentry and townspeople alike filled any extra living space with friends and acquaintances. And with an extra day between game, the number of visitors increased.

Staunton stood by the tavern door keeping an eye out for anyone to return with news from the game. A large carriage arrived in town and stopped at his establishment.

"Kind sir, can you tell us—"

"Two miles down that road." Staunton was growing tired of dandies arriving from London. He had counted five carriages and even more men on horseback.

A minute later, one fortyish gentleman arrived in town on a spirited spotted brown and white mare and dismounted at the Black Bull. He walked toward Roger Staunton.

"Is everyone at Netherfield Park? The town seems a bit deserted."

"Yes, they have been there hours before the game began. If you are interested in the outcome, you had best hurry. I have heard they just finished the third hole. It will not take much longer now."

"I would prefer to wait here. Is your establishment open?"

Staunton held the door for the man. The stranger had the walk of a man who had seen much of the world; he seemed confident, yet relaxed. He grew cautious as the gentleman surveyed the empty room in the tavern, but once he settled on a bar stool, Mr. Staunton poured him a drink and they spoke about the game. The man just nodded and a twinkle in his eye flashed at the mention of the five men at Netherfield Park. Almost all his questions pertained to Mr. Darcy. Staunton fidgeted with the glasses, answering what he could without revealing anything important.

"I suggest you best find a seat closer to the action." Staunton pointed to the table nearest to the one reserved for the Netherfield party. "The competitors will be sitting there when the game is over."

"Thank you, no. I prefer to watch from back here."

Staunton said nothing. He wiped the bar several times more, cleaned the glasses twice, and kept the man within his line of sight. He refilled his glass.

"Are you here for the games?"

"No, I am here on business."

"With the gentlemen playing golf?" Staunton asked, hopeful to gain some information.

The stranger paused before saying, "No, not with them. I read about the games in the papers, which mentioned the men were involved in a competition for a horse."

"London papers?"

"Yes. It is all the talk in town. Many wagers have been made," the stranger said as he sipped his drink. "The stories were replete with Mr. Kent's tavern games, Mr. Rawlings' chariot race, and most humorous retelling of Mr. Darcy's Tup running. Lord Blake's game had been finished by the time anyone got wind of the competition."

"Which gentleman is most favored in London?"

"It is tied between Lord Blake and Mr. Darcy."

"Lord Blake and Mr. Rawlings are tied here. The book is open. Would you care to place a wager?" Staunton asked as he reached for the betting book.

"No."

He closed the book just as a swarm of men entered the tavern. "Finished? They are finished?" Staunton asked.

One of his regular patrons shouted, "No, we were commanded to leave once the men reached the final hole. Blast. It was exciting; I had no wish to go."

Another patron interrupted. "Mr. Bingley did not want the men distracted by some folks talking too loud and cheering excessively. He said that was not allowed."

"You'd best be prepared, Staunton. The lot of them onlookers will be here soon. There will not be a drink left before this night is through. Is the book open? I want to wager on Lord Blake. I believe he will come in second and lose the horse. Everyone will want to bet on this one."

There had been many bets made for the golf game, but the amount was insignificant compared to the wagering on the victor for the stallion. Not even the gambling fever raging in London could compare to the zeal which had overtaken Mr. Staunton's little establishment, although the size of the wagers were dramatically different.

Lord Blake was favored to win not only the golf match but the horse. Mr. Rawlings was second, and Kent was third. Since many people did not like Mr. Darcy, he was last in the betting pool. Bingley was the most admired by everyone, but anyone with a bit of sense understood that after the last game, Bingley could not win without all the competitors succumbing to a fatal accident of sorts.

The Black Bull filled quickly. Staunton spent his time filling drinks and recording bets since all his workers attended the game. He was relieved when they arrived to handle the bulging crowd.

"Our Mr. Bingley hit the ball in the rut. Lord Blake kept chuckling as they walked down the fairway. You could tell Mr. Bingley was none too happy. He did well though. The Lord beat him by the one stroke so now they are tied for the last hole."

"Well, how about Mr. Darcy?" the stranger asked. The regular patrons viewed the man with puzzled faces. Staunton nodded for them to continue.

"He is in a mess of trouble. I do not see how he can even finish fourth now."

"He does fine going down the fairway until it comes time to hit the ball in the hole. He cannot get it done."

"He will come in last for sure. He was down ten strokes from Mr. Rawlings. He cannot make that up on the last hole."

"Does that mean there may be a four-way tie?"

"Yes, sir, it does. That is why everyone is testy. No one bet on Mr. Darcy anyway, well, no one important that is." The patron said as he glimpsed at the pocket on the man standing next to him.

"If Mr. Bingley wins the match, Mr. Darcy would be tied for the stallion with Lord Blake. I stand by my wager until the final hole is played."

"Have a drink, boys. We will soon know who won, or if they all tied," Mr. Staunton said.

As they waited, everyone could feel the excitement at The Black Bull. The crowd lingered impatiently as the men finished the game. When they believed enough time passed for the round to end, the talk grew louder, and the men became rowdy. They expected the gentlemen from Netherfield Park any minute. Soon, everyone would know who the golf victor was, and which man would be the proud owner of Heracles. Even more important to the patrons, they would know which of their friends would collect their winning bets.

At last, as the door opened, the gentlemen entered followed by a few London friends. Mr. Staunton noted that the stranger remained in the back and appeared to slink down in his seat. *He does not wish these men to see him*, he thought.

The assembly of men at the Black Bull could not discern from the faces or actions which gentleman had won. When asked about the game, they refused to respond until the five judges arrived.

Finally, they entered and the entire room hushed.

Sir William surveyed the now hushed crowd. "Ah, it is so good to see all my fine friends and neighbors. I suppose you would like to hear the results?"

"Yes, speak up man! Tell us who won the stallion."

"Not I. We will let Mr. Bingley share the story while eating dinner."

It did not take long before the conversations commenced. The patrons queried Mr. Staunton if they could continue to wager. When he shook his head, they bought drinks, and thus, the drinking added to the merriment of the crowd. They did not calm down again until all the competitors sat down for dinner and someone shouted—

"Tell us, Mr. Bingley, tell us how it went."

Bingley toasted the competitors. All four friends nodded their heads in acknowledgement.

"All in all, my good friends' attempts were impressive. My first time exceeded fifty points for the initial five holes. I had been fortunate that my father was a very patient man." Bingley remembered the day his papa had introduced the game to a gangly thirteen-year-old. He loved golf because it was the last activity they did together.

"Please, Mr. Bingley, who won?"

"On the fifth hole, all my friends had a chance to win, perhaps not the most points for the golf game, but for the overall win. Mr. Darcy has discovered why short putts are not easy. Nonetheless, I believe he enjoyed the game." Bingley looked to his friend.

"It is not a game, Bingley. It is a torture." Rawlings shouted out. Everyone laughed, including Darcy.

"Please continue, Mr. Bingley," someone shouted.

"The fifth hole was five hundred yards long. I hit first off the tee. My ball flew straight, and I knew I needed to repeat it to be on the green. This was a long hole, so I surmised it would take four strokes." All the men followed the story. They had spent two days learning the rules and understanding how to play.

"The other men's shots were not as straight as mine. Now, Mr. Rawlings, landed on the green in two shots. His chances of winning were now exceedingly slim. Nevertheless, he did a remarkable job for his first effort."

Rawlings nodded then lifted his glass at the compliment.

"Mr. Kent's ball ended up in a deep ditch. I can attest it takes three whacks sometimes to get your ball back on the course. That was not his fate—it took him four strokes."

"What happened to Lord Blake."

"We both reached the putting area in just two strokes with very long shots. Many golfers will tell you the game is won or lost with the putts."

Bingley canvassed the room, and realized every single man was leaning forward with their focus fixed on him. No one moved; the time had come to reveal the winner.

"Mr. Darcy arrived on the green, and he did admirably to finish the course with thirty five strokes even though that meant he came in last. Mr. Rawlings ended the game in fourth place, and Mr. Kent finished third."

"Bingley, do not be such a rump-fed dewberry. We played horribly. Just say it!" Rawlings said. Everyone laughed.

Bingley, ignoring his friend's interruption, waited for the crowd to quiet.

"First place was undecided and would go to whichever one of us, Blake or me, who got their ball into the hole first. Lord Blake putted within two inches. I was not so successful, but I was close, perhaps five inches away. I went first. I smacked it with a firm stroke, which rolled towards the hole and ..." the patrons leaned forward as Mr. Bingley completed his sentence—

"Straight out again. Missed. Now, Lord Blake understood if he sunk his next putt, he would win the game. The pressure was on him. He cleaned away some debris between the ball and the hole. He squatted down to study the pathway until he was ready to take his shot."

"Do not keep it too yourself, man. Tell us what happened."

"He made the putt. Lord Blake won the game."

A few men cheered.

"And the stallion? Did he win the Andalusian?"

"No. Mr. Darcy, Mr. Kent, and Lord Blake are tied. Is that not right, Mr. Bingley?" another patron shouted.

"Yes, they ended the five games with sixteen points. There is a tie. Mr. Rawlings finished with fifteen points, and I have twelve points. Other than my score, you can see how close the competition turned out to be."

"What happens now? Who will get the stallion?"

"The judges will choose a game for the three men. They will play the game at my Harvest Feast. The Andalusian will be available for anyone desiring a look. The judges promise it will end with a clear winner."

All the men murmured amongst themselves. No one had given much credit to Mr. Kent and none to Mr. Darcy. Now they would have to consider their apparent skill at many things in determining who to bet on for the final contest. Lord Blake was still preferred, except now with the final wagers on the line, no one overlooked Mr. Kent. The prejudice against Mr. Darcy remained.

"Lest you think hitting a golf ball is easy, I invite the good citizens of Meryton to come to Netherfield Park to try the game at the Harvest Feast. You will learn that Mr. Darcy spoke the truth."

The tavern crowd cheered. They did not want to miss the opportunity to play golf, and besides, there was a competition of their own to win.

Bingley returned to his seat but before he could take a bite, Staunton approached him. Bingley turned to Darcy and whispered to him who in turn shook his head, shrugged, and quietly asked the others. All five friends stood man and searched the crowd. Each man shook his head, except Darcy who had caught sight of a stranger snaking through the crowd and slithering out of the tavern.

The visiting Londoners planned to spread the stories about the contest in every parlor, ballroom, club, and assembly once they returned to town. They admitted how much they envied the five men at Netherfield Park, and warned Bingley that all of London would seek ways to be acquainted with the entertaining young man who hosted the event.

Dinner continued, and everyone listened to the stories about the missed hits, the balls that flew off to the right or left. The four gentlemen alleged Bingley had created ruts purposely just to make them use those blasted iron clubs. The men talked and laughed long into the night.

Tomorrow, they would rest.

Chapter Twenty-three

"Care to race? Darcy said while patting his horse, Bouchain.. The hairs on his neck bristled when Blake's frown turn into a forced smile. Nevertheless, he was determined to speak to him today.

Blake nodded, and then summoned the young stable hand to fetch Chesterfield.

The sun was just beginning its ascent when the two men left the stable and headed for the open meadow, not in a gallop but in a slow trot. They agreed upon the spot to begin the race, the moment when to start, and the number of coins to pay the winner. While they made their way to the field, Darcy did not miss Blake fidgeting in his saddle or that his eyes darted from the path and then on him. He wondered what caused him to be so edgy.

Darcy coughed to gain his attention. "Once Bingley announced golf, I accepted the probability I would place last."

Blake glanced at his friend. "I must tell you, I was surprised you did not do better. I believed you were my biggest challenge. Kent turned out to be a tough adversary as well. I had not given him a moment's thought."

"I focused all my attention on beating you. Still, Kent earned the privilege to compete in the tie-breaking game." Darcy chuckled. "He did manage to slip into the tie without our noticing. In fact, I thought you had won the horse when you sank your final putt. Did you?"

"No. You forget I can do calculations in my head." Blake paused. "I will never let the tradesman's son rule me."

"Of course, the matter of the thirty percent persists and I am not a tradesman."

Blake shrugged.

"Kent is a fierce competitor. Will you be willing to allow him to lead the alliance if you do not win?" Darcy asked.

"I agreed to the deal. Look, I do not wish to lead the group at all. If I win, I will insist you continue to lead. You are the one with the vision.

Kent, on the other hand, would relish it, I think. Will you be able to relinquish control to him? "

Darcy looked over the open field and the wooded area beyond. "I will find it hard, but I did agree. I, too, will abide by the results."

"As I explained many times, Darcy, Heracles will be mine! I shall not be denied so this conversation is moot."

The two men reached the spot for the start of their race. On the pre-arranged signal, they bolted straight across the meadow, towards the wooded area. Darcy had no difficulty arriving first.

"Enjoy your breakfast?"

Blake brushed the dirt from his jacket and wiped his face. "You shall discover what dust tastes like soon, my friend. I demand a sunrise race following the harvest feast."

"Agreed, but I shall hold you to it whether you win Heracles or not. I insist we race for double the wager. You will not beat even the young upstart entrepreneur as effortlessly as you proclaim, and I cannot envision you besting me."

Blake placed his hand upon his chest. "You wound me, for surely you jest. I shall be the one atop the Andalusian for our race. The coin is already heavy in my pocket."

The two continued to banter and discuss the judge's possible choices for the final games, while Blake's eyes drifted to the woods, and then suddenly he took in a deep breath. He steered Darcy towards Netherfield and returned the conversation back on the alliance.

"Why, Blake? I have yet to figure out why you demanded this. I refuse to accept the reasoning you proclaimed."

"Why not? I am critical, as you say, to the whole operation."

"Humph! I suspect there is more. If money is your need, I—"

"Do not presuppose the reason for my demands." Blake interrupted. "A loyal friend would take me at my word. Accept what I say and do not question my motives as if I was a man like Cuffage." Blake turned his horse around in an abrupt manner. He kicked his heels into Chesterfield's sides.

They did gallop, although this time they did not race. Blake did not look or speak to Darcy the entire way back to the stable.

***

With the addition of Caroline to Netherfield Park, the families of the surrounding area were now able to make their welcome calls. Ten o'clock, the time considered proper for calling, had come; and, to the Bingley sisters, all Meryton seemed to have turned up on their doorstep.

Men attended too, except they came to get a glimpse of Heracles. The ladies pretended they wished to meet the sisters and convey their best regards to Mr. Bingley's family and to express their appreciation for the exciting games. In actuality, they came under the guise of friendship for gaining a connection with Miss Bingley for their sons or any of the five single men residing at Netherfield for their daughters. A marriage alliance was on their agenda. Mrs. Bennet was the personification of this tactic.

Everyone was in the parlor when Whitson announce Mrs. Bennet, Miss Jane Bennet, and Miss Elizabeth. Darcy cringed, but maintained the mask of indifference he had learned at as a toddler. Introductions and the usual civilities occurred.

"You have a sweet room here, Mr. Bingley. I do not know a place in the country equal to Netherfield. You will not think of quitting it in a hurry, I hope, though you have but a short lease."

Mrs. Bennet sounded a little too sweet to Darcy's ears. He sent a quick glance to Miss Elizabeth, who was not embarrassed, but was nodding in agreement. Humph. He studied the three women. Jane did not resemble her mother at all. Elizabeth's figure was similar to her mother's, but it was her eyes that matched exactly. He wondered if Mrs. Bennet captured her husband with her own impertinent glances. He could not imagine any other reason Mr. Bennet married so decidedly beneath him. He moved backwards and left the others in control of the conversation.

"Whatever I do is done in a hurry," Bingley answered. "Therefore, if I should resolve to quit Netherfield, I should be off in five minutes."

"Yes, that does describe you, Mr. Bingley, always scurrying off on one path or another." Lord Blake smiled to Miss Elizabeth.

"At present, however, I consider myself as quite fixed here." Bingley glanced at Jane.

"Exactly what I should have supposed of you," Elizabeth said.

"You begin to comprehend me, do you?"

"Oh! Yes. I understand you perfectly."

Bingley turned to Jane, his hand placed over his heart. "I wish I might take this for a compliment, but to be so easily seen through, I am afraid, is pitiful." He hung his head.

"I am sure she means it as a compliment, sir." Jane said.

"I do. A deep, intricate character is no less estimable than such a one as yours," Elizabeth said.

Mrs. Bennet glowered at her second daughter. "Lizzy, remember where you are, and do not run on in the wild manner you are suffered to do at home."

"I did not know," Lord Blake said, "you were a studier of character, which must be amusing, but I would have imagined you more a studier of, umm, flowers."

Elizabeth arched her eyebrow. "Yes, but intricate characters are the most inconspicuous ones, similar to wildflowers."

Darcy was quick to notice the secret exchange between the two. He took a step closer to Elizabeth, his attention focusing on her brightened eyes and inhaling the lavender fragrance surrounding her. "The country can in general supply but few subjects for such a study. In a country neighborhood you move in a confined and unvarying society."

"But people themselves alter so much something new may be observed in them forever," Elizabeth responded.

"Unlike those people who deliberately offer a well tended appearance for all to see and admire, much as, say, a garden rose?" Blake imitated her teasing manner by tilting his head and raising his right brow. He moved to her other side drawing her attention away from Darcy.

"Yes, indeed, my lord," Mrs. Bennet said,. "I assure you there is quite as much of intricate characters in the country as in town."

Everybody was surprised, and Darcy, after looking at her for a moment, turned away wordlessly, and strode the window. He stood with his back to the room, biting his lip. He cared not that he appeared rude to the Bennets. He wished he could have watched the activities in the room through the reflection on the windowpane. Alas, it was not night so he must imagine the scene as he listened to every word.

Mrs. Bennet continued, "London does not have any great advantage over the country, for my part, except for the shops and public places. The country is a vast deal pleasanter, is it not?"

"And in town no secluded forest paths exist where you can enjoy nature's entertainment or even admire its decorations," Lord Blake said, bowing to Mrs. Bennet.

Darcy stiffened. Secluded forest paths? Is that what Blake was avoiding this morning? Was she there?

Bingley chuckled. "When I am in the country, I never wish to leave it; and when I am in town, it is the same. They have each their advantages, and I can be equally happy in either."

"Ay. You have the right disposition. But that gentleman," Mrs. Bennet said, looking at Darcy, "seemed to think the country was nothing at all."

"Indeed, Mama, you are mistaken," Elizabeth said. "You quite mistook Mr. Darcy. He only meant that there is not such a variety of people to be met with in the country as in town, which you must acknowledge to be true."

Darcy started, but felt an unexpected sense of pleasure at her defending him. His normal custom was not to react when any one came to his defense, especially not a lady. They had ulterior motives. He pondered her reply.

"Certainly, my dear, nobody said there were," Mrs. Bennet replied. "But as to not meeting with many people in this neighborhood, few are larger. I know we dine with four and twenty families."

Nothing but concern for Miss Bennet and Miss Elizabeth could enable the gentlemen to keep their countenance. Miss Bingley was less delicate, and directed her eyes towards Mr. Darcy and once she captured his attention, she rolled them without caring who witnessed it. He turned back to stare out the window.

"I am sure, madam," Mr. Rawlings said, "the families you dine with are all most unique and provide an interesting study for your daughter., Nevertheless, Mrs. Bennet, and unlike Mr. Darcy, I do not think the people in town are decidedly more intriguing. I find them to be too similar." He gazed at Miss Bingley. "In public they all think the same and act the same. I have discovered that many in Hertfordshire are, as Mr. Bingley would say, pleasanter people."

Darcy stopped himself from nodding. He kept his focus on the unchanging scene out the window. Yes, they are like twins, and if any person replaced someone, no one would know. Humph. But pleasanter people here? They just want something. Mrs. Bennet wants husbands for her daughters. Mr. Goulding wants to sell horses, Mr. Phillips wants the payments we give him, and Sir William wants to brag about our acquaintance. That is why they are more pleasant. They are but sycophants.

"Mr. Rawlings, would you not say Sir William is an agreeable man? So much the man of fashion! So genteel and so easy! He has always something to say to everybody. He possesses my idea of good breeding; and those persons who fancy themselves so important, and never open their mouths, quite mistake the matter."

Humph, Darcy thought. Sir William is a babbling bore.

When no one spoke, Mrs. Bennet continued. "The Lucases are a good sort of girls, I assure you. It is a pity they are not handsome! Not that I think Charlotte so very plain, but then she is our particular friend."

"She seems a pleasant young woman," Kent said.

"Oh! dear, yes, but you must own she is plain. Lady Lucas herself has often said so, and envied me Jane's beauty. I do not like to boast about my own child, but one does not often see anybody better looking. Everybody says so—do not trust my own partiality. When she was a mere fifteen years old, a gentleman was so much in love with her that we were sure he would make her an offer. However, he did not. Perhaps he thought her too young. Still, he wrote some verses on her, and pretty words they were."

"And so ended his affection," Elizabeth said, abruptly. "There has been many a one, I fancy, overcome in the same way. I wonder who first discovered the efficacy of poetry in driving away love!"

Darcy whirled around, tilted his head, and raised his brows. "I have been used to consider poetry as the food of love."

"Of a fine, stout, healthy love it may. Everything nourishes what is strong already. But if it be a slight, thin sort of inclination, I am convinced one good sonnet will starve it entirely away."

Darcy smiled, her reasoning surprised him; no one had concluded this before. He admired the light flickering in her eyes and in particular its vividness whenever she spoke of her beliefs. He could not discern if she said outlandish things merely to be entertained by the listener's reactions. His eyes fixed upon her face as he attempted to resolve the question. It was a pretty face and fine eyes. He returned to staring out the window, intrigued as she continued to defend her position..

Rawlings stepped closer to Elizabeth. "You believe a sonnet expressing great love will not open up a heart. Do you then think poetry of great humor may have worked on a fifteen year-old girl?"

"No, sir, not even that. If there is not the inclination in the beginning, I do not believe anything can result in the sort of affection desired by the gentleman. But I concede, an amusing poem will stand a better chance."

Rawlings raised his brows. "Since you believe it is possible for one to fall out of the beginning stages of love, might there be also the possibility for a volte-face? Cannot one start to fall in the other direction as well? Especially with one so young, whose heart cannot be so decided?"

"Of course, but that would take something other than a love sonnet when there is no inclination. Perhaps the best way to change one's heart is to show the steadfastness of his feelings."

"So flowers and other gifts would not work?" Rawlings eyed Blake.

"I believe the inclination still must be there as well." Elizabeth said.

"Even if the lady's purpose is to seek an improvement in her situation in life?" Darcy asked, turning his head. Defend this truth now, Miss Elizabeth..

"We were not speaking of deceit, Mr. Darcy, but of one's heart. A love sonnet, as with any form of attention, would work on any lady so mercenary." Elizabeth glanced at Caroline when she spoke the final words.

Fearing Caroline would target her sharp wit upon those he wished to remain steadfast in their opinion of him, Bingley forced his younger sister to be civil, and say what the occasion required. She performed her part but without much graciousness.

Mrs. Bennet soon afterwards ordered her carriage and she and her daughters then departed.

***

After morning calls were completed and all the visitors had left the parlor, Caroline hurried to discuss the Harvest Feast and ball with the housekeeper. Mrs. Nicholls proved her worth; only minutes had passed when Caroline discovered she had nothing she needed to do. She ventured to the garden where Mr. Kent came upon her sitting on a bench. While they had met years ago, neither one recalled much of the time spent together. At eight years old, she hated boys and she remembered saying he was her brother's most annoying friend.

"How is the planning for the Harvest Feast, Miss Bingley?"

"Quite well. The timing of my arrival was fortunate, for I do not think the locals would have been able to handle such an affair successfully."

"Oh. I had thought highly of Mrs. Nicholls. She seems to be a most proficient housekeeper. I would be surprised if you spoke ill of her to others. I heard Mr. Darcy compliment her several times."

Caroline started. "Um, yes, she is capable, I suppose. I was speaking about the others that must be involved."

Kent slid in the seat next to her. "I can help with the preparations if you like."

"You can remove the ballroom embellishments. However, I am tempted to leave the room decorated in such a manner! What would Meryton say to a ball in a tavern? Oh, I forgot. That experience is not unusual for them."

"Now, Miss Bingley. That was too cruel. But, yes, I will ensure the room is restored to its original grandeur as soon as may be."

"How do you find Meryton society? Is it to your liking?" she asked.

"I prefer London. The fashions, the manners, the etiquette, and the wonderful gossip are far superior to here."

"I can find no fault with what you say. Nonetheless, have you discovered any enjoyment here?"

Kent nodded. "You brother has seen to my every comfort. And he found a perfect way to avoid boredom, would you agree?"

"Yes. The games were quite the topic in town. I suppose you, too, want to win the stallion."

"Yes, most decidedly so. Heracles is a mighty fine horse and a symbol of wealth and power."

"Is wealth and power what you seek?"

"Of course." He narrowed his eyes. "We are the same, you and I."

"Excuse me? I think not." Caroline leaned away from him.

Kent chuckled. "You are the daughter of a tradesman as I am the son of one. Does that not make us the same?"

Caroline stayed silent. She turned her head towards the house.

Kent leaned in, whispering, "I appreciate what it is like, being viewed as a lesser mortal. I never forget how the gentlemen in the best circles find ways to hold their status above me."

"But Lord Blake, Mr. Rawlings, and Mr. Darcy—are they not your friends? They belong to those best circles."

"I possess something they want. I am not foolish enough to think I am wanted for anything more than that. I do like them, for they are pleasant enough chaps, but they still maintain their status. Keep an eye on them tonight when we go into dinner. Examine how they walk about the room, demanding everyone's attention. These are little things, but I grant you they reveal the men's true feelings. Do not ignore how they address each other, and then listen when they speak to your brother or to me. You will detect the subtle condescension; you have experience the same from Darcy."

"You are trying to put your prejudice in my eyes and mind, Mr. Kent. I have never witnessed Mr. Darcy as anything but gracious."

"Darcy is an honorable man, but he is excessively proud. Rawlings is less condescending than the other two, although he has his moments as well. Lord Blake learned to be ostentatious from his birth. How could he not act so pompous when one is constantly treated as if he is above everyone?"

Caroline cast her darkened eyes into his. "What do you want from them, Mr. Kent? Surely, you would never allow the men to treat you this way unless you wanted something."

"True. Again, I repeat, what I want makes us the same. I, too, wish to be elevated into higher society." Kent smiled at Caroline's reaction. He darted his eyes around the garden and towards the house, lowered his voice, and said, "We can help each other. I will be continually in Darcy's company, and I will be your champion. Let me help you, Miss Bingley. I will ensure that he does not leave you out nor forget your charms."

"What do you want from me? You are the not the sort of person who returns any favor without your own gain in return. Am I correct?"

He nodded. "I am as you surmise. I wish you to champion me as well. I have my own plans for the future, and I want to succeed. And I, too, do not wish to be left out when others are around Darcy. I need him to lean on me for friendship and advice."

"You think he leaves you out?" She asked.

"Yes, I do. You and I are aware the members of their circle do belong to a secret club. Perhaps not an explicit one, but they shut out those not born into their world. I wish to be included, and I suspect so do you. You know exactly what the key is to the locked door for me, for you, and for your brother."

Caroline looked away.

Kent stood. "I promise you that the rulers of the social order will one day change. Families from trade will reign over the likes of them. Our grandchildren will be the ones with the secret society, and they will long for entry. Alas, it will take too long for us. We must find a way into theirs."

Caroline clasped her locket and lowered her head. "Marriage."

"Yes. Please consider my plea. I wish to be your friend." He stared at her. "We are the same, Miss Bingley. We are the same."

After he left to find the other men, Caroline sat for a while squeezing the jewel around her neck. Mr. Kent is correct. She narrowed her eyes and shook her head at her brother's laughter inside the house. She left to find the butler. "Whitson, I need to send a letter."

"Very good ma'am." Bowing first, he then led Miss Bingley to the desk in the study. Caroline wrote, sealed, and handed her message to Whitson.

"See that this is delivered tomorrow morning."

***

Bingley suggested a game of twenty points and his friends agreed, happy for something to do. The excitement of the games had died away and the nothingness of the days had begun to bore the men. Caroline was working on the Harvest feast and the Hursts had chosen to rest in their bedchamber. The men left for the ballroom tavern where Bingley directed the doorman to be extra tenacious in guarding the entrance against his relatives.

They had played for a while when Bingley sent his butler for a package in his study.

"With such a grin, I suspect your mind is on your Miss Bennet," Kent said.

Bingley shook his head. "Well, no, I was not thinking about her, and she is not my Miss Bennet."

Whitson placed the package on the table, careful not to let it drop. Bingley pulled back the covering, revealing three modified Baker rifles—one for Rawlings, Kent, and Darcy. He chuckled at Blake's questioning expression and reminded him that he had received his earlier, and, no, he was not getting another.

"I want to thank you for your participation in my little Olympics. It was great fun, and I appreciate your effort. However, I do have one stipulation."

"What? Are we not allowed to fire them?" Rawlings asked.

"You must not tell my brother-in-law. I am giving him one for his birthday, and I do not wish to present it this soon. I cannot think of any other gift suitable for him."

They mumbled their agreement.

Blake watched Darcy admire the firearm. "I was surprised you did not choose fencing for your game."

"My choice was intended to score me the most points and you the fewest. As for fencing, you and Rawlings are much too good for me to take such a chance, and anything could have happened. If my sword slipped just a hair I would easily lose."

"Were you not afraid of me?" Kent asked.

"I did not say you were not a good fencer. Since we never fenced, now was not the time to discover any of your unknown abilities. So, you see, that was one more reason for me not to choose it."

"You excluded me, Darcy," Bingley said, chuckling.

"I will be kind and remain silent."

Kent nudged Bingley. "Do tell. We want to hear."

"Every time we fence, Darcy wins in record time. I am no match for him, not even good practice material," Bingley whined.

"I was alarmed at the golf game when you announced it." Darcy said.

"But I was relieved." Blake added.

"I wish you had not been so pleased!" Bingley replied.

"Did you play pub games while drinking at them, Kent," Blake asked, "or did you just play? Perhaps you skipped your studies at school to master them."

"My family sells them all over England. I tested them before they sold them. During our university days, when you all were studying, I was in the local taverns beating the locals. I played for money. Did you not wonder how I had all those extra funds?"

"I would have liked to join you," Blake said. "I was seeking something to do, since I completed my assignments almost upon assignment."

"Would it have been from a desire to be in my company, or just boredom?

"A little of both." Blake chuckled. "I do so like to compete, and I do so like to win."

Kent nodded. "I, too, like to win."

"Bingley, I understand you and Kent raced each other when you were growing up?" Rawlings asked.

"Ah, so you know the truth. Yes, I would spend school breaks with Kent's family, especially after my mother passed. My father was so busy and Caroline was away at her ladies' seminary or staying with friends. Louisa married young." Bingley looked over to Kent. "He was kind to invite me. There was always something exciting to do."

"But racing, Bingley? How were you allowed to race carriages?" Blake asked.

"Kent's family makes them, were you not aware of this?" Rawlings asked.

"Oh. I thought they made ships." Blake said.

"We dabble in many things. Building ships is just one endeavor."

Rawlings tipped his head. "I want to thank you, Bingley, for the entire competition. It has been the most entertaining activity I have enjoyed in many a year.".

"Hear, hear" rang a chorus of voices,With their drinks held high, they sang loudly—

For he's a jolly good fellow, for he's a jolly good fellow
For he's a jolly good fellow and so say all of us
And so say all of us, and so say all of us

Bingley watched the men pay him this compliment. He discovered that he was content in *his* home, providing hospitality to *his* friends, who were enjoying *his* wine and talking about enjoying their stay on *his* estate. He may lease Netherfield Park, but this was how he envisioned life. He had found his dream of a good home, good friends, good drink, and good sport. Best reason of all, the most handsome woman of his acquaintance lived a mere three miles away.

Chapter Twenty-four

Blake rose a half hour earlier than usual to avoid any unwanted company. When he left his bedchambers, he stopped abruptly and then turned and called back to his valet. "Pack up. I will be leaving here at the completion of the competition. I will not stay for the ball or anything else. Wait. If I win I will delay my departure until after the ball, but we must leave after the morning after."

Once his man nodded, Blake continued down the hallway on the way to the stable and his morning ride.

Kent, hidden from view, heard the plan and thought about the ramifications, With Mr. Phillips bringing the papers to sign before the ball begins, Blake must be intended to avoid the signing if he loses. He will reject the alliance. He hurried away to warn Bingley.

Blake rode to a location the locals called Oakham Mount. He pushed his horse to a gallop, attempting to reach the pinnacle before the sky's colors faded from view but, in truth, he raced to arrive first to the second place he and Elizabeth had come upon one another. He no longer deemed going to the open meadow viable, and instead chose this spot unknown to everyone at Netherfield, especially Darcy.

A pattern developed over the last fortnight. Elizabeth walked towards the forest path until out of sight when she would scurry to the mount. Blake rode his horse in different directions each day, but he, too, headed for this destination. Autumn sunrises created the brilliant colors the two used as their excuse to discuss.

They never planned their meetings. In fact, several days crept by where one or both remained indoors. The weather did not always cooperate and the competition got in the way. Some mornings, Mr. Bennet woke at dawn, desiring to talk to his beloved daughter; occasionally Darcy had waited at the stables to join him for a ride. He and Elizabeth had not agreed to meet so the missed opportunities were distressing but not without understanding.

This morning Blake rode faster than his horse wanted to go. The filly complied, sensing her rider was angry. Chesterfield pushed forward with each heel nudge in the side and headed towards the now familiar resting spot.

An express messenger had arrived late last night, and the letter for him did not contain good news. He hoped Miss Elizabeth would come soon, for today he needed a diversion.

He tied his horse to a tree and searched the area for any uninvited guests. Satisfied, he found his spot on the ledge, which had somehow become theirs, and waited. Even after the sky turned into its solid monotonous daytime blue, a spectacular view existed. He was so high he could survey most of the Netherfield Park estate. Today, the scent of burning leaves filled his nostrils, although he believed the workers were foolish for doing so with rain approaching. He found the comings and goings interesting as the workers tended the fields. He located several men and boys to the left, attempting to keep the blaze in check. For the first time, he wondered what the commoners' life was like.

Miss Elizabeth approached him without disturbing his concentration. She stood on her tiptoes to see what held his interest. "Lord Blake," she whispered, trying to wake him from his thoughts.

"Miss Elizabeth." Blake rose to greet her and presented her. "I am pleased with your presence this morning. I hoped to see you today." He offered his hand to help Elizabeth to the ledge.

"And why is that?"

"So you can cheer me and make me pleased to be in this place overlooking someone else's estate."

"Oh, and what do you wish to discuss? I imagine nothing as mundane as the latest play or music or even a book will do?" She asked.

"I assure you, any subject will suffice."

"I wish to assist you. How shall I remove your reason for needing cheering?"

"No person can help." He turned his head away.

"It cannot be as horrible as all that! Oh! Excuse me; this is not my concern I will discuss any topic you like."

"My father." Blake said in a barely audible voice

"Is he to be the subject?"

"Yes. I am undecided on where to start."

Elizabeth lowered herself on the ledge in a single graceful flow and waited for him to join her. He found a place not too close to be improper but near enough to revel in her scent. They swung their legs over the edge. Neither one attempted to still their feet, although they laughed about the child-like action. Blake grabbed a handful of pebbles, pouring them from one hand to the other.

"He is a mathematician, the same as I am. We both possess this ability to do things with numbers which only a small percentage of people can match."

"I did not realize math was a talent of yours."

"Yes, I was awarded Senior Wranglers Honors at Cambridge. Are you aware of the program?"

"No, my lord. If you would be so kind as to explain, I am willing to learn."

When Elizabeth tilted her head to the side and gave him an encouraging smile, he relaxed. "The singular way to achieve intellectual distinction at Cambridge is by placing first in an examination called Mathematical Tripos. The Senior Wrangler is the candidate with the most marks. Each mark is a correct answer." Blake flung a pebble towards the valley below.

"Does the exam take long?"

"Ha! My tests lasted five and a half hours a day for eight days, except time was not the major problem."

"How so?"

"They hold the Tripos in January, in a building without chimneys or stoves or fires of any sort." Blake stopped speaking, closed his eyes and shuddered. "The air is so cold the ink one uses to answer the questions may well freeze. No warmth exists in the room at all. The marble floor is like ice, a radiating chill burns through your boots; everyone wears every stocking they own."

Blake raised his legs from the swinging position to stare at his feet. He then sought Elizabeth's gaze, and once he caught it, he exaggerated a shudder. She laughed, and he felt encouraged to continue. "The ceilings are so high; the heat seeping out of all the gentlemen's body did not help. You understand heat rises? It was the most difficult goal I ever achieved, but it did teach me if I remain steadfast in my pursuits I can be successful."

Elizabeth nodded her head. After a moment of silence, she tapped his arm. "Thank you for telling me. To be the best is quite the honor. You should be proud of your accomplishment."

"Well, yes, I am. My father was a second wrangler."

"Did he put pressure on you?"

"No. I am happiest when I am involved in math, and I found mathematical formulas are the one constant in my life. Everything else is uncertain, which brings my story back to my father." Blake's expression returned to the disheartened one he wore before.

"How so?"

"I received an express from him last night."

"I hope the message did not contain bad news."

"Word from my father is always dreadful, particularly when he sends his demands by messenger. He wants me to return to London. I have no choice. I must obey."

Elizabeth's eyes grew wide. "Oh. Will you be leaving soon?"

Blake studied the small pebbles still in his hand as if he imagined the tiny stones to be his problems, some small and others heavy and dirty. He waited a second before flinging them to the sky. He turned and gazed at her. She seems worried. . "Not before the competition has been decided. I do want to win and I shall remain steadfast."

Blake watched her as she observed the tenant farmers below tending to the bonfire. and when she turned to face him, he received her smile, satisfied. No one else could ever create such a tranquil impression.

"Let us think of the things in our lives that give us pleasure." She said. "Your story today about the wranglers is a pleasant one of mine. Surely, my amusement will lighten any unease you feel."

"Yes, it does. Now what pleasantry shall we discuss?" Blake thought for a moment. "Chess—a perfectly pleasing topic to me. Have you ever played?"

"No my lord. I tried backgammon, but my father refused to teach me the game."

"Would you like to learn? I can instruct you." He leaned in closer, his head almost touching hers. "You own a quick mind, and I believe you might do well. You are an observer and studier of people, correct?"

"I did admit to that characteristic."

"Think about the chess pieces as if they were intricate characters. Pawns are the least complex, and the queen is the most. Wait," Blake paused, screwing up his face. "I guess you would identify the king as an uncomplicated one, too."

"Unlike our own King!"

Blake laughed.

"What are you, Lord Blake, which piece, that is. A pawn or a king?"

"I am a knight. I shall always protect my queen. Even at the risk of being captured."

"And who would dare capture you?"

"It is not possible for any enemy to imprison me, *my lady*. But my heart could be locked up by the queen." Blake's gaze caught hold of hers, the gold flecks in her brown eye sparkled. "Of course, the queen is aware two different knights exist; one black and one white. The black knight is a rascal, and he would not always appear righteous in his actions. In fact, he is a scoundrel at heart."

She gasped.

Blake leaned back. "I suppose that is where the term blackguard came from."

"And the white knight?" she whispered.

"He is all gentleman-like; all his actions are principled. He never allows himself a dishonorable word or deed."

"And are not black knights noble too?"

"It is hard to fight and kill the dragons whilst being polite and on your best behavior. A black knight feels free to take what he wants without regard to rules."

"Oh?"

Blake glanced around before leaning in close to her neck, and in a soft whisper in her ear, said, "Now some queens do not mind a rascally black knight." He held his breath.

"Oh." Her eyebrows rose, and her body tensed.

He sat upright, shrugging his shoulders. "Most queens prefer the white knight, at least they claim so publicly."

Blake continued to speak about chess and strategies. Elizabeth proved to own a quick mind. Impressed with the questions she asked, he promised to teach her how to play. After she departed, he stayed and watched the world at work.

He was astounded that Hertfordshire was the place he found a queen named Elizabeth. How did this happen? He sighed. She possesses the intelligence, the wit, the grace, and the most beautiful, welcoming eyes.

He glanced around to determine if anyone watched him, refrained from speaking aloud until he felt secure in his solitude. "Now I must plan the day for declaring my love. I shall stay for the ball. I care not what my father wants. What better place to speak to her than at Bingley's ball! Why, I shall dress my best, and she will look divine, of that, I am sure. We will dance the last dance before I lead her out to the balcony, where I shall reveal my feelings. I must tell her how much I want her."

Blake conjured up an image of Elizabeth's expressive eyes challenging him and her curls bouncing by the night's crisp breeze. "I will explain my situation with her in a calm manner. I must make her understand. She must accept. How can she not? I am a marquess and the heir to a dukedom."

He practiced the words to use, he remembered what she had said about poetry killing a romance. He tried humor but could not string together acceptable words that made light of a serious request. In the end, he would hand her a gift, a special present only she would understand.

**

"Blake, you left too soon this morning. I had hoped to race out in the meadow again." Darcy peered up from his breakfast plate.

"I needed a ride to calm me down."

"Worried about the game?"

"No. I am anxious about my plans after the competition for something I must finish before we return to London. It is important to my future."

"Oh?"

"I also received an express before dawn." Blake lost interest in continuing the conversation and finished his breakfast in silence. After a while, Darcy tried to engage him again in a discussion about horses. "Sorry, I was not attending. If you will excuse me, I must answer the letter."

Darcy rose from the table when Blake left the room. My God. What plans? He strode over to the window. He noticed the birds flying in a v-shaped formation towards the south. There was something in Blake's tone of voice leading him to think it affected Miss Elizabeth and not the alliance. Consider what you are doing, Blake. Think. You are titled; she is not. You have responsibilities and a duty to your family. You will fly away soon from Meryton and leave all this. A different world awaits you. Do not be unwise, my friend.

He continued to stare out the widow, his hands clasped behind his back. What can I do? Why do I care? She is a mere passing fancy. Um... for him. She is another flirtation to fill his leisure time. Damn. He and Bingley should learn to control their urges.

Within clear view of the window, two servants walked away from the house—a footman and a young woman he had seen cleaning the library. They stole a moment to touch fingers, brief and intentional; their gaze indicated a secret flirtation or liaison existed between them. The visualization of Blake and Elizabeth sharpened in his mind, in which he identified a similar expression they shared.

She is from a small country estate, and her father's rank is no higher than minor gentry. The Bennets are without style or discipline. They show no sense of propriety. The eldest two girls do, but the rest do not. Think man. They would become your family. You must accept how unsupportable such a connection would be. She is not of your sphere or even mine.

Darcy noted the couple parted, sighing as they waved goodbye. I do not believe you will connect yourself to persons so far beneath you, so what do you need to finish first? What Blake, are you planning?

The young maid stopped to watch the footman leave; her sweet appearance and pleasant figure visible to Darcy. A reflection of a different pretty face danced on the windowpane, the sunlight sparkling through her fine eyes. He shook his head but could not clear the vision from his mind. Blake, I do agree with you. Miss Elizabeth does present the most beautiful expression in a penetrating gaze, lively and carefree, his mind traveling down the visual recollection of her body. Yes, her figure is light and pleasing. How did I not see her as she is? My God, she is more than tolerable. Why did Blake become infatuated so quickly? Why did she respond to his charming ways? Why did I not dance with her?

Darcy stepped backwards from the window and returned to the table to refill his cup. As he sipped, he thought of his family and how, like Blake's father, they planned to select his future marriage partner. He wondered if the young poor couple outside faced parental dictates, or if security drove their decisions. Security is what compels the ladies wanting my wealth, home, and status. Pray tell, what does any woman bring me? He exhaled a deep breath.

The idea crossed his mind about Blake taking on a mistress, which caused him to wince. No, no. I must not let him propose such an arrangement. I brought him here for business, not to trifle or toy with any maiden. I will be at fault and besides—"

"Ah. You are up early. Good morning, Darcy." Kent filled his plate. "I have received some information from my uncle you may be interested in, all about exporting linens to Russia."

Darcy nodded, and then he spoke about business for the next hour, although the words barely registered on his mind. He could not purge the image of a particular young lady, twirling a garden rose in her hand, presenting the sweetest smile to Blake.

***

On her walk back to Longbourn, Elizabeth mulled over her conversation with Blake. She considered him the most charming of men and appreciated every attention he paid to her.

"So little bird, dare I hope for more?" she sighed. "Is this a mere flirtation? Might a man of such high rank consider me for his wife? Bah."

She hugged a large oak tree. "I am confused. He pays me great attention, does he not? Yet, he does not show the same attentiveness when others are around. Why is that? He shows politeness and nothing more. Mr. Bingley is friendlier to Jane."

Elizabeth kicked a few stones away as she moved further along the path to her home. She picked up an orange colored leaf, searched the area before she spoke aloud again.

"Well, I must think and be practical! Does he wish something honorable or…" She found her favorite fallen tree trunk to sit on. With her foot, she pushed away the dead leaves for several minutes. "I wonder what he meant when he talked about the knights. Blackguard indeed."

After sitting a moment lost in reflection, she tossed the leaf away, rose and headed towards her home.

She arrived back at Longbourn in time for breakfast, joining her family at the table.

"Did you have a pleasant stroll this morning?" Jane asked.

"Yes, just a few days are left to enjoy the scenes before winter sets in. I must walk when I can."

A footman with a note for Miss Bennet interrupted breakfast; it had come from Netherfield, and a servant was waiting for an answer. Mrs. Bennet's eyes sparkled in suspense until her daughter read—

"Well, Jane, who is it from? What is it about? What does he say? Well, Jane, make haste and tell us; make haste, my love."

"It is from Miss Bingley." Jane read the message aloud.

> My dear Friend,
>
> If you are not so compassionate as to dine to-day with Louisa and me, we shall be in danger of hating each other for the rest of our lives, for a whole day's tête-à-tête between two women can never end without a quarrel. Come as soon as you can on the receipt of this. My brother and the gentlemen are to dine with the officers.
>
> Yours ever,
> Caroline Bingley

After a short discussion about the availability of horses and carriages, Mr. Bennet allowed Jane to ride on horseback to Netherfield Park, even though the fast moving gray clouds in the sky warned of rain headed their way. Elizabeth, disturbed by this decision, followed him into his study.

"Papa, you were quiet at breakfast, much more so than usual." Elizabeth sat in the chair next to his desk. She did not need permission to sit down.

Mr. Bennet sighed. "Yes, my child. Today is not a day of grand levity."

"Why so? You find humor in all the situations surrounding us."

"I received a letter this morning, which saddened me especially. It concerns yourself so you ought to know the contents. There is no chance the situation will change."

"Change? I do not understand."

Mr. Bennet leaned back away from his daughter, stared straight ahead, his fingers joined in a steeple manner and pressing against his lips. To Elizabeth's surprise, she spied the growing wetness in his eyes. She grew alarmed; nevertheless, she waited for her father to speak. Abruptly, he turned to his daughter and announced—

"It is all gone."

"Gone? What is gone?"

"Your dowries. Yours and your sisters'."

Elizabeth's eyes grew wide and her jaw dropped. "Does mama know?" She asked, and then she heard her mother's laughter rang out. "No, I suspect she does not."

"I have yet to share this sad state of affairs, except with you. Here is your Uncle Gardiner's final letter describing the entire misfortune. You may read the vile words if you wish." He released a heavy sigh and handed her the message.

"Once the news spreads, we will become the latest entertainment in a place overflowing with amusements. For what do we live, but to make sport for our neighbors, and laugh at them in our turn?"

Elizabeth opened the letter, her eyes flying through the page. "Gas Light Company? You gambled all our inheritance in a gas light company?"

"Yes, my brother Gardiner warned me not to invest all our funds in this singular venture. I did not conceive as to how it would fail. I only saw the world lit up bright. I envisioned reading a book at night in light as strong as the day. Bah! Progress they say. It is best to keep everything the way things stand now."

"Is all the dowry money gone?"

"No, my child. Your mother's five thousand from the marriage settlement is still intact. That provides a mere thousand pounds for each of you." Mr. Bennet shook his head. "I must inform her soon."

"Yes, I suppose she should be told. Papa, do not distress yourself so. The man for our sad turn of events is the evil person. Mr. Cuffage is to blame, not you."

"Evil? Human nature is so prone to fall into it! No, Lizzy, let me, once in my life, suffer how much I have been at fault. I am not afraid of being overpowered by the impression. My shame will pass away soon enough."

"Shall I tell Jane?"

"Tomorrow you may inform your sister while I enlighten your mother at which time everything becomes a parade. It gives such elegance to misfortune! Another day I shall rest in my library, in my nightcap and powdering gown, and give as much trouble as I can."

Elizabeth patted his shoulder and kissed the top of his head. "Everything will be fine, dear Papa."

They spoke no more, for father and daughter understood each other.

Chapter Twenty-five

The darkened clouds seen earlier on the horizon now hugged Netherfield Park, releasing its pelting rain without regard for the unlucky souls below. The refreshing crisp November air had transformed into a bone chilling dampness. The birds huddled in their nests and the squirrels sought refuge in the nearest tree. Not all God's creatures were fortunate in locating a safe haven before the storm began.

The drawing room at Netherfield had grown dark enough to require the candles lit even though the timepiece on the mantle indicated afternoon had now begun. The rain drops dripped on the windows and the flickering sparks from the blazing fire crackled in the formal drawing room where Caroline Bingley rested on the sofa with her head held high, hands folded loosely in her lap, and without the smallest slump in her posture. Her furrowed brow and frown marred the lady-like picture as she stared at the gold threads running through the royal blue carpet. The light from the fire caused the amber hued rose, hanging around her neck, to send similar golden sparkles throughout the room.

Mr. Kent was correct, Caroline thought.

Long ago, she conceded the inconsequential existence awaiting those not born into society's upper echelons, or otherwise intimately connected to someone from that rank. Her awakening to this unwritten but unquestioned truth of life occurred when she attended the first private ladies' seminary in London.

Once her father enrolled her into the private school, her affable spirit had changed irrevocably. Her initiation into class distinctions and true prejudice began the day she stepped in the lesson room. Every girl— including the personal servants of the girls—sneered at her. She was the only tradesman's child in a school for daughters and nieces of dukes, earls, and barons. No one spoke to her, preferring to cut her at every opportunity. She fought hard for the scraps of acceptance she had earned. Still, she recognized the importance of a family name in the world. Bingley was not a name valued by those families she wanted to please.

Caroline sat waiting for a woman with no fortune and no connections. If Charles wed a country wife, the laughter and whispers in every London ballroom would bring back those she had received at the ladies' seminary. The only means available to stop the indignity required her or her brother to marry a Darcy or someone of his stature. And Darcy was being stubborn. So, today she needed to learn everything before she could attempt to undermine any marriage offer her brother Charles might make. She vowed to take any action, even if she must befriend her and pretend to find her worthy.

She, thinking about her own future, continued to stare at the gold threads running through the blue carpet until Whitson showed Miss Jane Bennet into the parlor.

***

The gentlemen returned from their dinner with Colonel Forster and his officers in high spirits. They savored the tales of military exploits against the French along with good food and overflowing steins of ale. The men depicted the battles in exciting words, although the officers never spoke about the hideous side of war. They preferred to share the most comedic incidences: a horse giving premature birth during the intensity of a battle, catching the enemy with his breeches down in the literal sense, and the many pranks played by a mysterious soldier whose identity remained undiscovered.

"I do not remember when I enjoyed dining in a room filled only with men." Bingley grinned, teasing his friends while a servant took his coat. "Do not gawk at me in such a way. I jest. You have been excellent company, nonetheless I admit I enjoyed this evening."

Darcy handed his gloves to the servant. "I am sure you did. You grumbled about how I focused on literature and philosophy at Cambridge, but you favored the Greek studies. I suppose it was the sports and the wars you preferred and tonight was all about war!"

"I admit it. I find tales of warfare exciting."

Rawlings winked. "The past fortnight we provided sufficient action here at the Netherfield Park Olympics even for you." "We have been your sport!"

"I still am." Kent glanced at Blake.

"As Darcy and I are. Let us trust, however, our efforts do not resort to a war." Blake patted Kent on the back. "Regardless of my win, I hope we can all remain friends."

"Your win?" Darcy and Kent said in unison.

"Excuse me, sir." Whitson bowed, and announced, "Miss Bennet took ill while dining with your sisters. Miss Bingley provided her with a place to rest until you returned."

"She is here?" Bingley asked, and without expecting an answer continued, "Has my sister retired for the night?"

Whitson confirmed she had not and directed Mr. Bingley and his guests to the parlor where the sisters sat waiting for them.

"Caroline, what is this about Miss Bennet being here in my house?"

"Louisa and I invited her to dinner. We wanted to become better acquainted in a less public situation. We would not secure her attention with you flitting around," Caroline glanced at her sister.

"It is true, Charles." Louisa shook her head.

"And am I correct that she is not well?" Bingley's hand trembled at his side before he clenched it into a fist. "What did you feed her?"

"Her slight chill is due to the wet clothing she wore. Why, she came on horseback during a downpour!" Caroline exclaimed more to her brother's friends than to him.

Bingley furrowed his brow. "Should we call the doctor?"

"She has a trifling cold, Charles, and she is resting now. I am sure her ride home will be drier."

"Ride home? Nonsense. You are to arrange for her to stay the night. I will not risk, nor be responsible for, any worsening of her condition." Bingley jerked the cord to summon a servant.

Darcy, pointed out the risks in sending the coachman and groom back out in such weather.

Caroline gave in and called for the housekeeper to send word to Miss Bennet and her family.

Bingley slid into his favorite chair. "Now that this has been settled, may I ask your opinion of her?"

The other gentlemen followed their host, and found seats around the room.

"I have an excessive regard for Jane Bennet, she is a sweet girl, and I wish she were well settled. I am afraid there is no chance with such a father and mother, and low connections."

"Their uncle is an attorney in Meryton," Louisa said in a half whisper

"We have met Mr. Phillips," Blake replied, his words sharp.

"They have another uncle too, who lives somewhere near Cheapside," Caroline said, followed by a giggle. "Cheapside! Perhaps he lives in one of his warehouses?"

"If they had uncles enough to fill all Cheapside," Bingley tapped the table, "it would not make them one jot less agreeable." He glanced at Kent.

"But it must materially lessen their chance of marrying men of any consideration in the world," Darcy injected.

"Why?" Rawlings asked. "Are you suggesting a wedding is inconceivable for such a woman? Or do you believe gentlemen are unable to grasp their value? You imply a lady's charms cannot prevail over low connections."

"I am saying lower status will make a marriage difficult and unlikely, but not impossible."

"So, you believe a gentleman can surmount society's conventions and marry one beneath him?" Blake said as he moved across the room to help himself to a drink. He stared at the painting above the sideboard depicting an unknown family. He glanced over his shoulder and directed his gaze on Darcy. "Or do you hold the opinion the man should follow another option?"

Darcy pointed to the two ladies in the room with his eyes and furrowed his brow. "Blake, any man not seeking connections or fortune is free to *marry* where he chooses. Of course, he must still consider his family obligations. A young man should seek advice from his elders."

"You did not answer my question with completeness, but no bother." Blake shrugged. "Yes, some men do what their dear fathers and uncles want! I need not hold a discussion with His Grace, because I am well acquainted with my father's aspirations for me."

Kent smiled at Caroline first, and then turned to Darcy. "But if there is no need for, as you say, connections and money, how can a gentleman's family object. On what grounds would they do so?"

"Why, being acceptable is more than possessing fortune and connections," Darcy answered. "Such circumstances can be overlooked if one does not need these things. A lady must come from good stock, show proper decorum in her behavior, and skilled at managing a large household. Those qualities are not found in women outside certain levels of society."

Caroline whispered to her sister, "Well, at least our Mr. Darcy thinks accomplishments overrule fine eyes." Louisa nodded.

"Please Caroline," her brother said, interrupting, "could you entertain us tonight? Everyone would enjoy some music, I think."

She rushed to the pianoforte. She may not possess upper echelon connections; however, she was an accomplished lady with a considerable dowry.

After a few hours of recitals and light conversations, the ladies and Mr. Hurst retired for the night. Bingley and Kent chose to continue their nightly game of billiards. Blake removed himself to the library to find a book. Rawlings and Darcy remained in the drawing room.

"Darcy, do you believe in your own gibberish about marriage?"

"Yes, one cannot be too careful. Marriage should enhance one's life not a distraction."

"Enhance? You speak as if wedlock is nothing more than an alliance between families. Should there not be more?"

"Yes. A man should respect his partner, and I suppose it would be helpful if he enjoys her company, as well."

Rawlings scoffed. "Marriage is more than a business transaction. Respect is necessary, I grant you, and enjoying one's company is helpful, but a man needs a connection of a different sort."

"Oh, are you speaking about a novelist's notion of love? Marriages happen for other reasons. All I seek is respect and pleasant company. Over time, our feelings will deepen for one another."

"Be careful. You may be unfortunate enough to marry such a woman."

"And you? What do *you* seek?" Darcy asked.

"Love, lust, laughter, gaiety, and fun to name a few. I, too, would like to respect my partner; yet, good company is more important to me now. I shall overlook much silliness and impropriety if lightness and fun filled the rest of my days and nights."

With one brow raised, Darcy asked, "Are you not afraid such things will fade over the years?"

"Perhaps a little. But it is a chance I am willing to take take in order to obtain any degree of happiness. I did experience a union of different sorts. Now, I yearn for a silly girl looking up to me laughing and teasing the night away, although it must be true affection. I will excuse much for love: in fact, I would forgive anything if a woman freely chose me."

Darcy waited while his friend stared into his drink with a seriousness not often seen.

"Am I so evil when I admit I am glad I am no longer married to Margaret, even if it meant she died to bring about my freedom?" Rawlings rested his head on his right hand and closed his eyes.

"No. I understand. Perhaps I would feel the way you do if I had wed her." Darcy rose from his chair patted his shoulder before moving to get coffee.

"Bah! You accept what befalls you and continue on as if you planned it." Rawlings said.

"Oh? What do you envision for me?"

"A man focused on your estate business, our alliance, and I assume other avenues for increasing one's wealth."

"Yes, I admit I am too attentive in that regard." Darcy took his seat, stirred his coffee, and leaned forward. "Um. I have been perplexed on a different matter." He slumped in his chair. "I need your advice on my reactions to a certain la—"

"Pardon me, is this a private conversation?" Blake interrupted as he entered the room carrying William Cowper's *The Morning Walk*.

"Not at all. Come join us in a nightcap." Rawlings said, hoping he had concealed the disappointment in his voice.

***

The next morning Mrs. Bennet received a message explaining Jane's illness continued and that she would be staying awhile longer. Elizabeth left in haste, hurried thorugh the wet grounds until she reached the doorstep of Netherfield Park, all muddy and frazzled from the three-mile long walk. She wished to visit her sister to determine how bad her cold was if she felt well enough to hear the news about the dowries. She needed her sister's calming perspective.

"Miss Elizabeth Bennet," Whitson announced when she entered the breakfast room. The long table permitted the Hursts and Darcy to sit on one side and the remaining three gentlemen sat across from them, Bingley, at the head. At the opposite end, Caroline and Lord Blake were leaning towards each other, sharing a humorous story, and exchanging smiles.

"Miss Bennet, it is so good of you to come. How did you arrive? I did not hear a carriage," Caroline inquired.

"I walked. The distance is not far."

"It is nearly three miles," Caroline said, tartly.

"Please pardon the interruption. I have come to see my sister."

Bingley approached her. "Miss Bennet is resting. She would take pleasure in your visit, Miss Elizabeth. I understand she is still feverish. I will send for the doctor if she does not improve."

"Mr. Jones is our apothecary. May I see her? I must determine if he is needed."

"Certainly, and without any further delay." He called for a servant and retuned to his seat when she disappeared into the hallway. He fiddled with his food for a moment, and was barely attending to the conversation until Louisa said—

"I shall never forget her appearance. She looked almost wild."

"She did indeed." Caroline said. "I had to fight to keep my countenance. How nonsensical to come at all! Why must she be scampering about the country, because her sister has a cold? Her hair, so untidy, so blowsy!

I am afraid, Mr. Darcy," Kent said in a half-whisper. "This adventure has rather affected your admiration of her fine eyes."

"Not at all," he replied. "They were brightened by the exercise."

"She has nothing, in short, to recommend her, but being an excellent walker." Caroline said.

"Yes, and her petticoat, Louisa jumped in. "I hope you saw her petticoat, six inches deep in mud, I am certain; and the gown overtop did not hide it."

"Your picture may be exact, Louisa," Bingley said, casting his glower at his older sister. "But this was all lost upon me. I thought Miss Elizabeth Bennet looked remarkably well when she came into the room. Her dirty petticoat quite escaped my notice."

"She walked three miles, her ankles in dirt, and alone, quite alone! What could she mean by it? It seems to me to show an abominable sort of conceited independence, a most country-town indifference to decorum," Caroline said.

"It shows an affection for her sister which is exceedingly pleasing," he said.

"Or affection of a different type." Caroline sneered "I suspect it is not a dissimilar than riding horseback in the rain. The results are the same." She dabbed her mouth with her napkin.

"I, for one, agree with Bingley," Blake said. "She is close to her sister. I would not object to someone walking even one mile to care for me. Miss Bennet is fortunate to have such a sister."

Rawlings swallowed the first bite of his morning sweet treat. "I, too, agree. These are the only sisters in my acquaintance who show true affection to one another. It has been my experience most sisterly love is all pretenses.".

Mr. Darcy said little more and Mr. Hurst nothing at all. The former was divided between admiration of the brilliancy which exercise gave to her complexion, and doubt as to the occasion justifying her coming so far alone. The latter was thinking of his breakfast.

Later, the apothecary did come at Bingley's request, and having examined his patient, said she caught a violent cold, and they must endeavor to get the better of it. He advised Miss Bennet to return to bed, and promised her some draughts. Pressured by her brother, Caroline invited Elizabeth to stay, and sent a note to Longbourn. Miss Bingley, Mrs. Hurst, and Elizabeth stayed with Jane for the entire afternoon.

The gentlemen spent their day indulging in sport, and did not meet again until dinner at half-past six. Elizabeth sat between Mr. Hurst and Mr. Rawlings.

The men showered Miss Elizabeth with questions regarding her sister's health the moment she entered the dining room. She informed them Miss Bennet had not improved, but the draughts would need time to take effect. The sisters, on hearing this, repeated three or four times how much they were grieved, how shocking it was to have a bad cold, and how they disliked being ill themselves; and then thought no more about the matter. Their indifference towards Jane when not before them restored Elizabeth to the enjoyment of all her original dislike.

Elizabeth noted Miss Bingley sat the end with Blake at her left. She selected the seat next to Blake. She looked up when she sensed someone's gaze upon her and discovered Darcy's penetrating dark eyes staring at her from across the table.

Darcy sipped his wine. "Do you like to read, Miss Bennet?"

"Yes, I do and almost as much as a walk to view the surrounding area."

Lord Blake leaned in close. "Speaking about walking, have you read Cowper, Miss Bennet? I finished book five, *The Morning Walk.*"

"My father does own several of Mr. Cowper's books; however, I prefer William Wordsworth. His writing about nature is a pleasure to read.

"I agree; Wordsworth is the better author."

"I did not say better, Mr. Darcy, I merely stated I preferred his subject matter." Elizabeth replied.

Darcy could not inject himself in the conversation; he was cut off each time he opened his mouth to speak. Blake monopolized the conversation with Elizabeth. How was he to discover her reading habits. Well, she at least liked the same author as he did. When the conversation turned to poetry, his attention was piqued.

"Miss Elizabeth," Blake said. "Cowper touches on the natural world as well, but I grant you with a different meaning. He wrote,

'Tis liberty alone that gives the flower
Of fleeting life its lustre and perfume,
And we are weeds without it.

"I appreciated the book and how Cowper used nature to describe many ideals." Blake waited for Elizabeth to respond and rolled his eyes when he heard Caroline say his name. Reluctantly, he turned to hear her comment.

"I was not aware you enjoyed poetry. I brought Lord Bryon's *Hours of Idleness* and Sir Walter Raleigh's *Lady of the Lake*. I will make them available to you, if you would like."

Lord Blake nodded without comment before returning his attention back onto Elizabeth.

"Why, Miss Bingley, I was not aware you were so well-read," Kent said as he gazed at her over his wine glass. "Darcy, have you read those books?"

Conversations continued thusly during all courses. Darcy started a topic, and then Blake would disagree. Miss Elizabeth gave her thoughts, thereafter Kent moved the conversation towards Miss Bingley's own merit, and challenged Darcy to object. Rawlings ate his meal wordlessly; content to watch the tradesmen's offspring maneuver the discussions.

Elizabeth returned to Jane's bedside at the conclusion of dinner, and Miss Bingley began abusing her as soon as she departed. She pronounced Elizabeth to be dreadful indeed, a mixture of pride and impertinence, possessing no conversation, no style, no sophistication, and no beauty.

All the men listened, none choosing to respond in word or expression, except Kent. He continued to highlight Caroline's favorable accomplishments. And every compliment was preceded by "Darcy, did you know that Miss Bingley..."

Chapter Twenty- six

Elizabeth, along with the Bingley sisters, spent much of the day upstairs tending to Jane's needs. The gentlemen choose the outdoors pitting their wits and their Baker rifles against the well-stocked covey of grouse until it began to rain. Upon returning to the house, they settled into the billiards room to educate Hurst on how to play Twenty Points.

As daylight gave way to dusk, Caroline and Louise left to prepare themselves for dinner. Still concerned for her sister's state, Elizabeth requested a dinner tray. She had spent a long day in Jane's bedchambers, so, when her sister fell into a restful sleep, she felt sufficiently at ease to join the others.

Entering the parlor, she found Lord Blake reading on the sofa, Mr. Darcy at the writing table with Miss Bingley fluttering about him, Mr. Rawlings resting in a comfortable chair by the fireplace, and the other four members playing loo. She declined an immediate invitation to join them, suspecting them to be playing high, and made her sister the excuse. She replied that she would amuse herself with a book for the short time she could stay downstairs before returning to Jane.

Rawlings sympathized with Miss Elizabeth as she deflected the various volleys aimed at her. Miss Bingley would have been an adept adversary for most country misses. He had known many women like her: elegant, with a contrived, sophisticated air, a wit as sharp as a tack, clothes befitting a queen, and enough intelligence to tell a wickedly good story. She, however, was the exact sort of woman he despised.

Anyone paying the slightest attention to the sparring between the two ladies could easily discern that Miss Bingley did not impress Miss Elizabeth. When Elizabeth made her way towards the books lying on the table Rawlings caught Blake and Darcy following her every movement.

Bingley lifted his eyes from his cards and offered to fetch her other books—all that his library afforded. "I wish my collection were larger, for your benefit and my own credit. I am an idle fellow, and though I have not many, I have more than I ever look into."

"Do not be too harsh on yourself, Bingley. I have had success." Blake held up a book. He showed the title to Elizabeth with a polite little nod.

"I am astonished," Caroline said, haughtily, "that my father should have left so small a collection of books. What a delightful library you have at Pemberley, Mr. Darcy!" Holding her body erect, and with a swaying of her hips, she walked around the desk where Darcy focused on the letter he was writing. She kept her chin high, showing off her amber-hued topaz necklace.

Mr. Rawlings kept his eyes on Elizabeth when she sat down on the sofa to read. Before turning two pages, she set the book aside, and joined the card players, standing between Mr. Bingley and Mrs. Hurst. Ah, he thought, and here comes Blake. This should be interesting.

Blake positioned himself behind Mr. Hurst and next to Mr. Kent. Elizabeth and Blake continued to alternate between watching the game and stealing glances at each other.

Rawlings shifted his attention away from them when Caroline changed the topic to something that caused Elizabeth to divert her attention onto Darcy.

"Is Miss Darcy much grown since the spring? Will she be as tall as I am?"

"I think she will." Darcy said, sneaking a peek at Elizabeth and then added, "She is now about Miss Elizabeth Bennet's height, or rather taller."

Well now, Rawlings thought, what is this? I am astonished he brought Miss Elizabeth into conversation, and in front of Miss Bingley and Blake! He was the one that warned us about toying with the ladies. He continued to focus on Darcy, fascinated. Tonight is as entertaining as anticipated.

"It amazes me," Bingley said, "how young ladies can have patience to be as accomplished as they all are."

"All young ladies accomplished? My dear Charles, what do you mean?" Caroline asked.

"Yes, all of them, I think. They all paint tables, cover screens, and net purses. I scarcely know any one who cannot do all this, and I am sure I never heard a young lady spoken of for the first time, without being informed that she was very accomplished." Bingley played his card with a flourish as his opponents sighed.

Surely you jest, Bingley. These are not grand undertakings. Rawlings scoffed.

Darcy stopped writing and set his gaze on Bingley, yet it slipped towards Elizabeth several times. "Your list of the common accomplishments has much truth. The word is applied to many women who have done nothing more to deserve the epithet than by netting a purse or covering a screen. I am very far from agreeing with you in your estimation of ladies in general. I cannot boast of knowing more than half a dozen, in the whole range of my acquaintance, that are really accomplished."

Rawlings nodded. Yes, my friend, you have made yourself clear on that point more than once during our stay, and have declared the *Ton* the only place to find such remarkable ladies. He leaned forward with greater interest wondering what would happen next.

"Then Mr. Darcy, you must comprehend a great deal in your idea of an accomplished woman." Elizabeth said.

"Yes, I do comprehend a great deal in it."

"Oh, certainly!" Caroline moved to stand closer to the writing desk. "No one can be considered accomplished who does not greatly surpass what is usually presented as esteem. A woman must have a thorough knowledge of music, singing, drawing, dancing, and the modern languages, to deserve the word; and besides all this, she must possess a certain something in her air and manner of walking, the tone of her voice, her address and expressions." She glared at Elizabeth. "Or the word will be but half deserved."

"You seem to fit the particulars of your description, Miss Bingley." Kent said.

Oh my, what is Kent up to tonight? Rawlings thought. Shall we repeat last night's spectacle over dinner? What is his purpose in championing Caroline? Thank goodness, I am not in their line of fire.

"All this she must possess." Darcy leaned to the right to bypass Caroline and directed his gaze on Miss Elizabeth. "And yet to all this she must add something more substantial, in the improvement of her mind by extensive reading." He graced Caroline with a smile.

Oh, I think Darcy has entered the race for Miss Elizabeth. Rawlings smiled.

"I am no longer surprised at your knowing only six accomplished women. I rather wonder now at your knowing any," Elizabeth said.

"Are you so severe upon your own sex as to doubt the possibility of all this?" Caroline squealed.

"I never saw such a woman. I never saw such capacity, and taste, and application, and elegance, as you describe, united."

Rawlings shook his head. Oh no, Miss Elizabeth. He is complimenting you. Even Blake recognizes his admiration, and, now, he is wearing his calculating face he uses when processing new information. Darcy, my dear friend, the marquess will not be so oblivious to your interest in Miss Elizabeth from now on.

Blake moved to join Miss Elizabeth while maintaining his hard stare at Darcy's back who had returned to writing his letter. After glancing around the room, Rawlings felt confident no one else noticed the growing tension between the two. Perhaps Kent did. He, too, is an observer of people, albeit a quieter one.

Caroline and Louisa continued their discussion of an accomplished woman's attributes, and then began naming women they knew who fit their description. Mr. Hurst called them to order, with bitter complaints about of wife's inattention to what was going forward with the hand of cards.

The card players returned to their game; freeing Caroline to pursuing Darcy. He concentrated on his letter as she continued to glide about the room, trying to engage him in conversation.

Rawlings enjoyed witnessing this little game of cat and mouse. Caroline deviously set out a piece of cheese and a skillful Darcy avoided the mousetrap by either providing short answers or nothing at all. Compliment after compliment she tossed his way—admiration of his quickness of writing, skill at mending pens, and the evenness of his lines—until she gave him an admiring comment that would not go unchallenged—

"It is a rule with me that a person who can write a long letter with ease cannot write ill."

Bingley chuckled. "That will not do for a compliment to Darcy, Caroline. He does not write with ease. He studies too much to find words of four syllables!"

"Humph. I believe how I seek the best word or phrase is an established fact, even if it means a four-syllable word is used. My writing style is decidedly different from yours," Darcy quipped.

When Elizabeth began defending Bingley, Rawlings leaned forward in his chair. My goodness. She is again challenging Darcy. Rawlings caught sight of Blake smirking. He is rather enjoying this too.

Darcy sat erect with his gaze glued on Elizabeth. "Nothing is more deceitful than the appearance of humility. It is often only carelessness of opinion, and sometimes an indirect boast." He smiled at Bingley. "I remember you stating recently if you ever resolved on quitting Netherfield you should be gone in five minutes. You meant it to be a sort of panegyric, of compliment to yourself -- and yet… "

All eyes turned towards Darcy.

He cleared his throat, diverted his eyes away from Bingley, and rested them back on Elizabeth. "What is there so very laudable in a hurriedness which must leave very necessary business undone, and can be of no real advantage to yourself, Bingley, or to any one else?"

And where would that leave our sweet Miss Bennet? Rawlings sighed. Watching Elizabeth intently, he was disappointed she did not catch Darcy's warning. Would Bingley leave Miss Jane without a proper goodbye?

"And which of the two do you call my little recent piece of modesty?" Bingley challenged his friend.

"The indirect boast; for you are proud of your defects in writing, because you consider them as proceeding from a rapidity of thought and carelessness of execution, which if not estimable, you think at least highly interesting. The power of doing anything with quickness is always much prized by the possessor, and often without any attention to the imperfection of the performance," Darcy explained.

Rawlings sighed again. We all know you never act quickly unless forced to do so. You mull things over forever. Did you not tell us you thought about the alliance for six months before acting upon it? Nevertheless, if you are not careful, my friend, your lack of rapidity of action will cause you to lose something you secretly want, he mused as he turned to catch Miss Elizabeth's reaction.

She raised her brow. "You have only proved by this that Mr. Bingley did not do justice to his own disposition. You have shown him off now much more than he did himself."

"I am exceedingly gratified," Bingley said, "by your turning what my friend says into a compliment on the sweetness of my temper. I am afraid you are giving it a turn which that gentleman did by no means intend; for he would certainly think the better of me if, under such a circumstance, I were to give a friend that asks me to stay a flat denial, and ride off as fast as I could."

"Would Mr. Darcy then consider the rashness of your original intention as atoned for by your obstinacy in adhering to it?"

Touché, Elizabeth. Now, Darcy, you must answer her. Once your mind is set, will you be able to change later? Rawlings leaned forward in his chair towards his friend as he listened to his reply

"You expect me to account for opinions which you chose to call mine, but which I have never acknowledged." Darcy's brow shot up. "Allowing the case, however, to stand according to your representation, you must remember, Miss Bennet, that the friend who is supposed to desire his return to the house, and the delay of his plan, has merely desired it, asked it without offering one argument in favor of its propriety."

"To yield readily -- easily -- to the persuasion of a friend is no merit with you," Elizabeth shot back.

Whoa. Is that not what this alliance is all about? Darcy, are we to yield to your plans based on your persuasion powers? Rawlings wondered.

"To yield without conviction is no compliment to the understanding of either." Darcy glared at Blake. "But to accept due solely to the other's higher status is equally repugnant."

So, might we challenge you? But what if all we have to confront you with are our instincts? I wonder, will you allow us to say no to a business proposition without a well research and rational argument? Rawlings noted the interplay of cold stares between Darcy and Blake. Is Darcy trying to warn Miss Elizabeth not to succumb to his friends' charms? Is he calling Blake's actions repugnant? Oh my God, he is.

"You appear to me, Mr. Darcy, to allow nothing for the influence of friendship and affection. A regard for the requester would often make one readily yield to a request without waiting for arguments to reason one into it. In general, and ordinary cases, between friend and friend, where one desires the other to change a resolution of no very great moment, should you think ill about that person for complying with the desire, without waiting to be argued into it?"

Blake moved to stand beside Elizabeth. "I might add, there may not be a need to argue with a friend." He turned his gaze on her. "The desires may be mutual; therefore, there is no reason to defend one's request. The higher ranked person need only ask, as is his right, or shall we say entitlement, for the person to agree with his request. Perhaps the friends are close intimates, which would also make a difference."

Rawlings noticed everyone's attention focused on Darcy. Answer carefully, man. All your partners are listening to your answer and they assume this conversation is all about business, but I daresay, Blake is speaking of another purpose.

Darcy grabbed the arms of his chair so tightly his hand veins enlarged. "Will it not be advisable, before we proceed on this subject, to determine the degree of importance, as well as the degree of intimacy subsisting between the parties? Should the demands be accepted without thought or the opportunity to reject the request by the other, regardless of rank?"

Good job, Darcy. However, I do not believe Miss Elizabeth understood the hidden meanings to the conversation between the two men. What does Blake wish to demand? Is there much intimacy subsisting between her and Blake? I am positive Darcy is concerned.

Before anyone could answer, Darcy turned back to his letter. "Bingley, I know you dislike an argument, and suspect you want to silence this."

"Perhaps I do. Arguments are too much like disputes. If you and Miss Bennet will defer yours till I am out of the room I shall be very thankful; and then you may say whatever you like of me."

"What you ask," Elizabeth said, "is no sacrifice on my side; and Mr. Darcy had much better finish his letter."

Mr. Darcy dipped his quill in the inkwell and scribbled away.

Rawlings was disappointed when the conversation ended. He had not been quite so entertained before. Miss Elizabeth indicated she was not impressed with Darcy either. She spoke with subtle sarcasm, and yet Darcy did not understand. Regardless, this young miss from a minor country estate appeared to be the one person in England capable of challenging Mr. Darcy—other than Bingley, that is, but he never went beyond an unimportant tease.

When Bingley applied to Miss Bingley and Elizabeth for the indulgence of some music, Rawlings chuckled at how rapidly Miss Bingley moved to the pianoforte. Elizabeth politely, and more earnestly, declined to play first. Miss Elizabeth is a woman of exceptional worth, and I hope my friend overcomes his prejudices to seek her out before it is too late. Although, I doubt she wants his attentions. He must do more than peer at her with that damn hard stare. Admit it, my friend, you want her. What is stopping you? Must you mull over everything? Do not be so conflicted. But then, she would be an advantage to Blake if he should win her hand. Of course, that is, if it is her hand he is seeking. Is she the reason for the thirty percent? Do you need money to keep her in a nearby cottage to your father's estate?

Rawlings continued to monitor the actions of the people in the room. He was not surprised to see Darcy again staring at Elizabeth; however, her reaction to his stares troubled him. Please, Miss Elizabeth, try to understand the purpose behind his looks. Not all men speak about their feelings with pretty words and flirtatious ways. Look deeply into his eyes, Miss Elizabeth, for there is something important for you to grasp.

After playing some Italian songs, Miss Bingley varied the charm with a lively Scotch air; and soon afterwards, Mr. Darcy, drawing near Elizabeth, said to her --

"Do not you feel a great inclination, Miss Bennet, to seize such an opportunity of dancing a reel?"

Blake was close enough to overhear the question. His hands balled into fists, and his eyes narrowed.

I daresay, he does not have a single good thought for his friend at this moment, Rawlings reflected.

Smiling, she made no answer, preferring instead to turn and smile at Blake who relaxed at once. Darcy with some surprise at her silence repeated the question.

"Oh!" I heard you before. I could not immediately determine what to say in reply. You wanted me, I know, to say yes, that you might have the pleasure of despising my taste. I always delight in overthrowing those kind of schemes, and cheating a person of their premeditated contempt. I have, therefore, made up my mind to tell you, that I do not want to dance a reel at all -- and now despise me if you dare."

Darcy replied, "Indeed, I do not dare."

Rawlings watched her reaction to his gallantry. Having thought she would affront him, her expression showed her surprise. Her manner is a mixture of sweetness and archness in her manner, which made it difficult for her to cause offense to anybody. He knew Darcy had never been as bewitched by any woman as he was by her. And if he were to ignore the inferiority of her connections, his friend would be in some danger of falling for her. Whoa! Darcy must be merely trying to shield her, and keep her from harm. Pity, he does not understand himself. For now.

When Blake offered his arm, suggesting they discuss his book from the comfort of the sofa, neither saw the cold, intense stare aimed at their backs.

Miss Bingley was busy at the pianoforte, fidgeting with the sheet music, her gaze taking in everything, with Kent by her side. Rawlings walked by them on his way to the sideboard for some refreshments just as Kent whispered, "Did you notice her fine eyes, Miss Bingley. It seems that Mr. Darcy has. Fortunately for you Miss Elizabeth did not understand the tease; I cannot promise you that she never will."

Rawlings' interest in the intimacies between Blake and Elizabeth increased when the marquess leant close to her to share something private. She laughed, which Rawlings recognized was not her way with Darcy. Blake handed her a book with a flower bookmark sticking out. Blushing, she glanced at the others in the room, and in particular, darted her eyes towards Darcy. Nodding her head to Blake in just the tiniest motion, she caressed the book. Thereafter, she stood, and expressed her desire to return to her sister. As all other conversation was at an end, Elizabeth left the room, keeping his book with her.

As she moved to the door, Rawlings read the title on the book, *A Morning Walk,* and now felt positive about what was happening on Blake's early morning gallops. *I wonder which passage is it that he wants Miss Elizabeth to read. Are they planning to meet somewhere? I must keep a close eye on Blake.* He glanced at Darcy, and noticed he, too, had witnessed the entire scene. *I must ask Logan to see if Blake rides out in the morning as is his normal habit, or does he forgo riding now that Miss Elizabeth is here. And I want a copy of his book.*

"Eliza Bennet," Miss Bingley said, when the door was closed on her, "is one of those young ladies who seek to recommend themselves to the other sex by undervaluing their own; and with many men, I dare say, it succeeds. In my opinion, it is a paltry device, a very mean art."

"Undoubtedly," Darcy replied, "there is meanness in all the arts which ladies sometimes condescend to employ for captivation. Whatever bears affinity to cunning is despicable."

Good show. Rawlings was surprised when Miss Bingley continued the subject. As she spoke, he observed Blake flitting from one place to another. First, he sat on the sofa, next he stood by the window, and lastly he spent an unnecessary amount of time stirring the burning wood in the fireplace. All the while, Caroline was unleashing her cruel wit about Miss Elizabeth, her family, and the whole of Meryton. Darcy, however, never once removed his darkened gaze from Blake.

Slap her, Blake. I dare you. Rawlings chuckled. *I know you want to. Are her comments about Miss Elizabeth the reason for your unease? Or is it because you are not the only man sorry for her return to her sister's room? Ah, Miss Bingley, it is fortunate for you we are all gentlemen, for I too grow tired of your talk. Someone, please, change the subject.*

Bingley, with his uncanny ability to respond to any uncomfortable situation, observed that the hour was late. All the men concurred, causing Caroline and the Hursts to retire to their bedchambers. Once his family had left the room, a grinning Bingley turned to his friends and suggested a game of Twenty Points, which they agreed to with alacrity.

"Not too late for a little sport, I take it," Rawlings said, "although there was plenty going on this evening. He laughed when two of his friends turned and glared at him. "Come, come, and let us work out our aggressions on the billiard table."

The men played several games before calling it a night; however, before Darcy left, Blake motioned him to stay. "Shall we have a go at a different game? This time though, we must choose one pocket, and only shots that fall into it will count."

"Do we both select a different pocket or do we shoot for the same one?"

Blake raised his brow. "Do you wish to chase after mine?"

Darcy crossed his arms. "Since neither of us has chosen yet, it would be hard for me to answer at this time."

"Not true. I have already chosen." Blake pointed to the right end pocket. "I have selected this one." He caressed the end pocket. "You see, I choose quickly and decisively!"

"Humph. Unlike you, I consider all the ramifications before selecting my choice. It is the better way."

"Ramifications such as?"

"For one, the location of the pocket is a significant concern. If you chose a pocket on the outskirts," Darcy pointed to the outer pockets at the end of the table, "then you must consider the difficulties in following through. It is too far from the center of everything."

"Perhaps the location is an obstacle, but not to one who is willing to overcome such trifling things as that. The outer pocket is not beyond my reach. I have enough of what it takes."

"Would not the center pockets make life easier for you? Banking is much easier when aiming for a pocket in the center. All the easiest shots are there for the taking."

"Well, banking is not the only consideration. I grant you it can be important, nevertheless, anyone with a straight approach can achieve success. I suspect the outer pocket is, shall we say, satisfied with the quickly moving ball coming toward her and taking possession of the desired territory."

"You may be correct. However, the pocket's position is not your only concern. The location of the other balls on the table must be considered, Blake. Where do they stand? Would not those located in the center impede your long shots to the outer pocket? They can be quite formidable, I believe."

"Phew. I would just blast right past them. I no longer find them restrictive in any way, even with their connections to me. I seek only the pocket. It is all that matters."

"I find the true game goes beyond one pocket. The entire table must be studied before one can advance in the proper direction."

"Advance? Let me inform you my friend, I have already advanced forward, and with great success, I might add."

"Are there not balls surrounding the outer pocket, too? Would not those balls follow your rolling ball wherever it went?"

"Hah! I would leave those other balls behind. Only when I chose to allow them to follow, then it be permitted. I have no need for them, nor does my pocket. We could be happy just by ourselves."

"I think you are not considering all the implications. Are you not fearful that the pocket is open to anyone wishing to come to the table armed with plenty of shots?   Or at least, being pushed in that direction from elsewhere."

"That is not possible with my pocket."

The two men stared at each other before Blake narrowed his eyes, and spoke with conviction. "Once I choose, I do not relent, and as I said, I have chosen. I fear no rival coming to the game armed with, as you say, plenty of shots of his own. Any competitor may have a better game than I have, but I do not cower from him." Blake leaned closer to Darcy, and in a half whisper added, "He comes too late."

"Perhaps you should consider why the pocket is so enticing to you."

"Pockets do not like the shooters that merely stare and never take their shot. You ignore the pocket while you mull everything over. I, on the other hand, offer quickly."

"Offer what? Do you offer a quick victory, and then, you are off to play another game with another pocket?"

Blake grabbed hold tightly to his cue stick. "How I place my shots, and with which pocket is none of your concern."

Sighing, Darcy bowed slightly.

The two men spent the next half hour making shots and glancing repeatedly at each other. In the end, Darcy won the game. Blake, losing the desire for any more sport, retired for the evening.

***

The aroma of this morning's cooked ham was in the air when Elizabeth entered the empty dining room. She spied the table filled with eggs, ham, breads, and some familiar pastries. Bingley's cook had sold these to Meryton's locals for years. She moved to the buffet, turning when she heard footsteps behind her. Her ready smile receded once she saw Mr. Darcy entering the room.

"Miss Bennet, good morning. May I ask how your sister is faring?"

"She is still ill with a slight fever but I am hopeful it will pass today. I thank you for asking."

"Should we call the doctor?" Darcy moved closer to her, breatheing deeply to inhale her lavender scent. "Mr. Bingley would not hesitate to summon one from London. He could be here tonight. Just let either of us know. I do not know if the apothecary's skill is sufficient." He wished to share with her how Bingley's father caught pneumonia from a cold, which caused his death; however, he would not reveal anyone's private information nor was he comfortable with unduly raising her concern.

"Thank you, no. I suspect once her fever breaks, she will be on the mend, and rather quickly. Mr. Jones has treated all our colds with great success in the past. I have no doubt this time will be no different."

Darcy bowed his head.

The two continued to the buffet table. Darcy was amused at the quantitiy of food she added to her plate. In addition to heaping on ham and eggs, she supplemented her breakfast meal with three sweet lemon pastries. Elizabeth glanced up at his chuckles.

"Mr. Rawlings may need to stand guard over his pastries."

"Oh, I beg your pardon." A red-faced Elizabeth reached to return the sweet treats.

"No, no, help yourself; there are plenty. Nonetheless, my friend cannot go a morning without such a pleasant indulgence. He vows no other pastry in town is as agreeable."

"All of Meryton is familiar with them. In fact, my sisters and I grew up on them. My father would use them as a reward for good behavior."

Apparently, sweets did not work with the youngest two, Darcy mused when he filled his plate with equal amounts of food.

They sat across from each other. Elizabeth ate her breakfast in silence; he admired her elegance and grace. She patted her lips with the napkin after each bite, kept her elbows off the table, remained in an upright position, and tilted her head somewhat as she often glanced at the door. Neither spoke, she preferred to concentrate on the consumption of the meal; he chose to gaze with admiration at her gracefulness. A few times, he caught himself attempting to reach over and pat her hand.

Pushing away his empty plate, Darcy motioned for the servant to refill his coffee. "When you have finished, would you care for a walk in the garden? The morning is accommodating. You could continue to defend Mr. Bingley."

"And you, sir, would you continue to provide insight into his character?"

Darcy leaned forward, and in a solemn tone said, "Or perhaps insight into another friend would serve you better."

With her eyes glowering, Elizabeth rose abruptly. "Thank you for the offer; however, I must return to my sister now. I will let Mr. Bingley know if a doctor is needed." With that, Elizabeth curtseyed, and left the room, leaving her pastries on the plate.

He felt that old dullness overtake him as he watched her retreat to the hallway where he spotted Blake . He quickly offered to escort her back to her sister. Once they were out of view, Darcy directed the servant to send a plate of pastries to to Miss Bennet's room. When the servant left with the plate of treats and a pot of coffee, Bingley walked in.

"Good morning, Darcy. I trust you slept well."

"Thank you, yes. You have risen early this morning."

"I admit I tossed and turned all night. Should I send for a doctor? I have thought about nothing else except the health of Miss Bennet. Even last night, I could not concentrate on the card game."

"You were playing high last night. Perhaps it would be wise not to set up the table tonight." When everyone had convened in the drawing room the night before, he spotted Elizabeth's startled expression at the amount of money wagered on the game. "I will not be playing tonight. I also believe Miss Elizabeth may be more comfortable with other entertainment. Some quiet time to read might prove soothing to her. The ladies will have spent their day caring for Miss Bennet."

"Good, very good. We shall have no card table tonight."

The two men took advantage of their time alone by discussing business arrangements, and finalizing plans for several trips up north. They exchanged words, but neither man listened with any serious attention.

Chapter Twenty-seven

The ladies occupied themselves with another day keeping the now improving Jane company; the men set about another morning of leisurely pursuits. Yesterday, the inclusion of a sixth opponent at the men's morning bird shoot and afternoon billiards game proved costly. Jonathan Hurst had confirmed himself as an excellent shot when loaned a Baker rifle, and victorious with a cue stick. Kent and Rawlings often cried foul for Bingley allowing his brother-in-law to join the fray. "Keeping the spoils in the family," they said in jest.

Blake and Darcy had other thoughts occupying their minds. Neither man shot a bullet or a cue ball particularly well this day, as they spent the entire afternoon exchanging glares.

Bingley appeared to be in a happier mood when all the guests convened in the evening—Miss Bennet had overcome the critical aspect of her cold, and joined the group in the drawing room. He buzzed around her the entire time as if she was his personal Queen bee, fulfilling her every need. He shared not a single word with any other person. He placed her close to the fireplace, ensuring the logs remained lit by taking charge of the responsibility. He had hot chocolate prepared for her, a treat she seemed to enjoy. He directed servants to bring in blankets and a hot brick for her feet. When she declined a second cup, he ran to fetch a glass of wine as soon as the request escaped her lips. Worried about her continued recovery, he told her that no service was beneath his dignity this night.

However, unlike the previous evening, everyone did retire earlier. Miss Bennet needed only to indicate she had grown tired before the entire assembly made the appropriate excuses and departed for their rooms. Bingley was quick to escort Miss Bennet and Miss Elizabeth. All day he had appeared unaware of the growing tension between Blake and Darcy, but his action belied his ignorance. Kent and Rawlings had also detected the strain between the two men; but, as true gentlemen do, they imparted an impression of ignorance, which proved helpful in lessening the friction.

When Rawlings entered his bedchambers, he found Logan sitting in his usual comfortable chair, having accomplished his nightly tasks. He had stroked the fire, placed the brandy and cigars near his master's seat and prepared the bedclothes. Rawlings spied *A Morning Walk* on the table.

"Thank you, Mr. Logan. I cannot be nonchalant at your resourcefulness."

Without providing an explanation of his methods, Logan nodded his head at the compliment.

Rawlings settled back and lit his cigar. He leafed through the book to the vicinity where the flower bookmark stuck out in Blake's book. Unable to identify the passage, he tossed the volume on the table.

"Was the entertainment tonight as enjoyable as yesterday?" Logan asked as he poured Rawlings his evening brandy.

"Most decidedly so. Miss Elizabeth is unquestionably Darcy's equal. Well, perhaps not in fortune or connections, but in wit and cleverness, I should say so. There is only one failure on her part."

"And what, perchance, is that?"

"Her inability to understand Darcy's true feelings toward her. I find this remarkable since she is a most perceptive person."

"I suspect he requires a good kick in the breeches. He must do more than just stare and engage her in verbal challenges." Logan relaxed in his chair, swirling his brandy in the glass.

"I doubt if he even understands his own inclinations. I have never been so delighted with watching two people converse." Rawlings drained his glass and poured himself another drink.

"And Blake. Did he do anything?"

"Blake did not say a word, never looking away from them while the two wrangled. Tonight, he held back because I suspect he believed Miss Elizabeth was bettering Darcy.

"So, she was triumphant in her thrusts and he with his parries?"*

"Taking up fencing now? There were many Counter-Ripostes and he engaged in a magnificent Counter-Parry. In the end, she did retreat, I suspect in order to fight another day. Darcy is still the king of the argument. Surprisingly, he does allow Miss Elizabeth much liberty in her opinions. Poor Miss Bingley." Rawlings closed his eyes and shook his head. He leaned back in his chair and sipped his drink.

"I assume you mean she is poor in kinds of treasures that do not include fortunes and dowries." Logan said, smirking as he took another sip.

"She, like Blake, was forced into the role of spectator. When Darcy and Miss Elizabeth are sparring, no one dares to interrupt."

"How did the conversation go? I mean, what was their topic tonight."

"Him," Rawlings said, chuckling at Logan's stunned expression. Rawlings took another puff on his cigar. He blew the smoke towards the ceiling.

"You mean Blake, or was Darcy himself the topic?"

"Darcy! I relied on all my training on self-control not to lose my countenance when Miss Elizabeth suggested Miss Bingley tease the man."

"Tease him? She asked Miss Bingley to do this? Impossible! I wager such a suggestion shocked her."

"I do believe we all were. 'Tease calmness of temper and presence of mind' was Miss Bingley's answer. She said she could not do so. Darcy proved her correct. He remained calm even when Miss Elizabeth attacked his vanity and pride."

Rawlings poured himself a third brandy, even as Logan gave him a cautious stare with each ounce filling the glass.

"She called Darcy vain? Proud he is, but vain?" Logan shook his head when Rawlings offered to pour him a second drink.

"Oh, he muttered something about vanity being a weakness, but where there is a real superiority of mind, pride was not to be laughed at. Miss Elizabeth had to turn away to hide her smiles over that pronouncement. I had to drink my wine slowly. I was fearful I would spit the damn stuff out."

"You do not drink slowly. I am always suggesting you should imbibe less, as well as at a leisurely rate." Logan gave a pointed glance at Rawlings' finished brandy.

Shrugging, Rawlings placed the glass on the table without refilling it. "I am a big man. I can drink more than you small framed ninnies can. Nevertheless, let me finish. That cheeky girl had the nerve to proclaim Darcy as a man without defect. She looked straight in his eyes when she made her declaration. Can you picture him after such a challenge?"

"Well? Did Darcy agree?"

"He most assuredly did not. He said he was not deficient in understanding – imagine calling yourself clever after having stating that he was not vain; however, he did own that he had a resentful temper. Remind me never to lose his esteem. Do you know why?"

Logan shook his head.

"He admitted once his good opinion is lost, it is lost forever. Now his declaration correlates to his conversation yesterday, do you not agree?" Rawlings leaned forward with both eyebrows raised and hands on his knees.

"How so?"

"He said 'To yield readily -- easily -- to the persuasion of a friend is no merit'. Do you understand now? He has not only a temper, but immovable opinions as well." Rawlings settled back into the chair, took a few deep breaths, and added, "This may cause problems for the alliance, and that is my utmost worry. Oh, let us hope Blake does not lose Darcy's good opinion."

"I understood you to say yesterday if the details were well explained, found reasonable and the parties were honorable, than his judgment could be swayed."

"Yes, true. Someone he respects can change his regard with rationalization, I suppose; but he must respect them without doubt."

Logan nodded.

Rawlings abruptly leaned forward, his brow raised. "There was one final verbal thrust by our duelists. Miss Elizabeth then reversed her taunting jab by charging him with having a defect after all. Can you guess?"

"I am thinking it was not his arrogance. I do not believe Miss Elizabeth would be so bold."

"No, she did not call him arrogant. She said he had a propensity to hate everybody. Just what Bingley accused Darcy as owning when we went hunting! Again, Darcy did not let this comment pass. He retaliated by accusing Miss Elizabeth with her own defect – a willingness to misunderstand everyone. I do not think Darcy knows how correct he is."

"Ah, the blindness of love."

"With regret, the ladies return to Longbourn tomorrow, and my entertainment will be lost." Rawlings exhaled a deep breath, puffing his cheeks out. Relaxing in his seat, he finished his cigar, blowing smoke rings while contemplating the change.

"Will they be gone in the morning?" Logan asked.

"Yes, by ten. Their father insisted upon it. With his recent misfortunes, he should be pushing his daughters towards us. I do not believe Mrs. Bennet knows the truth, otherwise both the Bennets ladies would remain here until an offer was made, the settlements signed, and the new dresses ordered." Rawlings recollected his own wedding arrangements. "I do respect Mr. Bennet for not forcing his girls on us. Still, he wants them home, and I shall be sorry to see them leave."

"Do the other gentlemen know about the Bennet misfortunes?

"No. I have not even discussed the situation with Darcy. No one has dropped any hints either. I cannot imagine what impact the loss will have, and on Blake in particular. Once he finds out Elizabeth's dowry is gone, I suspect his attentions might be diverted to another."

"Ah. To the fortunes of Miss Bingley."

"I doubt she would interest him! Blake is a discriminating fellow. More likely, the lady he chooses will reside in London with the right connections and wealth."

"Any lady in particular?"

"Last season he appeared to be courting someone. I cannot recall whom, although he had spent all his time wooing her. It was the subject of the gossips and old dowagers!"

~*~

Mr. Bennet did indeed miss his two eldest daughters. The ratio of men to women concerned him, even though the Hursts provided proper chaperonage. At eight and forty, he could still remember how men reacted when beauty was in so close a proximity, and no father present. Mr. Jones had provided him with a thorough report on Jane's condition, allowing him to send a note requiring them to return home. The carriage would arrive at ten the next morning. He even wrote that he would brook no argument.

Elizabeth, concerned with the growing intensity between her and Mr. Darcy, feared Lord Blake would speak uncivilly to him. Lord Blake had hinted at his displeasure with his friend the day before. She reasoned if she were absent, there would be less tension between them, and no harm would come to their friendship.

At this moment, however, she was more concerned about her mother. She believed her father would wait to reveal their recent misfortune until they had returned home. She had told Jane everything before breakfast this morning. Both sisters dreaded the uproar and silliness soon to descend upon Longbourn. Sighing, they wished to delay the news by remaining at Netherfield for another day or two. At least, that was what they told each other.

While Jane finished overseeing the packing of her things, Elizabeth decided to wait in the library for the carriage to arrive. Surprised by Mr.

Darcy's presence, she lowered her eyes and curtseyed. "Excuse me. I did not mean to interrupt your privacy."

"Please stay. I was just seeking a book, and then I will be on my way," He waved her in without turning her way, and continued to peruse the books. Miss Elizabeth was amused as he reached for a book, mumbled, and then replaced it in its slot. He repeated this several times before she laughed aloud.

"What amuses you, Miss Elizabeth?" Darcy returned her bemused expression.

"Your diligence in trying to find a book. I daresay it should not be hard here." Her eyes roamed the shelves, noting the sparseness of reading material. "Perhaps my father may have what you seek. I will inquire about it when I return home."

"Thank you." Darcy bowed his head. "I would not be surprised if he did. I was looking for a book on gas lighting," As Darcy spoke he presented her with a smile she had not seen before.

"I have no doubt, as you apparently well know." Mistaking his smile for a smirk, she spoke curtly and with her dark gaze boring into his eyes she curtsied abruptly, and then spun around to leave the room.

Darcy started and then raised his brows while she rushed to the doorway.

Elizabeth was pleased Blake was standing and watching in the doorway and and when she accepted his offer to escort her to the waiting carriage, she took it. However, she was not pleased when he sent a sideways chilling glance back towards Darcy.

***

The daughters were not welcomed home with any affection by their mother. Mrs. Bennet wondered at the quickness of their return, and was sure Jane would catch cold again. Their father, though very brief in his expressions of pleasure, was pleased to see them; he had felt their importance in the family circle by their absence.

In addition, Mr. Bennet, just as Elizabeth assumed, needed his two eldest daughters at home when he informed their mother of the loss of all her children's dowries. So it was, within the hour after their arrival, he sent for his wife. Jane and Elizabeth roamed the hallway, preparing for the inevitable eruption. As the moments slipped away, they were surprised how subdued it was inside their father's study, and they repeatedly sent questioning glances to one another. They heard a muffled voice or two.

Bolting from the room, Mrs. Bennet did not speak to her daughters, although she almost knocked them down rushing to her bedchambers. She did not call for Hill. She did not shriek. She did not ask for her smelling salts. She entered her room, deposited herself in the chair by the window, and stared at the garden below. After three quiet hours of uncommon stillness, Mrs. Bennet insisted Hill fetch Jane and Lizzy.

After knocking on the opened door, the two eldest girls stood guardedly in the doorway, waiting for her to respond. She was pacing around the room when she heard the knock. She surprised them with a smile and waved them inside.

"Jane, Lizzy. I would like a moment to speak with you; here in my chambers. It is private here, and we need to talk."

"Yes, mama," the two said in unison as they entered.

Mrs. Bennet closed the door behind them. She invited them to sit as she continued to pace. Glancing at each other, they sat still while waiting for their mother to speak. When she did, it was with the calmest voice they ever heard from her.

"It is a sad state of affairs, this business about the dowries. It is not the end of the world. We have a little time. You, Jane, will secure Mr. Bingley, of that I am sure. I do not believe your beauty was for naught." She held her eldest's face in her hands. "He is quite smitten with you."

Mrs. Bennet turned towards Lizzy with a concerned expression not often shared with her least favorite daughter. "You, too, have an admirer in Lord Blake. I do not know why, but we must work diligently to secure an offer from him as well."

Mrs. Bennet paced a little more until she stopped in front of her daughters with a calculating stare. "We have no other choice except to pursue these men. We must succeed quickly before everyone in Meryton finds out. We must take drastic steps. The harvest feast and ball is a good place to start."

Jane and Lizzy remained perfectly still, except for their expressions. While they listened to their mother enlighten them with her campaign, their brows rose gradually, and their eyes grew wider and wider. They glanced from their mother to each other. After a time, Jane sent a silent plea to her sister to stop her. Shrugging in response, Lizzy smiled mischievously. This was the first time, she had ever considered allowing her mother to go on so without so much as a clever retort. She was entertained by it.

It appeared to her that Mrs. Bennet had decided it was time to concentrate on helping her second born. Turning all her energy towards Lizzy, she leaned in close to her daughter's face. "Now, you need to be less, well, independent. You must learn to flatter him, and tell him how well he looks in his coat. Look down when you say this."

"At my feet?" Lizzy shook her head in wonder.

"No, my dear. Do not vex me." Mrs. Bennet narrowed her eyes, and stared at Elizabeth. Raising her right eyebrow, she continued. "You know exactly where to cast your eyes. And when you do, you must not smirk, which would take away any chance you would ever have. Do you hear me, missy?"

"You mean like this?" Elizabeth presented an exaggerated smirk as she stared into her mother's eyes.

"Yes. Now practice showing a proper smile."

Lizzy copied Jane's smile.

Her mother nodded her approval, and then continued with the lesson. "And the next issue, do not go on with your teasing ways. You must tell him how handsome he is, how smart, how kind, and most of all you need to tell him how strong his arms are, and how big his hands are. Compliments of that sort always work. Men imagine they must have strapping arms, and they seem to smile most assuredly when you tell them about their enormous big hands."

"But mama. What if his arms are not strong? What if Lord Blake has tiny hands? Should I lie?"

"No, he would know what you say is a lie." Mrs. Bennet shook her head. "You must phrase your words as such: if his hands are tiny, then mention how you think they are the most wonderful size. They are neither too big nor too small to hold your heart."

It took great effort for Lizzy not to laugh aloud. Jane stared at the floor to hide the blush she could feel burning her cheeks.

"Is that all?" Lizzy practiced her non-smirking smile. When Jane's eyes pleaded with her to stop, she rewarded her with another exaggerated smirk.

"No. You must also tell the man he is the smartest, cleverest man you have met. Say, if the whole world was as smart as he, then there would be no wars, no poverty, and no unhappiness."

Lizzy shook her head. "I have seen such a ploy used by another; I assure you, mother, it does not work. Men are not that vain."

"Yes, Lizzy, believe me, they are. Oh, I have one more thought. If Lord Blake wins or especially if he loses that horse, you must be the first one to be at his side. Quickly walk to wherever he is at the end of the game." Mrs. Bennet gasped. "Good Heavens! We need to work on your walk."

"My walk? Do you mean I am missing that certain something in my manner of walking, and a certain air about me? Someone has already hinted at my failings of this nature to me."

"What are you gibbering about? No, I mean you walk like a boy. Now Jane, show her how to walk." Mrs. Bennet took Jane's hand, pulling her to her feet. "Yes, get up and walk around the room."

Jane did as she was told, walking from one end of the room to the other.

"Look, Lizzy. Watch her. Do not turn away; now watch Jane's backside. See how her hips move; they tend to sway ever so slightly. Not much, mind you but just so. Yours, I daresay, do not.

"What do mine do?" Elizabeth asked with her eyebrows raised.

"They just sit there on top of your legs as you move about. Now try it. Sway your hips."

Mrs. Bennet placed both hands on Elizabeth's hips. She pushed them to the right and then the left. Jane bit her lip and closed her eyes and turned her head away. Still, Elibeth spotted the tears falling uncontrollably down her sister's cheeks. Jane always cried laughter tears when she was concealing her amusement. She never cried sad ones.

"No, do not sway so much. Here use this fan."

"Fan? Am I supposed to fan my hips?"

"No, silly girl. You are to use the fan to hide that hideous smirk. You have pleasing eyes; the fan will highlight them."

"So I sway and fan?"

"And tilt your head. To the right. To the right. Oh my, your hair. What are we ever to do with your hair?"

"Cut it short?" Lizzy used her fingers as scissors in her hair.

"I will ensure Sarah spends at least one hour each morning fixing that hair. You know what that means?"

Lizzy shook her head. This time she was dumbfounded.

"You cannot go walking about in the woods. Your hair is so wild looking when you get back. No more walking for you."

"What if Lord Blake likes to walk? Especially in the woods."

"Well, that is a good point." Mrs. Bennet placed her fist on her chin while she thought of a solution. Answering, she shook her finger at Elizabeth. "You may walk with him, but do not go scampering off in the woods alone. I fear that would send the wrong signal."

"Signal?"

"That you are a wanton woman. In order to catch this man, you must make him chase you."

"Oh, so I am to run instead of walk?"

"Do not speak so. Lizzy, I told you to use your fan to hide that smirk you are wearing. Of course, you are not to run. Ladies do not run. They walk slowly, fluttering their fans, tilting their heads and swaying their hips. Now practice."

With both hands, Mrs. Bennet pulled Elizabeth from the chair on which she had just sat. As Elizabeth walked, Mrs. Bennet stared at her. "Blink your eyes. No, no, no, not so quickly. That looks like you have something caught in your eyes. That only works when you are alone on a balcony at a ball. He will stand ever so close to try to remove something from your eyes. Wear your best perfume for that kind of occasion, and place it between your breasts. Oh, and we must lift your breasts."

"With my hands? Like so?" Lizzy pushed them upwards and inwards. "Do I do this while he is removing the imaginary dust from my eyes?"

Jane had to look out the window. She had no self-control left and was no longer able to hide her own toothy smiles. She covered her mouth with her hand to stop the snickering from escaping.

"Silly goose. We need to get you a better corset, one that lifts your assets much higher."

"If they were any higher, I could place my fan there as a resting spot."

"And we need to have a few of your dresses cut down further." Mrs. Bennet stared at Lizzy's chest.

"You have chosen low cut dresses as it is. Will not my, well, you know, show?"

"It is called a nipple. We are mother and daughter and can speak openly here. Of course, I am not suggesting you reveal it, well, not the whole of it. I did raise you girls to be proper ladies. He will think it is a glimpse of heaven but his thinking of what lies below will increase his excitement."

"A glimpse of heaven?"

Noticing Elizabeth's ashen face, Mrs. Bennet muttered, "It is just the tiniest bit of a glimpse—a sliver is all. We are in desperate straits. This may be just the push he needs."

Lizzy looked over to Jane. "So Jane, I see that little piece of heaven sneaking out of your dress. No, your left one." She chuckled when a blushing Jane covered her neckline with her hand. "Is that why all the men favor you so? In the future, I shall watch Mr. Bingley to see where he aims his eyes."

"We need to keep Lord Blake's eyes aimed up high, away from your boyish hips. You have beautiful eyes and wonderful breasts. These are your best assets my dear. The rest is just horrid."

Mrs. Bennet grabbed Elizabeth's hand, pulling her to the door. "Let us go to your room and find all the dresses that require fixing. Hill! Hill!"

Chapter Twenty-eight

Mr. Bennet sat at the breakfast table, letter in his hand, informing his family of the impending arrival of a visitor. After the habitual silliness had settled, he revealed the the caller as a Mr. Collins. Once his wife figured out this man was Longbourn's heir, her shrill cries flooded the room. He read the letter aloud, announcing Mr. Collin's intention of finding a wife from amongst his daughters, transforming his wife's venom-laced words into peals of laughter and shrieks of happiness.

As promised, at precisely four o'clock, Mr. Collins came to Longbourn. A tall, heavy looking young man of five and twenty entered the house with a grave and stately air about him, and with the most contrived manners.

Mr. Bennet delighted in the man's ramble through the rooms. evaluating the furniture and all of the household items. Mr. Collins offered exaggerated comparisons to similar objects found at his patroness' home, Rosings. While he talked, he interspersed minutiae about her generosity, the great Lady Catherine de Bourgh.

Mr. Collins turned out to be as absurd as Mr. Bennet had hoped, and he listened to him with the keenest enjoyment, maintaining at the same time, the most resolute composure. However, he did not hide his displeasure when he caught his guest repeatedly gawking at his two oldest daughters, although Mrs. Bennet showed no concern over the direction of his stares.

Even his daughters' charms did not keep this ridiculous man from occupying many hours in his study during the first several days, each day too rainy to encourage walks to town. In his library sanctuary, he had wanted but failed freedom from Mr. Collins. However, he hated to hear any of the folly and conceit that this self-important buffoon had displayed in every other room in his room. For days, he had listened to Mr. Collins speak a great deal: of his house and garden at Hunsford, his two weekly dinners with the Lady Catherine DeBough, and how this great woman had promised to visit his humble abode upon his installation of a wife. At the exact moment the sunlight streaked through his window, he suggested Mr. Collins join his daughters in their walk to Meryton. His reason was a simple return to a quiet sanctuary. He elicted his wife's help, and without delay, Mrs. Bennet agreed with the plan, pushing Mary towards the guest.

Even though they left as a group, Mr. Collins lagged behind the youngest Bennets, whom had skipped ahead as fast as possible, giggling as they went. In deference to the man's future position, Jane and Elizabeth walked a bit slower, although they too attempted to walk apart from him. With only pompous nothings on his side and polite civilities on theirs, the not so subtle clergyman devised a new strategy.

"Miss Bennet, Miss Elizabeth, did you not wish to stop to admire this peculiar little rock?" Mr. Collins spoke only loud enough for the eldest girls to discern. His eyes did not part from Elizabeth's figure, and his breathing grew heavier, making the end of the sentence difficult to discern.

When he received no reply, other than the two ladies moving forward, he called out "Please I beg you. I have a cramp in my leg and must stop. Will you be so kind as to wait a moment?" Leaning down, he rubbed his right calf, taking many deep breaths. He noted they had stopped just ahead, whispering to each other and, in his mind, sending him sly looks. The youngest daughters had quickened their pace. He blotted the sweat from his brow with his already soaked handkerchief. Regaining his strength, he hobbled to catch up with the eldest Miss Bennets.

"It was most kind of you to wait. I rarely get cramps in my legs even though I am so used to walking."

"I am sorry for your pain." Elizabeth dropped her eyes to his left leg. "Why, Mr. Collins, you must be suffering excessively, for I see you are now hobbling on the other leg. Perhaps you should rest there?" She pointed her eyes to a fallen tree just off the road.

"Yes, that would be acceptable." Reaching the tree, he patted the lower end of the trunk, signaling the ladies to sit with him, and smiled in anticipation of the pleasant view to come. He glimpsed up, just in time to understand they had ignored his request and proceeded towards town.

"Wait! The cramp has passed. As you see I can walk now." He hurried to reach them by taking long strides.

They turned onto the main avenue, catching up to the younger sisters who were gaping at several men across the street. They recognized Mr. Denny, a favorite officer of their acquaintance, but they did not recognize the handsome gentleman with him. The stranger's air impressed the eldest Bennets, and even they wondered who he could be. Kitty and Lydia, determined to find out, led the way across the street, exclaiming a desire for something in a shop across the road, and fortunately had just stepped on the pavement when the two gentlemen, turning back, reached the same spot.

Mr. Denny addressed them, and obtained permission to introduce Mr. Wickham, who had returned with him from town. He announced that his friend had accepted a commission in their regiment. The youngest girls admired his appearance, believing it was greatly in his favor; he had all the best part of beauty and stateliness—a fine countenance, a good figure, and very pleasing address. In their eyes, the soon to be addition of regimentals would make him uniformly charming.

When the rest of the Bennet party joined them, they shared a most civil and proper conversation that kept the girls engaged, except for Jane. She searched every horseback rider coming into town for a familiar face, finding disappointment at every glance. Soon the group parted company, after Mr. Wickham indicated he had an urgent matter that needed his attention. What business awaited him, he did not reveal; but as soon as the Bennets had moved out of sight, Wickham nudged his friend for a small loan to use inside the Black Bull Tavern.

***

Blake longed to visit Oakham Mount, but assumed the rainy weather would keep Miss Elizabeth home. There was no point in riding if the only view was wet grounds surrounding Netherfield Park. He paced the library floor sighing as he walked until he grew bored. He sat quietly for a short period before he picked up a book and stared unseeing at the pages. Setting it aside, he sipped tea before striking up a conversation with one of his friends. He fell silent again when he caught himself responding absently to questions he had not heard. He fidgeted in his seat and twiddled his thumbs, and when that did not appease him, he tapped his fingers on the arm of the chair. In the end, he gravitated towards the window and silently cursed the rainfall. After a while, Blake began the pattern again.

"Worried about the Andalusian? I will take good care of him, Blake," Kent said.

"That will be difficult with him living in my stables." Blake returned to the window and released a long sigh.

"Does anyone wish to bet on the game the judges will come up with?" Rawlings asked. "I am personally hoping for a boxing match."

"Surely, not boxing. There are three competitors. Not knowing is maddening. I cannot conceive which game they will choose." Blake smiled at Bingley and said, "I admit I was most fortunate you chose golf."

"I do not think my strategy for coming in third will work this time!" Kent held the cards up for Bingley to see, who nodded his agreement, and the two began a game of Picquet.

Blake returned to his pattern of pacing, reading, sipping and looking through the window.

Darcy watched Blake, although he attempted to keep his scrutiny hidden from the man. He, too, had reread the same page over many times. Miss Bingley pretended to search for a book while eyeing Mr. Darcy. Mrs. Hurst sat with the blank expression of boredom and played with her bracelets. Occasionally, she joined her sister in some outlandish discussions. Rawlings and Hurst discussed the wines and brandies they had enjoyed before. They even tried a bit of Bingley's scotch, neither man finding it to his liking.

Just when it seemed the tediousness of the day would continue into another night, the clouds gave way and the sun appeared. Blake jumped up from his chair and announced, "I need some fresh air."

Darcy fell in behind Blake before he could escape. "I will join you. Shall we ride our horses to town? We could visit the Black Bull, now that our private club has been dismantled and returned to a ballroom."

"Yes, that is an excellent suggestion. I shall come as well." Bingley leapt from his seat. Kent nodded. He, too, said that he found the confines of the house boring. But when he discovered the destination was not a nearby estate, Rawlings waved the others off. He preferred to remain in the comfort of this dry room with Hurst, and the many carafes of warmth the library offered.

Losing their reason for lingering in the room and with the harvest feast and ball beginning in just three days, Miss Bingley and Mrs. Hurst left to check on the preparations.

***

The four men rode into Meryton and, each man lost in thought. The rain had kept the men captive in a house with little to do except think. Without the excitement of the games, they yearned for a gentlemen's activity, even if it meant mingling with the locals. So, when they unexpectedly stood in the doorway of the Black Bull, there was a clamor from the patrons and they were surprised but pleased.

"To Lord Blake, Mr.Kent, and Mr. Darcy. May the best man win the stallion," one of the patrons yelled out. Both men bowed. Another patron ordered ale for them.

Before entering, Bingley noticed Darcy had stopped abruptly when he stepped inside the doorway, and glared at a man sitting with an officer at a table along the back wall. The man stared back at first before jerking his face to the wall.

"Where are you going?" Bingley asked when Darcy turned to leave the tavern.

"I have no desire to drink in this place," he answered brusquely.

"But the patrons would wish to talk with you and we have been stuck in the house for days. We need the diversion.".

Darcy turned, Bingley followed on his heels.

Several patrons overheard his remark and shared it with all the others in the tavern. What little respect Darcy had earned during the games was lost.

Darcy and Bingley rode back to Netherfield Park in silence. Every time Bingley tried to broach the subject, Darcy scowled at him until Bingley closed his mouth. Finally, as soon as they reached the drive, Darcy proclaimed the man at the table was by no means a respectable young man. Mr. Wickham had been very imprudent and had lost any regard he might have previously held. Darcy refused to elaborate any further; and Bingley allowed the discussion to end there.

When they entered the house, Darcy stormed up the stairs, informing him he did not wish to be disturbed until dinner. Bingley left to find the other men.

Mr. Kent returned to the Netherfield Park after a few drinks and pocketing a few coins won from several rounds of skittles, a game he had recently sold to Staunton. He also possessed startling information and desired to share it with Rawlings as soon as possible. When he entered the library at Netherfield, he found Rawlings, Hurst, and Bingley discussing the accuracy of the Baker rifle. When informed Darcy had gone to his chambers, Kent signaled Rawlings to meet with him in the billiards room.

Once they were alone, he explained what had happened in the tavern. "I was shocked to hear what that man alleged."

"Exactly what was said?" Rawlings asked, calmly. He had heard many unkind remarks about their friend over the years, finding most to be without cause.

"Darcy had cheated him out of a living. The idea of Darcy cheating anyone is unbelievable to me."

"I agree." Rawlings sighed as he ran his fingers through his hair. "Who is this man?"

"He said his father was the steward of old Mr. Darcy."

"Which does lend his story a truthfulness, but I do not believe it even if Darcy came home in a state. I heard him stomping up the stairs and slamming his bedchamber door from where I sat in the library."

"Should we do anything?"

Rawlings shook his head. "No, let us follow his lead. Kent, where is Blake?"

"I suppose he is still at the Black Bull. I must apologize to him. I was so focused on the gossip; I neglected to let him know I was leaving.".

"I doubt he would be bothered by your defection. I rather suspect Blake was pleased. I would even wager that he went to see the pert Miss Elizabeth. He had been like a caged animal and it was not because he worried about the competition."

Meanwhile, Blake, oblivious to the gossip surrounding him, had been sitting in the tavern plotting ways to sneak off for the short ride to Longbourn when he noticed Kent had left. He did not see either Bingley or Darcy. Paying for his drink, he smoothed his clothes, nodded to the patrons, and nearly ran out the door. Arriving at Longbourn, he was delighted to find Elizabeth at home.

Mrs. Bennet watched Blake struggle to look somewhere other than at her daughter's womanly charms. She sent a smile to Lizzy.

Seeing her mother's gloating expression, Elizabeth felt the sudden heat on her cheeks and tried to cover her neckline with her hand.

"Miss Elizabeth, are you feeling well? You look a little flushed. Do you need some fresh air?" Blake asked, his voice anxious.

Mrs. Bennet interrupted. "Yes, Lord Blake. A walk in the garden would do her much good. She has been confined in this house for days."

Blake led her out the door before Elizabeth could object. "Are you feeling better now?" He whispered. He leaned in when he asked and inhaled her perfume.

"Yes, thank you." Elizabeth caught her mother standing by the window tilting her head to the right, blinking her eyes and swaying her hips. Elizabeth gasped; not at her mother, but where Blake had focused his eyes.

Flushed, Blake lifted his eyes to meet hers. "Have you found Wordsworth's book? I remember you said he was your favorite and you would reread it as soon as you returned."

"Yes, I did." Elizabeth steered Blake towards a bench in the part of the garden unseen from any window.

"You do look especially lovely today." Lord Blake swept his hand across the bench to make sure it was dry.

"You have done very well in the competition. I believe you fared much better than you expected before Mr. Bingley's game. I did not know you played golf."

Lord Blake's eyes sparkled. "Neither did Mr. Bingley. I was quite shocked when he announced his game. And I suspect it was quite a shock to him when he discovered my skill at the game." Blake grabbed her hand as she slipped on the wet grass when taking her seat.

"Mr. Kent did well to tie for the stallion."

"Yes, he did, surprisingly. However, I would have liked Mr. Darcy to be my only opponent. I did so want to best him directly." Blake lowered his head as he admitted, "He is my fiercest rival."

"Mr. Darcy?" Elizabeth asked. "I do not think many townspeople wagered any money on him."

"We were always battling each other at Cambridge." Blake paused, and then said, "Now on the other hand, Kent has picked up a few skills since school."

"Miss Bingley has one to cheer for, then? Mr. Kent seemed to champion her while I stayed at Netherfield."

"I suppose, however, I am convinced she would have wished to cheer another." He turned his body towards Elizabeth causing his knee to touch hers. He had a vivid memory of that moment before, and longed to recreate it again. He could not think of a single proper way to caress her arm. He fought against looking down at the place where the soft material at her neckline ended.

"Perhaps." Elizabeth blushed when she noticed Blake dropping his eyes again. She quickly raised her hand and placed it over the enticing spot. She had noticed Jane doing this when Mr. Bingley spent too long fixated on her glimpse of heaven. "Have you discovered the final competition yet?"

Lord Blake lifted his chin. "No. I understand the judges are making that decision. Perhaps you father might have dropped a hint?"

"He would never tell if he knows."

"Mr. Bennet does appear able to keep the competition games to himself."

"And he is good at keeping secrets and confidences, my lord," Elizabeth said. "You would not wish otherwise."

"No, you are correct. However, I do have a request."

Elizabeth raised her brows and signaled for Blake to continue.

"Would you honor me with the first two dances at the ball?"

"I am afraid I must decline." She watched Blake's shoulders slump. "I am engaged for those dances."

"Mr. Darcy?"

"No." She leaned back and with a shocked voice exclaimed, "I daresay he would not desire such a thing."

"Oh." He waited patiently for Elizabeth to continue.

"My cousin, who is visiting us, has claimed the first two dances." She leaned in and whispered, "I am not engaged for any other."

"Excellent. Then I request not only the second set but the last one as well."

"I accept." Elizabeth looked away to hide her blush she felt rising on her cheeks.

For a while, the two spoke about the harvest feast, the competition, the ball, and Heracles. Blake assured Miss Elizabeth that the horse was very gentle, even though his size was great. They continued speaking in this manner until they saw several Militia officers and a well-dressed gentleman approaching the house, bringing Blake's visit to an end.

,While waiting for his horse, he overheard the man telling Mrs. Bennet he was from Derbyshire and knew Mr. Darcy quite well. After a quick introduction revealed his name was Mr. Wickham, Blake took his leave and returned to Netherfield Park.

When dinnertime arrived, Darcy reappeared from his self-imposed seclusion. Both he and Blake ate their dinner quietly and remained lost in thought. The others allowed the two men to remain unsociable, and instead spoke about the upcoming events. Miss Bingley regaled them with stories describing the humorous difficulties the staff had encountered—from the rams running loose in the stable yard to the struggles they had had removing a bar that was too large for the ballroom door— and everyone shared a laugh or two.

After the ladies departed for the drawing room to plan the evening's entertainment, the men continued to speak about the upcoming ball until Blake cleared his voice.

"Darcy, there was a gentleman visiting the Bennets this afternoon. He said he was from Derbyshire and knew you."

Darcy clenched his jaw, his hands curling into fists around his brandy snifter.

"I did not know you went to Longbourn." Bingley said.

"Yes, when Kent left me on my own in the tavern."

"I do apologize, Blake." Kent responded. "I had some news I needed to give to Rawlings. I quite forgot you were still there. It was unpardonable of me."

"Truth be known, I barely noticed your absence, so I was not offended."

"I am sure you were not, Blake." Darcy said coolly. "You were free to go to Longbourn."

"Do you know this man?" Blake asked.

Kent interrupted. "I overhead heard some scathing remarks he was whispering about you. He told an officer sitting with him at the tavern about how you cheated him,"

"And?"

"Yes, something about your father had willed him a living at a parish and you denied it to him when he died. He claims to have suffered a great deal as a result."

"What is he doing here?" Darcy asked.

"I believe he has joined the militia."

"His name is George Wickham. Do not give implicit confidence to any of his assertions; he used me ill. His allegations are perfectly false. Anything due him was conditional at best. I have always been remarkably kind to him, and have lived to regret it." There was such repressed anger in Darcy's tone, no one dared to respond.

The men did not even dare to glance at each other when Darcy exclaimed, "I cannot bear to hear his name spoken, and I beseech you never to say it to me again." He squeezed the glass so tightly it shattered into many pieces, causing an intermingling of red wine and blood to spatter down his coat.

Wrapping a handkerchief around his hand, Darcy apologized and retreated to his chambers.

Chapter Twenty-nine

Fortunately, this November morning arrived sunny and bright; a perfect day for an outdoor autumn feast. Caroline had fretted about a rain soaked day, for naught. She had imagined ruffians clomping through the house, defiling everything in sight with muddy boot and dirty petticoats. And what they did not foul, she was sure they would steal. She had gone as far as hiring extra footmen to stand guard, which proved an unnecessary expense as the day wore on.

Darcy stood on the steps outside the front door of Netherfield Park. For a man rarely impressed, he was astonished at the transformation. The Bingley family had outdone themselves. The layout of the grounds rivaled those held at London's Vauxhall or even Ranelagh at its height.

Netherfield Park had been partitioned into activities for men, women, and children. The golf course remained in the meadow to the north. Men crowded around and lined up first thing, all wanting a turn. Bingley provided extra clubs at the practice field, along with young lads to chase down the local citizen's attempts at the longer strokes.

The area reserved for the younger guests was to the south of the house, where the game of Joust proved to be a favorite. Children, in order to win the prize, mounted ponies to ride around in a wide circle and used a long stick to spear the ring hanging along the path. Bingley had a table set up for some of the Kent family world puzzles. Small-sectioned pieces of each country fit into their proper place on the game board. Kent's family had fashioned some extra puzzles, these depicted trees, mountains, flowers, and similar scenes of nature.. If the children found them enjoyable, they would consider adding them to their growing list of manufactured goods. They sought no payment other than an indication of its popularity.

The pen for Tup Running was still intact in the East Meadow. Mr. Darcy had allowed one soaped and greased ram inside the circle for anyone wishing to try his game. To his surprise, a long line of men had formed.

Darcy, still standing on the portico, watched the carriages, wagons, horseback riders, and even walkers approach the grounds. Rawlings joined him, coffee cups in hand. He offered one to Darcy. "Quite the affair," he said waving his now freed hand across the yard.

"I agree." Darcy tilted his head to the right "Look over there. I assume that is the competition area set up for the locals. Is that the dart game?"

"The large tree trunk with lines painted on it? I suppose it is."

"Have you ever played before?"

"No I have not, although I have tried many new things during my stay. Grabbing the arse of a ram was one such activity." Rawlings threw Darcy a mischievous smirk with his sideways glance.

"Perhaps we should try now. I suspect the game will be impossible to play later."

Rawlings agreed. They handed their cups to a nearby servant and made haste. Once they found the darts, they set about hitting the center ring of the target, situated twenty paces away. After several failed attempts, a loud chuckle from behind caused them to turn around.

"You are fortunate you did not compete in this event." Mr. Goulding bowed. "Mr. Kent and Mr. Bingley have set up all the pub games on the other side of the house along with the outdoor versions for the men."

"Miss Bingley was elated when Mr. Kent removed the tavern decorations from the ballroom." Rawlings said.

"Are they making use of everything?" Darcy asked.

"Yes they are, including hanging the Five Alls sign on a nearby tree. And they have an outdoor version of skittles for the men. A long line has formed."

"I propose we should give those games another try, Darcy. Will you join us, Mr. Goulding?"

"I cannot, Mr. Rawlings. As the judge, I must remain here. Mr. Long is judging the archery and Sir William is in charge of the shooting competition." Goulding pointed to the other two areas as he spoke, cringing as the first shots of the day exploded in the air.

"Mr. Bennet? Is he not judging? Darcy asked.

"He and Mr. Phillips are setting up the game for the stallion."

"Oh." Darcy's brows lifted. "Perhaps I can offer some help."

Mr. Goulding laughed. "No. The game is still a secret. As you see, the judges are very busy today. I suspect I will be here for quite awhile.

Many men spent their days practicing since the announcement for this competition. The dart game will start in a quarter-hour, and I expect the efforts should be entertaining."

"Good luck, Mr. Goulding." Rawlings said.

"Luck? Why would I need luck?"

"Why, to avoid being hit by any misdirected darts!" Rawlings laughed as he and Darcy left, heading towards the vicinity of the pub games.

Darcy spotted Wickham immediately. He was demonstrating to the Bennet ladies how to play quoits. He muttered a curse word while his hands formed fists, relaxing only after Rawlings grabbed his arm and whispered encouragement to remain calm. "He is a human canker sore on all the Bennet daughters."

But it was Rawlings who then tensed and twitched when Wickham leaned into Miss Lydia's neck and repeatedly touched her back as he demonstrated how to hold the loop.

"Shall I throw a dart at that redcoat of his, Darcy?" Rawlings sneered. "Or should I just smash the frig pig's head in?"

"Whose head?" Blake asked as he joined the two.

Rawlings tilted his head toward the group and mouthed, "Wickham."

Blake spied Wickham, now standing a little too close to Miss Elizabeth, and when he stood too close to merely whisper in her ear his hands balled into fists. He watched as Wickham stared down at her breasts when he touched her back and moved in closer to her, his eyes never leaving her chest. Blake's every muscle tensed, he clenched his hands into tighter fists. "Is this man a threat? Should we have Bingley throw him out of here?"

"He is just trying to anger me." Darcy eyed his previous childhood friend. "Take notice of his smirk while he studies your reactions. I assume he has heard of our acquaintance with the Bennets."

Rawlings agreed. Wickham did appear to be taunting them with a menacing-looking tight-lipped smile. He stood at his full height, and seemed to be challenging them as he moved another step closer to Miss Elizabeth. He glared at Darcy before dropping his gaze upon her neckline.

Blake took a step forward.

"No! Do not show any reaction. The cur enjoys cuckolding gentlemen. He does it for sport. He cares not for the lady in the scheme. I suspect his actions are aimed at me, a revenge on his part." He did not reveal his own gullibility. Like his father, he once believed Wickham only needed friendship, although Darcy and his sister suffered for embracing this foolish opinion.

"Thank you for your warning, but I do not like the way he is behaving around the ladies. If you chose to do nothing, that is your concern, but I have had no past with the man."

Darcy grabbed Blake's arm. "If you show him you are concerned, he will surely target the Bennet girls. Do not overreact. It is us what he seeks. Let him believe these women are of no serious interest to you. It is the only way to protect them."

Blake shrugged off Darcy's hold. "Bah! He would never dare to treat me this way. I believe he was staring at you." He moved towards the Bennet group. He did not stop even when Mr. Wickham scooted away.

Rawlings watched Lydia turn and wave her handkerchief at the retreating redcoat. "Someone should warn Mr. Bennet his daughters may be at risk."

"Unless, we give Wickham reason to use them, they are not in any serious harm. I suppose he is most interested in who may be my favorite." Darcy shook his head as Blake approached Elizabeth. "Thankfully, they have no monetary allurements. Wickham is a fortune hunter, and these ladies do not fit his needs."

"I believe seven thousand pounds would turn the any officer's head," Rawlings said.

"I beg your pardon, Rawlings. You had retired early. Miss Bingley informed me last night that their father has lost his daughter's dowry money."

"Oh, what did she say?" Rawlings asked, he attempted to keep the tone indifferent.

"Mr. Bennet's brother-in-law, Mr. Gardiner, in Cheapside squandered a fortune on some risky investment. He was involved in some scheme and the investment failed. According to her intelligence on the matter, Mr. Cuffage, a competitor to Mr. Gardiner, is the person the Bennets blame for their misfortunes."

Rawlings stiffened at this new information. Logan had not discovered that bit of news. "Did Miss Bingley know which venture? I would hate to discover too late that we are following the same path."

"No, nor do I believe she cared to uncover anything more than the fact there was a financial loss." Darcy paused, his gaze drawn to the Bennet daughters. "I sent an express to my secretary, Mr. Rogers, in London cancelling my request to investigate Cuffage now that we have identified the real culprit. Mr. Phillips should be told as well."

Rawlings nodded. "Oh. Do not forget Mr. Phillips has as much a connection with the Bennets as Mr. Gardiner. Shall we say we are in possession of information exonerating Cuffage?"

"Yes, you raise a good point, and naming the man would be a bit embarrassing for him. I will not mention his Cheapside relative at all."

Satisfied, Rawlings turned his attention back on Blake and the Bennet ladies. He studied Blake flirting with Miss Elizabeth and wondered if he had been present when Miss Bingley spoke about their misfortune. He imagined she told the story with great enjoyment. He dared not ask Darcy what Blake knew. "When is the announcement for the competition between you, Blake and Kent?"

"Not until two this afternoon."

"Well then, shall we continue on to the pub games? I spy a few ladies in need of some assistance." Rawlings chuckled at Miss Lydia's pretense of failure. He contemplated the best approach to gain her attention.

Darcy nodded and they moved quickly to join the group. He placed himself near to Elizabeth, and although he listened to their talk, he did not offer anything to the conversation. He held his eyes steady, staring off into the distance. Once or twice, he nodded or shrugged while displaying his haughty, nonchalant manner. Occasionally, he snuck a peek at Wickham, and was satisfied his ploy had worked.

Lydia turned to Kitty and whispered among her giggles. "Look! Mr. Rawlings is looking at us. Shall we tease him about the golf game?"

"No! That would be too cruel even for you." Kitty said, her voice raising above a whisper.

"I will laugh at him just the same."

"Good morning, Miss Catherine. Miss Lydia." Rawlings politely bowed to the both the ladies.

Darcy nodded to the young girls. He stood aside, his concentration focused between Blake and Elizabeth and Wickham.

"Mr. Rawlings, is it not funny that both you and Mr. Darcy lost at golf? I mean, did you expect Lord Blake to be able to play so well?"

"I was most surprised, I assure you, Miss Lydia." Rawlings said and then diverted his attention to her sister. Miss Catherine did you enjoy the game?"

"Yes, I did indeed."

"You are looking quite lovely this morning. Is that perchance a new bonnet?" Rawlings smiled openly at Kitty while keeping his eye on Lydia.

She squealed. "It is an old one of Kitty's. I am wearing the new one, Mr. Rawlings. See?" When Rawlings peeked at Lydia, she twirled around so he could view it from all angles.

"Very pretty, but I like the blue ribbon," Rawlings returned his gaze to Kitty and said softly, "that Miss Catherine used to trim her bonnet."

"Well I prefer a different color. Red is exciting!" Lydia directed her stare over to the men's skittles game where Wickham was challenging another officer.

"Miss Catherine, have you tried to play the games? I did fairly well in the competition. I could show you some tricks." Rawlings turned to Lydia. "Oh, and you too Miss Lydia. Shall we try our luck at the ladies' Skittles?"

Kitty quickly maneuvered herself to be the lady on Mr. Rawlings' arm. In doing so, she almost knocked her sister down. With a backwards glance, Kitty smirked at her youngest sister when Rawlings, with one eye on Lydia, placed his free hand on Kitty's. Lydia, standing behind them, glared at him through half closed eyes and stuck her tongue out. He observed the fuming girl. He sent her a grin before commenting to Kitty on how lovely she looked in her pretty gown.

Rawlings walked off with Kitty, abandoning Lydia. Darcy took note and offered the young girl his arm. As they followed behind, Lydia exaggerated her flirting and with every step loudly teased him. Darcy caught Wickham studying them. He feared he had sent out the wrong impression and tried to envision a way to demonstrate his dislike for the girl. Wickham may view his indifference as some manner of understanding between them. He pushed his fear away. Wickham knew his tastes well enough to realize this child and her outlandish behavior is not the sort of woman he favored.

Blake and Elizabeth recognized their chance and headed to the croquet game, although she watched Mr. Darcy's kindness to her sister with a befuddled expression.

"This game is easy Miss Elizabeth. Hold your mallet like so." Lord Blake spoke sharply to get her attention. When she refocused her eyes on him and he smiled playfully and then demonstrated how to hold the club.

"I believe I understand." Elizabeth approached her ball, raised her mallet, and smacked it through the wickets. "I play often, Lord Blake." Grinning, Elizabeth confessed, "In fact, I can best all my friends."

"Unfair, Miss Bennet."

"I believe you did the same with the golf game! Was that unfair as well?" Elizabeth raised her brow.

"True. I am guilty. It is never wise to reveal all your strengths to your competitors. Now, shall we make a friendly wager?" Blake matched his raised brow with hers. She nodded agreement. They discussed a prize worthy of such a contest, and agreed upon his retrieving a few sweet pastries from Netherfield for her if she won and her granting another performance at the pianoforte if he did.

They played the game while Mrs. Bennet kept her eye on them. When Elizabeth won, she felt her daughter had forfeited her opportunity to gain this man's favor. Her feelings remained unchanged until Lord Blake smiled at Lizzy. Her thoughts raced forward. I suppose he let her win. He is chasing her I just know it! That's a good girl, Lizzy. Blink your eyes. Tilt your head. Bah. She will never learn to sway her hips!

The crowd appeared, through their laughter and smiles, to be having a wonderful time. Many men had lined up for their competition. First, they must participate in the target-shooting contest. Once a man completed his allotted number of shots, he moved on to the darts. Archery was last. At each event, the men with the highest totals played again until there were three top scorers. They would compete for their prize in the late afternoon.

The men were free to try Tup Running and golf. Bingley permitted women to try golf as well, but no lady showed any interest. They preferred the tavern games, croquet, and helping the young children with the puzzles, none of which damaged their hair or dresses. There were more unwed men at this event than had ever before been assembled. Every single girl had carefully prepared her appearance in the hopes she would win her own type of competition.

Much to Caroline's consternation, she could not find her brother. She needed him to preside over this spectacle, as she called it to her sister. Mr. Darcy had not even noticed her effort in ensuring the event was a success, and Charles' disappearance was hampering her plans to spend many hours learning how to play the games with her particular favorite as her instructor.

She went to the golf course first. She had incorrectly assumed Charles would be showing the locals how to hit those stupid little balls. Much to the surprise of his Meryton neighbors, Mr. Robinson volunteered for that responsibility, since he had played many times before.

Caroline checked the pub games area next, and then the croquet field, and finally the Tup-running pen, but she was unable to locate him anywhere or even Miss Jane Bennet's whereabouts. Exasperated, she found a spot under an awning reserved for the host family where she and her sister whispered many unkind remarks about the attendees.

A crowd surrounded Bingley and Mr. Bennet, who stood ready to name the game. When Darcy, Blake and Kent joined them, the gathering cheered while Mr. Bennet introduced the men.

Standing alone and slightly hidden amongst the crowd, Rawlings waited while Mr. Bennet tried to quiet the crowd. Lydia had left him to flirt with several officers. Kitty followed her sister since Rawlings attention on her had faded.

"Quiet everyone, please." Bingley raised his hands turning to Mr. Bennet when the crowd had finally ceased murmuring.

Mr. Bennet said as loudly as he could, "Now these fine young gentlemen attended Cambridge together." He peeked at the men with a twinkle in his eyes. "Since all the judges are graduates of the better school…Oxford," Bennet waited for the snickers to die down before continuing, "We wanted a race that was customary for *our* alma mater."

The crowd laughed and then settled down, waiting for the announcement.

"The three men will compete in a rowing race in one man boats."

Mr. Bennet pointed west. "Within a short walking distance on Mr. Bingley's property is a one-mile section of the Colne Brook where they will race, and the first gentleman to reach the finish line will win the stallion.

Darcy, Blake, and Kent eyed one another. They did not know the experience level of their competitors. They left to change into appropriate attire. Rawlings watched the men enter the house just as his valet brought him a few messages that had arrived from London.

"Curious is it not, Logan. I had not noticed the irony of this competition until I saw them just now." Rawlings said as he glanced at the three competitors.

"How so?" Logan asked

"The Duke and a tradesman's son are competing for a prize. Darcy is like a bridge between the two. It is a new world, as Kent is always saying. When two persons as far apart socially as they are in a friendly competition, but who can join together in business together, we are witnesses to a significant change in the social order."

Logan sighed. "They have both worked hard to overcome their prejudices. They seem to be more affable to one another lately."

"Yes, those *two* seem to have overcome their prejudices, and Kent has appeared to overcome his anger at Blake's demand. And, I might add, it is fortunate for the alliance," Rawlings said.

"Kent believes he will win, keeping Blake from gaining his thirty percent. I suspect he believes he will be the new leader when this race is done."

"Well, Kent may think that way, but I wonder which one of the three men will win. The tradesman has our future in his hands and the marquess has the past. But who holds the present? Is it Darcy? Come, come. I have a shilling to spare. I select—"

Logan interrupted him. "Blake. I do not think the time has come for the changing of the guard. He will prove that the nobility is still in charge."

"I will take that wager. I suspect our days as leaders are dwindling, and just like Kent slyly tying for the horse, I believe others are inching their way up. They may have already arrived while we were busy skirmishing amongst ourselves. A shilling it is."

"And which man do you wager on?"

"Darcy, of course.

"Did you know the judges were all Oxford graduates?

"No, but it explains why they were not known to us."

They walked at a quickened pace in order to stake out the best spot. "Yes, and I suppose they had a few merry laughs about the Cambridge boys." Rawlings said. "They have chosen well. None of our friends have rowed competitively before. Do you wish to change your wager? I am giving you one final chance!"

"I suppose the winner will be the one with the stronger arms and legs. "Blake is more the athlete than Kent, so instead of changing it, I propose we increase the bet. I will be pleased to take a pound from you."

"He does have the leisure time to waste on sport, but Darcy is determined. He will expend everything he has to stop Blake from winning. A pound it is. Well, here they come." Rawlings pointed to the two walking towards them.

"This should be interesting," Blake said as he glanced at the water. "It is good I know how to swim. I hope you two do too."

"I can swim." Darcy replied.

"I learned as a child," Kent said. I heard that rowing is popular at Oxford and even Eton has begun competitions this year."

"I wonder if it will endure though." Darcy said.

"It will last long enough for one of us to win Heracles." Kent laughed. "Good luck, Darcy. You too, Blake. You both will need it."

"I need no luck. I fully intend to win the beast, as Miss Elizabeth calls it." Blake remarked with unbridled confidence.

The competitors made way to the starting line. They bowed first to each other and then towards the cheering spectators. The boats were identical, except for the number painted on its side. Mr. Phillips was making his way through the crowd with three slips of paper, each one with a boat's number, for the drawing. No pulling straws this time.

Darcy studied the two men standing beside him and pondered the possibilities. He would avoid risking Pemberley if Blake were to win. Then again he worried, if Kent wins, Blake might flee. Blake would never be subservient to Kent. But then would he? Would he allow Kent to take command? Faced with this possibility, he felt trapped.

Had Rawlings possessed the connections to secure the Baker rifle sale, he would have not searched for a solution. The way to secure the sale was to ensure Blake's win elsewise he would mortgage Pemberley. There was no other course. But do let Blake win is dishonest, and he always presented himself as an honest man. Besides, how could he cheat his other friend? Would Kent bolt if he allowed Blake to win the damn race? The thought that pounded in his mind these past two weeks, bellowed again—should I even try to win? Other than the Baker sale, Kent was more important than Blake. At this instant, he wondered if he should win and then offer Kent the thirty percent. The questions continued to plague him as it had since the three-way tie occurred. His hands began to sweat.

You will never defeat me, Darcy," Blake said, his words taunting. "I shall neither fail in defeating you in this rowing contest nor in securing a particular lady as my own. I shall enjoy watching your regretful face." Blake leaned towards him. "You come too late."

The hair on Darcy's neck pricked him.

They settled in their boats, grasped the oars, and prepared to begin the race. Mr. Phillips raised his gun, and the crowd grew calm.

Darcy glared at Blake. "I shall welcome you at the finish." He grabbed the oars and slammed them into place.

Blake gripped his own oars. And she shall welcome me." His last word was spoken louder than the others. "Me," he yelled again.

Stillness overtook the crowd. The rowers sat perched, muscles tense in anticipation.

Bang.

The crowds cheered equally for the men.

Kent was slightly in the lead, but he was barely able to maintain it. Darcy pulled even beside him. Blake let them forge ahead and remained a short distance behind, planning to overtake them in the end.

Rawlings and Logan quickly moved down the riverbank. They cheered on their man, but intuitively believed more than the horse was on the line. The crowd made way for them as they hurried along the path; Rawlings yelling instructions to Darcy.

At the finish line, Mr. Bennet stood with a flag ready. He did not have a preference on who he wanted to win, having now sworn off wagering for the remainder of his life. Turning to look at the crowd, his eyes narrowed as he spotted the man who had come for his daughters' dowries money later that day. Mr. Bennet sighed as Mr. Cuffage tipped his head and tapped his pocket.

Staunton blinked he eyes. So the stranger who came to his tavern during the golf match had come for business with Mr. Bennet. Well, *I will not bother Mr. Bingley, since it does not seem to be his concern.* Roger Staunton had arrived early to record the final wagers in the Black Bull Tavern betting book. He spied the three men rowing furiously. He felt a colossal loss. There would be no further games. The small, unknown little parish would return to its dull and boring ways. His tavern had become the place to go; his clientele increased substantially with each event. He had enjoyed the increase in profits and the excitement of the competition. He, at least, hoped his new patrons would come again in the future without the need for games; but he knew such visits were unlikely.

"Here they come! Look!" someone in the crowd yelled when he spotted the competitors. Mr. Bennet held the flag up high, although his hand shook a little too obviously as Cuffage snaked his way through the crowd towards Longbourn.

The boats came around the bend in view of the spectators standing along the riverbank at the finish line. Darcy was leading. Mr. Bennet stood on a large rock holding a flag, causing the rowers to step up their efforts. With each stroke, the men challenged each other. The oars lifted almost in a synchronized manner; but only the deeper reach of one man would control the outcome.

"Kent, check behind you. Blake is moving. Push, Darcy, damn the oars, push!"

Rawlings and Logan reached the finish line at the same time as the rowers. Darcy was ahead until Kent's boat slid into his. Darcy's oar dropped in the water. Blake, having reserved his strength for making the final and longest stroke, crossed first. Mr. Bennet named Lord Blake the winner with Darcy second and Kent third.

Kent panted heavily. "Congratulations, Blake" he yelled, his voice breathless. "You now own the stallion, and here I was hoping for once to have something you wanted!"

"But you already do," Blake answered through his own heavy panting. "Do you not know?" When Kent shook his head, he said, "You own the freedom to follow your desires."

Kent sighed.

Darcy remained quiet. He did not take his eyes off Kent's back. He could hear Rawlings cursing nearby. It was deliberate. Kent purposely hit his boat and allowed Blake to win. He felt his face tighten as he imagined possible scenarios. He would knock Kent flat on his back to get the truth.

The competitors left the boats for solid ground. After much backslapping, handshaking, and smiles all around, Mr. Bennet grabbed and raised Blake's hand in the air. One spectator yelled out, "Three cheers for Lord Blake." Everyone roared their approval regardless if they won the wager or not.

He bowed to the crowd.

Kent slid into the crowd after catching the cold black stare Darcy had aimed at him. He located Rawlings and headed his way.

Rawlings handed Logan his winnings and tilted his head towards Blake. "Well, he proclaimed his victory all along. The stallion is now his."

Kent's eyes shot up as he joined them. "Rawlings, did you wager on me or Darcy?"

"Darcy. I was not prepared for him to be rammed so surprisingly. His victory came only at the last moment when he overtook you at the finish line."

Logan slipped away, loudly counting his winnings.

"Yes, I was surprised at the end," Kent said, the tone of his voice even. I had my eyes on Blake when I bumped into Darcy. I cannot complain now about the division of profits. Damn."

"I am sorry for your loss, Kent." Bingley said as he approached the two men and patted him on the back.

"It is a beautiful horse, and I wanted to win. Nevertheless, I will not take anything away from him." Kent looked at Darcy standing directly in front of him. "There is no dispute; he was the victor."

"And he has now acquired the thirty percent." Darcy replied, "And control of the alliance. You must do as he says now."

"No." Blake said, joining them and making the group complete. "I told you before, I do not wish to lead this alliance. You should continue. You were the one with the vision." Blake placed his hand on Darcy's shoulder. "I have no wish to take your place."

"Perhaps Darcy should charge you ten percent!" Rawlings said, and then laughed. "It would be fitting."

"But now Blake you must make the sale." Darcy said.

"I will, I promise you it will be done."

Everyone focused their attention on the driveway at the house as the servants brought forward the famous stallion, saddled and ready to turn over. A boisterous cheer sounded as Blake bounded towards the horse and vaulted onto the saddle. As he walked him down the road with a slow gait, he waved to everyone, fighting the urge to gallop. After returning to the front steps, he handed the reins to the groom and permitted access to anyone wishing to inspect him. Blake joined his friends as they all waited for the Harvest Feast's final competition to begin.

Darcy signaled for Kent to meet him in the house.

Kent shook his head. "Shall we watch the other competition?" Bingley, Rawlings, and Blake walked ahead. Darcy blocked Kent's movement and waited until the others disappeared from view and out of hearing range.

"Why did you sabotage me?"

Kent tilted his head in Bingley's direction. "I did it for his family. They are desperate for this sale. Otherwise, I would have never let him win. Do you think this was an easy loss for me? I have been rowing boats in races for years!"

"I do not understand why you think you had to do this."

"Blake would have bolted had he not won. I heard him and his valet making plans. He is packed and ready to leave. Did you know that? He said if he lost, he would leave immediately. He said if he won, he would stay for the ball, and that he had something important to do. So I... did what I did."

"He has been called back to town by his father. It has nothing to do with the competition."

"Bah. He said if he won, he would stay for Bingley's ball. You see. Returning as his father demanded was not keeping him from the ball... if he won. We are to sign the documents making us partners right before it begins. He was going to bolt, I tell you. Why would he not wait until he signed the papers if he lost?" Kent muttered, "And I saved your beloved Pemberley, too, you fool."

Darcy noticed Blake speaking to Miss Elizabeth and he pushed what Kent mumbled from his mind. He was too tired to argue and now his thoughts focused on new concerns. *Blake has something planned for the ball? It must be more than signing the papers.* The words Blake said before the race bellowed in his ears: *You came too late.* Did he need the money for her? What was he planning? If he lost, would he have just left her here? Now that he won, is the purpose for the extra money to secure her as his wife or… He winced. He will cause Miss Elizabeth a great harm. I must find a way to warn her.

"Darcy?" Kent asked. "Do you agree with me about Blake?"

"I suspect only he knows the truth, and he would never willingly reveal it. Very well. But if you are wrong, you cost us a great deal of money." Darcy said.

"What is done cannot be undone. Let us catch up with the others." They nearly ran until they reached their friends.

"Bingley, I was so focused on my own race; I admit I do not know what is expected of them." Kent said.

"The three finalists are given one dart, one arrow, and one shot. The one with the highest score will win," Mr. Bennet explained as he joined the group. "An exceptional race, Mr. Kent, Mr. Darcy. Admirable effort."

"Do we know who the finalists are?" Kent asked.

"Well there is one you probably do not know. He is one of Bingley's tenant farmers, a young man called, Pruitt. He is quite a good shot even without owning a Baker rifle."

"Is his farm located on the west side?" Darcy asked.

Mr. Bennet jerked his head towards him, "Yes, how are you acquainted with him?"

"I am not at liberty to say." Darcy recalled the visit he and Bingley had made to the man's home. A serious problem with his roof had caused him to apply for assistance. Covertly, he had suggested Bingley provide the materials, but demand the man repair his roof and pay a small fee with the proceeds of the harvest sales. After that incident, both men had met daily with several other tenants having similar needs and problems. The tenants gave undue credit to Bingley for solving the problems, and not to the aloof gentleman standing with him.

"One man you have met, I believe—Mr. Robert Goulding." Mr. Bennet noted the changed expressions when they recognized the name.

"Only some of us met him." Rawlings said looking to Darcy. "I believe Kent and I were absent from the visit to Goulding's Farm."

"And the third person?" Kent asked.

"A military officer, which I assume thrills my two silliest, youngest daughters." A bemused Mr. Bennet cast his eyes on Darcy. "I believe his name is Wickham."

"Wickham!" the men cried out in unison.

Chapter Thirty

Mr. Long climbed up on an upturned crate to address the burgeoning crowd. "After two rounds Mr. Goulding has one hundred points; ninety five for Mr. Wickham and ninety for Mr. Pruitt." He nodded to Sir William to begin the shooting contest.

The crowd mingled around the area slated for the local men's competition. The three finalists were preparing to start the final round. They stood abreast for the firing segment, a servant handed each man a loaded standard flintlock. As the competitors inspected their firearms, Rawlings cringed when Lydia yelled out, "Good luck, Mr. Wickham."

The targets were all numbered and placed on a makeshift railing. The smallest object was fifty points and the largest twenty. The man with the highest score shot first. The spectators cheered for each man: the gentry encouraged young Robert Goulding; the militia yelled their support for Wickham; and everyone else shouted out for Mr. Pruitt.

Rawlings whispered to Darcy, "Can you feel the tension in the air, and I am not talking about the contest. Look around. Even this competition has its class distinctions, with the spectators lining up behind its representative."

"Yes, the world does seem like it is partitioning into particular groupings. However, I doubt if a harmonious society ever existed. Nowadays, people of similar minds and thoughts can easily group together and cause havoc."

Rawlings sighed. "You do describe what is happening in London. All these folks cramped into what anyone would call squalor. The parliament must do something other than talk. I fear where all this togetherness is headed. I am beginning to accept that Kent is correct; a new world is emerging, and I see our class doing little to prevent this coming reversal of fortunes."

"Well, my approach to bring this next generation of entrepreneurs into our world may help prevent any aggressive behavior against us. We will not stop them with threats or edicts."

Before Rawlings could answer, young Robert Goulding took his place at the firing line. His eyes swept over the crowd, and rested on Miss Jane Bennet's lovely face. She returned his smile and nodded. He aimed his gun. His hands were sweating. His heart pumped furiously. He pulled the trigger.

Bang.

"Thirty points for this round. Mr. Goulding's total is hundred thirty points. Next turn goes to Mr. Wickham."

Wickham bowed to the cheering officers and one loudly shrieking young girl. He aimed his rifle, and waited until he had the crowd's full attention. He squeezed the trigger.

Bang.

"Forty points," Sir William proclaimed as he picked up the object and returned it to its position. Mr. Wickham now has a total of one hundred and thirty five points. Mr. Pruitt must now shoot a fifty-point target to win; otherwise, Mr. Wickham is the victor.

The military officers hooted and hollered. The tenant farmers shouted down the redcoats.

"It is well that the spectators are not armed!" Rawlings chuckled as Darcy kept his eyes on Wickham.

Mr. Pruitt readied himself to take his turn. This time the crowd fell silent. All eyes were on the tenant farmer as he aimed and pulled the trigger.

He shot a hole through the smallest object. If the shoe buckle was tagged as fifty points, he won, but if only forty-five points then the game would be tied.

Sir William studied the object and then yelled, "Mr. Pruitt is the winner with one hundred forty points."

The farmers shouted approval and much coin exchanged hands among the onlookers. When Mr. Pruitt received the prized Baker rifle, Bingley remarked how he was pleased one of his tenants won. He also handed the victorious man the guinea prize money. Cheers and calls for showing the gun from the spectators followed.

Rawlings applauded Pruitt before nudging Darcy with his elbow. He nodded towards Lydia Bennet. "I believe I am needed to cheer up a particularly forlorn young lady."

"She is too young for you."

"I doubt if she will be available in a year or two. She will not take her time choosing a husband nor will I choose to let my opportunities slip past me. Besides, a man my age courting a girl not yet twenty is not extraordinary."

Darcy scoffed.

"Ladies make their debuts at almost her age. Countless marriage contracts are signed before the girl has become a woman; some agreements are made while the child is still in the cradle." Rawlings eyed Darcy and chuckled at his embarrassment. "Fortunately for me, Miss Lydia is a woman, I grant you a young one, but a woman she is!"

"Humph. Can you not see the trouble she could cause you? She taunts you!"

Rawlings smiled. "And she is merciless! I enjoy her female wiles and, as you say, arts and allurements too. Is there not one lady that taunts you and keeps you awake at night?"

"Go."

When a chuckling Rawlings left to find Miss Lydia, Darcy thought about his friend. He wanted more for him than a silly child without discipline or grace. He had fortune enough, his family line was acceptable, and he felt of him like a brother. His face brightened and his eyebrows shot up. *He would not care about my sister's past.*

Setting aside this inspiration, Darcy searched the crowd, seeking the fine eyes in a pretty face he had often studied with great interest. *Yes, Rawlings, one lady keeps me awake at night, as you have full well figured out. But, I have responsibilities that you do not. I am master of Pemberley with hundreds of persons dependent upon me, and you, a second son, in comparison have nary any cares. I must find a woman worthy of my status.*

Darcy whipped around at the sound of laughter. He gasped at the sight of her eyes sparkling in the late afternoon sun. She tilted her chin down slightly when she laughed and appeared to be insensible of how that small dip highlighted her eyes. *One whiff of her lavender scent and I feel as though I could succeed at anything. Is this what he feels? Oh, why did you notice her, Blake? Your father will never approve of her and will be harsh in his actions. If she is not of my sphere, then certainly she is not of yours.*

He closed his eyes and steeled his resolve when he heard the two voices headed his way.

"Mr. Darcy, there you are! Mr. Kent and I are making our way to the East Meadow. Will you join us?"

"Miss Bingley, Kent." Darcy bowed, agreeing to their plan when he spotted Blake and Elizabeth headed in the same direction.

"I was astounded by Miss Bingley's acquaintances in town." Kent sent Caroline a smile. "I suspect her accomplishments set her apart from the other ladies. I do not know when I heard anyone play the pianoforte better."

"Thank you." Caroline waited for another response that did not come.

"Miss Bingley," Kent continued, "I must congratulate you on this spectacular event and organized in such a short time. I am impressed. I know of no other lady, especially not in this little parish, with the ability to manage any gathering of this magnitude. I applaud you! Don't you not agree, Darcy?"

"What? Oh yes. Very well done, Miss Bingley." Darcy tipped his head. His focus returned to another woman, one with sparkling eyes that she directed towards another man. Questions continued to plague him; still, he found no answer to what Blake's plans could be.

Kent snuck Caroline a slight shrug and a tilt of his head. "Miss Bingley and I were discussing our favorite colors. I mentioned how much I liked the color of her gown; it is perfect for this time of year. What is the name of it, again?

"Amber. I am pleased you like it."

"Which is your favorite color for a gown, Darcy?"

He searched the crowd until he spotted Miss Elizabeth on Blake's arm and then glanced sideways to Kent and said without hesitation, "Pale yellow." His mask of indifference remained when he returned to watching Elizabeth. He admired the graceful way she moved, and how the light affected her dress, heightening its sunny tint.

Kent followed his gaze. "Come, come, Darcy. Pale? Do you not prefer a more substantial hue? Might a gown that is rich in color and shimmers in the light be better suited to you?"

"You asked my preference. It is pale yellow." Darcy studied Kent as they made his way to the Tup Running pen. What the hell blazes is he up to now? Why is he pushing Bingley's sister my way? Humph. I will never understand these tradesmen families! Can they not see how obvious they are? Bingley was adopted, I am positive of it now, perhaps they stole him off some estate up north. Or he might have been some by-blow child of a duke or earl, and he was sold to the highest bidder. I wonder if any young lord went missing three and twenty years ago. Or he could have been brought to the shores of England from a pirate ship. A stolen babe from America.

"What holds your mind so intently, causing you to suddenly smile so?" Caroline said, imitating a cooing bird. "Perchance you have a particular person in your thoughts?"

"Perhaps."

"Darcy, do I know her?" Kent asked.

"Her? No, not a lady. It was someone of the opposite gender that held my interest!" Darcy enjoyed their brows popping upwards and jaws dropping open. "If you will excuse me, I have a need to speak to Bingley." He laughed as he heard them sputter.

Darcy caught up to Bingley, surprised he was standing alone. "Did you ever take an ocean voyage as an infant?"

"What? No, not that I am aware of."

"Did your parents preserve any unusual clothes or strange family keepsakes from when you were young? A favored blanket, perhaps? Or even a journal or letter?"

"Darcy, you do ask the oddest questions at times. Is this important?"

"No, purely a thought or two. Pay it no mind."

Bingley left to escort Miss Bennet around the festivities, much to his sister's chagrin.

The Meryton guests whispered about the obvious preference he had for their dear sweet Jane. It would benefit the parish if a union between the two took place. Mr. Bingley had brought a sense of pride and community to the area and everyone wished he would remain at Netherfield Park. Without uttering a word, they set about doing all they could to foster the relationship, even to the point of listening to a particular mother crow.

The crowd remained in a festive mood while they enjoyed the food made available to them. There was plenty of ale, and musicians filled the air with many songs. Now that the time for trying Tup Running had ended, Bingley had the area cleared and wooden floor planks placed in the pen, which would then serve as the center of the activities. Music, dancing, drinking, and gaiety ensued, while everyone waited for the sky to grow dark and the fireworks display to begin. The children grew restless, refusing to behave.

Darcy located Rawlings standing alone watching the youngest Bennets flirting and teasing several officers. He joined his friend just as Colonel Forster approached them.

"It was kind of Mr. Bingley to extend his invitation to the militia," the colonel said. "Soon we will depart Meryton. We have been preparing the young men in the hope of finding some of them willing to switch from the militia to the regular army. We will need good soldiers. The situation on the continent is one of grave concern."

"Oh? Is there any particular officer in mind?" Darcy said when Wickham came in view. He imagined the man wearing a regular army uniform lying slashed to pieces.

"Perhaps. We will move to Brighton once our training is finished here. However, I expect at least four more months are necessary and perhaps even longer before we leave. These young men need to be prepared in the unlikely event that our shores find some unwanted and uninvited guests! There is the possibility of rioting. Tension resides everywhere nowadays."

"It was good then that all the officers had the chance to enjoy the day. I see your man almost won the Baker rifle. Although, I admit I did not support him." Rawlings darted his eyes to Darcy.

"Mr. Wickham is my most skilled lieutenant. He rides well and, as evident by this competition, he is as fine a shot as I have ever witnessed. I understand he had a privileged upbringing of sorts. I believe he was a great master's favorite.

"I daresay he was, but Colonel you would be wise to…"

"Use him as his skills dictate." Darcy shot Rawlings a glance that demanded he withhold any warning about Wickham. I am not responsible for his actions here. Damn, Rawlings, if the Colonel punishes Wickham in any way, he will turn his revenge on all of us!

Bingley and Caroline opened the dancing along with the tenants and some townspeople. Everyone else clapped as the musicians began the first tune. Darcy even relaxed when Rawlings indicated Wickham had left; however, he did conceal where he went and with whom.

Once the dancing commenced the judges and their family members slipped indoors for private refreshments and a drink or two. Bingley and his sister walked with Darcy as they made their way to the drawing room.

"I do not see Mr. Bennet, Caroline. Did you extend an invitation to all of the Bennet family? Bingley asked.

"Of course! He has made his apologies. Urgent business is his excuse. Bah. Is that not what all men say when they choose not to do something? He has left his brood here."

"Do not speak so. I warn you Caroline. I will have them treated with respect, and you must get to know them better since they are one of the principle families of the neighborhood." Bingley stomped away from her, seeking out Miss Bennet.

Caroline gasped. "Oh my goodness. Oh my." She hid her red face from Darcy.

Darcy offered her his arm and she accepted it as they entered the drawing room together, causing everyone to notice. He ignored Caroline when she returned to her usual manner of holding her head high; however even he noted that she walked with more haughtiness than usual. His eyes searched the room until he spotted Elizabeth wearing her pale yellow dress near the fireplace. *Blake, must you always be near her?*

"Darcy, come settle this argument." Rawlings waved him over to his small group, which included Miss Lydia, Miss Catherine and Mrs. Bennet.

Once Caroline saw the grouping, she discovered a task needing her attention. He released her and joined them group.

"What is the problem, Rawlings?"

"Ah, Darcy! You must settle an argument for us. Miss Lydia does not believe you participate in Tup Running often. I assured her you do, annually."

"Yes, it is true." Darcy cringed when she shrieked her disbelief. *How does he stand that voice? And her exuberance? Can she never speak softly or listen quietly? Rawlings, I must introduce you to a higher class of women. This girl is silly. Although I am pleased Miss Bingley is no longer hanging on my arm. I must thank him for this ploy.* Darcy chuckled at the thought of Miss Bingley spending two seconds with Miss Lydia. *Well, Miss Catherine seems more sedate. Look at her, Rawlings. Even she would be better than the one you chose.*

Darcy left the group and headed to the sideboard. He filled a large glass with wine. *I do not think Bingley has enough drink to help me through this evening.*

"Mr. Darcy," Mr. Phillips said as he fixed himself a drink, his eyes darting around the room. "I have some news about…"

Darcy was quick to hold up his hand. "Mr. Cuffage. I have heard. I have"—he tried to remember the words they had agreed on—"information that exonerates the man. I have cancelled any further investigation. When might our partnership papers be ready?"

"As agreed earlier, you can sign them tomorrow afternoon, or if you prefer, before the ball. But, good sir, I wish to caution you about—"

"Bring the papers" Darcy interrupted. "We will sign them and ensure that Mr. Cuffage's contracts are ready. I believe I have made myself understood." He rose to his full height, glowering down at the country lawyer. *Must I speak ill of his brother-in-law to make this man understand. Does this man think I am a fool? Do not force me to broach a subject that will cause embarrassment to you!*

"Very good, sir. Your papers will be ready tomorrow." Phillips bowed, sneered, and walked away.

Darcy paced slowly while keeping his eye on Blake and Elizabeth. Every time he drew closer to them, Blake led her to her mother or sisters. He knows what he is doing by avoiding me like this. Blake, I shall speak to her, regardless of your tactics.

"Let me refill your drink." Kent apprehended his glass and retreated to the sideboard before he had time to refuse, thus leaving him standing alone with Miss Bingley.

"We are in tedious company, Mr. Darcy, would you not agree?"

"I find the company quite mixed in this room. But as you say, yes, there is tedious company at every angle." Darcy gaze drifted towards the corner where the two of them stood.

"I suspect you, good sir, would prefer a more refined party. Sometimes it cannot be helped when the guests do not comply."

Upon his return and with drinks in hand, Kent remarked on how successful the festivities had been and how the locals spoke fondly of the Bingleys, claiming them to be the ideal family. Darcy noticed Kent and Miss Bingley sharing smiles when he handed a glass to her. Darcy excused himself to speak to Bingley; Kent and Caroline whispered as he walked away.

Bingley had huddled with Miss Bennet by the fire the entire evening, ignoring the other guests to the point of being rude. They chose instead to maintain their discussion in half whispers and laughter and let everyone fend for themselves.

"Bingley, I believe the sky is black enough for the fireworks. The children are restless.

"I see you are correct. I will inform the men to begin the show.

"Oh, and Blake had mentioned that he was interested in speaking to the person in charge of the fireworks. Remember, he mentioned having such a display at his father's next shooting party. His Grace would enjoy it immensely'I believe is what he said, '. Now is a good time for him to talk to the man, before he packs up and leaves.

"Yes, yes. I will take him there."

"Perhaps I can escort Miss Bennet to her sister?" Darcy smiled at her. Now if Miss Elizabeth is willing, I shall have a few words with her, he thought as Jane placed her delicate hand on his arm. He had the same reaction he had when any of the ladies from London had taken his arm—nothing, not a tingle, not a stirring. He recalled the one time at Longbourn, the day he visited to receive Mr. Bennet's approval for his rules, when Elizabeth placed her hand upon his arm while they walked in the garden. His arm crackled with excitement. A dull ache remained when she had pulled her hand away and gave it to Blake's waiting arm.

Abandoned. He had felt the same when his mother had died, and then again when his father passed away. But she is very much alive. He pushed a breath out through his puffed cheeks.

His plan did not go well. In fact, upon arriving at the viewing area Darcy found Elizabeth seated with Blake by her side and her mother on the other. Blake had declined Bingley's offer. Darcy chose his seat poorly, leaving the spot next to him open, Kent seized upon the opportunity and escorted Miss Bingley to the seats placing her beside Darcy.

The crowd now happily relaxed, found a comfortable spot to view the display and they clapped when the music escalated to a crescendo as each burst of light exploded against the black sky. The Harvest Feast ended when the last firelight faded from view. A parade of families, on foot and in carriages and wagons, silently and tiredly gathered their broods and returned home.

The Black Bull Tavern had provided an alternative attraction for the men not wishing to view the fireworks; offering their own festivities to celebrate their victor for the Baker rifle. Patrons purchased many drinks for the three finalists with Mr. Pruitt garnering the most attention. While the crowd swarmed around the two local men, Logan engaged the charming Wickham in a private conversation, played cards and paid for an endless flow of strong drink. More precisely, it poured in only one person's glass.

Earlier, before the finalists appeared, Logan had requested his drinks fixed in a secretive way, which was unusual but not unprecedented. Since he would benefit the more for it, Staunton voiced no objection and slipped the shilling incentive into his coat pocket.

Wickham was winning at cards. His opponent appeared unperturbed and with every victorious hand, the lieutenant became more animated in his speech. Logan called for another round of drinks and threw more coins on the table.

The two men gambled, drank, and, most importantly of all, chatted until the officer collapsed on the floor. Logan picked his pockets clean and headed out the door and headed back to his master waiting for him at Netherfield.

Rawlings paced around his room. Where is he? Damn. It should not have taken this long. He glanced at the timepiece on the mantle and huffed. My God, it is four in the morning. I hope you left me with some capital left.

Returning to his chair for an uncounted number of times, he tapped his fingers on the table until he lost the battle and poured another full glass of brandy. As he gulped the amber liquid, he ignored the burn cascading down his throat, and stood up when the door opened. Logan's face was unreadable.

Rawlings spat out the words, "What, pray tell, did you discover?" He scoffed. "If you discovered anything at all. It has been all night!"

Logan spied the glass on the table. "Here, I drank false drinks, but you," he glared as he pointed to the near empty decanter, "indulged fiercely in the strongest brandy in the house."

"And?"

"Wickham is a cautious person. He chooses his words carefully, although, his tales poured out as quickly as the whiskey did. I did have a time getting him to reveal more than the story he has repeatedly told."

"And did he?"

"When he believes he is winning at cards, he can be very revealing. With each hand, he said a little bit more. He is a braggart, believing himself to be self-important and in complete control. I had to laugh when he passed out. It was easy to pick his pockets clean." Logan placed the money on the table.

"Logan! I insist you stop delaying, and tell me what you found out. Will this man create problems for us, or not? Why does Darcy despise this fellow?"

"Despise him? If it were me I would have shot the bloody sod in the back."

Rawlings jerked his head up. "What?"

"Yes, I am astonished that Darcy keeps his temper. By all rights the rogue should have had a bullet in him long ago, or perhaps slashed to pieces with a sword after a lengthy torturing."

Rawlings slumped in the chair. "Will it impact us at all?"

"I do not think so. Mr. Darcy is angry, rightfully. It is a personal matter."

"Did this man steal from him?"

"It is more along the lines that he tried to." When Rawlings raised brows up and waited, Logan continued. "He nearly seduced his young sister."

With his jaw dropping, and eyes widening, Rawlings leaned forward, grabbing the arms of his chair tightly. "Did he harm her in any way?"

"He was after her money. I am sure he would be dead if he had touched her. Fortunately, he merely attempted to elope with her, and gain full possession of her thirty thousand-pound dowry. She is still an innocent girl today because the cad knew how far he could push a judicious man such as Darcy before his life was in real danger."

"Taking money from a young girl is despicable unless, of course she is a conniving, scheming charlatan. I daresay that Miss Darcy is the former and did not deserve such treatment."

"We are talking about an innocent young girl of fifteen, not a shrewd woman of one and twenty."

"True. Six years can make a difference in a woman's actions as does a lower place in society."

While he recounted to his master all the particulars between Wickham and Darcy's sister, Rawlings poured Logan the remainder of the brandy. He wondered why Darcy allowed the man free reign in Hertfordshire. What was it that Darcy said? 'I suspect his actions are aimed at me, a revenge on his part.' "It is providential the Bennets girls lost their dowries or that blackguard would certainly set out to seduce one of them. It is also fortunate that the Bennets are ladies." Rawlings sat erect. With a pounding heart and sweaty palms, he had a single thought—Lydia! Regaining his composure, he turned to his valet. "Mr. Bennet must be warned. Lydia is in jeopardy!"

Logan nodded. "There can be no two opinions on that, but Darcy favors Miss Elizabeth. Would not Wickham be more interested in her?"

"Today he escorted Lydia while I was busy making her jealous with Kitty. Wickham must suspect Darcy favors Lydia! Damn. What have I done? She adores men in redcoats."

"That explains Wickham's particular attention he paid to Miss Lydia."

"I suspect he means to seek his revenge through her." Logan gulped his brandy and placed the glass on the table as he glanced to the clock on the mantel. "Bingley's ball is tonight and you look unfit to be seen by gravediggers. You must sleep if you wish to present a handsome face for Miss Lydia. The scoundrel will not enthrall her with his spurious charm if you can offer her the better choice."

***

Netherfield Park was quiet this early in the morning. The only sound was boots climbing the stairs. Blake and Darcy had held their day after race as agreed, the winning coins jingled noisily in the former man's pocket.

Mrs. Nicholls knew about the private races between the men, and she sensed the tension in the house when a certain Longbourn lady graced Netherfield Park. It was her job as housekeeper to know these things. Nevertheless, with only her instinct to guide her, she believed her position was secure by the obvious way Mr. Bingley dotted on the eldest

Miss Bennet. Everyone in Meryton desired the match if no other reason than to keep Mr. Bingley in the neighborhood. They pressed her regularly for confirmation.

Walking the halls, she wondered when the the other guests would rise, and in particular Miss Bingley, to whom she needed to give a report. She had everything prepared for this evening's ball. The white soup was ready. The house, scrubbed from top to bottom, looked flawless. The many flowers in vases filled the ballroom with the scent of yellow Banksia roses and delicate lavender irises wafted throughout. The musicians would arrive later this afternoon from London in time to set up and tune their instruments.

The servants, she noted, were groggy from last night's fireworks display. Most had never witnessed such an array of fireworks. All the same, she did expect, and had demanded with firmness in her voice, they must be sharp for the ball. When the crowds had dispersed, it was too late for the necessary clean up. This morning, the servants were hurrying to dismantle all the games and clear out the mess left behind. Mrs. Nicholls hoped they would finish in time.

As she climbed the stairs, she thought about the last fortnight and all the previous activity surrounding the competitions. Even if the extra work had meant many full days and late nights, she was somewhat sad now the end had arrived. Well not all the competitions. There are still the ones where the gentlemen are the prize! Mrs. Nicholls laughed to herself. Those games will be going strong tonight.

Mrs. Nicholls stopped and knocked on Miss Bingley's door.

"What? Who is it?" Caroline said curtly.

"Mrs. Nicholls, ma'am. You asked me to meet with you this morning. You wanted to review the final preparations for the ball. Shall I return later?"

"Yes, in one hour, if you please. Oh, and prepare my bath water." She answered.

Her response did not surprise Mrs. Nicholls. Miss Bingley was not a morning riser even when she did not stay up late, as was the situation last night. The drawing room had been where much merriment and the conversations grew more animated as the evening progressed. Lord Blake was a gracious winner, only gloating a little bit, while his friends sipped their whiskey. They had refused to share with him. The jesting continued, aimed at Mr. Bingley, when his sister scolded him several times concerning his disappearance earlier that day. His silly grin disarmed her without ever accounting for his whereabouts. Miss Bingley and her sister played merry tunes on the pianoforte as the men reminisced over the games. Mr. Rawlings jested they should have been naked like the early Greeks. Now that would have tempted even me to watch the competitions.

Mrs. Nicholls entered the kitchen and informed the cook that no one other than Lord Blake and Mr. Darcy stirred. She could hold off making the breakfast for a while since those two had departed for a morning ride.

Without looking up from the ham she was preparing for the morning meal, the cook smiled. "I am not surprised his lordship went for a gallop, what with him winning that stallion and all."

"I am sure it is none of our business," Mrs. Nicholls said, her tone gruff. "Miss Bingley will want her bath water now."

Mrs. Nicholls entered the housekeeper's quarters and began the tedious job of reviewing the final preparations for Mr. Bingley's first ball. She had worked hard to guarantee its success.

Chapter Thirty-one

Darcy stood at the window, absentmindedly brushing off his coat, as he examined the carriages arriving at Netherfield Park. The footmen held torches to light the way, thus he was able to discern the identities of those stepping down from each particular conveyance. The elegance of the dress surprised him; the ladies showed more style for this ball than he had witnessed at the assembly hall dance. They dressed in fine silk gowns with turbans or feathers adorning their heads, copying the London fashion.

A long line of guest waited to alight from their transports. Not all were carriages; some emerged from curricles and gigs, and several officers rode in on horseback while the others walked. Darcy wondered if the Bennets, with so large a family, would arrive in two conveyances. The carriage that carried away the two eldest Bennets from this house seemed insufficient in size for seven people. From his own sister's pains, he knew how combative a lady became to ensure her best gown remained wrinkle free. He pondered which of the daughters received the preference of the carriage and assumed age had its privileges, although with the Bennets he was not as confident in his conjecture. He maintained his observation of the carriages while each vehicle made its way to the front door.

From the third floor window, he continued to scrutinize each arrival, and with such intensity, that a flawlessly dressed Rawlings was able to join him unnoticed. Unlike Darcy's black outfit, he wore his blue coat and his favorite waistcoat—a matching indigo with golden threads weaved into the fabric. If they had worn the same color, they would have been indistinguishable, except for the appealing curl in Darcy's hair and the clever spark in Rawlings' silvery green eyes. They had agreed years ago that they would never dress identically.

"Darcy, are you seeking out someone? Or are you planning your attack?"

Startled, Darcy turned away from the window, shrugging. He presupposed his friend knew which lady was the object of his search. "Attack? Come now; speak in plain words... if you are able."

"As you wish. Whenever two forces meet on the battlefield, the generals follow a plan for success. Both cannot lay in wait, otherwise, there would never be a victory, or a loss for that matter, but let us focus on taking possession of the territory. One must attack, and I am presuming you are planning to surprise your opponent tonight."

"Sometimes, Rawlings, you bore me. Why can you not just accuse me and be done with it?" Darcy flashed a smile as he tipped his head.

"What fun would that be? Where is the other general, by the way? Ah! There he is."

Darcy glanced around the room, searching every fair-haired man. "I do not see him." He detected the furrowed brow on his friend's face. "What concerns you now?"

"Just trying to find the right four syllable word. Alas, a smaller word must do. Even you cannot find a larger one." He directed Darcy's attention to the window. "Look down. He is on the front step! As I stated, step is a one-syllable word." Both men leaned in closer until their heads brushed the pane. Rawlings chuckled. "He is lying in wait; but if you allow for where he stands, he is not waiting for you!"

Darcy found Blake without much effort. Even in the hazy torch light, he was able to spot the marquess fidgeting on the steps, and if he needed a word to describe the man, he would call him exhilarated. Damn. A five syllable word. Must I always seek such words? Excited means the same, and yet that word is but three syllables.

"Chuckling, Darcy? You find the other general amusing?"

"No. I laugh at my word choice." Darcy's countenance changed to one of seriousness. "I am not a general, Rawlings; I do not seek the same territory, regardless of your opinion."

"I find that surprising. I will let it pass, for now. However, please enlighten me and explain exactly why you are lying in wait."

"I need to impart some information to the lady about the, shall we say, other general."

Rawlings gasped as the hair on his neck stood on end. "Do not do this. Do not attempt such a thing! You have no standing. I appeal to your good judgment, and plead for you not to jeopardize everything. We signed the partnership agreements just today."

"I am responsible. I brought him here." Darcy looked up into the starlit sky. "You do not know how beleaguered my life has been recently. I vowed never again to allow an innocent young lady of my particular acquaintance fall prey to pretty words. Now, if you will excuse me, I must get Blake to hold off on his ... um... plan of attack."

The muscles in Rawlings' neck tensed. He immediately grabbed Darcy's arm, stopping him from heading down the stairs. "Wait! He will not respond well to *your* good intentions. Let me go for you. I shall divert his attention. I shall be your colonel."

Darcy nodded and watched him dash down the stairs. He returned to the window in time to glimpse the last carriage pulling into the long line in the driveway. Before long, he spotted Rawlings as he approached Blake, and after a few spoken words, they went inside and out of view.

I must obtain a few moments of Elizabeth's time. But how? He paced back and forth, stopping when a thought occurred. He concentrated on arranging a meeting in the library, on the balcony, or even at the refreshment table. How can I speak to her without Blake hovering around?

"There you are, Darcy!" Bingley patted him on the back. "Tonight, do not hug the walls as if they are your only friends. I insist you enjoy the ball. You must dance this evening. Come, come. I have seen you occupied thusly before; I know you are capable. Oh, I beg your pardon, Caroline is waving. I must return to greeting my guests."

Dance? Why yes, of course! That is my answer. Darcy returned to spying out the window as the passengers were descending from the final carriage. His brows shot up at the sight before him. Miss Elizabeth wore the most welcoming smile, and unlike the fashionable turban the hostess chose, she had adorned her curls with what appeared to be delicate white flowers and pearls. He found it bewitching and a far superior choice than large peacock feathers extending out of a lady's turbin, he sent her a small nod of approval He felt his chest tighten as she glided up the front steps, he struggled for breath when her eyes lifted up to meet his. My god, she is... beautiful. I shall be honored to dance with her. He turned his head away as he refocused his mind on the somber task before him. He stepped inside the ballroom.

Miss Bingley had demonstrated her exceptional skill at managing this event, or more precisely, directing Mrs. Nicholls, the hard-working housekeeper. The ballroom shimmered; the multitude of candles cast a flickering radiance indiscriminately throughout the space. The sounds of random notes, plucked from the string instruments, pervaded everywhere as the musicians from London readied themselves for the flawless melodies soon to fill the air. A bouquet of fresh baked breads, roasted beef and poultry, and fruity scents seeped from the nearby dining area, barely overtaking the fragrances of the winter flowers arranged and placed on every available vertical service. A crush of guests shifted about with an increasing loud progression of whispers and laughter as the servants poured the wine freely, ensuring no glass remained empty long. All this awaited the cream of Meryton while they passed through the receiving line and entered the room, wordlessly announcing to the guests their esteemed status and place of respect within the parish.

Bingley, now joined by his four friends, waited patiently for the Bennets to make their way up the staircase. As these final guests reached the landing, each man, in unison, snapped into an upright position when the young ladies came into view.

Rawlings whispered to Darcy, "Mrs. Bennet certainly knows how to dress her daughters. She has proven to be a military strategist as well. So there will be no laying in wait. She sent her soldiers straight to the front line with, ahem, their weapons loaded. All hope is lost."

Darcy spied Elizabeth's gown, and at once felt his heartbeat quicken. He breathed several deep breaths before glancing sideways at Blake, whose smile had broadened and stretched the entire width of his face, not unlike Bingley's grin.

After Rawlings admired the cut of the Lydia's gown, he leaned closer to Darcy, and in a half whisper said, "We are merely brigadier generals, while Mrs. Bennet is the generals' general, my friend; she is the field marshal over us all!"

Nonetheless, as Elizabeth made her way down the receiving line, Darcy defeated the marquess in this first skirmish of the night by swiftly offering his arm to escort her into the ballroom.

Bingley, as expected, escorted Miss Bennet, Blake followed with Miss Mary while Kent led Miss Bingley into the room.

Rawlings had no opportunity with Miss Lydia. She had flitted inside before he could even approach her. When he held his arm for Miss Catherine, she ignored him, preferring to walk towards the two officers waiting beside her sister. Standing alone and staring at the teasing wench, he announced albeit quietly, "Do not run away from me Miss Lydia. Tonight you shall dance in the arms of someone worthy of your passions, and he will not be wearing the color red."

Bingley spoke to Rawlings when they entered the ballroom. "Do not worry if she denies you early in the evening, just make certain you dance the last one with her." Bingley winked. "Do not let the opportunity pass."

Bingley turned to Jane, rewarding her with a tender expression. "Miss Bennet, I must tell you how lovely you look tonight."

Jane blushed, lowered her eyes, smoothing the wrinkles in her dress from the ride. They had squashed into the carriage, her sisters pushing against one another while her father and mother sat in comfort with just Mary between them.

"Miss Bennet, may I request the honor of the first set?" Bingley asked. "And before anyone else can claim it, may I apply for the final dance as well. If I could only be accepted for one, then I would wish it be the last dance."

After Jane agreed to both, the two took their places at the head of the line. Each musician held his instrument in position while Bingley waited for his friends to choose their own partners.

Although Darcy led Miss Elizabeth into the room, he had to check his arm to confirm that she had accepted the escort. The lint he brushed away earlier felt heavier than the slender elegant fingers curled around his sleeve. He admired the lightness of her touch; although in conjunction with the distance she kept between her body and his, uneasiness would have been the more appropriate reaction. He charged ahead, without regard to the clear warning signs, requesting the first set, only to hear her rejection. He had come too late. His expression changed from confidence to concern when she stated, in a sharp tone, that she had promised the first and the second sets. Words stumbled from his lips until gaining her acceptance for the third set. Reeling from this surprise, he released her to Miss Lucas and stepped away.

When the other guests had lined up, Darcy searched the room until spying Blake, standing off to the side. No doubt Blake scouted the territory before today. I must stand guard. Damn. Why did Rawlings put battle words in my head? Expecting his friend to make his move, he inhaled sharply when a clumsy, ill-dressed man came to claim Elizabeth. The man's mouth moved with no sign of stopping while she disregarded his babbling to search the faces in the ballroom. Darcy relaxed and chuckled at the scene.

However, he took a step back when he caught Blake studying him. His recovery was quick. He threw his shoulders back, sucked in his stomach, and raised to his full height as he returned to patrolling the perimeter as he watched the dancers line up.

Darcy chuckled again when he focused his attention back on the couples waiting to begin the dance. Ah, the beauty and the beast! Perhaps a troll is a better term for the man. Good god, she rolled eyes when he turned his head. Miss Elizabeth, it is never wise for a lady reveal your dislike of anyone so openly. It just encourages a man to pursue her. I wonder who he is and if he is capable of even dancing!

Rawlings approached Lydia, but before he could speak, an officer wearing a well pressed redcoat and polished insignia arrived to claim her. Lydia flashed a mischievous grin back towards him as she took her place on the dance floor. He narrowed his eyes, sending her a silent message. She threw her chin up and laughed. He shook his head, returning her laugh, and retreated to find one of his friends. The moment the officer whispered in her ear she lost interest in him, giggling while they waited for the musicians to start the dance.

Once Kent escorted Miss Bingley to the line, Bingley sent the anticipated signal. The long awaited first note sounded; the men bowed, and the ladies curtseyed in their most practiced manner.

Darcy circled the dancing area, while Blake anchored himself in the spot he had calculated Miss Elizabeth would end the dance. Blake remained entrenched; Darcy continued to patrol the room, maintaining surveillance on both Blake and Elizabeth. He sought a tactic to break the marquess' plan. Amidst his thoughts, his eyes repeatedly drifted away from the sullen Blake and towards the lady with the amusing expressions escaping when her dancing partner turned away.

Before the first dance of the set ended, Rawlings approached Darcy. "General, sir. There is one fewer enemy in red attending tonight. I believe his colonel sent him away on a mission. This evening begins well."

Unruffled, Darcy maintained his unyielding stare at Elizabeth and answered in a nonchalant tone. "Oh? I had not noticed."

"Bah! You were aware of this, and I suppose you were instrumental in sending him on some important mission away from Meryton?"

Darcy sighed. "I did not. It is not I who fear a confrontation."

"I am also here to report, sir, that as we speak, the other general is surveying the same territory you seek. I shall stand guard until relieved of duty by a well endowed foot soldier who has been ordered to do so by the field marshal." Rawlings chuckled. "What is it with these Bennets? Unquestionably, they can drive a man daft."

Darcy shook his head. "I have expressed my opinion to you before. Miss Lydia is too young for you. Perhaps, I should speak in your terms. You are a general, and she is the drummer boy; too great a difference in age and in rank.

"Is that all? Neither is an insurmountable obstacle. And I am but a colonel."

"She does not show proper decorum nor hold herself above reproach. Think, my friend, about Londons' reaction to her." He sighed at Rawlings' grin. "I do not comprehend what interests you."

Rawlings inclined his head, sending a pointed glance to the haughty lady dancing among the locals, casting condescending sneers at every opportunity. "Miss Bingley and her London manners should indicate why I prefer the delightfully flirty Miss Lydia. I have had enough of perfect, sophisticated proper ladies. The *Ton* is infested with them."

"Still, you have responsibilities. Do not push those aside."

"And you? Are you not ignoring your own expectations? Miss Elizabeth is not your ideal."

"As I told you, Rawlings, I seek to speak with her, nothing else." Darcy paused to compose his next words.

"Bah! I do not believe safekeeping her from harm is your true reason. Do not try to mislead me, Darcy. You look upon her differently than other ladies."

"Fine. I will admit she has caught my fancy as you presume; you know me far too well." For the briefest of moments, Darcy closed his eyes. "And you are correct, she does keep me awake at night; but," he turned to face Rawlings, "I must consider more than myself. My sister and the Darcy duty and family stand in the way."

"Do not be a—"

"Drinks anyone?" Kent interrupted. "Shall we partake of some refreshments?"

"I thought you were dancing?"

"Miss Bingley was needed to resolve some problem requiring her skills. I am sure she will not take long. She is quick thinking." Kent steered his friends towards the refreshment table while sending a secret signal across the room.

When Kent turned to pick up several glasses of wine, Rawlings whispered to Darcy, "You have been ambushed, General."

After the men sipped their drinks and spent a moment conversing, Miss Bingley, prompted by Kent, approached. "It is fortunate tonight was such a lovely evening." Glancing around the ballroom, she added, "The locals seem pleased." She batted her eyes at Darcy.

Kent bowed. "You have arranged a wonderful ball, Miss Bingley."

"Decidedly so," Rawlings added.

Caroline hid a smirk behind her fan as she targeted her eyes on Mr. Darcy.

"Miss Bingley, you are especially lovely tonight, do you not agree, Darcy?" Kent darted his eyes from Caroline to his silent friend.

"It is kind of you to say so."

Darcy limited his response to a nod.

She waited for him to say something while fanning her self with her open fan.

Rawlings took pity on him and claimed his promised dance with her as his penance due to his rude behavior at the golf practice picnic and whisking Miss Bingley towards the dance floor. She accepted in a gracious manner, although she glowered at him through narrowed eyes. They joined the dancers just as the band started the second set.

"Darcy, will you be dancing tonight?" Kent asked.

"I plan on dancing the next set." He did not elaborate.

"May I ask which fair lady has won the honor?"

Rising to his full height, Darcy turned to Kent. "I would appreciate you not encouraging Miss Bingley. I do not understand your ploy, but I warn you, do not endeavor to sway me along those lines. Any further attempt will not be met with any fragment of a cordial response."

Kent took a step back. "As you wish. I shall leave you to your own devices." He turned and walked away.

Blake was quick to claim Elizabeth for the second set. Darcy, expecting this, found a strategic spot to observe them. His eyes bore into the two with a strange, black stare as they touched hands. The two dancers, however, were unaware, or rather uninterested, as their eyes remained focused on each other. Darcy cringed every time she smiled at Blake or laughed at his whispered words. His hands curled into fists when they leaned too close, and then again when the dancing couple was slow to release their entwined fingers. *I must talk to her, warn her,* he thought as he unknowingly began to pace around the room; his gaze never wavering from their position on the dance floor. Darcy moved around the ballroom floor, speaking to no one. He glared at the musicians, willing them to play faster, until the dance ended.

Kent followed the direction of his gaze, assuming Miss Elizabeth would be at the end. *Well, as I surmised, she is who he wants. But without her sizeable dowry, it may very well fit my purpose if Darcy were to secure her hand. Perhaps not as helpful as it would had it have been Miss Bingley, but it will do."* Kent's eyes narrowed. *"And Darcy would take Miss Elizabeth away from Blake, wounding him. I would not be at all sorry for that man's loss.* Rawlings joined him and they stood in silent contemplation for a few moments while watching different friends.

Darcy claimed Elizabeth for the next set, but he did not see what Kent beheld—the scowl upon her face, at once concealed, when she turned to face him for the dance. "Does Miss Elizabeth not like Darcy? She seems to cast cold stares at him when he is not looking."

"I should not know. I have been more interested in watching Blake. He does not appear pleased."

"I suspect he feels he is still competing. Although this time, he may not be so confident about his chances. He did trifle with me with the rowing contest."

"I believe it was you who trifled with Darcy." Rawlings replied.

Kent, ignoring the pointed jab, tilted his head towards Darcy. "He needs to understand, Blake is a tenacious and relentless challenger. I do not think he would quit any race without a fight." Kent paused when the tune changed. "Do you believe Darcy is partial to Miss Elizabeth?"

Rawlings glanced at the two dancers. "He is dancing with a local country miss. He rarely dances, and only when he is compelled to by proper etiquette."

Kent chuckled. "Ah. She is challenging him again. He seems amused by her verbal contests."

"I doubt he has ever been challenged, since mostly sycophants follow him around." Rawlings glanced sideways at Kent.

"True." Kent shrugged. "Miss Elizabeth does not hang on his every word, unlike a certain other lady of our acquaintance." He located Miss Bingley across the room. She, too, was engrossed in watching the two dancers.

"And therein is his attraction with Miss Elizabeth."

The two men watched while the two dancers continued their unique verbal challenges.

Elizabeth mumbled as they separated in the turn. "I shall not find him amiable."

"Miss Elizabeth, I beg your pardon. Your words escaped me." Darcy reached for her hand as they married up again for the next few steps of the dance.

"It is your turn to say something now, Mr. Darcy. I talked about your, umm, performance, and you ought to make some remark on the size of the room, or the number of couples on the dance floor."

"I do have a matter of extreme importance to discuss with you."

"Here, in the middle of a dance with music flowing and laughter all around? I cannot think seriously, as we take our turns and perform our steps. My head is full."

"The present always occupies you in such situations, does it? Should you not consider your future? Should you not be cautious?"

Elizabeth, without missing a step, presented him with what he assumed was the loathing look of a combatant slowly aiming a modified Baker rifle at a despised enemy. "Cautious? I remember hearing you once say, Mr. Darcy, you are very cautious, and you hardly ever forgave; that your resentment once created was unappeasable. I suppose then you are most vigilant as to your forming your dislike in the first place.

"I am." Darcy felt a sharp pain, his neck muscles twitched as if a bullet had just passed through it.

"And never allow yourself to be blinded by prejudice?"

He ducked his head. "I hope not."

"It is particularly incumbent on those who never change their opinion, to be secure of judging properly at first." She smiled at his furrowed brow

They separated as required by the dance, continuing the steps apart from one another. Darcy furrowed his brow. Does she think I am prejudiced against her? Prejudiced? I am not prejudiced at all. She is beautiful, witty, and intelligent, but I must know what is on her mind."

They turned towards one another; his hand capturing hers.

Raising himself to his full height, Darcy tightened his hold on her hand. "May I ask to what these questions tend?"

"Merely to the illustration of your character. I am trying to make it out."

"And what is your success?"

"I do not get on at all. I hear such different accounts of you as puzzle me exceedingly." Elizabeth stared at his hand caressing hers. When she looked up, she studied him with the hint of a question in her eyes.

"I can readily believe that any report may vary greatly with respect to me and be prejudiced against me; and I could wish, Miss Bennet—"

"Do not speak of Mr. Wickham in this way."

She had discharged the name like the razor-sharp shot of a skilled and highly trained sharpshooter. He felt her jerked her hand away from his. "Mr. Wickham? You were speaking about Mr. Wickham? I thought you were referring to another." Darcy shot a look towards Blake, who was glaring back at him.

"Lord Blake? He sung only about your goodness. Why would he speak any other way? Are you prejudiced against him as well?"

"But Mr. Wickham has done differently? You did say you have heard differing accounts."

They took another turn. Darcy's hand flew to massage the back of his neck. Wickham? No, not him! Tread carefully. She is infuriated. What did he tell her? My God, not him. I must warn her about him as well.

When they rejoined hands, Darcy leaned closer, taking in the lavender scent surrounding her. "Mr. Wickham is blessed with such happy manners as may ensure his making friends; whether he may be equally capable of retaining them, is less certain."

She glared at him. "He has been so unlucky as to lose your friendship, and in a manner which he is likely to suffer from all his life."

At that moment, Sir William Lucas appeared close to them, meaning to pass through the set to the other side of the room; but on perceiving Mr. Darcy, he stopped to bow.

"I have been most highly gratified indeed, my dear sir. Such very superior dancing is not often seen. It is evident that you belong to the first circles. Allow me to say, however, that your fair partner does not disgrace you, and that I must hope to have this pleasure often repeated, especially when a certain desirable event, my dear Miss Eliza, shall take place." Sir William glanced at Miss Bennet and Bingley.

Elizabeth and Darcy turned to observe the couple sipping their drinks and sharing a laugh with Rawlings and Kent.

"What congratulations will then flow! I appeal to Mr. Darcy—but let me not interrupt you, Sir. You will not thank me for detaining you from the bewitching converse of that young lady, whose bright eyes are now upbraiding me."

Sir William smiled, clapped his hands, and moved to the other side of the room, where he whispered to the gleeful listeners. While the gentleman regaled the crowd, all eyes turned towards Bingley and Miss Bennet. By the nodding of the heads and the contented smiles on their faces, they appeared in much agreement. These reactions were not lost on Darcy.

"Forgive me, Miss Bennet. Sir William's interruption has made me forget what we were discussing."

"I do not think we were speaking at all. Sir William could not have interrupted any two people in the room who had less to say for themselves. We have tried two or three subjects already without success, and what we are to talk of next I cannot imagine."

"What think you of books?" he said, smiling.

With her right brow raised, Elizabeth took aim and fired another blast towards him. "Books—Oh no!—I am sure we never read the same, or not with the same feelings. You, sir, wish to read books on gas lighting, and I find that I cannot speak on such a matter."

"I am sorry you think so; but if that be the case, there can at least be no want of subject. We may compare our different opinions." He leaned in close and tightened his grip on her hand. "You may find we have differing thoughts on other topics. Perhaps we could meet in the library and speak for a moment or two. I—

"This is ball, Mr. Darcy. I have not the desire to speak on serious subjects." Elizabeth pulled her hand away with such force it caused the dancers beside them to take notice. "I cannot figure you out at all. You puzzle me exceedingly."

Humph. I am not the one who needs your concern! "Miss Elizabeth, I wish that you not sketch my character at the present moment, as there is reason to fear that the performance would reflect no credit on either." Darcy gazed down at her curious expression. You do not understand me at all.

"If I do not take your likeness now, I may never have another opportunity."

"I would by no means suspend any pleasure of yours," Darcy answered curtly. Why are you thinking about me? Damn stubborn girl. Worry about Blake or Wickham. He returned to his aloof posture, his head held high, his shoulders back, and his eyes, darkened by his thoughts, bore into hers. Well, I shall not try to protect you again. You are… unmanageable and unmovable in your opinions. Yes, I spoke the truth—you misunderstand everyone and do so willingly. Humph.

She did not speak again. They went down the other dance and parted in silence; each one dissatisfied.

As Darcy watched her approach Miss Lucas when the set ended, he felt a powerful urge to grab her by the hand, pull her into the library and… He snapped to attention. Do what? I was not thinking of shaking her, I want to take her in my arms and give her a reason not to fall for… "Wickham. Damn him! What did he say to her? What lies is he spreading this time?"

The moment the dance ended, Rawlings picked up some wine for Lydia. However, when she turned to walk away from her partner, she nearly knocked the drink from his hand.

"May I offer you a glass of wine, Miss Lydia?"

"Thank you." She fluttered her eyes as she looked up at him.

Bowing, he requested the honor of the supper dance, and was disappointed to learn another had claimed it. Remembering Bingley's caution, he asked for the last set of the night, hoping she had not given them all away. She accepted, although her sigh was louder than he would have wished.

Undaunted he said, "I do so admire your gown tonight. You look lovely."

"The blue ribbon matches my eyes, do you not think so?" Lydia blinked her long lashes as she tilted her head.

"Yes, it is a beautiful color as are your eyes, Miss Lydia."

"You are wearing your blue coat." She cast her eyes on him. "Why, we are a match, are we not?" When he smiled at her statement, she continued. "You know you have such big hands, Mr. Rawlings. I do not recall anyone with hands that size. You must be very strong."

Rawlings smiled as broadly as he could. *If you want this little flirtation to work, my dear, then I will play along.* When Lydia walked away for the next dance, Rawlings studied the womanly sway of her hips. *Whew. Greased up rear parts, indeed.*

Turning her head slowly, Lydia smiled at him before curtseying to her partner.

***

Once the supper dance ended, the gentlemen moved to the dining room. Kent led Miss Bennet to the seat reserved for her next to Bingley. He chose the seat on her other side but not before sharing a nod and smile with his grinning friend. Darcy had been unsuccessful in claiming a place near Miss Elizabeth; and even though Blake had not partnered with her for the dance, it was he who had maneuvered to take the chair next to her. Darcy, displeased at the inability to speak privately to her, selected a location that permitted his continued surveillance of the two.

Supper was a disaster. Lydia and Kitty raced about, chased by several officers. Without regard to the loudness of her voice, Mrs. Bennet spoke of the future possibilities when Jane would become Mistress of Netherfield Park and Elizabeth became a Marchioness. She added, and in an equally loud voice, her belief that the eldest girls' fortunes would help her younger ones find rich men of their own. Miss Mary entertained the guests with a very poor rendition of Mozart's piano sonata in A minor. Even Mr. Bennet contributed to the fiasco by embarrassing his own daughter at the end of the musical piece, demanding she not continue.

Without concealing her discomfit about her family, Elizabeth ate her supper in silence, blushing at each humiliation. Darcy understood the meaning for the blushes, unlike Blake, who seemed oblivious to anything except that she was the woman sitting next to him. One time she lifted her gaze from her plate, and her body shuddered when the gawky talkative man from her first dance introduced himself to Darcy.

Darcy's eyes darted from Elizabeth to the clergyman. Who is this man? And why is Miss Elizabeth so mortified by him? What is he to her?

She closed her eyes before swallowing the remaining wine in her glass. When the meal was over, and the dancing was about to resume, she did appear to relax. Mr. Rawlings and Mr. Kent were among the first to seek her out for a dance.

The ballroom activities continued along the same manner as before: Darcy paced the room; Blake stared at all the men dancing with Miss Elizabeth; Rawlings watched Lydia with much amusement; and Bingley and Jane remained close all evening; talking when they could not dance, and only parting when a gentleman came to claim his angel for her promised sets. Kent's behavior was the only exception; he now avoided Miss Bingley.

The mood in the room remained unchanged until the musicians announced the last dance; Rawlings claimed Lydia while Blake escorted Miss Elizabeth to the floor. Darcy, surprised the marquess had secured her hand for this dance, grabbed a glass from the table, and drained the contents in one gulp. Two sets. He knows better than to dance twice.

Bingley, Blake, and Rawlings lined up together. Bingley gave the signal. When the musicians began to play the waltz, Darcy's heart pounded as he held his breath. He felt his stomach knot as Blake placed his arm around her waist. Even though the couple maintained a proper distance between them, he glared at Blake in the same manner as a magistrate would intimidate a little boy caught stealing candy. His right eye twitched and his leg muscles flinched. He moved closer to the dancers. This is unsupportable!

Darcy noticed Blake did not seem surprised at the dance choice and explained why he did not request dancing with her for the supper dance. Bingley always shares his damn secrets with Blake. Why did he not tell me? Feeling a sharp twinge, Darcy flashed his scowl upon Bingley who merely lifted and lowered his brows before turning back to gaze at Miss Bennet.

The Meryton neighbors did not fuss one whit. They determined if Mr. Bingley wanted this scandalous dance at his ball, then they would allow him to do so without comment. A few guests spoke unkindly of the waltz, turning their eyes away from the couples on the floor.

Mr. Bennet was not smiling; he did not turn away. He stood close to the dance floor casting his own dark stares at each of the men.

Darcy watched Blake and Elizabeth; his thoughts, as they had all through supper, returned to her pointed questions during their dance. Wickham! What is that reprobate up to now? Nevertheless, he forgot

Wickham; his imaginings replaced with other feelings when half way through the dance, he witnessed the sweet smile Elizabeth gave to Blake and the vibrancy of her gaze upon his face. Unable to do more than stand and watch, he clenched his fists so tight that markings from his nails left impressions on his palms. He paced with more determination. *I must stop Blake. This has gone too far.* He paid no attention to the guests moving out of his way until he almost knocked Mr. Bennet down. The two men stood abreast, holding their own competition, both glaring at the dancers.

Darcy released a long held breath when the music ended and maintained his close watch when the couple made their way off the floor.

Rawlings, Blake, and Bingley, each man wearing wide smiles, escorted the ladies to their waiting mother. Rawlings did not look anywhere except at his partner. She smiled up at him with a toothy grin, snuggling closer to him than he had ever hoped. Nonetheless, and just as quick, Lydia left to join Kitty. He could hear her giggles throughout the room and chuckled at the smug look upon her face when she gazed his way.

Catching up to Bingley, Rawlings whispered to him. "I shall be forever grateful, my friend. I understand now why you insisted on us learning the waltz so many weeks ago." Bingley moved to the musicians' area. He requested they strike a note, and he waited patiently for the remaining guests to quiet down.

While Bingley was thanking everyone for coming and wishing them a safe journey home, Rawlings approached Mr. Bennet. "Sir, might I have a word with you? It is of some importance."

Wordlessly, Mr. Bennet nodded agreement and followed Rawlings to the library. He accepted a brandy before displaying his harshest glare at the young man, and without concealing his contempt, he asked, "Mr. Rawlings, did you enjoy holding my youngest daughter in such an intimate way? Is she the reason for our private talk?"

Rawlings froze; sweat poured from his forehead. He took a long moment to set his glass down before responding in a calm voice. "Ahem. Any such talk between us would not be undesirable on my part; however, I have another reason to speak to you. Miss Lydia may be in grave danger."

Mr. Bennet's body stiffened. He tightened his fingers around his glass. After steeling himself, he nodded for Rawlings to continue.

"Mr. Wickham is not to be trusted with—"

"Phew! Wickham? You have come to warn me about Wickham?" Bennet relaxed.

"I assure you, sir, she is in danger from him. You must be watchful when he is around."

"Bah. He has been polite to my family, perhaps a little too charming, but courteous at all times." Mr. Bennet sipped his drink while sizing up Rawlings. "I recognize you are a great friend to Mr. Darcy. I shall warn you to be watchful while in that great man's company? I have heard of his treatment towards the young officer."

"Let me recommend, no, let me strongly suggest you do not listen to his charming story. As for Mr. Darcy's using him ill, it is perfectly false. He has been remarkably kind to him." Rawlings narrowed his eyes. "Though Wickham has treated my friend in a most infamous manner. Mr. Darcy is a gentleman, and in every sense, is the most honorable of men. Do not listen to the rumors."

"Oh, and are you privy to all his deeds? You stand by your friend. That is admirable; still, you have told me nothing specific against Wickham. Do you possess information that I should know?"

Rawlings opened his mouth to speak, quickly closed it, realizing Darcy had not given him permission to reveal that the cad had seduced a fifteen-year-old Miss Darcy. In fact, Darcy did not even know he knew.

Mr. Bennet continued, "You are much mistaken if you expect to influence me by such a paltry attack as this. I see nothing in it but your own willful ignorance and the malice of Mr. Darcy."

Rawlings bowed abruptly, the depth of which concealed his sneer. "I beg your pardon. Excuse my interference. My warning was kindly meant. I was merely acting as a friend to you and your daughters." Rawlings furrowed his brow, narrowed his eyes and with a coldness said, "Mark my words, Mr. Bennet, he is not to be trusted with any young girl, and especially your two youngest." Slamming the drink down, he left.

When Rawlings returned to the ballroom, he noticed Blake leading Elizabeth to the balcony. He froze as a chill ran down his spine when Darcy, taking long quick strides from across the room, headed in the same direction. He heard Miss Lydia calling him from the other side of the room. He turned to acknowledge her; she was waving him over. His feet would not move. His attention switched from her to Darcy and back to her sweet smiles. He forced his feet free and and moved toward Lydia.

Darcy, stopping at the balcony door saw Blake standing too close to Elizabeth. He was caressing her body with his eyes, all the while speaking softly to her, his mouth close to her ear.

Darcy could not make out the words, but he startled the couple when he found his voice and called out loudly. "Ah. There you are, Miss

Bennet. I believe your family is looking for you." He glared at Blake with a determined look.

"Thank you, Mr. Darcy, I will be along in a moment," Elizabeth said curtly. Darcy noisily held the door open for her.

Blake raised her hand to his lips, placing a light kiss upon it. He spoke quickly. "Miss Elizabeth, please will you do me the honor of meeting me tomorrow at Oakham Mount. I wish to—

Darcy heard the words clearly. "Your father is ready to leave." He raised his voice a little louder, using his hand to point to the ballroom.

Elizabeth sighed, shrugged her shoulders, and made her way back into the ballroom.

Darcy shut the door and approached Blake. They stared at each other for a moment before Blake moved to follow Elizabeth. Darcy grabbed his arm, spinning him around.

Blake demanded, "What is your meaning, barging in like this? I told you before; stay out of this."

Darcy took a breath. "I may ask, what is your design? Where do you propose this is will end?"

Again attempting to exit, Darcy grabbed his shoulder. Blake turned back to glare at him. "It is none of your concern." He paused and with a calculating expression said harshly, "Or is it? You favor her; admit it, man. I warned you, you come too late."

Ignoring Blake's question, Darcy chose to change tactics and spoke with a softer voice. "It is irrelevant whether you or I have a preference for her. Do not look at me with such pretense. Do you know what has happened to the Bennets?" When Blake shook his head, Darcy sighed. "When you find out, you may regret any decision you have made."

Blake moved closer to Darcy with his arms held stiffly at this side. "What happened? What are you trying to say?"

Darcy leaned his back against the railing. "Miss Elizabeth's dowry. Her seven thousand pound dowry is gone."

"Gone? How"

"Yes. It was squandered by her relative in Cheapside in some dishonest scheme of some sort."

Blake's eyes grew wide. "She has nothing?"

"I heard one thousand pounds might be left."

Blake gasped. "Damn. Damn. Are you positive?" He looked at Darcy, who nodded in answer. "Blast. When was this?"

"Recently. I believe the news was traveling around the parish while the eldest Bennets stayed here."

Blake paused to contemplate this new information. "I do not think this has affected Miss Elizabeth. She still seems the same witty, lively lady."

"Perhaps a little more so than usual." Darcy said while looking over Blake's shoulder at the light spilling out from the just opened door, a woman's silhouette appeared.. He did not modulate his voice lower instead raised it louder. "I know your father is nearly bankrupt. I have heard, his debts are so great that he may be forced out of parliament this year. He may not even be able to keep his estate. He owes Kent's family a large sum of money. Think, man, you cannot afford to marry Miss Elizabeth."

"You know? I knew his gambling was out of control, but I did not think the extent of the problem was general knowledge. Oh God. Damn him." Blake closed his eyes.

Darcy spoke with more consideration, although he did not lower his voice. "You must seriously consider how hard it would be for Miss Elizabeth. There will not be enough income for you two to live on. Your title is not enough. You do not wish to live at Longbourn, do you?"

Suddenly the door closed, and the balcony grew a shade darker. Darcy controlled the small smile attempting to appear on his mouth, successfully keeping his serious mien in tact. Elizabeth is safe now.

Shrugging, Blake spoke with confidence. "See here, Darcy, just because my father is in dire straights does not mean I am. In the wedding settlement, my mother left her fortune to me and not to my brother or sister. I always suspected it was my grandfather's demand. He never approved of mother's choice. I own her country estate that is doing well, and I have her home in town as well. I have an income of six thousand a year. So you see, I can afford Miss Elizabeth. Not that this is any of your concern."

"Six thousand a year. I did not know. And yet..." Darcy grasped the railing until his knuckles turned white. "You stay at your father's house in town and in the country." The knot in his stomach returned and the dull pain in his chest struck spread through his body.

"It is at his request." Blake straightened his posture before glowering at Darcy and with a rising voice demanded, "As I said, stay out of this." Blake turned to leave.

Darcy frowned. "Then you are proposing an honorable attachment? Your father will never permit the connection."

"None of this is your concern," Blake shouted angrily as he hurried to the door leading into the ballroom. Glancing backwards, he yelled, "Stay out of it!"

Darcy grabbed the railings, when Blake slammed the door shut behind him. His breathing slowed as all light faded from the balcony matching his mood.

Chapter Thirty-two

Nigel scanned the area, stopping at the ledge overlooking the Netherfield Park estate while he had waited for the two young lovers to appear. In the pre-dawn darkness, he had walked with ease along his own well-worn path, even with little light to guide his way, and located the fallen tree serving as his forest chair. By his third week in Meryton, he had discovered the meeting place between Lord Blake and Miss Elizabeth Bennet, as well as this particular discreet, comfortable spot where he sat and observed the pair. The trees provided enough cover for him to remain unseen, except with winter approaching, the bare branches would soon deny him privacy for any future surveillance. The two young people had flirted, talked, and behaved in the most proper manner, attempting nothing different than the conduct deemed appropriate in the strictest drawing room in England. The two lovers were not lovers at all, not yet. At least, this is how their actions appeared to him.

The previous evening, from a strategic location beneath the Netherfield Park balcony, he overheard Lord Blake request Elizabeth Bennet meet him for an important conversation. Hence, today, he waited on his familiar tree trunk, having arrived long before the sun rose, with his eyes and ears focused on the opening beyond the trees.. Before long, his man arrived.

Blake dismounted the Andalusian and patted his neck prior to tying him to a tree. "Today is the day, Heracles. I could not sleep one minute last night."

The horse neighed.

He rubbed the stallion's nose. "I hope I can convince her that my title is of no importance—love is all that matters." He held a carrot in his hand when Heracles reached for it.

Hearing a rustling of the leaves, his eyes searched the area, sighing when he spotted a squirrel scurrying up a tree.

"Will she understand? Will she say yes? Will she accept my offer? Regardless of my father's opinion of women like her, I will never believe she is a fortune hunter or a social climber." Blake allowed the horse to nuzzle his shoulder. "She must agree... I love her. Titles are not important to her, I am sure."

Heracles shook his head and snorted.

"I do love her." Blake walked to the edge of the mount. He remained motionless while he monitored his friends' carriages headed down the driveway towards London.

Nigel kept his eyes on the now restless young man, fidgeting after spending the morning talking aloud, although Blake stood too far away for him to hear the actual words. The young man paced, kicked the leaves, and threw pebbles over the ledge.

"I am waiting for you, Elizabeth."

***

Of the five partners, only Darcy and Blake remained at Netherfield along with Bingley's family. The other three men had journeyed to London on matters of business. This morning, Blake had left before sunrise for his customary morning ride. Following an evening out, the Hursts did as was typical for them and ordered a breakfast tray sent to their room. Thus, Caroline had lain in wait for Darcy's arrival for breakfast. When he entered the dining room, he caught her practicing a speech aimed at persuading him to provide her his support and assistance. He poured his coffee and filled a plate with eggs, the spicy hodgepodge that he enjoyed, and two of the cook's special fruit pastries. He chose the seat at the other end of the table, seeking some way to avoid Caroline's pleas to stop her brother from making a grand mistake.

"Mr. Darcy, we must do something, and soon. I fear what has taken Charles to London."

"Oh? What do you suspect?" Darcy bit into the apple filled pastry.

"He plans to retrieve my mother's pendant, her favorite piece, a blue topaz. The one my father gave him to present to the lady he selects as his bride. I heard him tell Louisa yesterday. He will propose upon his return. We must not allow him to return."

"Your brother is his own man. I am in no position to interfere with his plans." Darcy took a bite of egg, grimacing when the cool yolk slid down his throat.

"He listens to you. You can explain how such a connection would not help him advance his position in London"

Barely lifting his head up, Darcy peered at Caroline. "If he is not bothered by the connection, Miss Bingley, then—"

"And what an embarrassment her family will be to us. We would never be able to invite anyone worthwhile to our home if the Bennets are visiting. My fondest wish is to save my brother from the humiliation that will follow once the *Ton* has met them all."

"How he handles his own family is his concern. Miss Bennet has shown impeccable manners. She would not embarrass him. I cannot—"

"Yes, I agree. Jane is a sweet girl. I do admire her, and if she cared for Charles—"

"You think she does not?" Darcy interrupted. He sat upright.

"I understand the female mind, and when she is around him, she has not shown any sign of being violently in love. She seems the same to you and the other gentlemen here." Caroline hid her smile behind her napkin as Darcy's expression changed from the blank face of indifference to the exact reaction she sought—deep furrows appeared across his forehead.

"Has she spoken to you at all about your brother?"

"No. In fact, she mentioned only one gentleman in my presence. It is my belief she prefers Mr. Goulding, the person in the contest for the silly firearm. I noticed how they shared looks with one another." With both brows raised, she leaned towards him, although the table was long, and they would remain far apart. "When he missed his shot, she hurried to his side. Why would she do so if she did not have deep feelings for him?"

Without taking his eyes off his breakfast, Darcy pushed the food around the plate. He, too, had witnessed the exchange between them, but until this moment, he had not considered it important.

His silence gave Caroline courage to continue. "Mr. Goulding did dance twice with her last night. Does that not again show his preference?"

Darcy placed his fork down and picked up his cup. He nodded for her to go on.

"And if it was not for their loss of fortune, I believe her dowry would have made the difference to Mr. Goulding. He is a second son." Caroline waited for this information to settle on his mind. She smirked at his flinch.

"They may just be—"

"Friends? No. She seeks him out whenever he enters a room."

Darcy leaned back into his chair. He recollected every instance where he had witnessed them together. He was not in complete agreement. He noticed no specific action on Miss Bennet's part. Of Mr. Goulding, he had no doubt of his desire. Miss Bennet's heart could not be touched; many men had sought her attention to no avail. As Miss Bingley suggested, she had presented the same smile to everyone, male or female.

Caroline continued. "Her mother is desperate, Mr. Darcy. Did you hear her plans last night? She wants my brother to put other rich men in her daughters' path. I heard her, and I suspect you did too."

Darcy nodded.

"I must save Charles from an unequal marriage. I could accept her if she loved him. She does not. She would have told me if she did. We have had many private conversations."

Darcy sipped his coffee. *She does not love Bingley? Damn. Ladies and their falsehoods! I do not understand them at all. This will not do.*

"Mr. Darcy, will you assist me in this endeavor?"

Darcy released a long sigh. "What do you propose we do?"

"We shall close up the house and return to London. He would have no reason to return."

"A return to London would be acceptable to me. But why would that dissuade him from returning?"

"My brother falls in love with whichever lady is nearby. As long as he remains in London, he will find another with whom to spend his time. There are many worthwhile and very pretty young ladies of our acquaintance in town."

"What part do I play in your plan?"

"Convince him. She does not care for him, and Mrs. Bennet is pushing her daughter to accept without regard to Jane's wishes. They are desperate now."

"Are you positive Miss Bennet is merely acting as her mother wishes?"

"Did you not notice the change in, um, their style of gown with the change in financial status?"

He tried to place when Elizabeth first wore the lower cut gown. *Yes, it changed at the same time the rumor about their lost dowries was being discussed. Damn. Mercenary woman.*

"Of course, if you feel that I am mistaken, then I would not expect you to become involved."

"No, no. I do not doubt you. I will speak to him. I do not wish to see him hurt."

"Nor I, Mr. Darcy. Shall we pack up today?"

"Blake is out riding, and I do not know when he will return. I suggest we wait for him before any decision is made."

Nodding, Caroline tried to smile through her frown.

He excused himself, using business as an excuse, and left to wait to hear from Blake in the library.

***

Following the ball, Mrs. Bennet had not slept at all. What she had heard Mr. Darcy say on the balcony about Lord Blake's poverty had kept her awake and worried. All night she had paced, sipping wine from a decanter that had required filling several times. She had nibbled on cheese and fruit while she contemplated the resolution to her family's situation.

Mr. Rawlings seemed interested in Lydia, but her youngest had only officers on her mind. Neither Mr. Darcy nor Mr. Kent were interested in any of her girls. That left Mr. Bingley. She had believed he would offer for Jane, but he did not request an interview and indicated he would be leaving for London early this morning and without explanation. She could not count on his return. Men were such fickle creatures, falling for the nearest woman. And there were many women in London throwing themselves at him. Lord Blake, she feared, was merely flirting with Lizzy. He must marry a woman with a large fortune and one thousand pound dowry was insignificant for such a high ranking man. He could easily marry a woman with fifty times that amount.

In the early hours of the morning, she had arrived at a solution. She had watched Mr. Collinsvery carefully during his visit and in particular which of her daughters had caught his eye. She believed he desired only Jane or Lizzy. She had tried to encourage an arrangement with Mary. Unfortunately, her third daughter did not entice the man at all, nor would she try to use her female wiles on him. And he appeared to be a man in need of womanly charms.

I am thankful that Mr. Bennet is leaving to go to town. He would never lend his support to my scheme.

The customary noisy activities were missing from Longbourn with the girls sleeping late to recover from the ball. As planned, Mr. Bennet readied himself for his journey to London for that important business he had told everyone that could not wait. He had, however, told his wife that payment was due for his most foolish investment on gas lighting. He must travel to London to convert the funds into cash. Mr. Cuffage was adamant payment be made immediately.

Mrs. Bennet approached Mr. Collins the moment the front door closed behind her husband. "Might I have a word with you this morning? Please, before the girls come down for breakfast."

Collins nodded, and the two made their way into Mr. Bennet's study.

"It is my hope you have had a pleasant stay."

"Yes, very agreeable. You have received me with the utmost civility. Your hospitality rivals my dear patroness, Lady Catherine de Bough's. She is the model for extending hospitality to her guests. Not a single issue is left to others; her humble manners and Christian kindness are beyond anything I can describe."

"Yes, yes. I have asked to speak to you about a reference in your letter you sent to Mr. Bennet."

Collin's eyes widened. "Oh?"

"Yes. It did reveal you as a most honorable and good man."

"I am confused. Which part?"

"Ah. You expressed your desire to choose a wife from among my daughters." Mrs. Bennet glanced at the closed door. "It is also my wish. We can talk openly here."

Collins smiled, nodded, and relaxed into the chair. "I was under the impression you had understood my wishes after we shared the little tête-à-tête upon my arrival."

"Yes, I was, and have kept a close watch on my girls. I felt we should speak since, as their mother, I am privy to their wishes." Mrs. Bennet leaned forward, glanced at the door, and spoke in a voice slightly louder than a whisper. "Mr. Collins, I have one daughter that wishes, secretly, for a connection."

"I must admit I, too, have a secret desire. I have hinted to you, most strongly, that I do not find Miss Mary or the two youngest acceptable for Lady Catherine de Bough. I need a woman of elegance and grace. I seek someone who can entertain her ladyship with cleverness, and be a comfort to her most charming daughter, Miss Anne de Bough. My wife must be able to temper her wit and vivacity with the silence and respect which my patroness' rank deserves."

"Oh, I see no problem with my charming daughter. I have raised her to be a proper lady. Now the one interested is…"

Collins leaned forward, his hands and brows sweaty. With a single blink, he stared into Mrs. Bennet's eyes.

"I have it on good authority Elizabeth has had secret feelings from the moment you arrived."

"I am relieved. She is a dear sweet girl, and would do me a great honor as my wife. But, I beg your pardon; are you sure? As much as I might wish otherwise, Miss Elizabeth has not shown me even the slightest encouragement."

"Mr. Collins, you are an only child, raised by a father. You have not had the experience of understanding ladies' ways since you have no sister and no mother to reveal these things. Shall I share a few secrets of the female mind when it comes to proposals of marriage?"

Collins nodded eagerly.

"You, sir, do not wish to have a lady immediately willing to accept your offer."

Collins head shot up and he sat tall in his chair. "I do not?"

"No. You must understand, all true ladies must show a little unwillingness. If she agrees quickly, then a gentleman must consider her attempting to secure her future or he may think that she is a wanton woman seeking, well, I shall not say the word."

"I am beginning to see your point. Is there more I should know?"

"Well, yes. A proper lady will reject the offer not once but at least twice. And if she truly desires the match she will say no, even to a third proposal."

"I do not understand at all. Why would a lady say refuse so many times?"

"She must hear your arguments for her. If she feels you are not willing to persuade her to accept you, then she will believe you do not care for her at all. A young lady needs assurance of your true feelings. It is sad, but it is the true delicacy of the female character. In this you can trust me."

"Three times? I must propose three times? I object. This is nonsensical!"

"Mr. Collins! It makes perfect sense. You, sir, do not understand how a lady thinks. You must prove your hand is worthy of her acceptance, and that the establishment you offer is highly desirable. You must put forward your connections with the family of De Bourgh as additional evidence of your worthiness, and you must not forget to mention her loveliness and amiable qualifications."

"Is this important? Why, this is preposterous. I should just propose, and she should accept. I am offering her Hunsford and the de Bough connection and one day Longbourn."

"Lizzy is no different than any elegant lady. She wants to increase your love by suspense. It is a silly game, I know, but it is the usual practice of my sex when a proposal is desired. Do not fear the seriousness of a rejection at first. Think of it as a charming response and her rejection will prove her love!"

"Then does she accept?"

"Well, first, you must let her run off to her room. Remember, young ladies like to be dramatic. After marriage, they must behave in a sedate and proper manner at all times. This is the only opportunity they have to demonstrate their silly girlish ways. It is the last stage of courtship."

"Then she will come down and accept me?"

"Not yet. I must go to her, as her wise mother, and counsel her. I remember when my mother came to me when Mr. Bennet offered. This time will be no different. I look forward to this, as a mother. You do not wish to deny me this one little moment, do you? But remember if she smiles and accepts right away, you should withdraw your offer. Do not be misled into thinking this is how it is done!"

Collins nodded. "So it shall be. I shall offer today, but I will reluctantly play this game, and only for a short period." He rose from his chair and headed to the door. "Mrs. Bennet, I shall be forever grateful for this insight. I would not wish to make such a mistake as you have pointed out by a quick acceptance."

Mrs. Bennet turned and stoked the fire, smiling to herself. Yes, all is going as planned. I have no doubt Lizzy will refuse him every time. Her head is full of Lord Blake.

She looked up when this gullible man cleared his throat and held the door for her. The two made their way to the dining room for breakfast, and without an invitation or permission, Mr. Collins attempted to act as the head of the house. He demanded the girls quiet down and asked that they show some modesty. Lydia and Catherine merely giggled. Jane blushed. Mary delivered some advice to Mr. Collins with quotes straight from Fordyce's Sermons.

While the others were enjoying their breakfast and reminiscing about the previous night's activities, Elizabeth had woken up late and with a start. The room was too bright. She had intended on going straight to Oakham Mount before sunrise. She called for Sarah.

The morning sun caused a glare on Lizzy's reflecting glass. "Hurry, Sarah. I wish to walk while there is still sun. I stayed up too late last night talking with Jane."

"Miss Elizabeth, the sun will shine the rest of the day. I do not think any rain is coming. See, no clouds at all." Sarah picked up the brush and began to style her hair in her usual simple fashion.

"Sarah, could you fix my hair in the same curls as last night. I, um, liked how they felt. And could you add a few of the flowers again?"

"Now Miss Elizabeth. I do not have time to spend on such things. I have many other chores that need to be done." Sarah chuckled when she spied a blush rising on Miss Elizabeth's checks. "You have plans this morning? Do I need to splash a little extra lavender water on you?"

Lizzy ignored her maid's teasing, choosing instead to focus on getting to Oakham Mount as quickly as possible. "I need to hurry, Sarah. I need to select a proper dress."

"Mrs. Bennet insisted you wear the rose gown this morning. She demanded I not let you outside your room without it."

Elizabeth looked at the gown draped across the bed—one of the newly designed dresses. She had avoided wearing any with the exception of once when Mr. Collins arrived and once when Lord Blake visited, both at her mothers command. She felt the fire burning her cheeks when she recalled how Lord Blake did his best to avoid the neckline of her gown while Mr. Collins could not place his gaze anywhere else. Sarah finished styling her hair and she was pleased. She moved to the closet, pulling out dresses in a succession, discarding each one on the bed. Finally, she located a beautiful pale green gown, one that her mother had missed. The neckline was perfect, not too low to cause embarrassment but not too high either.

"This one. I shall wear this one today."

Sarah sighed but helped her with the dress. "Your mother will not be pleased."

Fully dressed for the day, Elizabeth checked the view outside her window. Oakham Mount was visible, but she was too far away to distinguish if anyone was waiting there. *Why did I let Jane talk about Mr. Bingley all night?*

Hearing Mr. Collins and her mother's voice in the dining room, Elizabeth attempted to creep past the door undetected.

"Lizzy, come in here."

"I feel the need for some fresh air this morning after last night's ball. I will return later."

"No. Lizzy. You are to come and eat your breakfast. I insist."

Elizabeth entered the dining room, took her usual seat and placed a few items on her breakfast plate. Swallowing a few bits, she hoped to satisfy her mother. She needed to leave soon in order to meet up with Blake as she had agreed. However, her heart skipped a beat when the very instant she stood to leave, she noticed her mother signal to Mr. Collins.

Announcing his desire for a private interview with Miss Elizabeth, Mrs. Bennet gleefully complied. She pushed all the other girls out of the dining room.

"Lizzy, I *insist* upon your staying and hearing Mr. Collins," she demanded as she left the room. With a backward glance, she glared at her daughter to let her know she, just like her father would, on occasion, brook no argument.

And so, no later than mid morning, Elizabeth and Mr. Collins were left in the dining room alone, while Mrs. Bennet congratulated herself on a task successfully completed. She dawdled in the vestibule, eavesdropping through the slightly open door. After a short while, she grew impatient. It was with a quickness, she began to re-enter the room, only to stop when she heard her daughter say—

"I thank you again and again for the honor you have done me in your proposals, but to accept them is impossible. My feelings in every respect forbid it. Can I speak plainer?"

Mrs. Bennet charged into the room, speaking quite animatedly and much too loudly. "Depend upon it, Mr. Collins. Lizzy shall be brought to reason. I will speak to her about it myself directly. She is a very headstrong, foolish girl, and does not know her own interest; but I will make her know it." Mrs. Bennet sent a small nod to Mr. Collins. He returned the nod.

Elizabeth chose to remove herself to her own room once she discovered the servants guarding the doors that lead outdoors with the deliberate purpose to stop her from leaving. Her mother followed her up the stairs. She had not even been able to close the door to her bedchambers in time to keep her mother out.

"Lizzy! You have declared you will not have Mr. Collins. Well, missy, Mr. Collins begins to say that he will not have you."

Elizabeth stood and faced her mother defiantly. "Then we are in agreement."

Mrs. Bennet tried to reason with Lizzy, but found her to be exactly as she had described; obstinate and headstrong. She explained how an alliance with Mr. Collins would save the family. When her defiant daughter implied that she could do as she pleased, her equally defiant mother decided to try a different approach. She sat in the chair and calmly patted the bed for Lizzy to sit down.

"Did I ever tell you about a Lieutenant in the army I once favored?"

Elizabeth sat down but did not respond. She would not look at her mother.

Mrs. Bennet spoke her words soft. "Your grandfather Gardiner, would not allow me to follow my heart with the lieutenant."

Gaining her daughter's interest, she revealed a story never shared with her daughters. "My dear father made me marry Mr. Bennet. He was the one with the estate and, at that time, had fifteen hundred a year." She looked tenderly upon Elizabeth. "He impressed upon me what great responsibility a daughter in the family has—namely, she must choose whichever future that will take care of others."

Mrs. Bennet paused as she watched Lizzy's eyes flash with distrust.

"And do you know what my mother did?" Mrs. Bennet waited until her daughter shook her head. "She encouraged me to choose your father as well. Both my parents taught me that my place was to do as I was told. So, as much as I loved the lieutenant, I understood that he could not offer me security. My brother, Edward, was away at school, and could not plead my case for me. And when he came home, I told him the situation. Do you know what your favorite uncle said?"

Elizabeth looked up at her mother; she shook her head more visibly.

"He said I must marry the better man."

Elizabeth's eyes grew wide, and her mouth dropped open.

"Yes, it is true. Your Uncle Gardiner told me to choose Mr. Bennet. And he said I would be foolish not too. I did not want to appear foolish in his eyes. Perhaps that is not the case now, for I do not care what his opinion is of me. I have had to live with the decision, not him. Well at least he knows he is indebted to me. Did you know it was your father's status that elevated my dear brother and made it possible for his success today?"

Elizabeth's interest grew, and was evident by her softened gaze at her mother. This was the first honest conversation they had ever shared.

"It is true. If I had followed my heart, he would not have been able to marry whom he chose, nor would he have had the comfort of a fine house." Mrs. Bennet took Elizabeth's hands, looked her in the eye, and in a most calm voice said, "Lizzy, dear. I know you do not wish to marry Mr. Collins, and I see your point about how silly a man he can be, but you must consider the truth of life. I have great expectations for you and your sisters."

Elizabeth gave her mother a questioning look. She continued to remain silent.

"You are not as beautiful as Jane; well, no one is." Mrs. Bennet patted her hands when she noticed her daughter cringe. "You are a pretty sort of girl. You have a nice figure and pretty eyes." She smiled tenderly at her second born. "You, however, do not have the right charms to entice gentlemen. You are willful, you are not dutiful, and you even refuse to behave as a lady by walking all over the country. You do not flatter men, and my dear, they do like to be flattered. Men are stupid creatures really. They walk around so high and mighty, but you will learn they are unsure of everything. That is why you must flatter them."

"Flattery does not always work, mother. I have seen an example of how it failed."

"Perhaps the occasional gentleman is not so easily fooled. But, Lizzy, you are too smart. They do not like that. You must learn to hide that side of you. You father did not help you by encouraging you this way."

"I cannot behave any other way."

This is why you will not get the right sort of proposal from any worthwhile man. They prefer ridiculous and stupid women. Look at your father. He chose me and is always saying how silly I am and how little understanding I have. I let him think that because you see, dear, he chose me. He did not have to, but your beloved father, that you hold so high, chose me."

"You used your charms on him, but I daresay they would not work today. Did you reveal a little glimpse of heaven to him?"

"I know you wonder why. He chose me because I flattered him, and I was silly around him, and I made him feel smart and strong. Those were the qualities he looked for in a wife. He was the new master of Longbourn, and so unsure of himself. So I said the words he needed to hear. Now today I have a fine home and live in a fine neighborhood, and I am important in this part of the county. If I had followed my heart, I would have none of those things. My life would have been a struggle even now. My lieutenant is no longer in the army. He is a tradesman now, and not a very good one at that. The path I chose was better for me."

"But what about love and respect? That is what I want."

"They come and go, and sometimes they come again. That is what we all live for. You will see one day. Even love matches lose their passion. It is the daily living that wears us all down."

Elizabeth withdrew her hands from her mother's and with her shoulders squared, defiantly turned her head away. Her mother continued—

"Mr. Collins pays you a great compliment. He is willing to overlook this side of you because he finds you very pretty. It is a great thing for a man to have a pretty wife. Other men are jealous, and having other men envious is always good for a husband's temperament."

Elizabeth smirked. Mrs. Bennet shook her head.

"Now, life with Mr. Collins would not be so bad. Perhaps not as nice as life with Lord Blake, still my dear, he will never offer marriage to you. You are just not in his social sphere. Surely, you must see that. He may offer something else, and then your father will not allow that, even if he has to shoot the man." Mrs. Bennet waited. She knew she was correct that Elizabeth was waiting for Lord Blake.

"You pushed me toward Lord Blake! Why have you changed?"

"Your father explained to me how great men marry from their own circle, and he demanded I speak to you today. He is worried after witnessing you and Lord Blake dancing that scandalous waltz. He fears the sort of offer he will make.

"Jane is not equal to Mr. Bingley either. They danced the last dance. Does he not fear him?"

"Mr. Bingley is free to choose Jane because he is just the son of a tradesman, and his reputation would not suffer. Lord Blake cannot afford to take a country wife with no money and connections. It is just not done."

"I believe Lord Blake will propose marriage, mama."

Mrs. Bennet worried that there had been an agreement. She held Lizzy's chin in her hand and looked into her eyes. "Has he spoken of marriage? Or has he merely hinted at some sort of future?"

Elizabeth jerked her head away from her mother's hand. She shrugged.

"Well, missy, he will break you heart. You must remove him from your mind and accept life as it is, not as you want it to be. He will not offer marriage; it is just the way of things. I know you have tender feelings for him. I see how you look at him. I remember that feeling."

Lizzy stood by her bedroom window overlooking the backside of Longbourn. Looking out into the distance, she could see the faint rise of Oakham Mount as a grey mass on the horizon. She sighed when she turned back to her mother.

"This is the problem, Lizzy, and it is a serious one. If Mr. Bingley does not marry Jane, then we are in a very bad way. We will not be able to live here when Mr. Bennet dies. At this time, my dear brother cannot help us; he has to take care of his own family and his own business. There is no one else. Mr. Collins will not consider Mary, Kitty, or even Lydia. It is you he wants. So, if you insist on rejecting Mr. Collins, then we face a very hard future. You do not know what poverty is, Lizzy. You do not know. You have been spared that because I did as my family demanded. Think on that."

Mrs. Bennet rose to leave. She was almost to the door when she turned and said, "I will leave you to your thoughts, and I promise to say no more. You must decide your fate by tomorrow morning."

"I would like to take a walk and think over what you said."

Mrs. Bennet had been waiting for this plea. "No, Lizzy. You will stay in your room. I will station John outside your door if necessary. You must not leave until you have come to a decision, and I will not accept a quick decision. You will think upon it until you agree to marry Mr. Collins, even it takes all night. I will have a tray sent up to you."

"May I please see Jane?"

"Jane is needed elsewhere today."

With that, Mrs. Bennet left the room and called for John. I must one day thank Mr. Darcy for revealing Lord Blake's financial problems on the balcony last night. I know he saw me. To think, I almost let Lizzy make a horrible mistake, pushing her on such a penniless man.

***

The sun traipsed across the sky; the oranges and pinks of the early sky fading into shades of blue and white. The glaring bright yellow sun, having risen high in the sky, now made its way to the west. Blake had lingered a long time. Mid-afternoon had arrived when he gave up waiting at Oakham Mount, although he had not given up on her. He headed for Longbourn. He needed to discover if she was ill, or whether there was another reason for her absence. The day would not pass without an answer.

The pleasure he derived from holding her in his arms was still fresh in his mind. When he pulled her close to take the turns of the waltz, he had nearly fainted like a silly girl at the experience. He could still smell the lavender scent, making his head swim a day later, and he shuddered when he thought of her breath bathing his body when he pulled her to him. Her hair tickled his cheek; he had wanted to yank out the pins and let it fall down her shoulders. Oh, God. Sighing, he took control of his body reacting to his thoughts when he neared Longbourn.

"Lord Blake, you honor us with your presence," Mrs. Bennet said. She curtseyed as elegantly as she knew how.

"Good day, Madam. I am here to visit with Mr. Bennet."

"I am sorry, my lord," Taking several quick breaths, Mrs. Bennet gained control over the tone in her voice. "My husband has gone away on business."

"I had wished to express my apology for my dance with Miss Elizabeth last night when they played the Waltz. I did not want him to think ill of her or me."

"Oh, phew. He had not a single bit of worry over the dance. Do not give it another thought."

"Well, now that I am here, perhaps I can visit with your lovely daughters."

"My Lord, I am sorry to inform you that my daughters have gone to visit their friends at Lucas Lodge. All except one." Mrs. Bennet watched Lord Blake's eyes light up. Without waiting for a response, she added, "Lizzy left for London this morning with her father. She is such an impulsive girl. She pleaded with him—she is his favorite, you know, and told him it was most important... critical is the word she used—for her to keep him company. It was almost as though she was trying to avoid something. My husband agreed to her request. He never could deny her anything."

Mrs. Bennet smiled when she heard Lord Blake's gasp.. "May I call for refreshments? They will return shortly."

"That will not be necessary." Blake followed Mrs. Bennet's gaze, and looked down at his boots. Shrugging, he continued. "Perhaps it may be better to return at another time."

Mrs. Bennet folded her hands in front of her, raised herself up tall, and smiled. "Yes, perhaps it would. I will not delay you any further, Lord Blake. You are such an important gentleman. I am sure you have much waiting for your attention. I will tell my daughters that you called when they return home."

"Thank you, madam. I will see myself out."

Lord Blake left without turning back or looking up. He mounted his horse, patted his pocket, and rode directly into the sunlight as he sped towards the open meadow west of Netherfield Park.

***

Hours had elapsed since Darcy settled in his chair. Although to him, the timepiece on the mantle ticked louder today and the logs crackled incessantly, yet what proved to be conspicuous, in an odd way, was the was the lack of other sounds permeating the room. At first, his mind remained focused on Bingley and Miss Jane Bennet. He had no desire for him to live in a loveless marriage. Witnessing one friend in a such a situation had been enough. He replayed the balcony scene in his head many times. What was Blake doing now?

Closing the book, he then ran his fingers through his hair, sighed deeply, releasing his breath slowly through inflated cheeks. Unable to remain seated, he rose to tend to the fire. More than half a day had slipped by since Blake left the house, which was long before sunrise. The sunlight no longer streamed through the east facing windows.

Suddenly, he felt a chill run throughout his whole body, even though the stoking the fire had caused the heat to reach him. With one hand leaning on the mantle, and the other poking at the diminishing fire, he cursed to himself. Damn him and his bloody charm.

Darcy sought refuge in a brandy as his eyes darted to the library door. With his back to the entrance, he filled the glass, which was twice what he usually poured, and swallowed the contents before pouring another. Sipping this drink while pacing the floor, he repeatedly diverted his attention to the door leading to the hallway foyer, and then to the driveway as it curved alongside that part of the house.

The emptiness outside the window drew him to the glass windowpanes. His lips turned downward as he studied the view only to see dust whipping up along the road, saddened it was the wind and not a powerful white stallion that caused the disturbance. His stomach tightened with each tick of the timepiece and every pop escaping from the grate, until he could no longer stand erect. Blake, you had better have made an honorable proposal or I shall... He stopped, and with his hand rubbing his forehead, exclaimed, "Shall what? Knock him out? Challenge him to a duel? Who am I to do these things? I am nothing to her."

Returning to his seat, he ignored the squeezing knot in his stomach and disregarded his hands sweating until he could no longer hold the glass securely. His cravat felt as snug as a noose circling the neck of a bloated dead man. His head ached, and every muscle twitched beyond his control. He gulped the remnants of his drink, slid back into the chair, and closed his eyes. He imagined Blake drawing her hand to his lips and the most expressive eyes shining when she whispered, "yes." His felt a strange emptiness take root, much deeper than the dullness that had been his visitor from time to time when his beloved parents had died.

At last, the sun had reached its final spot before hiding behind the horizon. Darcy had waited all day, but Blake did not appear. Surely, no man would be away this long for a mere tryst. Darcy debated what his friend was planning to offer. Marriage. It cannot be. He has a place to maintain in society. He felt his chest tighten as it had done with each thought of Blake and Elizabeth together. How can it not be an offer of marriage? He has been gone too long.

As a deep sullenness overcame his dullness, Darcy decided it was time to leave Netherfield Park, not for Bingley's sake but for his own. He wished to avoid Blake upon his return. With slumped shoulders and a slow walk, he climbed the stairs and, upon entering his bedchambers, informed his manservant to pack his belongings. They would leave after breakfast. He informed his valet that he was not to be disturbed for the rest of the night. His chest was tight, his throat was dry, and the fireplace smoke made his eyes mist, or at least that is what he told himself. Darcy spent the evening alone, visualizing the two lovers in an embrace tighter than when they danced the waltz. He imagined her lips upon his. "I came too late."

He bolted upright. "Concentrate on her family and her connections. I am fortunate not to have fallen into their trap."

He rang for a tray instead of dressing and going down for dinner. He did not wish to see anyone still residing at Netherfield Park. He realized he would not be able to escape his thoughts of her and had no desire to be with the Hursts, Miss Bingley, or Blake.

When Darcy's valet entered and found him sitting in a chair, bent forward peering out the window at the driveway, he offered to bring him anything he needed. His only words were, "A pot of tea." He moved to the desk, pulling out his writing paper and mended pens, and began to list things to do in town.

***

The next morning arrived finding the Longbourn house exceedingly quiet. Elizabeth entered the dining room where her mother was seated. Elizabeth squared her shoulders, lifted her chin, and coughed to get her mother's attention.

"No. My answer is no." Elizabeth rose defiantly before her mother could ask the question.

"It is just as well, child. Mr. Collins withdrew his offer. You waited too long, and he felt dishonored. You could not have him now if you begged him," Mrs. Bennet answered with a downcast smile. "That Charlotte Lucas has sunk her nails in him and dragged him to Lucas Lodge."

"Charlotte was here?"

"Yes, your particular friend has schemed against you. When Mr. Collins left with her, he was so angry with me that I fear what he will do. If Lady Lucas has her way, she will ensure her daughter will one day be the Mistress of Longbourn; mark my words. He is easily led. Oh, what are we ever to do now?"

"May I leave the house?"

"It is of no consequence to me now." Mrs. Bennet narrowed her eyes at Lizzy and shook her finger. "You have ruined us all. I never want to speak to you again." She stomped up the stairs, entered her bedchambers, and collapsed in the bed where she remained for the remainder of the day.

Elizabeth sprang out the door and ran all the way to Oakham Mount. She did not stop until she reached the top, calming herself by taking several deep breaths before she walked out on the ledge. She prayed he would be there, and was deeply disappointed he was not. She sat down and decided to wait. Surely, he would come today, even if only to assuage his curiosity. She smiled. When she heard what had happened, he would forgive her for not meeting him and laugh at the thought she could ever have accepted Mr. Collins.

She sat on the ledge for over an hour when a flash of movement caught her eye. She leaned forward and gasped at the sight at Netherfield Park and the driveway leading up to it. She focused her attention on the movement.

They are leaving. All of them. Every carriage. No! There goes Lord Blake on that beast of a horse.

Wanting to call out, and knowing it would be futile to do so, Elizabeth stood frozen on the ledge, her eyes squinting against the sun as she followed their passage until they were no longer visible. Abandoned. He abandoned me. Was he as Mama said? Just trifling with me? What exactly did he want?

Elizabeth turned back to return home when she came to an abrupt halt. Tied to a bush was something that looked like a handkerchief. She ran to retrieve it; her heart pumping at a quickened pace. She knelt down after pulling it from the branch. She knew it was from him. A smile crossed her face. He did not abandon me. He left me a message. As she touched the delicate linen, she felt something inside, something hard and so unlike a note. Untying it quickly, she recognized the very handkerchief she had embroidered for him, and inside were many tiny pieces, as if it had been stomped on until the structure collapsed. She studied the contents until awareness dawned which item had been crushed and broken and secured in her handkerchief—instinctively she knew it had originally been intended to be a gift—it was a very expensive and beautiful.

Elizabeth tried to control the mist in her eyes. She gingerly fingered and kissed the pieces of the crystal while reassembling it in her lap. A knight! A white knight! Engraved upon the front was the letter E with his insignia below. The tumult of her mind was now painfully acute. His words echoed in her mind. "He would have proposed to me! I was right; he was planning to offer marriage! Oh, why did he not come back today?"

Her astonishment, as she reflected on what had passed, was increased by every review of their time spent together. It was gratifying to have inspired so strong an affection, although his total lack of faith in her saddened her exceedingly. How could he leave without saying goodbye? Why did he not give me a chance?

She continued in agitated reflections until the sounds of Netherfield Park grew silent and her thoughts made her feel how unequal she truly was. She knew not how to support herself, and from actual weakness sunk down squarely on the cold, moist grass, holding the items close to her chest. It was not until she remembered her forced imprisonment did she react. Her face grew hot, her neck muscles tensed and her arms stiffened.

"Mother!" She yelled, her hands balled into fists.

Nigel gazed towards the troubled woman on the Oakham Mount ledge, sighing at the lady's distress, and, as quietly as possible, walked through the woods to his waiting horse. He left the area, but not before stopping in the East Meadow of Netherfield Park to pick up the final report from the hollow of the large oak tree. He placed the overstuffed package in his traveling bag, mounted his horse, and with a final look around said, "Cuffage will be pleased."

Chapter Thirty-three

A t half past three in the afternoon, a small-framed man entered one of the formidable houses on Grosvenor Street in London, known as the Peregrine. The doorman barely acknowledged him as he walked into the vestibule. Taking his hat and coat, the servant directed him to a chair, where he took a seat. He placed a bulging satchel on his lap, patted his jacket pocket several times while he waited for his meeting. After almost an hour, the doorman returned and led him into the study.

No one could mistake the wealth of the gentleman residing in this house. Magnificent paintings lined the wall. A gigantic fire crackled in the oversized fireplace at the far end of the room. Books filled the shelves, and a mountain of papers littered the desk with golden paperweights keeping them from slipping away.

The elderly gentleman rose from behind the documents and pointed to two chairs. His gold signet ring sparkled in the candlelight, highlighting its sky blue stone and the letter P with wings on both sides raised on top. There was no mistaking this seal.

Bowing to the distinguished gentleman standing before him, he accepted with a slight nod and chose the chair farthest from the fire. It was a warm day for November.

The old gentleman, bent over with age, made his way to the chairs. "I am glad you could arrive so quickly. Have a seat. Do I still call you Mr. Cuffage?"

Cuffage nodded. "Thank you, my Lord. Yes, I am still currently known as Cuffage." He sat down comfortably in the overstuffed chair.

A servant entered with a carafe filled with French wine. The distinguished gentleman poured two glasses, handed one to him and saluted him with his left hand. "Excellent bottle."

Cuffage nodded, sipped his wine, and waited.

"Have you obtained the funds from Mr. Bennet?

"I have. All thirty thousand pounds." He patted his pocket where an untraceable bank receipt hid among several other documents.

"Did you have any trouble? Is there anything I must be aware of?"

"No trouble at all." Cuffage watched as the gentleman sighed. He could not determine if it was in sympathy or disgust. "He is an honorable man. He gave his word, and, well, he simply turned over his daughters' dowry money. Well, he did not invest all their money. They each have one thousand pounds left. Of course, it did take him several weeks to convert the dowries into cash; but I have it safely deposited."

"Does Mr. Bennet relinquish all claims to the Gas Light Company?" the old master leaned forward with eager interest.

"Most assuredly, yes. He wants no part in any scheme, today or in the future."

"Did you get it in writing?"

"Of course. You are now free to move on with the project as he was the last of the ten investors to pay. I suspect your profits will soar now. The world awaits a brighter night. It was splendid of Mr. Bennet to help provide the financing, and I was able to extract revenge in the deal."

"Yes, the work will proceed as planned. Excellent. Now let us discuss a more serious matter—this alliance between the young men. "

"Ah. Mr. Darcy's brainchild," Mr. Cuffage said chuckling.

"He succeeded in getting the men to join him. I did not expect it.

"Nor me. Perhaps drastic measures were needed. Whitson kept me appraised by sending frequent messages. How convenient that Mr. Bingley allowed his butler access to the library where they kept the paper. Whitson did not need to resort to sneaking in there. He was able to view them all. I brought his reports with me." Cuffage lifted his satchel.

"They did not suspect him?"

"No, my Lord. He is very good at deception."

"Do any of the young men of the alliance have any concerns about you?"

"No. Whitson had no problem starting the rumor that Mr. Gardiner lost the funds in some scheme. He had determined it was best to have Mr. Rawlings' man discover only that Mr. Bennet had lost his daughters' dowry. He feared giving too much information out too soon. Later, he easily duped Miss Bingley's maid by leaving a note out in plain sight, and stood behind the drapes until she read it. In the end, he relied upon Miss Bingley to spread the word. Clever man, Whitson. Oh yes, he asks if there is a new assignment for him now the Bingleys have quit the place. He would prefer a different occupation this next time."

"I believe I do have one. I plan to place him with some industrialist up north, this time as a foreman. These entrepreneurs should respect their place in society, and not try to usurp real power away from the world's rightful rulers."

Chuckling, Cuffage tipped his head.

The old gentleman returned the nod. "Well, I am sure that little parish is feeling the loss today."

"Indeed so. Life in Meryton has returned to its dreary ways by now. Mr. Darcy hid behind the competitions to formulate the group. Quite smart."

"Now about Lord Blake's latest—"

Cuffage was quick to interrupt. "Lord Blake engaged in a harmless flirtation. My man reported the young man had left her gasping in the wind as he rode his horse to London. Apparently, it had not been hard to discover their rendezvous spot and he was able to spy on them regularly. They met often, but nothing improper took place. She has no charge to hold against him, nor any likelihood of any offspring to come."

The master nodded. "At least that is not another problem we need to fix. The future Duke requires a London wife, and one with considerable wealth. From the latest rumors, her fortune needs to be grand indeed to compensate for his father's losses. I understand His Grace is desperate."

"So I have heard. Oh, I took the liberty of removing my fee." Mr. Cuffage pulled the documents from his pocket and handed them to him.

The gentleman perused each page before he rose to place the papers in his desk. Retrieving a key from a chain around his neck, he locked the bottom drawer, replacing the key as he returned to his chair. "Oh, I must stay informed on this alliance. I will not allow them to succeed. When does Mr. Rawlings leave for America?"

"Soon. I arranged for a slight delay with the ship, as you requested."

"Good. And our observer will be onboard? Yes, good. Now, will Rawlings stay in contact with you?"

"Yes, he most assuredly will. I suspect he will not be long in writing once he arrives. I am to meet with him later today. He is bringing the contract for my signature. Perhaps I can use him to find out other ventures they plan to undertake."

The old master shook his head. "I have other means to ascertain what they are doing. I will not allow Mr. Darcy to succeed, and have taken all necessary steps. No need for you to take chances."

Cuffage bowed. "Very good, my Lord. Is that is all?"

"Yes, for now. Thank you for the good work, John, as always." The old gentleman stood, winked, and patted Cuffage on the back.

"My pleasure." Cuffage smiled. In the safety of his own head, he had come to call the man the Falcon, as called by his peers. Over the years, the Lord had proven to be tenacious when in pursuit of anyone, and the Peregrine Falcon was the most prized of all hunting birds, the fastest of its type. Commoners called tbe bird the Duck Hawk, but his lordship could never be called common.

This particular breed of falcons held a sense of power and mystery; it was the perfect symbol for the man. After watching its unsuspecting prey, the peregrine would abruptly dive, with astounding speed, hitting the victim with an impact typically knocking the bird unconscious, or often times killing it immediately. If the bird lived, the falcon would use its sharp talons to scoop up the prey, and with a single bite to the neck, quickly kill it.

While the lord's penchant for devouring his competitors was one reason for his partiality towards this bird of prey, the fact that the peregrine had few natural predators was why the Lord preferred the peregrine falcon to all others hunting birds.

Cuffage bowed. "Mr. Darcy is returning to London and will arrive later today."

"Now that they have succeeded in established their alliance, we must stop them. I expect you to disrupt his every move. He must not succeed."

Cuffage tipped his head, turned, and headed out to his New World Cigar and Wine Shop on Bond Street where he would await Mr. Rawlings.

To be continued in London —Book II Confrontation